3114300986753?
FIC Jackson, B
Jackson, Brend
Zane ;

D0445851

Main

Praise for
New York Times and *USA TODAY*
bestselling author Brenda Jackson

"Brenda Jackson writes romance that sizzles
and characters you fall in love with."
—*New York Times* and *USA TODAY*
bestselling author Lori Foster

"Jackson's trademark ability to weave
multiple characters and side stories together
makes shocking truths all the more exciting."
—*Publishers Weekly*

"There is no getting away from the sex appeal
and charm of Jackson's Westmoreland family."
—*RT Book Reviews* on *Feeling the Heat*

"Jackson's characters are wonderful, strong,
colorful and hot enough to burn the pages."
—*RT Book Reviews* on *Westmoreland's Way*

"The kind of sizzling, heart-tugging story
Brenda Jackson is famous for."
—*RT Book Reviews* on *Spencer's Forbidden Passion*

"This is entertainment at its best."
—*RT Book Reviews* on *Star of His Heart*

Other titles by this author
are available in ebook format.

BRENDA JACKSON

is a die "heart" romantic who married her childhood sweet-heart and still proudly wears the "going steady" ring he gave her when she was fifteen. Because she believes in the power of love, Brenda's stories always have happy endings. In her real-life love story, Brenda and her husband of more than forty years live in Jacksonville, Florida, and have two sons.

A *New York Times* bestselling author of more than seventy-five romance titles, Brenda is a recent retiree who now divides her time between family, writing and traveling with Gerald. You may write Brenda at P.O. Box 28267, Jacksonville, Florida 32226, by email at WriterBJackson@aol.com or visit her web-site at www.brendajackson.net.

BRENDA JACKSON

ZANE &
INTIMATE SEDUCTION

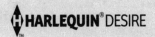

HARLEQUIN® DESIRE

If you purchased this book without a cover you should be aware that this book is stolen property. It was reported as "unsold and destroyed" to the publisher, and neither the author nor the publisher has received any payment for this "stripped book."

ISBN-13: 978-0-373-83790-8

ZANE & INTIMATE SEDUCTION

Copyright © 2013 by Harlequin Books S.A.

The publisher acknowledges the copyright holder of the individual works as follows:

ZANE
Copyright © 2013 by Brenda Streater Jackson

INTIMATE SEDUCTION
Copyright © 2009 by Brenda Streater Jackson

Recycling programs for this product may not exist in your area.

All rights reserved. Except for use in any review, the reproduction or utilization of this work in whole or in part in any form by any electronic, mechanical or other means, now known or hereafter invented, including xerography, photocopying and recording, or in any information storage or retrieval system, is forbidden without the written permission of the publisher, Harlequin Enterprises Limited, 225 Duncan Mill Road, Don Mills, Ontario M3B 3K9, Canada.

This is a work of fiction. Names, characters, places and incidents are either the product of the author's imagination or are used fictitiously, and any resemblance to actual persons, living or dead, business establishments, events or locales is entirely coincidental.

This edition published by arrangement with Harlequin Books S.A.

For questions and comments about the quality of this book, please contact us at CustomerService@Harlequin.com.

® and TM are trademarks of Harlequin Enterprises Limited or its corporate affiliates. Trademarks indicated with ® are registered in the United States Patent and Trademark Office, the Canadian Trade Marks Office and in other countries.

HARLEQUIN®
www.Harlequin.com

Printed in U.S.A.

CONTENTS

Dear Reader,

I love writing about the Westmorelands because they exemplify what a strong family is all about, mainly the sharing of love and support. For that reason, when I was given the chance to present them in a trilogy, I was excited and ready to dive into the lives of Zane, Canyon and Stern Westmoreland.

It is hard to believe that Zane is my twenty-fourth Westmoreland novel. It seemed like it was only yesterday when I introduced you to Delaney and her five brothers. I knew by the time I wrote Thorn's story that I just had to tell you about their cousins that were spread out over Montana, Texas, California and Colorado.

It has been an adventure and I have enjoyed sharing it with you. I've gotten your emails and snail mails letting me know how much you adore those Westmoreland men, and I appreciate hearing from you. Each Westmoreland— male or female—is unique, and the way love conquers their hearts is heartwarming, breathtaking and totally satisfying.

In this story, Zane, who is considered an expert when it comes to women, discovers that when it comes to his own love life, he needs to rethink some of his philosophies if he wants to capture the heart of the woman who has captured his.

I hope you enjoy this story about Zane and Channing.

Happy reading!

Brenda Jackson

ZANE

* * *

To my husband, the love of my life and my best friend,
Gerald Jackson, Sr.

To everyone who enjoys reading about
the Westmoreland family, this one is for you!

Happy is the man that findeth wisdom,
and the man that getteth understanding.
—*Proverbs* 3:13

THE DENVER WESTMORELAND FAMILY TREE

Raphel and Gemma Westmoreland

Stern Westmoreland (Paula Bailey)

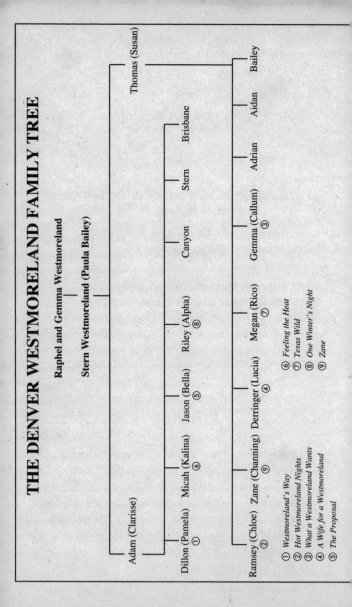

Thomas (Susan)

Adam (Clarisse)

Dillon (Pamela) ①　Micah (Kalina) ⑥　Jason (Bella) ⑤　Riley (Alpha) ⑧

Canyon　Stern　Brisbane

Ramsey (Chloe) ②　Zane (Channing) ⑨　Derringer (Lucia) ④　Megan (Rico) ⑦　Gemma (Callum) ③

Adrian　Aidan　Bailey

① *Westmoreland's Way*
② *Hot Westmoreland Nights*
③ *What a Westmoreland Wants*
④ *A Wife for a Westmoreland*
⑤ *The Proposal*

⑥ *Feeling the Heat*
⑦ *Texas Wild*
⑧ *One Winter's Night*
⑨ *Zane*

Chapter 1

"What do you mean Channing's back in Denver?" Zane Westmoreland dropped down in the chair across from his sister, a dark frown covering his face.

He fixed his gaze on Bailey, waiting on her response. Bailey knew that any mention of Channing Hastings would make him mad, but it seemed she was intent on ignoring him while she continued to eat her bowl of ice cream. Anyone else would have jumped at the anger that was apparent in his voice but not this particular sister. She didn't do anything until she was good and ready. While he waited, even more irritation bubbled up inside of him.

After what seemed like an enormous period of silence, Bailey finally angled her head. "I meant just what I said. I saw Channing today when I had lunch at the hospital with Megan. I understand she arrived in town last week. She looks good by the way."

Zane wasn't surprised. As far as he was concerned,

there was never a time when Channing hadn't looked good...even after a sweaty workout session at the gym.

Suddenly, unbridled fury worked its way along his stomach lining. Why should he care how an ex-girlfriend looked? More importantly, why did the thought of her being back in town trigger such deep-seated anger within him?

Zane could answer that question without much thought. It hadn't been their breakup that still pissed him off but rather *how* they had broken up. Usually he was the one who decided when one of his relationships ended, but Channing had surprised the hell out of him and ended it herself.

"Is Channing's fiancé with her?" He could have bitten off his tongue for asking.

"No, she's only here for six weeks, hosting a medical symposium at the hospital." Bailey didn't say anything for a minute and then, "That man got under my skin."

Zane lifted a brow. "What man?"

"Channing's fiancé. He was checking out the women at Megan's wedding reception, even with Channing standing right beside him. He had a lot of nerve."

Zane had noticed the man's roving eyes, as well. He really shouldn't care. If Channing was inclined to put up with that kind of foolishness, that was her business. It shouldn't concern him. But it did.

He glanced out the window while his mind wandered back in time. He had dated Channing longer than he'd dated any other woman—nine months exactly. Things had been almost perfect between them. But then she'd started hinting that she wanted more from their relationship. That was when he'd reiterated that he was not the marrying kind and never intended to be.

She never brought up the issue again, and Zane had assumed things were back to normal. But less than a month later, out of the clear blue sky, she told him that she had accepted a job at a hospital in Atlanta and would be moving away.

That had annoyed the hell out of him. She was trying to force his hand, and he wouldn't allow any woman to do that. So he'd called her bluff, refusing to offer a proposal. But then she'd moved to Atlanta as planned. That was almost two years ago, and he hadn't seen or heard from her until she'd shown up at his sister's wedding last month an engaged woman.

Engaged.

The very thought made him angry. She'd had the nerve to bring her fiancé to the wedding knowing full well Zane would be there. And like Bailey had said, the man had checked out other women even with Channing by his side. That she was so desperate to have a ring on her finger that she would settle for such a man—the realization made Zane madder.

"This is simply delicious."

Bailey's words intruded on his thoughts. He glanced over at his sister, and his frown deepened. He had come home to find her sitting at his kitchen table as if she lived there. In his current mood, her presence aggravated him. "And what do you think you're doing?"

She smiled. "What does it look like? I'm eating ice cream."

"*My* ice cream," he muttered. "How did you get in here, anyway? I changed the locks on my door."

Bailey leaned back in her chair and chuckled. "I noticed. Did you forget that I know how to pick a lock, Zane? Bane taught me ages ago. And as far as the ice cream, you only bought it because you knew I'd eat it. You don't even like ice cream, and this is one of my favorite flavors."

"They're all your favorite flavors," he said, forcing himself not to grin. The last thing he needed was for her to think he was getting soft. And as far as picking locks, he had forgotten that talent had been just one of the many ways she and their cousin Bane used to get into trouble.

Getting up from the table, he headed for the door.

"Hey, where are you going?" Bailey called after him.

"Since I can't find peace in my own home, I'm going to ride my horse a spell. I'll be gone for an hour or so and hopefully that will give you time to find someone else to visit."

He then walked out the door and slammed it shut behind him.

"Channing, wait up!"

Channing stopped and turned around. She smiled when she saw Megan Claiborne walking briskly toward her. Megan had been one of the first doctors she'd become good friends with while working at the hospital four years ago, and their friendship had remained intact. Last month, Megan married Rico Claiborne, a gorgeous Bradley Cooper look-alike who worked as a private investigator in Philly. To divide their time between Philadelphia and Denver, Megan worked six months as a doctor of anesthesiology in Denver and the other six months at a hospital in Philly.

Megan looked different. "Marriage agrees with you," Channing said when Megan came to a stop in front of her.

Her comment made an infectious smile settle on Megan's lips. "You think so?"

"I know so. There's a radiant glow about you. You seem happy. I mean truly happy," Channing said.

Megan's smile widened. "I *am* happy, and I have to

concur that marriage does agree with me. Rico is the best. He's everything I could ever want in a man."

"Then you have a reason to smile and look radiant." Channing was happy for her friend and she wanted that same happiness and radiance for herself.

Long marriages were common in Channing's family. Her parents had been married for more than thirty-five years, and her grandparents would be celebrating their sixtieth wedding anniversary next year. Her aunts and uncles had been in wedded bliss for more than twenty years, and her cousins and oldest brother, Juan, had all been married eight years or more.

When Channing had dated Megan's brother Zane a few years back, she had believed he was the one. Although he had told her more than once that he never intended to marry, she'd actually thought he'd change his mind. Over the course of their relationship, although he'd never spoken any words of love, his actions had convinced her he had feelings for her. He'd been so attentive, possessive and protective. She was the first woman he'd invited to his family's weekly dinner gatherings and the first woman he'd given a key to his place. So, quite naturally, she had assumed she meant more to him than all the women he'd dated in the past.

But as time went by, it became obvious that he had no intention of making their relationship more than the affair that it was. Then, one day after they'd dated exclusively for almost nine months—she'd come out and asked him how he saw their relationship evolving. He'd told her nothing had changed. He never intended to marry. He'd said that although he cared for her, he didn't love her—and never would.

She'd appreciated his honesty, but his words had hurt.

To protect her heart from further damage, she'd decided to move on. She wanted more.

A week later, she'd accepted the position as a neurologist at Emory Hospital in Atlanta. She didn't tell Zane about her plans until the week before she was ready to leave Denver. She knew Zane was still angry with her about the way she'd ended things, but it wasn't as if she'd left town without telling him.

"I wanted to ask you to come to my family's Friday night chow-down," Megan said, intruding into Channing's thoughts.

Channing winced. "You know I can't do that."

"Why not? Things between you and Zane didn't work out, and you moved on. As far as I'm concerned, it was my brother's loss."

"But I don't want to make things uncomfortable, Megan. I saw the way Zane was staring me down at your wedding. He didn't like the way I ended things between us."

"Forget Zane." Megan bristled. "Did he honestly expect things to continue between the two of you without him ever making a serious commitment?"

Channing shrugged, even though she knew Zane *had* expected that. They had been dating exclusively, and to him that was enough. "I guess he did," Channing said softly, remembering how hard it had been to leave him, to move forward and not look back.

"Well, it served him right to find out he was wrong." Megan took a moment and seemed to choose her next words carefully. "Channing, you were my friend long before you became involved with Zane. You moved away, and now you're back for a short time. There's nothing wrong with me inviting you to dine with my family."

Channing could see plenty wrong with it. "Thanks, but

I think it's best if I don't accept your invitation. I'll be in Denver for at least three weeks, six weeks if I decide to do a second symposium. Considering how Zane feels about me, he and I should keep our distance."

Megan didn't push…at least not right now. Channing knew her friend wouldn't let it drop. "You're welcome to come. If you change your mind, let me know."

Channing nodded, but she wouldn't be changing her mind.

By the time Zane had returned home, Bailey was gone. He headed up the stairs to shower, refusing to admit he missed his sister already. She was known for her drop-in visits not only to him but also to her other brothers, sisters and cousins.

Presently, there were fifteen Denver Westmorelands. His parents had had eight children: five boys—Ramsey, Zane, Derringer and the twins, Aiden and Adrian—and three girls—Megan, Gemma and Bailey. Uncle Adam and Aunt Clarisse had had seven sons: Dillon, Micah, Jason, Riley, Canyon, Stern and Brisbane. Over the past few years, nearly everyone had gotten married. Megan had married last month, and Riley would marry in September. The only holdouts were him, the twins, Bailey, Canyon, Stern and Bane.

His parents and uncle and aunt had died in a plane crash nearly twenty years ago, leaving Zane's brother Ramsey and his cousin Dillon in charge of the family. It hadn't been easy, especially since several of their siblings and cousins had been under the age of sixteen. Together, Dillon and Ramsey had worked hard and made sacrifices to keep the Westmorelands together. When the state of Colorado tried forcing Dillon to put the youngest four in foster homes, he had refused.

The deaths had been the hardest on those youngest four—the twins, Aiden and Adrian, and Brisbane and Bailey. Everyone had known that their acts of rebellion were their way of handling the grief of losing their parents. Now, the twins had finished college and were working in their chosen professions: Aiden as a doctor and Adrian as an engineer. Brisbane was in the navy and Bailey…was still Bailey. Considered the baby of the family, at twenty-six she worked for *Simply Irresistible,* a magazine for today's up-and-coming woman that was owned by Ramsey's wife, Chloe. But even with a full-time job, Bailey still managed to remind everyone she could be a force to reckon with when she put her mind to it.

When Zane reached his bedroom, he glanced out the window at the acres and acres of land surrounding him. Westmoreland Country. Since Dillon was the oldest, he had inherited the main house along with the three hundred acres it sat on. Everyone else, upon reaching the age of twenty-five, received one hundred acres to call their own. Thanks to Bailey's creative mind, each of their spreads were given names—Ramsey's Web, Zane's Hideout, Derringer's Dungeon, Megan's Meadows, Gemma's Gem, Jason's Place, Stern's Stronghold and Canyon's Bluff. It was beautiful land that encompassed mountains, valleys, lakes, rivers and streams.

Zane loved his home, a two-story structure with a wraparound porch. He had more than enough space for himself and a family—if he ever chose to marry. But since settling down with one woman was not in his plans, he had the place all to himself. Some people did better by themselves, and he was one of those people.

Except when it came to business. He, his brother Derringer and his cousin Jason were partners in a lucrative horse breeding and training business along with several of his Westmoreland cousins who lived in Montana and Texas. The partnership was doing extremely well financially, with horse buyers extending all the way to the Middle East. Ever since one of their horses, Prince Charming, had placed in the Kentucky Derby a few years ago, potential clients had been continually coming out of the woodwork.

He was happy with his work. Zane liked the outdoors. The only thing he liked better was women. He didn't have a problem with the revolving door to his bedroom, and he didn't intend for any woman to get it in her head that she could be the one. There wasn't a woman alive who could make him think about settling down.

A quick flash of pain across his gut let him know he wasn't being truthful about that. There *had* been one woman. Dr. Channing Hastings.

Zane's sister Megan had introduced them, and he had been attracted to Channing from the first time he'd seen her. In addition to her beauty, she had a luscious scent that drew him like a bee to honey. She was the very thing erotic fantasies were made of. He'd only intended to date her for a couple of months. Then, the next thing he knew, he was in an exclusive relationship.

Zane reached under his bed for the locked box he'd placed there. Using the key he kept on his key ring, he opened the box and pulled out the calendar that was inside. It was a personalized photo calendar that Channing had made for him as a gift on his thirty-fifth birthday. Had it been almost two years ago?

He flipped through the calendar, beginning with January. By the time he'd gotten to December, he had worked up a sweat. Seeing Channing dressed in such scanty attire—a different outfit for every month—had sent memories soaring through his mind. In January, she wore a floor-length red gown, the same one she'd worn to a charity benefit he'd taken her to at the hospital and the same one he'd loved taking off of her later that night. By December, she was wearing nothing at all while stretched across her bed in one damn hot position, her body barely covered by a white bedspread decked with colorful Christmas ornaments. She had one of those *I want you now* looks on her face. The photographer had been another female doctor whose hobby was photography, and she had captured Channing in some unbelievable poses. Channing Hastings was definitely a beautiful woman.

She had skin the color of rich mocha, a beautiful pair of hazel eyes, high cheekbones, a perky nose, full lips and a luxurious mane of golden-brown hair. The one constant in each photo was the necklace around her neck. It was the gold one he had given her. The same one she had returned when she'd told him she was leaving Denver.

Reaching into the box, he pulled out that same necklace, remembering the day he'd bought it. He'd been in Montana at a jewelry store with his cousin Durango, who'd wanted to buy a birthday gift for his wife, Savannah. Zane had seen the crescent moon and immediately known he wanted it for Channing. At the time, he had refused to question why, he'd just known that seeing it around her neck was important to him.

After Channing left, he'd flipped through the calendar and pulled out the necklace too many times, which was why he'd given the locked box to Megan for safekeeping. He'd been tired of torturing himself. Although Megan would have been curious about what was inside, he'd trusted her enough to know she would not open the box. He couldn't say the same for Bailey, who, as she'd reminded him today, had a fondness for picking locks. Megan had kept the box for almost a year, but he'd gotten it back from her when she'd taken that trip to Texas with Rico last year.

Megan had invited Channing to the wedding last month, even though he'd asked her not to. However, like Bailey, Megan had a mind of her own and didn't like her brothers telling her what to do. And what teed him off more than the wedding invitation was that he'd been over to Megan's place a few nights ago to welcome the newly-weds back to Denver, and she hadn't mentioned anything about Channing returning to town. He was convinced there was no way she hadn't known.

Zane placed the calendar and necklace back in the box, locked it shut and slid it back under his bed. He then stripped off his clothes to take a shower. His and Chan-ning's paths probably wouldn't cross while she was in town.

But...maybe they should.

It was time he looked at the situation differently, more objectively. He had gotten over Channing months ago, and she had evidently gotten over him. She was an en-gaged woman. He was happy with his life. She was happy with hers.

He stepped in the shower with his mind made up. He felt rather pleased with the decision and already he con-sidered it done. He would seek out Channing and pay her a visit.

There was nothing wrong with welcoming her back to town.

Chapter 2

Channing bent to lower the projector screen when a pair of dark leather boots came into view. The boots were followed by a rich, masculine aroma that she would recognize anytime, anyplace. Her stomach knotted as she slowly straightened.

Her eyes moved up past a pair of jeans-clad thighs, a lean waist, a firm stomach and muscled shoulders. Her gaze unerringly landed on a pair of gorgeous dark brown eyes, creamy chestnut-brown skin, an aquiline nose, sharp cheekbones, full lips and a strong chin.

Zane Westmoreland was almost too handsome to be real. She'd thought that very thing the first time she'd seen him three years ago, right here at this very hospital. He had come to repair his sister's flat tire, and Megan had introduced them. Channing's life hadn't been the same since.

She drew in a long breath and slowly released it. "Zane."

"Channing. I heard you were in town, so I thought I would come by and welcome you back."

Channing leaned against the podium she'd stood behind earlier. There were any number of plausible reasons for Zane to show up at the hospital's lecture hall, but for the life of her, she couldn't think of a valid one. He claimed he wanted to welcome her back to town, but just last month, when she'd seen him at Megan's wedding, he had refused to say a single word to her.

"Thanks, Zane." She could mention that she was only in town for three to six weeks but decided it wasn't any of his business. Two years ago she had left Denver to move on, and she had.

"So, you're still engaged I see," he said when she moved to the desk to place a stack of handouts in her briefcase.

She fought back a scowl. "Is there any reason why I wouldn't be?"

"I guess not."

"And what about you?" Channing asked, crossing her arms over her chest. "I take it you're still eluding serious commitments?"

She noticed the muscle that flicked in his jaw. "If you're asking if I'm still single, with no thoughts of settling down, then the answer is yes. That won't ever change." And without missing a beat, he asked, "Did Mark come with you?"

She frowned. Why was he all up in her business? "My fiancé's name is Mack, and no, he's still in Atlanta."

"He's a banker, right?"

Channing clicked her briefcase closed, wondering why Zane felt it necessary to go over information he already knew. Although he had avoided both her and Mack at the wedding, Megan had said Zane had questioned her at the wedding reception.

"Yes, Mack's a banker." There was no need to tell him the Hammond family owned several banks that were spread across Georgia, Tennessee and Florida.

She turned to Zane and tried to ignore how totally, utterly male he looked. She felt a deep fluttering in her stomach when her eyes connected to his. He had soft bedroom eyes, eyes that could educate a woman as to what true desire was all about. She, of all people, should know. Yes, some things in her life had changed, but it seemed the charge she got out of seeing Zane Westmoreland hadn't. Why was her body betraying her this way?

"Well, that's it for the day. It was good seeing you again, Zane."

"Same here. I figured sooner or later I'd run into you at one of those Westmoreland family dinners. I thought we should clear the air now so neither of us would feel uncomfortable."

So that's what this little visit was about? Channing thought. "I'm sorry you wasted your time coming here just for that. I thanked Megan for the invite yesterday but told her it would be best if I didn't attend any of your family functions."

"Why? Are you saying the only reason you got to know my family was because of me?"

"No, if you'll recall, I knew Megan and your sisters long before I met you. However, considering our history, I thought distance was best."

Zane stared at her. "I don't understand why you would think that now when you had no problem attending Megan's wedding and bringing 'Roving Eyes' with you."

Channing's frown deepened. "First of all, Megan is a good friend of mine, and I saw nothing wrong with being there to share in her happiness. And, for the second time, my fiancé's name is Mack."

Zane leaned back against a table and kept his gaze fixed on hers. "Didn't it bother you that *Mack* was checking out other women with you right by his side? And don't say you weren't aware of it, because you're too astute not to have been."

She shrugged. "All men check out other women. Big deal. Are you saying you never looked twice at another woman while we were together?"

He sputtered out a harsh laugh. "Hell, yes, that's exactly what I'm saying. I might be an ass when it comes to some things, Channing, but I would never have disrespected you that way. While we were together, I never once looked at another woman. You were everything I needed."

The next words were out of her mouth before she could call them back. "Evidently not, Zane. Had I been everything you needed then I wouldn't be engaged to marry another man."

She saw the anger that flared in his eyes and knew she'd made a direct hit. She might have been everything he needed in the bedroom, but she hadn't been in all the ways that mattered.

"Goodbye, Zane." She walked around him as she headed for the door.

A few days later, Zane stood on the porch of his cousin Dillon's home. It was Friday night chow-down, when all the Westmorelands in Denver got together. The women cooked, and the men came hungry. Although they all lived in what was considered Westmoreland Country, they didn't get to see each other every day. The chow-down was a way to bring everyone up to date on what was happening with each family member.

Seldom was anyone outside of family invited, but Zane hadn't thought twice about making Channing a regular during the nine months they'd dated. His family liked her, and she'd gotten along with everyone—especially the womenfolk. After a while, they'd begun to consider her one of them. That was when his troubles began.

Channing had gotten ideas about them sharing a future. Somewhere along the way, she'd figured he had fallen in love and was rethinking his position on marriage. She'd found out the hard way that Zane Westmoreland didn't change easily.

"You've been pretty quiet all evening."

Zane glanced over his shoulder as his brother Ramsey stepped outside to join him. After dinner, the women retired to the family room to watch a chick flick, and, like usual after such a delicious meal, the men gathered in the game room for drinks and poker. But Zane hadn't been in the mood. He had come out to get a breath of fresh air.

"I've had a rough week with the horses," he said, knowing that was only part of the reason for his mood. "Sugar Plum had to be transported to Casey, Visa Girl got loose and ran wild for a few hours, and Born Free had a difficult delivery."

Ramsey chuckled as he came to stand beside Zane. "That's all?"

"Isn't that enough?"

Ramsey didn't say anything for a minute and then, "Not for Zane Westmoreland, who thrives on challenges and difficulties. Why don't you tell me the real reason for your surly mood?"

Zane didn't say anything for a long moment. "Channing's back in town."

"So I heard."

Zane flashed an accusing gaze at his brother. "And you didn't tell me, either?"

"I only heard she was back this morning. Chloe mentioned it over breakfast. I understand she was invited to dinner tonight but declined."

"Nobody told me she was back. I should have been prepared," Zane muttered.

Ramsey lifted a brow. "Prepared? Why? You saw her last month at Megan's wedding."

"That was then. This is now."

"What makes 'now' different, Zane?" Ramsey asked. "I assumed you'd pretty much made up your mind two years ago when you let her go. You said you didn't want Channing in your life."

"That's not true," Zane snapped.

Ramsey lifted a brow, not anticipating such a strong response. "Then what is true?"

Zane paused and then said, "She wanted more than I could give."

Ramsey frowned. "Did she want more than you could give, or was it that you refused to give her more?"

Zane heaved out a deep, frustrated breath. "Channing knew the score, Ram. Love is not in my vocabulary. She knew that and accepted my terms. Then, months later, she tried changing the game, but there was no way I was going along with it."

"So, in other words, you wanted her as your lover but had no intention of ever allowing her to be more than that. You would have been satisfied to keep a casual arrangement for another two, three, possibly four years? Forever? Damn it, Zane, how would you feel if Rico would have wanted that kind of relationship with Megan, or Callum with Gemma? Yet you had no problem wanting one with Channing."

"I don't love her like Rico loves Megan and Callum loves Gemma," Zane said, narrowing his eyes. "And I wasn't going to lie to her and say I did."

Ramsey shook his head. "Then I don't blame Channing for leaving. You let her know she was nothing more than another notch on your bedpost."

"She accepted my terms like all my other lovers," Zane snapped. "She knew the score. We couldn't have the kind of future she wanted because I didn't love her."

"If you really didn't have feelings for her, you wouldn't have moped around for months after she left, and you wouldn't be all tied up in knots about her being in Denver now," Ramsey muttered. He shook his head and added, "Well, it doesn't matter now since she's engaged."

"He doesn't deserve her," Zane said in a voice sparked with anger.

"At least the man is willing to give her something you wouldn't—to make her a permanent part of his life."

"Damn it, Ramsey. You saw how he was looking at other women at Megan's wedding. He's going to end up hurting her."

"And you didn't?" When Zane didn't respond, Ramsey didn't say anything else for a minute and then said, "I wasn't going to mention this to you because it's really none of my business, but…"

Zane raised a brow. "What's none of your business?"

"I overheard a conversation between Megan and Chloe yesterday."

"About what?"

"Channing's fiancé. Tara called from Atlanta and told Megan she saw the man last week and remembered him from the wedding as Channing's fiancé. He was out on the town with women in intimate settings on two separate occasions." Tara was married to their cousin Thorn and they lived in Atlanta.

Zane swore through gritted teeth. In a way, he wasn't surprised about what Tara had seen. But what did surprise him was the fact that Channing refused to accept that her fiancé was a womanizer.

"Like I said, he doesn't deserve her," Zane said. "I might not have loved her, but I would never have betrayed her the way he's doing."

Ramsey nodded. "I'm going back inside. Are you coming?"

Zane shook his head. "No, I'm calling it a night. Think I might even sleep in late tomorrow. I haven't done that on a Saturday in a long time."

"All right. But you'll be joining us for Sunday's dinner, right? Susan's going to be upset if she doesn't see her uncle Zane there," Ramsey said, smiling.

Zane thought about his niece, who would be turning four soon. The niece he adored. "I won't disappoint her. I'll be there," he said, moving down the steps. "Tell the others good-night for me."

"Hey, babe, are you missing me? All you have to do is say the word and I'll fly out there and give you all the attention you deserve."

Channing rolled her eyes, bristling at Mack Hammond's words. "Cut it out, Mack. Need I remind you what happened last month at Megan's wedding? You couldn't keep your eyes off the women. Now you have everyone thinking I'm engaged to a womanizing jerk."

"Hey, you didn't warn me there would be so many beautiful women there. It was quite obvious your ex-boyfriend didn't like the fact that you returned to town an engaged woman."

Mack was right. Zane hadn't been happy about it. If their conversation at the hospital was anything to go on, he still wasn't. "But did you have to check them out so obviously? You don't believe in the word *subtle,* do you?" she asked, trying not to smile.

She had met Mack within weeks of arriving in Atlanta two years ago. They had dated a few times, but when he saw she would not put up with his playboy foolishness, they had become good friends instead. A few months ago, when he'd been invited to a cousin's wedding, he'd asked her to pretend to be his fiancée to keep his matchmaking parents and grandparents off his back. Then, when Channing had received the invitation to Megan's wedding, Mack had returned the favor. The last thing she'd wanted was to return to Denver alone and looking pathetic.

The only person who knew the truth about her fake engagement was Megan, who had found the entire ploy hilarious. She'd said there was no reason for Channing to end the charade since it really wasn't any of Zane's business.

"So, have you seen Zane Westmoreland yet?" Mack asked.

Catching her lower lip between her teeth, Channing eased down onto the sofa and curled up in a comfortable position. "Yes, he stopped by the lecture hall a few days ago. He figured I would be dropping by his family's place for dinner while I was in town, and he said we needed to clear the air so things wouldn't be uncomfortable."

"Uncomfortable for whom? You or him?"

"Both, I imagine. But I told him he didn't have to worry about that. I have no intention of attending any of his family's gatherings."

"Was he relieved to hear it?"

Channing shrugged. "Not sure, but it really doesn't matter. He's moved on and so have I. I'm over Zane."

"Are you?"

Channing frowned. "Yes. Why would you doubt it?"

"I'll give you my answer the next time I see you. Have you decided when that will be?"

"Not yet. Class enrollment here is high. I've been here almost three weeks already and Dr. Rowe wants me to consider doing another three-week class. I haven't decided on anything yet."

"Well, I know whatever decision you make will be the right one," he said. "Take care and be good."

"Same back at you, Mack."

Channing clicked off the phone and tried to force the conversation with Zane out of her mind. Nothing about him had changed. He still wanted to be footloose and fancy-free, and she still wanted the whole shebang—love, marriage and family.

She had lied just now to Mack when she claimed that she was over Zane. She'd honestly believed she was, but all it had taken was seeing him again to be proved wrong. Just being in the same room with him had stirred memories and emotions she knew were better kept undisturbed.

The most she could hope for was that her path and Zane's wouldn't cross again.

Megan caught hold of Chloe Westmoreland's arm and pulled her into the kitchen. "Do you think Ramsey took the bait yesterday?"

A smile touched Chloe's lips. "I'm sure he did. You and I were talking loud enough. And tonight was the perfect time for him to tell Zane just what he overheard. In fact, Ramsey just came back inside from being out on the porch with Zane, and when I asked where Zane had gone off to, Ramsey said Zane went home, calling it an early night because he'd had a bad week."

"I bet," Megan said, chuckling. "Especially since he found out Channing is back in town."

"I hope you're right about how Zane feels about her," Chloe said in a low voice. "What about Channing? Will she be upset when she finds out we stuck our noses into her affairs?"

"In the end, both Zane and Channing will get what they truly want, which is each other. Zane moped around like a sick puppy when Channing left for Atlanta, but he was too darn stubborn to recognize his true feelings. If he loves Channing like I believe he does, then the one thing he won't stand for is someone hurting her. Zane is very protective of those he cares about. He's going to come up with a plan to save her from Mack."

"What do you think he'll do?" Chloe asked.

Now that was a good question, Megan thought. Zane was the brother who was usually too logical for his own good. The same one who made it his business to know everything there was to know about women. The family should have known they would be in trouble when Zane decided to major in psychology in college. "I'm not sure. We'll just have to wait and see."

Chapter 3

The next morning, Zane sat on the edge of the bed, holding the locked box. After looking at it for a long moment, he slid it back underneath. He had been tempted to go through its contents once again.

He rubbed his hand over his face, feeling tired, although he had gotten into bed way before midnight. But he hadn't gotten much sleep, and upon awakening this morning, he had lain there, gazing up at the ceiling and thinking about Channing.

The thought of any man betraying her twisted his gut with anger. No woman deserved that, which was why he was always up front with any woman he was involved with. Channing hadn't been an exception. He had set the same ground rules with her as he had with other women, and, like he'd told Ramsey, she had accepted his terms.

He truly hadn't meant for their involvement to last as long as it had, and more than once he'd considered breaking it off sooner instead of later. But each time he felt pressed to do so—whenever he was getting too comfortable and relaxed—he would change his mind.

He enjoyed Channing both in and out of the bedroom. She had been fun to be with. Unlike others he'd dated, she wasn't a hard woman to please, which somehow made him want to please her more. She'd gotten next to him in a way no other female had: the way a smile could tease across her lips, her special scent that could drive him wild with lust or just plain spending time with her. She'd had a way of making him smile when he didn't want to be amused, a way of bringing him out. She was someone he could talk to for hours. One thing he missed more than anything else was their late-night phone conversations.

On those nights when she'd stayed late at the hospital, he would come home, shower and wait on her call. When it came, they would chat well into the night. She would tell him how her day went, and he would tell her about his. Then they would move into a number of other topics. It had been a special connection, one he'd hated losing.

And then there were those hot and sexy text messages she would send him during the day. They had come up with their own code, and she would tell him what to expect next time he saw her. And she would deliver.

Now she was engaged to marry someone else.

He should wish her well. She was just one woman, and he had dated others since her. But he would be the first to admit that his time with those other women just hadn't been the same. He had been enchanted by Channing from the beginning. She was a softhearted and passionate woman who brightened up any room. She was in a class by herself, and it bothered the hell out of him that she planned to marry a man who thought nothing of betraying her.

He stood and headed toward the kitchen. "Leave it alone, Zane. It's not your problem," he muttered to himself. He'd tried convincing himself of that very thing on his drive home from the family dinner last night. But as much as he told himself he wanted to wash his hands of Channing because she didn't matter, he knew she did.

Seeing her again a few days ago had reignited feelings he had tried to deny. He had missed her, and damn it all, he still wanted her. He'd never invaded another man's territory when it came to a woman, but this was different. Like he'd told Ramsey, the bastard didn't deserve her.

If he knew where she was staying, he would pay her a visit and try to talk some sense into her. But he didn't know, and he would not ask Megan. That meant he had to show up at the hospital again—with a plan.

Channing stopped when she saw Zane standing in the hospital parking lot, leaning on a light pole with his legs crossed at the ankles and his Stetson positioned low on his head. What was he doing here? Was he waiting for her? Why?

There had been a time when the sight of him would have had her heart jumping in her chest, and she was feeling annoyed with the fact that nothing had changed as far as that was concerned. She had been gone for almost two years, and at Megan's wedding, he'd gone out of his way to ignore her. Now she was back in town, and in only a week's time he had sought her out twice. And each time he'd done so, she was reminded just how deeply she had fallen in love with Zane.

She was finding it harder and harder to put aside her emotions when dealing with him. No one had ever warned her that falling in love would be so painstakingly complicated.

"Zane."

He straightened to his full six-foot-three-inch height. "Channing. I've been waiting for you."

She stared up at him. "Obviously."

"We need to talk." He pushed his hat back from his face, fully uncovering his eyes.

She wished he hadn't done that. Now she was staring into the eyes that had haunted her on so many nights. The eyes that would darken whenever they made love. The eyes with the intensity to turn her on with one heated glanced.

Channing drew in a deep breath when she felt a tingling sensation stir in her stomach. "We have nothing to talk about, Zane."

His brows creased in a thoughtful expression as he stared down at her. She couldn't help but wonder what he was thinking. It had been rumored that when it came to women that Zane was all knowing, and she'd pretty much discovered that to be true. He could tell each and every time she'd wanted him to make love to her, saying he could read her like a book. She wondered if he was trying to read her now. Lord, she hoped not. The last thing she needed was for him to know that just standing here with him made her nipples harden against her bra and threaded a tingling sensation through her bloodstream.

"I think we do," he said in a deep, husky tone that set her nerves on edge.

Bitterness tightened her lips. "Why?"

"I prefer to talk over a meal."

Her gaze lifted. "A meal?"

He cocked his head to the side. "Yes, a meal. You haven't had dinner yet and neither have I. There's no reason why we can't share one together. If nothing else, I'd like to think we're still friends."

Friends? Boy was he wrong. "Look, Zane, I don't know what this is all about, but the last thing you and I need to do is rekindle any friendship."

He crossed his arms over his chest. "Why? Are you worried what good old Mack will say if he finds out you had dinner with me? Seems to me that he probably trusts you a lot more than you should trust him."

She narrowed her gaze at him. "I'm not going to bother asking what you mean by that."

"No, you won't, but maybe you should."

Channing stared down at her shoes. She desperately needed to break eye contact with him. Zane was starting to wear on her last nerve. Thinking she had herself together, she returned her gaze to his. "Why are you so concerned about my relationship with Mack, Zane? You had your chance."

Zane sighed and dropped his hands to his sides. "Look, will it kill you to have dinner with me?"

"To talk?"

"Yes, to talk."

Channing studied her shoes again. What harm could come of her having dinner with him? Although he might not like Mack, the one thing Zane would not do was trespass on another man's territory. He assumed she was an engaged woman, so that would keep him in line. Besides, she was curious about what he wanted to discuss.

"Fine, we'll talk," she said, looking back up at him. He still carried a chip on his shoulder because of how she'd left. Maybe it was time they hashed things out once and for all.

"We can go in my car, and I'll bring you back here," Zane said.

There was no way she would say yes to being alone

with him in a car for any length of time. "No thanks, I can drive my own car and follow you."

He looked as if he wanted to argue, but she figured her expression made him think twice. "Fine, we're going to McKays," he said.

She went still. McKays was a well-known restaurant in town, and she had once considered it their place since they dined there often.

She lifted her chin. "I'll follow."

The moment they walked into McKays, Zane knew he should have suggested another place. Denver wasn't a small city by any stretch of the word, but the people who frequented McKays were regulars, and the Westmorelands were well-known in these parts.

The majority of these people had known Zane, his siblings and his cousins all their lives. And Zane figured most remembered him and Channing coming here together quite a few times. That was probably the reason the two of them drew so much attention as the waitress led them to a table in the middle of the restaurant.

"We need something a little more private, Tasha," he told their waitress when he saw they would be sitting across from a woman who was straining her neck to stare at them.

"No problem," Tasha said, smiling as she led them in another direction. "I have the perfect table for you two."

Channing glanced over at him and said nothing, althougth he knew what she was probably thinking. Tasha had been their regular waitress two years ago. No doubt Tasha saw some great significance with them eating together again after so long. And the engagement ring on Channing's finger was probably giving Tasha further misconceptions.

He smiled his approval when Tasha led them into a private room in the back. Although it was larger than what they needed, it was perfect. He would be able to hold a conversation with Channing without fear of being overheard. However, he could tell from the look on Channing's face that she didn't particularly like the intimate setting.

"I'm not going to bite, you know," he said, pulling out the chair for her after Tasha had left them alone.

Sitting down, she glanced over her shoulder at him, and he saw a fragment of a smile touch her lips. "Promise?"

Instead of moving away, he leaned down and whispered close to her ear, "Um, I don't know now. You do look good enough to eat."

A shiver passed through Channing when Zane moved away to take his seat. Erotic images flooded her brain, and she achingly remembered a time or two when he'd done exactly that—practically made a meal out of her.

She placed her napkin in her lap and noticed him staring at her. It didn't help matters that he had the most arresting eyes, and at that moment, they were filled with intensity. Zane was a powerfully sensuous man, and there was no doubt in her mind that he knew it. Men didn't draw women to them in droves the way he did and not know about their own magnetism.

Tasha returned and placed water, a bottle of their usual choice in wine and menus in front of them, said something about coming back later to take their order and then left them alone again. Zane continued to stare as he opened the wine bottle and poured them a glass, and—unable to do anything else—Channing stared back at him. She could feel the heat of his gaze touching every part of her, even parts he couldn't see.

Raw emotions she'd forced away for two years slowly returned. She felt her skin grow warm under the goose bumps forming on her arms. Then there was the smell of his cologne. She recognized the fragrance. It was one she had purchased for him as a Christmas gift. The masculine scent drove sensuous shivers up her spine.

What was he trying to do to her? What was he trying to make her feel? She was assailed with sensations she only felt while around him: that sinfully seductive consciousness washing passion through her, intense degrees of longing pulsating through her body.

Drawing in a deep breath, she broke eye contact with him and picked up her menu. Whatever it took, she must not forget that he was Zane, the man she had fallen in love with, the same man who had told her that he enjoyed sleeping with her but didn't love her. He could never love her, and she wanted a man who could.

When she glanced back up at him, he was still staring, which prompted her to ignore the racing of her pulse long enough to ask, "Have you forgotten that I'm engaged to someone?"

She watched as he took a slow swallow of his wine and then licked his lips before answering her.

"No, I haven't forgotten. Although I would like to," he said in a deep, husky voice. "I was just sitting here remembering all the good times we had together."

A shudder worked its way through her body as she remembered those good times, as well. Within a week of being introduced, they had shared a bed. That was unusual for her because she wasn't the type to become involved in meaningless relationships. But she'd been like most women who'd found him addictive: Zane's masculine charm had lured her in, conjuring up illusions that he was falling in love with her as much as she was with him. At the end, she'd found out the hard way just how wrong she'd been. Two years later and she could still feel the aftershocks of a broken heart.

"They were good times, weren't they?" he asked softly, breaking into her thoughts.

She gazed into dark, mesmerizing eyes. Whether she wanted to admit it or not, those had been good times. Candlelit dinners. Sex so hot it burned the sheets. And a closeness she'd never felt with any other man. "Yes, Zane, they were good, but those times are over and done with."

There, he needed to know she'd moved on. But had she really? She wanted to think she had, even though she hadn't been involved in another affair—serious or otherwise—since him. But that was beside the point. The main point was that Zane had never loved her and never would.

She was saved from any further conversation between them when Tasha returned to take their dinner order.

Zane took his time eating; he was in no hurry to broach the subject he had brought Channing here to discuss. At the moment, he was satisfied just indulging in small talk. He'd told her how the family was gearing up for his cousin Riley's wedding in September and how the horse breeding and training business was going. He talked about Bailey and how annoying his kid sister could still be at times, and he brought her up to date on Bane and how proud they were that his cousin was officially a navy SEAL.

Every so often he couldn't help but stare at her. She was so incredibly beautiful. How could any man not appreciate the woman she was? Now, two years too late, he himself could admit he had not appreciated her. He had enjoyed her, admired her and lusted after her. But he hadn't appreciated her. He would have been happy for their relationship to remain the same—without considering her wants and needs. Without considering what she deserved.

She deserved a man who appreciated her. He hadn't done so, and it looked as though her fiancé wasn't, either.

"I understand from Megan there might be some more Westmorelands out there somewhere," Channing said, breaking into his thoughts.

He looked at her, and another dose of desire tightened his groin. Her hair was pulled back and pinned on top of her head in a knot. A few tendrils had escaped confinement and brushed against her cheek. She was wearing a skirt and blouse; the color of both brought out the hazel of her eyes. There had always been a powerful attraction between them. He would have thought it had eroded by now. It hadn't.

She had to be aware of how charged the air was. She was trying to downplay it, but he felt that tug each and every time their gazes met. To know the attraction was still strong engulfed him in one hell of a delicious feeling. She might be engaged to marry another man, but there was no doubt in his mind she was still drawn to him. How was he supposed to concentrate on his meal with that kind of knowledge nudging up his testosterone?

"Yes," he said, taking a sip of wine. "During Megan and Rico's trip to Texas, they found evidence of a child my great-grandfather Raphel never knew he had. That child was given up to a woman right before the mother died in a train wreck. There was little for Rico to go on since few records were kept during that time. We're talking about more than seventy years ago. But Rico was able to get a listing of every passenger on the train—those who survived and those who didn't. He's still weeding through all of that information now. I'm told it was an extensive passenger list."

Channing nodded. "All of you must be pleased with how the investigation is going, though."

"Yes, we are. I'm confident Rico will eventually find our relatives. He's good at what he does, but it will take time. And there's still another woman who was assumed to be Raphel's fourth wife, Isabelle Connors. Rico is investigating any clues associated with her, as well."

As they continued their meal, he brought her up to date on all the babies who had been born to his cousins, the Atlanta Westmorelands. She had met most of them when they'd come to town for his sister Gemma's wedding.

"How's your folks?" he asked her.

He'd never met her parents or any of her family members since the Hastings lived in New Hampshire, but she would speak of them often and fondly. "They're fine. My brother's employer moved him to San Diego last year, and he loves it there."

Channing finished her meal and paused before asking, "So what did you want to talk to me about?"

She felt the intensity of his gaze once again.

"It's about the mistake you're making."

She lifted a brow. "What mistake?"

Zane took another sip of his wine. For some reason, she was willing to accept Mack Hammond and all his flaws, but Zane refused to let her be that generous. He placed his glass down on the table. "Marrying a man you don't love," he said calmly.

Fire flashed in her eyes. "And what makes you think I don't love Mack?"

A smile touched his lips as he leaned in closer. "Because I know you, Channing. If you loved him, you would not be sitting over there getting as aroused as I am."

Chapter 4

Channing gaped. "Aroused?"

"Yes."

She frowned. "I'm not aroused." The sudden rush of heat between her legs made a liar out of her, but she would never admit it.

"Yes, you are," Zane said with certainty. "Do you want me to prove it?"

"No, because you can't."

"You think not?" he asked, sliding his chair back and standing up.

Channing recognized that look in his eyes and drew in a sharp breath. "What is wrong with you, Zane?" She held up her ringed finger, slowly waving it for him to see. "Doesn't this mean anything to you?"

"Not a damn thing."

He reached behind him to lock the door before moving around the table. She quickly stood and backed up.

"I don't know what's gotten into you, but I refuse to put up with this foolishness. I'm leaving."

When she moved toward the door, he grabbed her hand. The moment he touched her, she froze, then a flood of desire rampaged through her bloodstream, making mush of her already stretched-to-the-limit senses.

"You think you're not aroused, Channing," he drawled, leaning in close. His tongue teased her lips, and she knew she had to stop things from going any further.

"I'm an engaged woman," she tried saying in outrage.

"You're an engaged woman who wants me," he countered. "Admit it."

"I won't admit a thing."

He shrugged. "Then feel," he whispered as his fingers traced up her arm.

Channing fought back a lustful moan as pleasure swept across the skin he touched. "I don't want to feel."

"Your body is saying otherwise. Why is that, Channing?"

She shook her head, fighting off the way his eyes were mesmerizing her. "You're wrong."

"No, sweetheart, I'm right, and I intend to show you just how right I am." He pulled her close, leaned in and swooped down on her mouth.

Push him away, damn it, Channing's mind screamed.

But at the first taste of his tongue her mind changed course and began chanting, *Devour him like he's devouring you, and don't let go.*

So she didn't.

Moments later, she wasn't exactly sure whose tongue was dominating or at what point they had begun pulling off each other's clothes. What was happening here? Invading another man's territory was not Zane's style.

Before she could question his actions any further, air hit her skin, and she realized she was halfway naked and so was he. She pulled her mouth from his. "Zane, you're not thinking straight. We need to—"

Whatever she was about to say vanished from her lips when he dropped to his knees and latched his hot mouth on her. Before Zane, oral sex had been something she read about in romance novels, but Zane had brought it to life for her. The man had a skillful mouth.

She clasped her hands on his shoulders, intending to shove him back, but at the feel of his hungry tongue, she let out a lusty moan. She instinctively arched her back and pushed herself into his mouth.

He knew all the erogenous spots to claim, conquer and satisfy.

"Zane!"

As sensations zapped her, he stroked his tongue across her, slanting his mouth at different angles. Each stroke had her moaning deep in her throat and whispering his name through her lips. And then it happened—an avalanche of the kind of pleasure she found only with him ripped through her. Instead of letting her go, he grabbed tightly to her thighs and held on as a cavalcade of spasms overtook her.

The next thing she knew, he was lifting her and placing her on one of the vacant tables and spreading her out. When she watched him rip open a condom packet with his teeth, she knew what he intended to do. Instead of stopping him, she reached down and grabbed his throbbing erection. It was just as she remembered—large, thick and nesting in a thatch of dark, curly hair. An urgency she hadn't felt in two years came over her, and she whispered in a heated breath, "I need you inside me. Now!"

He quickly slid on the condom and then, while staring into her eyes, he thrust inside of her, quickly setting a rhythm with deep, powerful strokes. He went deep, then deeper and took her to the hilt.

She moaned as her body became carnally reacquainted with his. Zane was a master at giving pleasure, and he was bequeathing a generous dose on her. She felt his swollen shaft each time he moved. She felt it all: how her feminine muscles clamped tightly on every inch of him, trying to drain him of everything he had.

Then, suddenly, an explosion of pleasure hit her. She would have let out a wail if he hadn't firmly locked his mouth on hers. Her response triggered him, and he pounded into her harder and deeper as her powerful orgasm ripped into her, nearly jerking her body off the table.

How could something so wrong feel so right? She pushed the question from her mind as his climax began and she was given yet another orgasm.

He snatched his mouth from hers and threw his head back, growling hoarsely, a sound she would admit she'd missed. She curved her arms around his neck to bring his mouth back down to hers. And then she kissed him—the way a woman was supposed to kiss a man who meant the world to her.

When she released him, he stared down at her, smiled and whispered, "Damn, I missed this. I missed you."

She didn't say anything but instead closed her eyes. Her common sense came reeling back with a vengeance as he eased himself out of her and then gently helped her off the table. They'd had spontaneous sex before but never in a public place. They were in a restaurant in downtown Denver, for heaven's sake! She didn't want to think about how many times Tasha might have tried to open the locked door. Had anyone heard them?

"Do you need help getting back into your clothes?"

She jerked her gaze over to where Zane stood. He had his clothes back on as if he had never taken them off. "No, I can handle it," she said softly, picking up her panties from the floor.

When she began sliding the undergarment up her legs, his next words stopped her. "How soon will you be breaking your engagement to Hammond?"

There was something about the way he'd asked, something about the tone of his voice that made her gut twist in a knot. He spoke as if her engagement had been a problem he'd solved. Had he? Dread consumed her.

"What makes you think I'm ending my engagement?" she asked, deciding to play her hunch and hope like hell that she was wrong. Surely he hadn't seduced her just to force her to break her engagement?

"Of course you're going to break it. You're not the type of woman who would be engaged to one man and mess around with another."

No, she wasn't. "And you're not the type of man to mess around with a woman who's not yours. A woman who belongs to another man. I guess we've both acted out of character today."

She watched his face take on a formidable look when he said, "I didn't act out of character, sweetheart. I was merely proving a point."

She had finished dressing now, and his words gave her pause. "Just what point were you trying to prove?"

He slowly crossed the room and pinned her against the table by bracing his arms on either side of her. He leaned in to get eye level with her. "The point I *proved* is that you're mine. There's no other man for you but me, and I don't intend to give you up."

Channing forced her heart to *not* leap with joy. Did that mean he loved her after all? He had yet to say the words.

She decided to ask him straight-out. "Does that mean you realized you love me?"

He actually seemed shocked at her assumption. He straightened. "No. It means I care for you, and I don't want to see you get hurt. Hammond would have hurt you."

Pain ripped through Channing, and her heart twisted. Did he not realize *he* was hurting her? "Let me get this straight," she said, fighting anger. "You don't love me but you brought me here to seduce me just to prove a point?"

Zane frowned. "I brought you here to talk some sense into you, but I ended up seducing some sense into you instead. Doing so brought back some damn pleasant memories, don't you think?"

She swallowed, suddenly feeling like the biggest fool on the planet. "So you only had sex with me because you figured I would have no choice but to break off my engagement?" she asked softly.

He shook his head. "No, I made love to you because I wanted you, and it was obvious you wanted me, as well. That made me realize you couldn't possibly love Hammond if you desired me. I was right. Your body wants me, so the way I see it, you belong to me."

She closed her eyes as blood rushed to her head. "Now that I belong to you, Zane, what do you plan to do with me? You just admitted once again that you don't love me, which means you don't intend to marry me. So what are you going to do with me, Zane?"

When he didn't say anything, when he just stood there staring at her with a deep scowl on his face, her anger exploded. "You selfish jerk! You don't want to give me all the things I want—love, marriage and a family—yet you don't want any other man to give me those things, either!"

"Damn it, Channing! Hammond is fooling around on

you. I didn't want him to hurt you. You don't need to marry a man like that."

"You're the only who has ever hurt me, Zane," she said as pain etched itself all through her body. "You don't love me, but you don't want any other man to love me."

Zane gritted his teeth. "Didn't you hear what I said? Hammond is being unfaithful to you."

"No, he isn't," she said sharply. "I was never engaged to Mack. I only pretended to be. Mack is a good friend and nothing more. But you didn't know that. For all you knew, he could have been my happiness, but you still went so far as to try to destroy that."

Shock shone on Zane's face. "What do you mean you were never engaged to him?"

Instead of answering, Channing moved toward the door. Fighting back tears, she unlocked it, snatched it open and quickly walked out.

Chapter 5

Later that night, Zane flung his front door open to find an angry Megan on his doorstep. "It's too late for visitors, Megan, and I'm not in the mood," he said in a low growl.

His sister pushed her way past him, strode to the middle of his living room and angrily whirled to face him. "If you weren't my brother, and if I had a gun, I would shoot you in the balls right here and now."

He felt the pain of her words and his balls ached in response. "Go ahead and say what you have to say so I can get some sleep."

"Sleep! How can you sleep after what you did to Channing?"

He crossed his arms over his chest. "She had no reason to call you. She lied about her engagement. She was never going to marry that guy with the roving eyes, but you knew that all along, didn't you? You not only invited her to the wedding when I pleaded with you not to but you let her make a fool of me."

Megan rounded on him, and he had the good sense to back up. An angry, out-of-control Gemma or Bailey he could deal with but an angry Megan he could not. Everyone knew about her penchant for self-control. On those rare times when she lost it, she was a force to reckon with.

"First of all, Channing didn't call me. Louise Mitchell did Megan snapped.

"Louise Mitchell?"

"Yes, as well as Emma Falk and Mavis Upshaw. They were all dining at McKays when Channing practically ran out of the private room in tears. I immediately went to see Channing when I got off work tonight. Thanks to you, she was completely devastated. She told me everything, Zane. *Everything.* And if you weren't my brother, I would shoot you."

"Not if I shot him first."

Zane looked toward his front door where an angry Bailey had let herself in. The hellion! That was all he needed. "You are supposed to knock, Bailey."

"Kiss it, Zane." She glanced over at Megan. "I heard. Wanda Grunthall's parents were dining at McKays."

Zane rolled his eyes. Was there anyone who hadn't been dining at McKays tonight? "If the two of you want to discuss my business among yourselves then go ahead. I'm going to bed."

"The hell you will," Bailey said, moving toward him. "You're going to sit and listen to what we have to say. And don't be surprised if Gemma calls you from Australia. Wanda Grunthall is a good friend of hers, as well."

Seeing that he would never get to bed until he heard what his sisters had to say, he dropped down on the sofa.

"Okay, I'm giving you both five minutes. Say what you have to say and leave."

Megan went first. "Have you even taken the time to consider why someone like Channing would fake an engagement?"

"I don't have to wonder why. She did it to piss me off."

"It's not all about you!" Bailey shouted.

Zane flinched. He was sick and tired of being yelled at. "If you use that tone of voice again in my presence, Bailey, I'm going to snatch up your little butt, take you to the bathroom and wash your mouth out with soap like I used to do."

Bailey glared at him. "Go to—"

"Bailey!" Megan interrupted. "Please let me finish. Then you can go for blood if you want."

Bailey nodded. "Sorry. Please continue, Megan."

Megan smiled at her sister. "Thanks." She then narrowed her gaze at Zane. "No, Zane, that's not the reason. Channing did it to keep her dignity and pride in check when she came to town for my wedding. Two years ago, when you were dating, people talked, made bets, laughed at her behind her back and figured you would eventually kick her to the curb like you did all the others."

Zane's jaw tightened. His eyes sparked fire. "Who told you that?"

"Doesn't matter. Everyone around these parts knows your reputation when it comes to women. But Channing hung in there because she thought she meant more to you than that. Most people knew better. They knew she really didn't mean a damn thing to you, that eventually you would drop her and move on."

Megan paused. "She was your steady girlfriend for nine months, Zane. Although I'm certain you gave her the same warning that you gave all your other women, at some point she began thinking she might be different. We all did. You treated her differently from the rest."

Zane didn't say anything for a long minute and then said quietly, "She was different."

"Then why would you hurt her, Zane? All you wanted to do was prove a point? What if Rico had done something like that to me?"

Before he could answer, Bailey spoke up and asked, "What did Zane do to Channing? All Wanda said was that they had a little spat. Is there more?"

Both Zane and Megan said simultaneously, "No."

Bailey narrowed her eyes. "You two are lying."

Instead of responding to Bailey's accusations, Megan returned her attention to Zane. "She told me the truth about the fake engagement, and I feel partly to blame for what happened because I deliberately let Ramsey eavesdrop on a conversation I had with Chloe. I figured he would tell you what Mack Hammond was doing and that you would get upset about it and come up with a plan to save Channing. Lord knows, I didn't think you'd go as far as you did."

"Damn, what did he do?" Bailey asked again.

A collective "nothing" was the response from Megan and Zane.

Then Zane said to Megan, "It wasn't planned. It just happened."

"Ahh Bailey said, figuring out what nobody was telling her. An angry frown settled on her face. "If you weren't my brother, I would castrate you."

Zane rolled his eyes, although he believed Bailey was more likely to carry out her threat than Megan was. "I never meant to hurt her," he said, when he began to realize just what had happened. He had tried to stop Hammond from hurting Channing, and he was the one guilty of causing her pain.

"I need to go see her and apologize," he said, standing.

"Too late," Megan said softly. "By the time I'd gotten over to her place, she had already canceled the rest of her symposium and packed her things. I sat and talked to her until it was time for her to leave for the airport."

Zane felt a gut-wrenching sensation in the pit of his stomach. "She's left town?"

"Do you blame her, Zane?" Megan asked.

He drew in a deep breath. No, he didn't blame her. "Doesn't matter. I'm leaving for Atlanta tomorrow."

Megan placed her hands on her hips. "To do what? Tell her you're sorry for what you did but that you still don't love her? Just let her go, Zane. You've done enough damage. Besides, she's not going to Atlanta."

He lifted a brow. "Where did she go, Megan?" he asked in a near growl.

"Don't tell him," Bailey piped in to say. "He will only hurt her again. Channing wants to be loved, and Zane isn't capable of loving any woman."

Zane ignored Bailey's words and continued to hold Megan's gaze. "Did she go to her parents' in New Hampshire?" he asked.

"Don't tell him, Megan!"

Megan drew in a deep breath. "No, she didn't go there, either."

Zane felt an intense need to ferret out her location. All of Channing's family lived in New Hampshire. He then remembered that she'd told him her brother had moved to San Diego. "Did she go to California?"

"No."

"Then where the hell did she go?"

Megan lifted her chin. "If you find out Channing's

whereabouts, it won't be with my help. Bailey's right.
You're not capable of loving anyone but yourself, so just
leave her alone."

She turned and headed for the door. After giving him
one hard glare, Bailey followed her sister.

Early the next morning, after a sleepless night—and
when he was certain Megan had left for work—Zane got
in his truck and headed over to Megan's Meadows to see
Rico. His brother-in-law opened the door with a sympa-
thetic look on his face. "I heard my wife tore into you
pretty damn good last night."

Zane grunted as he strolled toward the kitchen, following the aroma of coffee. He went still when he saw his
brother Derringer and his cousins Jason, Riley, Canyon
and Stern sitting at the kitchen table. "Somebody gave you
guys a day off of work or something?" he asked Riley,
Canyon and Stern. The three worked for the family-owned
business, Blue Ridge Land Management.

Riley chuckled. "It's still early yet. Besides, we heard
both Megan and Bailey chewed you out, and we wanted
to be here when you came and asked Rico for a bandage."

Zane set his chin in a frown. "Funny." After helping
himself to a cup of coffee, he slid into one of the empty
chairs at the table.

"That's not why they're here, Zane," Rico said, grinning, leaning against the counter with his own cup of coffee. "In fact, Ramsey and Dillon are on their way over, as
well. I called you earlier this morning to tell you about this
impromptu meeting, but you didn't answer the phone."

Zane shrugged. "I thought it was Megan calling, and
we don't have anything to say to each other until she tells
me where Channing is."

Derringer snorted. "Don't hold your breath for that to happen. Megan's pretty angry with you."

Zane opened his mouth to respond to Derringer's words when there was a knock at the door. "That's probably Ramsey and Dillon," Rico said, moving toward the living room.

Moments later, Ramsey and Dillon Westmoreland walked in and glanced around. Their gazes locked on Zane. Dillon smiled and said, "Glad to see you're still in one piece."

Zane cursed under his breath. Had everybody heard about Megan's and Bailey's visit?

Rico proceeded to get everybody's attention. "I wanted to give you guys an update on something I discovered with Raphel's investigation. I told Megan last night, and now I want to share the information with you."

"What did you find out?" Dillon asked. Since there weren't any more empty seats at the table, he and Ramsey settled their tall frames in stools at the breakfast bar.

"The woman who survived the train wreck and who adopted Raphel's son was Jeannette Outlaw. She named her son Levy—after her husband who was killed in the train accident. She moved to Detroit as a single mother and everyone assumed the child belonged to her deceased husband. She never told anyone anything different."

Rico paused and then continued, "Levy Outlaw married at twenty-five, and he and his wife had one son, Javier. That's where the trail stops. It seems Levy Outlaw, his wife and son moved away from Detroit, but we're not sure of their final destination. My people are working on it."

Rico leaned back against the counter. "The other news I wanted to share is that I found records on a woman by the name of Isabelle Connors who lived in Percy, Nevada. As you all know, Isabelle was documented as Raphel West-moreland's fourth wife."

"Percy, Nevada?" Dillon asked, lifting a brow. "That's where our great-grandmother Gemma was born and raised. Do you think there's a chance that she and Isa-belle knew each other?"

"That's a possibility I'm checking out," Rico said. A smile touched his lips. "Of course Megan is excited about the information I was able to find on Levy Outlaw."

Ramsey grinned as he shook his head. "I bet she was. She's determined to find more cousins to the West-morelands."

Rico chuckled. "Yes, and don't be surprised if I do."

"I want to know where Channing is, Rico," Zane said after the meeting had ended and everyone had left. "I'm sure Megan told you."

Rico took a sip of his coffee. "Yes, but Megan doesn't think you need to know where Channing is. Your sister believes all you're going to do is hurt her friend again."

Zane didn't say anything. Megan had pretty much made her thoughts damn clear. He had stayed up most of the night, walking the floor. Knowing he had hurt Chan-ning to the point that she had left town had kept him awake. His sisters were right. He had been wrong.

"Zane?"

He glanced over at Rico. "Yes?"

"If you found Channing, what would you do?"

Zane lowered his head and gazed down into his cup of coffee. He had asked himself that same question while walking the floor last night. He would apologize of course, but would that be enough? Lifting his head, he met Rico's gaze. "I'm not sure," he said honestly.

Rico nodded. "Then maybe you should be sure before

you go looking for her. When a man goes after a woman, he needs to know why he's doing it. He needs to have a game plan."

Zane didn't say anything, mainly because he'd never needed a game plan when it came to women.

"Do you know at what point I knew I loved your sister, Zane?"

Zane shrugged. He figured there was a reason Rico wanted to tell him this. "No. When?"

"I knew I loved your sister when I realized I couldn't live a single day without her." Rico took a sip of his coffee. "If you ever feel anything close to that kind of emotion, let me know and then I'll tell you where Channing is."

"I'm fine, Megan, really I am. Don't worry. I love it here," Channing said, stepping out onto the porch of her grandparents' oceanside villa in the beautiful Kindle Shores community of Virginia Beach. The house and five others were on a private section of land that developers had been trying to purchase for years. However, like her grandparents, none of the owners were interested in selling.

"It's been a while since I've been here, so maybe Zane did me a favor after all. In addition to reminding me what jerks some men can be, it made me realize I hadn't taken time off from work in a while to rest, relax and regroup," she said, sliding down into the porch swing.

The ocean looked beautiful. As a child, she enjoyed spending her summers here with her grandparents. Adele Hastings hadn't asked any questions when her granddaughter had called saying she needed to come to the house and stay awhile. But Channing had still heard the concern in her grandmother's voice when she'd told Channing where to find the key.

The moment Channing arrived and opened the door a sense of welcome had settled upon her. The memories of the summers she'd spent here were special. It was the time when she and all her cousins would get together to share their grandparents' wisdom and love.

She'd seen how her grandparents had spruced up the place with painted walls, gleaming tile floors and all-new furniture. She liked the look and all the vibrant colors. When it came to decorating, her grandmother still had style.

"Well, if you need anything—and I mean anything at all—call me, Channing," Megan said, interrupting Channing's thoughts. "Again, I'm sorry about everything."

"Don't be. Zane warned me how things would be between us in the very beginning, but I let myself fall in love with him, anyway. As far as the other night at McKays, the desire was mutual. I wanted him, Megan. Your brother proved he's still my weakness. I thought I had gotten over him, but evidently I haven't. He's not a man a woman can forget easily," Channing admitted. "But I will," she added with strong conviction.

"Well, it's going to be a long time before he gets back in my good graces. At some point, he has to come to terms with the fact that he's going to grow old alone," Megan said in a tiff.

A few moments later, after ending her phone call, Channing stood to stretch and look out at the beach. The beautiful blue water was inviting, and she decided she would take a dip later. But for now, she would make a sandwich and start reading the suspense thriller she had picked up at the airport.

But once she sat back down, she couldn't help thinking about what had happened over the past couple of days. Hurt and heartbroken, she had canceled her symposium with apologies and plans to reschedule and had flown from Denver to here. Upon arriving, she had gone shopping for enough food for the three weeks she intended to stay. On the first day, she had called Zane every god-awful name in the book. Then she'd called herself a damn fool and indulged in a good cry. The next day, she had gotten out and gone back into town to shop.

Her first stop had been a boutique where she'd found the most gorgeous pair of sandals. Deciding that she hadn't treated herself to a day of beauty in a while, she'd visited a spa. A couple of hours later, with several new beach outfits, new sandals, a pedicure and manicured nails, she had returned to the beach house feeling a whole lot better. Pain and anger were no longer at war inside of her. She had reached the conclusion that no man would ever take her joy.

She'd also faced a few realities. It seemed her dream of love, marriage and family was just that—a dream. Some dreams weren't meant for everyone. Zane had taught her that lesson. She couldn't put her love and trust in a man who didn't deserve it, a man who wasn't capable of loving, a man who couldn't make her happy. She wanted a man who simply adored her—the way she would adore him—a man who would love her, a man who wanted the same things she wanted, not because she wanted them but because *they* wanted them.

She'd meant what she'd told Megan. She appreciated Zane for making her realize just how naive she had been. She thought she had taken off the rose-colored glasses the last time she'd left Denver, but this time not only had she taken them off she'd tossed them into the sea. The next man she dated would have to work hard for her affections.

At that moment, she doubted she would ever fall in

love again. She'd tried and lost her heart, and now it was time for her to get out of the game.

Zane turned over in bed and glanced at the clock. It was two in the morning. Sitting up, he ran a frustrated hand across his face. Once the haze of his anger over Channing's engagement deception had shifted away, all he could see every time he closed his eyes was her stricken face. It hit him right below the gut each and every time he thought about hurting her.

Unable to sleep, he eased out of bed and went downstairs for a cold drink of water. However, when he opened the refrigerator it was a bottle of beer that he pulled out instead. Leaning against the countertop, he twisted off the bottle cap and took a huge swig, liking the feel of the liquid moving past his throat to hit solidly in his stomach.

He had built this house seven years ago, but this was the first time he'd realized just how lonely it was. His siblings and cousins visited often—and Bailey too much—but he never allowed women to consider his place as their home.

Except for Channing.

He had surprised even himself when he'd given her a key, but he had never questioned why he'd done so. All he'd known was those days when he would arrive home after working with the horses all day and see her car parked in his yard, sensations he couldn't describe tugged at his chest. His mood would brighten as soon as he opened the door and saw her, and he would sweep her up in his arms and kiss her as if his entire life depended on it.

He could remember the last time she'd sat at his kitchen table. It had been one morning after she'd spent the night and had awakened early to prepare breakfast for the both of them. They had eaten together, and it had been enjoyable, as usual. But it had been that same morning when Channing had come out and asked where their relationship was headed.

The question had annoyed him because he'd known she was about to bring up something he didn't want to discuss. He had told her he didn't love her and that nothing had changed. Afterward, he had quickly left for work, not wanting to stick around to see how she handled his response. A few weeks later, she had dropped the bomb that she was leaving town. Her decision to leave Denver had made him bitter. He hadn't even bothered to attend the going-away party Megan had thrown for her.

Taking another huge swig of his beer, he pushed away from the counter and walked over to the window to look out in brooding silence. Most people were in bed asleep, but here he was, right where he had been for the past three days, enduring sleepless nights due to a woman he should have gotten over two years ago. She was the only woman who could make emotions tug at him…like they were doing now. In fact, they weren't just tugging; they were eating away at him big-time.

He was still on Megan's and Bailey's bad sides. That much had been evident at tonight's chow-down. His sisters-in-law and his cousins' wives were sending him seething looks, as well. Even Gemma had called him from Australia to give him a blistering earful, saying, *How could you hurt Channing again, Zane? She is way too good for you. She is liked and well respected by all who know her, and she has a heart of gold. But that isn't enough for you, is it? Any other man would have appreciated the beautiful and heartwarming person that she is. One day you're going to realize just what you lost!*

Zane released a sigh of pure disgust with himself.

While shaving this morning, he had looked himself in the mirror and hadn't liked the person staring back at him. Everyone who had been on him for the past few days was right. Channing deserved a better man than him. She deserved the right to find a man who could love her, make her happy and give her the marriage and family she wanted. She deserved a man who would cherish her, who would show her every day how much she was adored and how proud he would be to have her at his side. Somewhere, that man was out there. The thought made Zane's gut clench. He would rather cut off his arm than lose Channing to another man.

He froze, stunned by what he was thinking. What man would willingly lose a limb for a woman he didn't love? Zane's throat suddenly went dry, and he tilted the beer bottle up to his mouth, quickly chugging down what was left.

It was then that Rico's words came back to haunt him… *I knew I loved your sister when I realized I couldn't live a single day without her.*

Zane drew in a deep breath. He could finally admit that he felt things for Channing that he'd never felt for another woman. He didn't want to let her out of his life. In other words…he couldn't imagine living a single day without her. His heart began pounding in his chest when he knew immediately what that meant.

"Ah, hell," he muttered to himself, glancing down at his empty beer bottle. "That means you've fallen for her, man. And you've fallen hard."

Everything suddenly made sense. Why he'd felt so down in the dumps after she left Denver for Atlanta and why every woman he'd dated after her seemed lacking. It also answered the question of why the thought of her being with another man constantly ate at him. More importantly, it explained why he'd kept that locked box under his bed for two years, unable to let go.

For the first time in his life, Zane Westmoreland loved a woman.

"Hello, Gramma, this is Channing."

"Hi, sweetie. I hope you got to the beach house all right and you're getting settled."

"Yes, I've been here for three days now, and I'm starting to unwind. I needed a break," Channing said, pushing hair back from her face.

"Yes, a break from work is always nice," Adele Hastings said.

Channing glanced out the kitchen window. She had gotten up early to go jogging on the beach. Then she'd returned, showered and prepared breakfast, which she'd enjoyed while catching up on the news on television. The meteorologist had reported a heat wave that was spreading all the way up to New England. This prompted her to check on her grandparents since they liked spending time outdoors. Her parents, who lived within five miles of her grandparents, would usually check on them but they had left last week for a two-week cruise to Hawaii, leaving out of San Diego after visiting with her brother.

"You and Gramps okay? I heard about the heat wave."

"We're fine, but what about you?"

She knew her grandmother was someone she could always talk to, and she felt blessed to have two confidantes, her mother and grandmother. "I'm through with men, Gramma," she said honestly.

There was a pause at the other end of the line, and then Adele asked, "Are you?"

"Yes. You love them, and they don't love you back. And

then there are those who claim they do but don't know the meaning of the word—like Emmitt."

Why she had brought up Emmitt Sawyer she would never know. Emmitt had been part of her college days. The first guy she'd ever slept with and the first guy she'd given her heart to. She'd thought he loved her; he'd even told her so a number of times. She'd believed him and had taken him home on spring break to meet the family. Then, at the start of their junior year, when they'd been dating for almost a year, she'd discovered he'd been messing around with a girl who worked as a waitress at some café in town…the entire time he'd been spewing words of love to Channing.

She had returned home brokenhearted. It had been her mother and grandmother who'd convinced her that not all men abused a woman's love. There were men out there who would cherish it. It had taken her five years before she'd put her heart on the line again for Zane.

She had moved from a man who told her he loved her all the time to a man who didn't hesitate to let her know he didn't love her at all. Both had been heartbreakers.

"So you think men are the problem, Channing?"

Her grandmother's question sliced into her thoughts. "No, I'm the problem. I expect too much and trust too soon. So I'm quitting men."

"Um, that sounds interesting," Adele said calmly.

Channing scowled. "Men aren't good for anything but sex." She suddenly sucked in a quick breath when she remembered who she was talking to.

She could hear her grandmother's chuckle on the other end of the phone. "I'll remember to tell your grandfather that."

Channing dropped down into a kitchen chair. "Oh,

Gramma. Gramps is like Dad. They are the greatest. They just don't make men like that anymore."

"Don't they?"

"I thought they did, but now I'm not sure. I'm tired of getting my heart broken. I'm locking up my heart and throwing away the key."

"Are you sure you want to do that, sweetie?"

No, but she felt she didn't have a choice. Like she'd told her grandmother, the problem wasn't with the men but with her. She was the one who had to make changes in the way she thought about love. She could see now that her problem was that she took relationships too seriously because she'd always had an agenda. Maybe it was time to loosen the shackles and be set free. Live a little and have fun.

"Channing?"

She blinked upon realizing she hadn't answered her grandmother's question. "Yes, Gramma, that's what I want to do. That's what I'm going to do."

Knowing she needed to get off the phone before her grandmother tried to talk her in to giving men another chance, Channing stood up. "I need to get dressed. I'm going to spend the day on the beach."

"Oh, all right. If you want to talk again, I'm here."

Channing tightened the belt on her robe. She had the best grandmother in the whole wide world. "Thanks, and I love you."

"I love you back."

Zane felt tired and drained. He didn't have to be told he wasn't pulling his share of the work today. It disgusted him even more when Derringer and Jason gave him pathetic gazes.

When they took a break for lunch, Jason left to meet

his wife, Bella. They were adding more rooms to her grandfather's home, which they'd turned into a bed-and-breakfast, and they were meeting with the contractors.

Zane glanced over at Derringer as they sat across from each other outside at a picnic table eating the sandwiches and drinking the tea Derringer's wife, Lucia, had made for them. "You're quiet," Zane said.

Derringer met Zane's gaze. "I was just thinking. I couldn't sleep last night and woke up around two. After checking on the baby, I went downstairs to get something to drink."

Zane nodded. That was what he'd been doing around that time.

"Do you know what happened when I walked into my kitchen, Zane?"

Zane frowned. "No."

"I swear I could smell gingerbread."

Zane didn't say anything. He didn't have to. All he had to do was remember the days when he and his siblings would wake up to the aroma of gingerbread. Their mother loved to bake, and gingerbread cookies were her favorite as well as theirs.

"Then it hit me that it's been almost twenty years, but damn it, I still miss Mom like yesterday," Derringer said, obviously trying to keep the pain from his voice. "Both her and Dad…but especially Mom. She had a way of making all our wrongs right."

Zane had to agree. Their mother had been special, and Susan Westmoreland had fostered a close relationship with all her children. He'd been in his late teens when his parents had died—in his second year of college. He recalled when he'd been around sixteen. At the peak of his dating years in high school, he'd thought he was a Casanova, the school's stud. His mother would warn him about breaking some girl's heart and claimed that if he wasn't careful someday a girl would come along and break his.

"I've been thinking of her a lot lately, too," Zane confessed. "I often wonder how different things would be if that plane hadn't crashed. Dillon would be retiring from the NBA about now, and Ramsey would have come out of college to become a sheep rancher and not have gone to work at Blue Ridge. And," he added with a smile, "we wouldn't have had the trouble that we did out of the twins, Bane and Bailey. The first time Bailey said a curse word around Mom her ass would have been grass."

"Yeah." Derringer chuckled. "Mom didn't play. But she also had a soft heart. All the neighbors loved her and Aunt Clarisse."

Zane had a feeling his mother would have liked the spouses her sons and daughters had married. Ramsey was happy with Chloe, Derringer was head over heels in love with Lucia and both Gemma and Megan had married good men who worshiped the ground they walked on. He drew in a deep breath, suddenly convinced his mother would have loved Channing, as well.

Neither Derringer nor Zane said anything for a minute, and then Zane asked, "When did you know you loved Lucia?"

If Derringer found the question odd, he didn't say. Instead, he took a sip of his iced tea. "First of all, I fought it like hell. The reason I never let any woman get close to me was because the very thought of falling in love and getting attached to someone sent chills up my spine. The thought of losing them the way we lost our folks and Uncle Adam and Aunt Clarisse was unacceptable to me. I had this fear of loving Lucia and then losing her the way we lost Mom."

Zane studied his brother. He wondered if Derringer

knew that Zane had similar fears. "How did you overcome them? Those fears."

"By realizing that life is full of risks. Things happen.
I couldn't live my life waiting for something bad to come
my way. Then I decided that nothing, especially not my
fears, weighed more heavily than my desire to be with
Lucia, to build a life with her and make a family. That's
when I admitted to myself that I cared more for her than
for any other woman before, that I loved her. And when
a man loves a woman he will move heaven and hell, if
necessary, to make her the most important person in his
life, regardless of the risks. She is worth the risk. She be-
comes your life."

Zane didn't say anything as he continued to sip his tea.
He knew in his heart that Channing was worth the risk.
She was a vital part of his life, but up to now he'd been
too afraid to admit it.

The thought of loving a woman was scary as hell, but
what was even scarier was the possibility that he'd lost
her and might not ever see her again. Or the thought that
wherever she was she hated his guts.

"Can I ask you something, Zane?"

Zane glanced over at his brother. "Yes."

"Do you love Channing?"

Zane sucked in a quick breath at his brother's question, but then only moments later he answered by saying, "I believe I do."

Derringer shook his head. "That's not good enough.
You need to know for certain. You owe it to yourself, as
well as to her, to know what your true feelings are. Do
you know what I think, Zane?"

Zane poured out the rest of his tea. "No, what do you
think, Derringer?"

"You're afraid to admit to falling in love for the same

reason I was. Losing people you love is hard. But you need to weigh all the options. Think of all the things that might happen and those that might not. Then ask yourself if spending time with Channing every day for the rest of your life is worth the risks."

Derringer glanced at his watch when he saw Jason returning. "I guess it's time for us to get back to work."

Zane found it hard to focus on work without thoughts of Channing and what his brother had said consuming his mind. For years, his brothers and cousins had considered him the know-it-all where women were concerned, and he did know a lot. But the one thing he *didn't* know was how to love and appreciate the one woman who should have mattered. The one woman who was meant for him.

Channing was meant for him. He could see that now.

A few hours later, telling Derringer and Jason that he needed to leave for a while, Zane got in his truck and drove over to Megan's Meadows at breakneck speed. He figured his sister was still at work and was glad it was Rico who opened the door. Before Rico could say anything, Zane spoke up and said, "I want to know where Channing is."

At the frown that settled on Rico's face, Zane held up his hand. "I love her, man."

Rico studied Zane, and then he nodded slowly.

"I figured you would come to your senses sooner or later. But be prepared. Love or no love, I don't think she's going to make things easy for you. Personally, I wouldn't."

Zane wasn't surprised by that. "Yes, but there's no way I'm not going to try."

Chapter 6

One of Channing's favorite spots in her grandmother's beach house was the window seat. She remembered when her grandfather had knocked down the wall to build it—a huge bay window with a padded seat long enough to stretch out on. One night in her teen years she'd even slept here. She'd woken up staring out at the ocean.

So here she sat with her legs stretched out in front of her while reading a book. The story had held her attention for the past two days, and she planned to finish it later tonight. After reaching a good stopping place, she placed her book aside, stood to stretch and decided to go to the kitchen to get something to drink.

Her brother hadn't called, which meant her grandparents hadn't mentioned anything to him and she appreciated that. The last thing she needed was for Juan to call wanting to know why she wasn't in Denver when she'd told him she would be there awhile. He was five years older and could be overprotective at times.

Although neither her parents nor Juan had met Zane, she had mentioned him on a number of occasions, so there was no doubt in her mind that they were aware she'd fallen in love. Just like there was no doubt in her mind that they knew the relationship had ended. No one had asked, but her family was astute enough to know her decision to leave Denver two years ago had something to do with Zane.

She was heading back to her window seat with a cold glass of lemonade when there was a knock at the door. She smiled, figuring it was the six-year-old girl she'd met yesterday on the beach. The youngster, Sandy Farmer, was an absolute doll. She and her parents and her adorable nine-month-old baby brother had rented the beach house next door for the entire summer. The parents were probably in their early thirties, and it was easy to see that they were in love.

Jennifer Farmer had let Channing hold her son, and the moment she had held the baby in her arms she recalled a time when she'd dreamed of marrying Zane and having his child. But then, in that same dream, she had fooled herself into thinking he loved her. The Farmer family was beautiful, and seeing them together made Channing realize just what she might never have.

But she'd decided not to take men or relationships seriously, she reminded herself, as she placed the glass of lemonade on the table and moved toward the door. Sandy had paid her a visit a few hours ago to see if Channing wanted to build sand castles on the beach.

Ready to tell Sandy she couldn't go out on the beach with her just yet, she opened the door.

"Hello, Channing."

* * *

From Channing's expression, Zane knew he was the last person she'd expected to see. She looked amazing with bare feet and wearing a short denim skirt and a lavender T-shirt. While she was still standing in the doorway, stunned, he figured he would ease inside before the shock wore off.

When he closed the door behind him, shock was replaced with anger. "Hey, wait a minute! I didn't invite you in. What are you doing here, Zane?"

"I came to apologize, Channing," he said, leaning back against the closed door. "The reason I did what I did that night at McKays was because I thought you were engaged to Hammond, and I didn't want to see you get hurt."

She gaped at him. "You didn't want to see me hurt? So seducing me just for the hell of it, to prove a point, wasn't going to hurt me?"

Zane crossed his arms over his chest. "I did not seduce you for the hell of it, Channing. I did it to make sure you would break off your engagement. At the time, I thought it was a good idea. Hammond was screwing around on you. How was I to know the two of you weren't really engaged?"

Channing clenched her jaw before saying. "That's beside the point! How Mack was treating me wasn't any of your business."

"The hell it wasn't. Was I supposed to stand around and let him mess with you?"

She looked livid. "Yes, that's precisely what you were supposed to do. It wasn't your business, Zane. *I'm* not your business. You didn't want me, remember? Who I became involved with after leaving Denver wasn't your concern. You can't have it both ways. You don't love me yet you didn't think twice about sabotaging what, for all you knew, was my happiness with another man."

Zane shook his head at their senseless argument. "I do love you."

Channing froze. And then seconds later, when he leaned in closer, she blinked. When he grasped her chin to tilt her face up to his, the only thing she seemed able to do was stare up at him. Did he really think she would believe that he loved her after all the times he'd denied it? No, Zane didn't love her. He just didn't want anyone else to have her. Hadn't he all but told her that very thing at McKays?

"I'm sorry I made you mad at me, but I'm here now, and everything is going to be fine, baby. You'll see."

Before she could respond, he licked his tongue across her lips slowly with deliberate strokes. He toyed with her mouth by sliding his tongue in and out between her parted lips. Her traitorous body let out a moan.

There were some things a woman couldn't get over, and that was how skilled a man could be at seduction. Zane was an ace. He could kiss the panties off a woman, and she of all people should know since he'd proved that skill on her a number of times.

Moments later, he lifted his head from her mouth, and she could hear his heavy breathing. But what made her breath catch were the dark brown eyes fixed on hers. He was staring at her in a way that made her insides melt.

"I want you," he whispered huskily against her lips.

Channing tried to ignore how quickly he had gone from loving her to wanting her. It was obvious Zane Westmoreland didn't know the difference between love and lust. And, for now, she didn't want to know, either. There was no denying she wanted him, and as long as she knew that love wasn't a part of the equation there was no reason she couldn't enjoy him.

Hadn't she told her grandmother a few days ago she was locking up her heart and throwing away the key? Zane showing up like this didn't change a thing. As far as she was concerned, his declaration of love was nothing but words. Words she refused to believe in.

"Channing, say you want me, too," he said throatily, holding her gaze with his dark eyes.

What he was asking of her was easy. "I want you, too, Zane."

A smile touched his face, and he drew her closer, putting his hands on her rounded bottom, cupping her in a way that placed an arch in her back and made her press tight to his middle.

She felt him, the heavy bulge of his erection through his jeans. Even through the denim she could feel him throbbing. She wrapped her arms around his neck, and they stared at each other as sexual heat surrounded them, stimulating them, charging the air. Erotic tension vibrated between them, and a gigantic craving rushed blood through her veins.

Then, soundlessly, he lowered his mouth back down to hers.

Zane felt his world rocking the moment their mouths locked. Tongues touched, entwined, twirled with a hunger that tugged mercilessly at his groin. Damn, he had missed this. He had lain in bed plenty of nights remembering. Channing had a mouth that was made to be kissed, and he had taken great joy in doing so. She had a taste that was unique, and his tongue was greedy, ready to make up for lost time.

She was kissing him back, tangling her tongue with his

in a heated duel, a sensuous motion that made his erection throb harder. There had never been a time when she hadn't met him on a primal level. There had never been a time when she hadn't both fueled and satisfied a need within him. Even now, his stomach muscles quivered as raw desire took control of him.

He shifted his stance so the apex of her thighs made better contact with his erection. He wanted her to feel it, to know what she was doing to him, to know just how much he wanted her.

Zane deepened the kiss, and the moan that came from deep within Channing's throat told him all he needed to know. He wouldn't have to grovel as he'd thought he would have to do. Like he'd been prepared to do. Like him, she was ready for them to move into the future together.

He pulled his mouth from hers and stared down into eyes glazed over in passion. How could he not have known he loved her? How could he have missed the truth when all signs pointed to those emotions he hadn't wanted to acknowledge? She had been the one even when he'd convinced himself that she was not.

He loved her. He needed her. And he never intended to let her go again. Derringer was right. The thought of not having Channing in his life far outweighed the fear of losing her to some tragic event.

Filled with love to a depth that was mind-boggling, he cupped her face in his hands. She looked absolutely beautiful, staring up at him with hazel eyes. Suddenly, something clenched in his gut. He saw desire in her eyes, but where was the vibrancy that was always there when she looked at him? He recalled seeing it that night at McKays. Perplexed as to why he would imagine such a thing, he asked softly, "You okay?"

She nodded. "Yes, why wouldn't I be?"

Good question. Zane grew thoughtful. But before
he could dwell on her response any further, Channing
placed her hands on his shoulders. At her touch, his heart
pounded furiously in his chest. Needing to have his mouth
connected to hers once again, he leaned down and feasted
on it like a desperate man. The only times he'd ever been
this hot for a woman had always been with Channing.

He moaned deep in his throat when he felt her hips
grind against his hard length, sending rapid sensations
rippling through him. The sensual pull between them was
too strong, more overpowering than ever before, and he
needed her now.

She released a startled gasp when he swept her off her
feet and into his arms. Glancing down at her, he asked,
"Where's the bedroom?"

"Straight ahead on your right."

He walked at a brisk pace, feeling the urgency in every
step. When they reached the bedroom, he placed her on
her feet beside the bed. "Do you have any idea how I
feel?" he asked, letting his fingers tenderly stroke the
side of her face.

"No."

Zane paused. She'd given him a quick and simple answer. "Then let me show you."

The one thing he'd always enjoyed during their time
together was his ability to pleasure Channing. Her body
would respond to him in the most sensuous ways. She
loved the taste and feel of him as much as he did her.

He murmured gently, telling her in plain terms just
what he planned to do to her. He heard how breathless
she became with every explicit detail.

He removed several condom packets from his wallet
and tossed them on the bed. Then, without wasting any
time, he quickly shed his shoes and socks before yank-

ing his shirt from his jeans and removing the rest of his clothing.

"Now for you to join me," he said, laving his tongue across her jaw. He then stripped her of her T-shirt, pulling it over her head and tossing it aside. He cupped her breasts through her lace bra, and his entire body felt an electrical charge. Then, with a flick of his wrist, the front clasp was undone and gorgeous twin globes were free, making his mouth water with heated male appreciation as he gazed at them.

"Beautiful," he murmured, heat stirring in his gut. Her breasts were perfectly shaped, enticing to the eyes and delicious to the mouth. Lowering his head, he buried his face between them and inhaled the luscious scent of her flesh.

Breathing thickly, Zane's mouth latched on to a swollen nipple and licked it with the tip of his tongue before sucking greedily. He felt and heard her body's response when she shivered and moaned, which triggered a similar reaction in him. Blood pulsed through the veins of his engorged shaft, making it ache that much more.

A thrill of intense pleasure ripped through Channing, and she held Zane's head to her breasts as his mouth had its way with them. Her nipples throbbed while being devoured by his tongue, and her belly quivered with intense arousal that moved lower, to the apex of her thighs. It was only a matter of time before he took note and gave her the kind of attention that only he could give.

Moments later, he lifted his head and inhaled deeply. She watched how his nostrils flared as they picked up her scent. In anticipation of his next move, thunderbolts of pleasure consumed her.

"I need to get inside you, bad," he said softly, reaching behind her to ease down the back zipper of her skirt. He gave it a little tug, and the denim slid down her thighs to pool at her bare feet. Her heart pounded furiously in her chest when he lowered to bended knees and removed her panties, easing them down her legs.

Instead of standing back up, he remained on his knees. He touched the curly hair covering her femininity. His fingers slid back and forth through the curls before parting her folds and easing inside of her.

Desire shifted into an urgency that Channing felt all the way through her bones. And when he added another finger and began working inside of her, stroking her with mindless precision, she threw her head back and moaned. She wasn't just wet; she was soaked—exactly the way Zane liked.

"I can't wait to taste you again," he whispered, his voice reaching her just moments before his tongue slid inside of her. Then, with his ardently skillful and proficient mouth, he licked, sucked and nibbled her right into an explosion.

But he didn't let up. All through her orgasm, he swirled his tongue inside of her, lapping her greedily as he held on to her with his mouth.

She cried out, screaming his name while bucking her hips, holding on to his firm, broad shoulders. She thought the same thing now that she'd thought the first time he had taken her this way. Zane Westmoreland's tongue should be outlawed and his fingers shackled.

It was only when the last spasm had left her body that he got to his feet, cupped her face in his hands and held her gaze. "I love you."

Channing's mind blocked out his words. She didn't want to hear them because they weren't true. He didn't love her; he loved this. He wasn't in love with her; he was in lust with her.

He kissed her, and she tasted herself on his lips while

his engorged length pressed hard against her stomach. Licking her lips, she pushed Zane down on the bed with the intention of savoring every inch of him. It had been two years, and she'd missed his taste.

He lay flat on his back as she eased over him, using her tongue to lick all the way from his ankles to where his shaft laid thick and swollen in a dense bed of curly hair. She used her fingers to stroke him before lowering her lips to his throbbing erection.

As soon as her mouth took him in, he let out a guttural groan. The sound sent heat surging through her. Her mouth tortured him, and she enjoyed the feel of him pulsating against her lips. Blood raced through her body when she felt him swell even more. He jerked, bucked and arched off the bed, but she refused to let go. This was what she wanted, what she craved, what she'd missed.

"Channing!"

Her mouth stayed locked on him even when he screamed out her name and his release flooded her mouth. She felt his hands in her hair, trying to pull her mouth away, but she refused to let go. His taste was setting her entire body on fire, preparing her for what was coming next.

She slowly eased her mouth off him, and before she could catch her breath, he had pulled her up and flipped her gently onto her back. Parting her legs with his knees, he looked down at her before reaching for one of the condoms he'd tossed on the bed earlier. He opened the packet with his teeth and quickly sheathed himself.

"I need this," he whispered before easing into her. He then thrust hard, and she wrapped her legs around him. He rode her, moving in and out, using powerful strokes, sensuous thrusts and a steady pace that had heat drumming through her at every angle.

The room filled with the scent of hot, sweaty bodies. Hard, gritty sex. And Zane was relentless. She responded by lifting her body to meet his downward spiral over and over again.

And then she went crashing over the edge, taking him with her. His body continued the steady strokes until the last remnants of climax had left her body, leaving her totally drained. She was convinced that what they'd shared today felt different from all those other times. She'd never experienced anything like it.

Moments later, Zane slowly pulled out of her and then eased out of the bed to go to the bathroom. When he returned, Channing lay stretched across the bed with her arms thrown over her eyes, pulling in deep breaths.

She lowered her arms so she could look up at him. He had put on his jeans but not his shirt. The woman in her couldn't help but appreciate his muscular chest. When he made a move to sit on the edge of the bed, she said, "You need to leave, Zane."

His brows rose in surprise. "Leave?"

"Yes. I enjoyed the sex as much as you did. We both got what we wanted, so there's no reason for you to stick around."

A dark frown settled on his face. "What are you talking about?"

"I'm talking about the reason you came here."

"I told you why I came. I wanted to apologize and to tell you I love you."

She shook her head as she eased out of bed and began putting on her clothes. She glanced over at him as she tossed her hair aside to slide her T-shirt back over her head. "I don't believe you."

He watched her every move. "What don't you believe?"

She eased her skirt up over her hips. "That you love me."

Zane was taken aback by what she said. "And why don't you believe me?"

"Because," she said, pulling her hair back and fastening it with a clip. "If you tell someone something often enough, eventually they'll get smart and believe it. You didn't love me a few days ago. I got that admission from your own lips. So why on earth would I believe that you love me now, Zane?"

Chapter 7

Zane stood there with his gaze fixed on Channing. He could not believe she was questioning what he'd told her. The first time he'd ever admitted his love for a woman and she didn't believe him? What kind of crap was that?

Somewhere in the back of his mind, he could hear Bailey gloating. *"The kind of crap you got yourself into."*

Drawing in a frustrated breath, he said, "The reason you should believe me is because I don't have a reason to lie about anything like that."

She gave a short laugh. "Sure you do. You've got it in your mind that nobody can have me but you."

He took it as an affront at what she said. "I don't think that!"

"Don't you?" Her eyes turned stormy. "Did you not seduce me in McKays to prove a point?"

"Yes, but I—"

"Doesn't matter," she said, interrupting. "You've explained yourself. You came to apologize, and you have. But please don't get love confused with lust, Zane. You can never love a woman. I get it."

No, she didn't get it. How could a man tell a woman he loved her and she not believe him? He drew in a deep breath when the answer slapped him in the face. Easily, if it was the same man who'd told her over and over that he didn't love her.

They stood there, eyes locked, while seconds ticked by. He needed her to understand. "I was afraid to love you until now."

Her brows rose. "Afraid? Please. Certainly you can do better than that. Zane Westmoreland isn't afraid of anything."

Boy, was she wrong. He rubbed his hand down his face in frustration. "Look, Channing—"

"No, you look," she said, her tone hardening as she tossed him his shirt. "You might not know what love is, but I do. I loved you, but you couldn't love me back. You *wouldn't* love me back. So I left Denver, and I stayed away for two years. Two years, Zane. And you didn't so much as pick up a phone to see how I was doing."

Her heart twisted, remembering the nights when she first got to Atlanta when, for some stupid reason, she actually thought he would come after her. She thought that he'd realize he loved her, he couldn't live without her and he would show up one day with a confession of his feelings. She had been so wrong, and when she'd finally accepted that Zane truly didn't give a damn about her, she'd tried moving on.

"I wanted to," Zane said and immediately knew it sounded lame.

Evidently she thought so, too. He could tell when he saw fire flaring in her eyes. "You wanted to? The Zane who does whatever he wants to do *wanted* to call me and couldn't? Why?" She held up her hand before he could answer. "That's right, you were afraid," she said, mocking his earlier statement. She crossed her arms over her chest. "And just what were you were afraid of, Zane? Were you scared that I would pressure you into marrying me?"

Zane knew women, and he knew you couldn't make them see reason when they believed there was none. And you definitely couldn't out-talk one who thought she had a case to make.

"You're upset, Channing. Maybe we should continue this conversation tomorrow."

"Don't count on it. Why don't you just head back to Denver? After that to-prove-a-point stunt you pulled in McKays, I don't want you around."

A dark scowl covered his face. "What do you call what we just did in this bed, Channing? We made love."

She gave him a smirking look, one like he'd never gotten from her before. "No, we didn't make love. We had sex. I'm sure you're very familiar with the act."

"Damn it, Channing. I could never have just sex with you!" he stormed.

"Then let me inform you that you just did." She slid her feet into a pair of flat shoes. "Put your shirt on so I can walk you to the door."

A nerve ticked in Zane's jaw. Not only did she think so little of what they'd just shared but she was kicking him out! He opened his mouth to say a few words, but when he saw tears welling in her eyes he muttered a curse under his breath instead. Tears she was fighting like hell for him not to see. At that moment, he was filled with remorse that he had hurt the one woman he should have protected from all harm.

"Channing, I do love—"

"No," she lashed out, halting his words in midsentence. "Just leave, Zane. Please, just leave."

Feeling helpless on one hand and like a total ass on the other, Zane pushed out a deep breath and put on his shirt. He kept his gaze on Channing. "You're wrong about me, Channing, and I intend to prove it."

"Don't waste your time trying to prove another point, Zane. I've taken off the rose-colored glasses and tossed them away. I did the same thing with the key to my heart."

He shoved his hands into his pockets, refusing to go down in defeat. "Then I guess my job is to find both and return them."

"Like I said, don't waste your time." She tossed the words over her shoulder as she led him out of the room to the door.

Zane's gut tightened when he heard Channing's door slam shut behind him. He paused when he reached the rental car. He had a mind to go right back up to her door and demand that she see reason, demand that she believe him.

Demand? Hell, he of all people should know you couldn't demand anything from a woman—especially one who felt she'd been wronged. He swallowed a deep lump in his throat at the realization that she *had* been wronged. So far he hadn't handled anything right with Channing. Feeling totally disgusted with himself, he opened the car door and slid inside, snapping the seat belt in place.

His hands gripped the steering wheel as he looked over his shoulder before backing out of her yard. He was in one hell of a mess and he—Zane Westmoreland who was considered the expert on any issues dealing with women—didn't know what he needed to do to fix things.

He'd figured showing up and confessing his love would

do it. He'd been dead wrong. A part of him was angry that she actually thought he would lie about something like that. Hell, he took those three words seriously. She'd suggested that he might be getting love confused with lust. Did she not think he knew the difference? Hell, he'd lusted after women since puberty. But he'd never felt the need to chase behind one and pour out his heart and soul.

The nerve of her, questioning his words of love. It was almost enough to make him want to drive back to the airport and catch the next plane to Denver. He didn't need this.

But he did need her. And regardless of what she thought, he did love her.

When he came to a stop at a traffic light, Zane closed his eyes and conjured up the image he'd seen when she'd opened the door for him to leave. The look on her face was the same one he'd see when he'd broken things off with other women. But he'd never seen that look on her.

Some women just couldn't accept, for whatever reason, that their relationship had come to the end. Seeing that look had never bothered him before because he'd felt it was the woman's problem and not his. Unfortunately, he couldn't think that way with Channing because he loved her. It *was* his problem.

He opened his eyes when a car behind him honked, letting him know the traffic light had changed. Moments later, he made a right at the intersection that would take him to one of the many hotels in the area. If Channing thought she'd gotten rid of him then she was sadly mistaken.

It was a beautiful day in July, and the ocean looked magnificent. As he drove along the beach's scenic route, his gaze took in the beautiful landscape. He'd been to Virginia before, with Derringer and Jason, when they met with a rancher in Richmond who'd been interested in purchasing a number of their horses.

As he was driving, his cell phone rang. Thinking it might be Channing calling to let him know she did believe his confession of love after all, his heart pounded in his chest. Entering the hotel's parking lot, he brought his car to a stop in one of the spaces and quickly shifted to pull his cell phone out of his pocket. He frowned when he saw the caller was not Channing but his cousin Canyon.

"What's up, Canyon?"

"Where the hell are you, Zane? I dropped by the Hideout last night and again this morning, and it looks like a ghost town. I asked Derringer and Jason when I saw you weren't working with the horses today. They both had locked lips for some reason."

Good for them, Zane thought, turning off the car's ignition. He'd told Derringer and Jason not to mention where he'd gone unless an emergency came up. The last thing he wanted was for Megan to get wind of the fact that he'd come after Channing. He didn't want her to try and sabotage things for him. He'd gotten Rico's word that he wouldn't mention it to Megan for a few days, to give Zane time to make his case with Channing.

Zane figured Canyon must be hunting him down due to some woman issue. He was tempted to tell Canyon that he had his own problems to deal with. "I'm out of town on business, Canyon." In a way, that was true. Channing *was* his business.

"Well, I need to talk to you about something."

Zane rolled his eyes. "Something or someone?"

"Someone. I told you Keisha Ashford was back in town."

Keisha was a woman his cousin had been involved with

a few years ago. "Yes, you mentioned she'd returned and had gotten rehired at that law firm in town."

"Well, I've been trying to get her to talk to me so we can clear up what drove us apart, but she won't give me the time of day."

Welcome to the club, Zane thought. "And?"

"And I don't understand how she could have thought I betrayed her with another woman."

Zane gritted his teeth. He understood Canyon's dilemma since he couldn't understand why Channing would think he didn't love her. "Well, she did walk in on you and—"

"Bonita and I hadn't done anything," Canyon said.

"Yes, but I can understand why Keisha had a hard time believing that since Bonita Simpkins was naked and all... and if I recall the story, so were you."

"I was wearing a towel because I had just taken a shower."

"Oh." He wondered if Canyon fully realized just how damaging that must have looked. "Let me ask you this," Zane said. "When the two of you were together did you ever tell Keisha how you felt about her?"

"Of course I did. I don't have commitment issues like you."

Zane frowned. "What do you mean by that?"

"What I mean is that I happen not to see falling in love as some sort of a curse. My parents, as well as yours, had good marriages. Solid and strong. That's the reason the thought of a wife and kids never threw me into a state of panic like it did you."

Zane took offense. "It never threw me into a state of panic. I just wasn't ready to settle down."

"And you won't ever be."

Zane's frown deepened. "What if I told you th
fallen in love?"

Canyon laughed. "Then I would tell you to go tell that
lie to somebody else. You're incapable of falling in love.
Now back to Keisha."

Zane took the phone from his ear and stared at it. If his
own kin didn't believe he was capable of falling in love,
then how could he expect Channing to believe it?

He put the phone back to his ear to hear Canyon ram-
bling. His cousin was thirty-two and an attorney at the
family firm. He'd started out as a medical student at Howard University and after the second year decided becoming a doctor wasn't for him. He'd switched to Howard's
School of Law instead. Now he worked as an attorney at
Blue Ridge. "Riley said I should make peace with her,"
Canyon said.

"And?"

"I tried, but she refuses to give me the time of day. I
don't even know where she lives, man. She refuses to tell
me. And the few times I've run into her, she acted secretive. Like she's hiding something."

Zane drew in a deep breath. "So exactly what do you
want from me, Canyon?"

"You're the expert on women. What do you think I
should do?"

Zane snorted. Yeah, he was an expert all right. An expert who couldn't handle his own damn business. "First
of all, she's probably not acting secretive, Canyon. She's
probably being coy. Keisha's sizing you up to see if you
can be trusted again. Trust is important to a woman." *So
is being told she's loved,* Zane thought.

"I didn't betray her," Canyon blasted.

"Doesn't matter. She thinks she caught you i

landed. You're going to have to prove Bonita Simpkins set you up."

"Why should I have to prove anything? She should have trusted me. I didn't do anything wrong, and I'm sick and tired of her treating me like I did. Goodbye, Zane. I'll see you when you get back to Denver. And where are you, anyway? You didn't say."

And he didn't intend to. "Gotta go, Canyon. I've just made it to the hotel."

"Oh, okay. When will you be back?"

Now that was a good question. He intended to stay for as long as it took to convince Channing that he was in love with her. "Not sure, but I'll keep in touch. Talk to you later."

Zane ended the call and decided he needed to come up with a solid plan. He'd gotten himself into this mess, and he would figure a way out of it.

What was this nonsense about them just having sex? Their time in the bedroom had always had more meaning than that. It had never been just sex for him.

He winced upon realizing that he'd never told her that. But somehow Channing had fallen in love with him anyway with the hope that one day he would love her back. Instead, he had looked her right in the eyes and told her— on more than one occasion—that he didn't love her, that he wasn't capable of loving women. And now he expected her to believe otherwise. Today, angry and hurt, she had shown him that things didn't work that way.

He opened the car door, thinking that no matter what it took, he would convince Channing that he did love her.

Whenever she got in a tizzy about anything, Channing had a tendency to cook…and not just a little bit of food. She released a sigh as she glanced around the kitchen at her handiwork. Ignoring the pots and pans stacked sky-high in her kitchen sink, she studied all the containers that littered her table, countertops and island. She had finished everything down to the chocolate chip cookies that had just come out of the oven.

She walked over to the refrigerator to grab a wine cooler, deciding to sit outside on the porch awhile. She'd cooked enough food to last her for the next two and a half weeks. But she couldn't help it. She needed to keep busy, and cooking had always been her solace. This time she'd ended up with spaghetti, two different casseroles, baked chicken, four kinds of veggies, rice, corn on the cob and green beans.

It was more than enough food to share. She immediately thought of the Farmers. There was no reason they couldn't benefit from her madness.

Had it been only a few hours ago that she'd engaged in incredible sex? If the tingling sensation between her legs was anything to go by, she would admit she could use some more. That was what two years without intimacy could do to a woman. She'd always enjoyed sharing a bed with Zane. The man was walking testosterone on legs. And in bed he was simply amazing. Truly unbelievable.

And yet he wanted her to believe that he loved her.

Yeah, right.

Channing shook her head as she opened the door and sat down on the porch swing. Zane must have forgotten who he was trying to convince. She had been the one, like the others, who'd gotten his spiel when they'd first started dating and the one who'd also heard it plenty of times in between. *I will never love any woman. I don't love you. I'm not capable of falling in love.*

And then he'd stop reiterating it, and she'd made the

mistake of thinking she was different. She'd wanted to mean more than the others.

Channing took a deep swallow of her wine cooler, deciding not to rehash the mistakes she'd made with Zane. She was trying so hard to get over him, but after he'd shown up here and made love to her, he'd probably only made things worse. He had stirred up wants and desires she'd convinced herself she didn't have, but what had happened last week in McKays had proved otherwise. She had let him take her on a table in a restaurant for heaven's sake. The only regret she had was that he'd only done it to prove a point.

What if he's telling you the truth about loving you? What if...

Channing pushed the possibility out of her head. There was no way. It was lust, not love. She got it now. She would never be confused again. And hopefully Zane was on his way back to Denver.

Chapter 8

The next morning, Zane pulled up in front of Channing's grandparents' home with a purpose and a plan. He'd never pursued a woman in his life, but giving Channing up wasn't an option. He hadn't gone to bed until he'd come up with this idea. And now he was back with a game changer.

If anyone had presented this problem to him, he would have told them, based on what he knew about women, that actions speak louder than words. Since Channing didn't believe a word he said, it was time to show it.

The next thing he would do was let her think she was in control. Some women enjoyed having the upper hand when a man fell in love with them. They had to see it happening before believing it was real. Especially when it came to a devout bachelor. The woman had to feel she'd succeeded in pushing the man into loving her. When she assumed she'd used her feminine wiles to conquer the man's heart, that made victory so much sweeter.

If that was what was needed, then he was game. And he planned to enjoy every single minute Channing thought she was winning him over, mainly because he would be winning her over, as well. And he knew just how to do it because he knew Channing—her weaknesses and her strengths.

By the time it was over and done, the how of it wouldn't matter because he'd loved her, anyway. And when he was through, there would be no doubt in Channing's mind that she was his woman and he was her man.

Her man.

Where was the shudder he was supposed to feel at being any woman's man? In fact, he felt pretty damn good when he considered the idea. And he also felt good about the fact that Channing still loved him although he was sure she would deny it with her last breath. What had happened yesterday in that bedroom wasn't just about sex like she'd claimed. It had been about making love.

To Channing, passion and love were synonymous, and there had been a lot of passion in that bed yesterday. But he wasn't stupid. Although she might still love him, that love was being held hostage by her mistrust, and he'd have to work hard to release it. More than anything he had to find a way to rekindle that love.

Smiling, Zane swiftly walked up the steps to the porch and glanced at the swing. He'd seen it yesterday but had been too focused on Channing to pay much attention to it. He could see her in the swing. He would be sitting there with her, his arms around her and her head resting on his chest. He'd whisper that he loved her while the motion of the swing rocked them. She would believe him when he said the words. And there would be no doubt in her mind of his sincerity.

He was about to knock on the door when he glanced

through her living room window. He paused, angling his head for a better view. When he got it, anger shot through him. A man was moving around Channing's kitchen. What the hell!

A deep scowl covered his face as he moved toward the door. He didn't know what was going on, but he was about to find out.

"Jennifer and I thank you kindly for all this food, Channing."

Channing smiled as she continued packing up the containers. "No problem, Ronald. You're actually doing me a favor. I hadn't meant to cook so much."

Ronald Farmer glanced around the kitchen. "Yes, I would say you did get a bit carried away."

Channing threw back her head and laughed. It was then that she heard the knock at the door. "Would you get the door for me? That's probably Dan Joyner. His grandfather owns the house with the gate down the road. I've known him for years, and he's stopping by to get some of this food, as well."

"Sure."

Zane was about to knock on the door again when it was opened by the man he'd viewed through the window. Dressed in a pair of shorts and a T-shirt, the man was as tall as Zane but with the body of someone who worked out often. The man had the nerve to be smiling.

"How are you doing?" the man greeted with a friendly air. "You're here for the food?"

Zane frowned. "No, I'm not here for any food. I'm here to see Channing." And without waiting to be invited inside, he moved past the man before turning back to him. "Where is she?"

The man looked at him curiously, as if to size him up. Then he said, "She's in the kitchen."

"Not anymore," Channing said, frowning as she stepped into the living room carrying an armful of food containers. She had heard Zane's voice and could not believe his audacity. Why was he still in Virginia? More importantly, why was he here?

"Let me help you with those," Ronald said, quickly moving forward to relieve her of the stack she was carrying.

"Thanks."

She glanced over at Zane and saw the deep haze of anger in his eyes. What was his problem? Deciding to wait until Ronald left before confronting Zane as to why he was here, she said, "Ronald, I'd like you to meet Zane. An old friend."

Juggling the containers in one hand, Ronald moved toward Zane with the other hand outstretched. "Nice meeting you."

Zane accepted the man's handshake grudgingly. "You stay around these parts, Ronald?" Zane asked.

Channing frowned. "Yes, Ronald stays next door," she answered for him. "His wife and kids are here for the summer."

"Wife?" Zane asked, shifting his gaze from Ronald to Channing.

"Yes, *wife*," Channing answered, annoyed.

She then smiled at Ronald. "I hope you, Jennifer and the kids enjoy everything."

Ronald returned her smile. "I'm sure we will, and again we appreciate it." Then with a concerned look on his face, he asked Channing, "You're going to be okay?"

Channing knew why he was asking. Evidently he'd picked up on Zane's anger and figured Zane might be an old friend but, at the moment, a bad-tempered one. "Yes, I'll be fine."

Satisfied with her response, Ronald glanced back at Zane. "Nice meeting you, Zane."

"Yeah, same here." Zane quickly moved to open the door for the man. When the door closed behind Ronald, he turned to Channing. Ignoring the scowl on her face, a smile curved his lips. "He seems like a nice married guy."

Her frown indicated that she had not appreciated his initial churlish attitude toward Ronald. "What are you doing here, Zane? I thought you'd be back in Denver by now," she said, turning.

He followed her into the kitchen.

"Not sure why you thought that. Besides, I've been doing a lot of thinking about our conver—"

He stopped talking as he looked around, seeing her kitchen table and counter littered with food containers. "What's going on? You're opening a restaurant on the side?"

Channing rolled her eyes when she began placing some of the containers in the refrigerator. "No, I was just in the mood to cook yesterday."

"All of this?"

She frowned over her shoulder. "Yes, all of this. I decided to share some with Ronald and Jennifer. They have a sweet little girl and a son who hasn't started walking yet. They're a beautiful family."

He nodded, thinking those folks were not as beautiful as his and Channing's family would be one day. Last night, after he'd planned his strategy, he'd envisioned them married with a couple of kids and living happily at the Hideout.

"So why did you come back, Zane?"

He leaned against the counter. "I couldn't help myself."

Channing drew in a deep sigh. She hoped he wasn't back to confusing lust with love again. "What do you mean you couldn't help yourself?" she asked, lifting one eyebrow.

He shoved his hands into the pockets of his jeans. "I got to thinking about our conversation yesterday."

"And?"

"I told you I loved you, but you didn't believe me. You said I'm confusing lust with love. For the sake of argument, let's say you're right about that."

"I am right," she said with absolute certainty. "No man, or woman for that matter, who's been against falling in love to the depth that you have can miraculously wake up one morning and decide they're in love. Falling in love doesn't work that way."

Zane nodded. "Okay, let's say you're right."

"And?"

Now to throw out the hook and hope she takes the bait, Zane thought as he moved closer. "And if it's only lust, like you claim, because of this strong sexual chemistry between us, then the only thing I have to say is that I feel that I'm close."

She lifted a brow. "Close to what?"

"Falling in love with you."

Channing closed the refrigerator, thinking that now she'd heard everything. "Falling in love with me?"

"Yes. Close. According to you, I can't be in love with you. If you're right about that, then how come when that guy opened the door I was ready to hurt him when I thought—"

"I know what you thought, Zane," Channing interrupted him to say. "And even if that was the case, it wasn't any of your business."

He straightened, rolling his head around and working his shoulders to slog out the kinks. "It might not be my business, but it's an example of one of those things that I can't help where you're concerned. I've never gotten jealous over a woman before, Channing, so that has to mean something."

She met his gaze. "It does mean something, and it has nothing to do with love. It means you're possessive. You don't want me, but you don't want anyone else to have me, either."

"You make me sound like a selfish bastard."

"Well…it's a description that fits," she said, moving around him to go into the living room. In fact, she was leading him to the door. She thought of a question she'd meant to ask him yesterday—something that had nagged at her all during the night. She turned, and he almost bumped into her. When he reached out his hand to steady her, her body tingled from the contact. She forced herself to take a step back when he dropped his hand.

"I have a question for you," she said, trying to downplay the sensations that were still moving through her body.

"What?"

Channing caught her lower lip between her teeth as she thought about what she wanted to ask him. She decided to come out and do it. "Would it have made a difference if you hadn't thought Mack was cheating on me?"

"What do you mean?" he asked, leaning against a wall in her living room.

"If you hadn't assumed Mack was cheating on me, would you have seduced me, anyway?"

He didn't hesitate. "Yes."

She stiffened. "Why?"

It seemed as if several long seconds ticked between

them before he responded. "I wanted you, and I could tell you wanted me. I know your body, Channing. I knew the moment you became wet for me. The moment your nipples hardened. I didn't have to wait for you to ask to know you wanted me inside of you."

Channing's stomach clenched. That wetness he was talking about, heaven help her. His words had it flowing again. She felt disgusted with herself for letting Zane have this kind of power over her.

Deciding she needed to take a stand against what he'd claimed regardless of whether it had merit or not, she said, "So you decided to act on your assumption? Even while believing I was engaged to marry another man? The Zane Westmoreland I know would not have done that."

He moved, coming within inches of her. "Then maybe I'm not the Zane you thought you knew."

Evidently not.

During those months they'd dated, she had been sure of him regardless of what he'd said about love. But he'd proved her wrong, which was why she couldn't believe his claim of love. Now it seemed she'd been right not to believe him. He was only on the verge of love.

"I think you should leave now," she said, moving again toward the door. When she opened it, he reached around her and shut it. She saw a muscle working in his jaw.

"What do you think you're doing?" she asked.

"I came back today for a reason, Channing."

She narrowed her gaze at him. "I know, you couldn't help yourself because now you think there's a chance that you're falling in love with me." Channing shook her head. "Deliberate or otherwise, you're confusing the heck out of me. Maybe you're right, and you aren't the Zane I thought I knew. If that's true, I don't want to know the Zane that you are now."

She gasped when he braced strong arms against the door on either side of her, effectively trapping her. "Maybe you should."

Zane knew what he'd told her was true. He wasn't the same Zane. First of all, the old Zane would never have fallen in love, and he loved this woman so much he ached all over.

"You're not making much sense, Zane."

He almost agreed with her, but he knew what he was doing *did* make sense. It was his strategy to win her over, to prove once and for all that what he felt for her wasn't lust but love. "Two years ago you thought you knew me, Channing. I enjoyed you, and you enjoyed me. In your neat and tidy world, you figured things should move from point A to point B by nobody's timetable but your own. However, what you failed to figure into the equation is that the worst thing a woman can do is push a man when he isn't ready. You did that. I wasn't ready then. I am now."

He saw irritation spread across her face. "Ready for what?"

"To be pushed into feeling things I wasn't ready to feel before. In fact, I'm open to endless possibilities."

Channing stared at Zane as her mind trickled back in time. The Zane Westmoreland she'd fallen in love with had never been a typical guy. There had been so many facets to him that she'd spent the first couple of months of their relationship trying to unravel him. There had been the reserved Zane. The forbidding Zane. The Zane who was devoted to his family. The Zane who said what he meant and meant what he said. Those were the qualities that had first attracted her to him, and those same qualities were what had captured her heart and made her fall in love with him.

She knew he still had those qualities, so who was the Zane she didn't know? As if the question was stamped on her forehead for him to read, he said, "You never get to know anyone completely, Channing, and the reason I'm willing to be pushed now is because I don't want to lose you again." He paused. "I admit I'm close. Closer than I've ever been in my entire life. Like I said, all I need is a little push."

He had to make Channing understand. He loved her, and maybe if she didn't believe he was there already, she would buy that he was almost there and take the chance of prodding him further.

"I admire you so damn much, Channing," he said honestly. "More than any other woman I've been involved with. I knew you wanted more from me, more than I could give. But that didn't mean I didn't care for you, because I did. I never led you on. I was always honest with you."

Channing said nothing as she thought about what he said. He was right. He had always been honest with her. He'd never told her he loved her, and she could admit that it wasn't his fault that she had wanted him to feel differently.

Now he needs a little push. What if I give him that push and nothing comes of it? Doesn't he understand he's asking me to play Russian roulette with my heart?

"Just what are you asking of me, Zane?"

"Something I probably have no right to," he said gently. "But I'm asking anyway because I want you more than I've ever wanted any woman. Don't give up on me. Get to know the real Zane, and don't be afraid to push me to the limit. You're the only woman who can. You're the only woman I will ever love."

Channing drew in a deep breath as she absorbed what Zane was saying. Although he didn't love her, he believed that she had the power to make him love her? All he needed was a little push. If that was the case, why hadn't he fallen in love with her when they were dating? Things had been good between them—the sex, the communication, the entire relationship. He hadn't been ready then. What would be different this time around?

She drew in another deep breath, deciding to call him out on something he'd said yesterday. "When you said you loved me, one of the reasons you claimed you didn't act on it was because you were afraid. What did you mean by that?"

Zane held her gaze for a long time, then in a quiet tone he said, "Let's sit down while I try to explain things."

She stared at him a second before nodding. What he was about to tell her was the complete truth. He hoped it would help her understand him. When she led him into the living room, he followed. She eased down on the sofa, and he took the chair across from her.

Channing sensed by the firm set of his chin that whatever Zane was about to tell her was a serious matter. He was sitting in the chair, stiff and straight, which indicated that he was not comfortable with what he was about to share. Gone were his familiar coolness, relaxed air and arrogance. Instead, she detected a sense of vulnerability in him—one that was controlled and guarded. Those were things she hadn't seen in him before.

He was tense, and she could feel the tension, as well. Why? "Zane?"

He met her gaze, held it for a long moment and then he asked softly, "Can you imagine losing both your parents at the same time?"

Channing's pulse almost stopped. She swallow deeply as she truthfully answered his question I can't."

He nodded slowly. "Well, I did. I was only nineteen and in my second year of college when it happened. But not only did I lose my parents. I also lost my uncle and aunt, who were like parents to me, as well. From that day forward, my life hasn't been the same."

Channing didn't say anything. Because of her friendship with Megan, she knew the story of how his parents and his aunt and uncle had lost their lives in a plane crash. She'd also known there had been several Westmoreland kids under the age of sixteen at the time and that Zane's brother Ramsey and his cousin Dillon had worked hard and made sacrifices to keep the family together.

"There wasn't a whole lot of time for grieving since we had to all pitch in to help the younger ones cope. It wasn't easy. A few of them worked through their grief by being rebellious, which caused unnecessary drama for all of us. But the one thing I decided never to do, because of that experience, was to get attached to anyone who I could lose in that way."

After a deep breath, he continued. "I loved my parents, and losing them was hard on me. The pain was deep— almost unbearable at times. Unless you've been through something like that, you can't begin to understand."

Channing believed it. She could hear the pain in his voice and could also see it in his eyes. "Is that the reason you can't fall in love, Zane? For fear of losing that person?"

"I thought so, but when I thought I had lost you after that night in McKays, for the first time I felt like I could take the risk. The risk of loving you was greater than the fear."

So he thought he could be pushed into falling in love with her, she surmised, because she was the first woman ~~· ~d~~ felt so strongly connected to that the positive emotions overrode his ingrained fear. Was his admission enough for them to move forward and try again?

Could she actually push him into loving her?

What he was asking went against everything she'd ever read in relationship books. A woman couldn't seduce a man into loving her. It took both people to make a relationship work. Was she missing some point here? Had she failed to take into account that all relationships weren't the same? Had she been so focused on what she'd wanted out of the relationship that she'd refused to see that he couldn't be rushed?

Zane had been a psychology major while in college and was rumored to have the ability to get into a woman's psyche and fully understand how females perceived their world. If that was the case, maybe it was high time for a woman to determine how he perceived his.

For nine months, they'd shared a traditional relationship. They had met, shared great chemistry, enjoyed mind-blowing sex, found it easy to communicate with each other and had a good friendship. No game-playing and no pressure. Yet in the end, love hadn't blossomed…at least not on his end.

But what if he doesn't fall head over heels in love with you? Well, if that happens, at least you'll have no doubt in your mind that he has issues that can't be solved. There is a slim chance that what he says is true, that he's capable of falling in love with you.

Are you willing to do whatever is necessary to find out? Even if it means putting on those rose-colored glasses and unlocking your heart again?

He stared at her with his mesmerizing eyes. Heat pooled between her legs because of his intense focus. The idea that he was asking her to help him fall in love was too much to take in at the moment. But if he hadn't fallen in love before because he'd been afraid to love, could she help erase his fears?

"Go out with me tonight, Channing," he said, his words floating across the room and touching her skin like a caress. "I understand there's one of those drive-in theaters around here."

When she parted her lips to turn him down, he held up his hand. "Before you say no, just think about what fun it might be. I haven't been to one in years. I remember my folks would pile us all into their car, and it was great. And guess what? It's John Travolta Night. *Saturday Night Fever* and *Grease* are in the lineup. I know how much you like the guy."

He was right. She was a big John Travolta fan. There wasn't a movie he'd made that she hadn't seen. "John Travolta Night?"

"Yes."

She knew that accepting his invitation to the movies meant she was accepting his challenge. Was that something she wanted? Should she turn him down and ask him to leave and not come back?

No, she couldn't do that. Doing so would be giving up on him, and if there was a possibility—even a slim one— that he was on the verge of falling in love with her, then she wanted to see it through. Who was it who said if you wanted something badly enough it was worth fighting for?

But this time if she wanted to do things differently, she had to shake up their routine.

"Yes, I'll go to the drive-in theater with you, but you can get rid of the condoms. I won't be having sex with you."

"You won't?"

"No."

Zane didn't say anything while he thought about her

request. Evidently she was still trying to understand this lust-versus-love thing. That was fine, because he would show her that his love encompassed everything—both the physical and the emotional. Besides, they wouldn't be having sex because they'd never had sex in the first place. They'd always made love, and it seemed he needed to show her the difference.

"Okay, Channing, we won't have sex."

As soon as he said the words, he saw what seemed to be anxiety leave her gaze. She stood. "I'll walk you to the door now."

He stood, too, and followed her. When they reached the door, they faced each other. Zane stroked Channing's hair while her gaze locked with his. How could he not have known the depth of his love for her before now? Why had it taken losing her a second time to make him realize that he could not handle losing her again?

"I'll be back around six." Deciding to give her something to look forward to, he leaned toward her, placed his hands at her waist and said in a soft, husky tone, "Go ahead and try it now, Channing. Push."

"I don't think—"

"Push," he encouraged again.

He heard her soft sigh and then a whisper when she said his name. "Zane."

When she boldly licked the tip of her tongue across his lips his breath caught and heat settled in his groin. He inhaled deeply and discovered her scent was as erotic and sensual as ever. Channing's unique aroma had the ability to drive him crazy… It was doing so now.

"You want to be pushed," she whispered across his moist lips. "Then you're going to get just what you ask for. When I finish with you, your heart won't be the same, Zane."

He had news for her. It was already different, and he would take great pleasure in proving it to her. When she took a step back and reached out to open the door, he reminded her, "I'll be back around six."

"Okay."

He walked out of her door knowing any moves he made on her would be the most important ones of his life.

His campaign would begin tonight. Already his mind buzzed with ideas for ways he could make the evening unforgettable.

Chapter 9

Channing picked up her cell phone when she saw the caller was Megan. "Hey, Megan, what's up?"

"Thought I'd ask you the same thing. Rico confessed that he told Zane where you were. Sorry about that."

Channing eased down on the sofa. "No reason to apologize and yes, Zane showed up on my doorstep yesterday."

"And?"

"And he claimed he loved me."

There was an undisputed gasp. "Zane told you that?"

"Yes. But of course I don't believe him."

"You don't?"

"No. It was less than a week ago when he looked me right in the eyes and told me he *didn't* love me, that what he felt for me was nothing more than possession. In other words, Zane thinks I'm his and doesn't want me to belong to another man. Now he wants me to believe he woke up one morning and miraculously realized he loves me. That's hogwash, and you know it."

"And you told him you didn't believe him?"

"Yes, and I asked that he leave." Channing decided there was no reason to mention she'd had sex with him before he left.

"So now he's on his way back to Denver?"

There was a pause before Channing said, "Not exactly. He showed up here again this morning."

"And?"

"And he did a flip-flop on me."

"Flip-flop? Now he's saying that he doesn't love you?"

Channing heard confusion in Megan's voice, so she tried to explain. "He's admitting to feeling things for me he hasn't felt for any other woman. I guess those emotions are confusing him, and he believes that if what he's feeling isn't love yet then it's close to it. He says all he needs is a little push."

"A little push by whom?"

"Me."

Megan frowned. She'd never heard anything so ridiculous in her life.

But the more she thought about it, the more she could see Zane's ploy even if Channing couldn't. First of all, there was no doubt in her mind that Zane loved Channing. He would not have dropped everything to go after her if he didn't. Then there was his admission of love. Zane would never admit loving someone if he actually didn't. And as far as him miraculously waking up one morning and realizing how he felt about Channing—well Channing might not believe it could happen that way, but Megan did.

Channing was dealing with a Westmoreland male, and most Denver Westmoreland males had put up roadblocks when it came to falling in love. Ramsey, Derringer and

Riley had fought the idea of falling in love tooth and nail. Even she and her sister Gemma hadn't given up their hearts easily.

Knowing how that analytical and psychological mind of Zane's tended to work, Megan knew his plan. He figured that since Channing didn't believe him, he would show her the evolution. He'd even gone so far as to encourage Channing to spearhead the transformation. Megan hated to admit it, but it was a brilliant strategy—if it worked. And she had a feeling it *would* work because Zane never failed at anything that he put his mind to. And he had an additional advantage. His heart was in it, as well.

"So, are you going to do it?" Megan heard herself asking.

There was a moment of silence and then Channing said, "Yes. I love him so much, Megan, even though I don't want to. Zane is a complex man." She paused then added, "He explained how your parents' and uncle's and aunt's deaths affected him."

Megan's mouth dropped open. "He told you that?" She was stunned that Zane would be that forthcoming about his fears. Over the years, she'd suspected he felt that way but had never been sure.

"Yes, he told me. And if that's really the reason he's been holding back then maybe I can help him overcome that. Do you think I'm crazy for thinking that way?"

Megan drew in a deep breath and smiled. "I see nothing wrong with a woman fighting for the love of her man, Channing." Just like she saw nothing wrong with a man fighting for the love of his woman. Crazy thing was, Zane and Channing were fighting for the same thing, and neither of them knew it yet.

"I'm going to keep my fingers crossed that things work out for you," Megan said quietly.

"Thanks, Megan. I appreciate it."

The rest of the day moved pretty fast for Zane. So he didn't feel like a slacker while he was in Virginia Beach and Jason and Derringer were back in Denver hard at work, the three of them had agreed that Zane could sort through the online files that had been piling up for months. Using his tablet computer, he had gone through all the emails, trashing a lot of spam and making appointments for interested horse buyers.

Now he glanced at the clock. He had a couple of hours before he picked up Channing, and he had a number of things to do. The hotel would be preparing a basket of food and wine. And when he had stopped at one of the gift shops downstairs he'd seen the perfect wine glasses and told the hotel he wanted them included in the basket, as well. When he was younger, his parents would take him and his siblings to Denver's only drive-in theater. It had closed ages ago, but those times had definitely been fun for them. Bailey had been in diapers and the twins were barely saying words that you could understand. Too bad Zane hadn't known that memories such as those were ones he would have to cherish forever.

As he slid into his jacket, he realized he wanted to share that special drive-in magic with Channing. He knew she wasn't keen on going to the movies with him—or to a drive-in theater of all places. But he thought that was just the kind of place they needed. At the drive-in, they wouldn't have to worry about anyone sitting beside them, invading their space. They would be in the car all alone.

He shook his head at his predicament. He figured after a week or so Channing would realize he loved her. If not, then he intended to sit down and try again to give it to her straight. Regardless of what she believed, he was a man who knew his mind and his heart.

Zane smiled as he headed for the door. She should have gotten the flowers by now. It wasn't the first time he'd sent a woman flowers, but it was the first time sending them had ever really meant anything to him.

"Ma'am? Will you be signing for the flowers?"

Channing blinked, but she still saw the man standing on her porch holding not just a vase of flowers but what looked like an entire friggin' bush. And they were roses. Red ones. The most beautiful flowers she'd ever seen. "Oh, yes," she said, coming to her senses. She quickly scribbled her name on the pad he'd given her.

"Where do you want me to place these? I doubt you can carry them."

She doubted it, as well. "This way," she said, leading the middle-aged man into her living room. "Right here will do."

She stared as he set the potted bush down and stepped back. "Whoever sent these probably meant for you to plant this outside. I've never seen anything so large. He didn't just send you long-stemmed roses. He sent you the entire rosebush."

Channing nodded. "Wait a second so I can give you a tip."

"No need," he said, heading toward the door. "It's already been taken care of. Your guy thought of everything. Nice fellow."

Yeah, nice fellow, she thought, closing the door behind the deliveryman and turning to stare at the bush again. She'd read the card already and knew exactly who'd sent them, and she couldn't forget what the card had said.

I love you.

What in the world was going on in that head of Zane's? Why was he trying to get a head start on falling in love when she hadn't even started pushing him yet?

She glanced over at the clock and then hurried to her bedroom. He would be here in fewer than thirty minutes, and she still had to put on her makeup. Good thing she never used a whole lot. Just a little powder and lipstick. Zane had often complimented her on her natural beauty.

She was wearing a pair of shorts and a tank top; she figured she'd keep them on. After all, she and Zane were going to a drive-in. If they decided to grab something to eat later, they could go to a fast-food place. Or they could come back here since she had plenty of food in the refrigerator.

She tossed her hair back from her face and tossed the idea from her head. She didn't need to give Zane any encouragement by inviting him to her house after the movies. She would push, but it would be on her time and in her own way.

She drew in a deep breath when she heard his knock. Giving herself one last check in the full-length mirror, she left her bedroom and headed for the door.

When Channing opened the door, Zane shoved his hands into the pockets of his slacks and looked down at himself. He then glanced up at her and smiled. "I think I might be a little overdressed."

A smile touched Channing's lips when she stepped aside to let him in. "Yes, I would say just a little. We're just going to the drive-in, Zane. No need for the jacket, shirt and slacks. You could have worn shorts or jeans with a T-shirt."

He shrugged. "I don't own a pair of shorts."

She lifted a brow. "You're kidding."

He chuckled. "No, why would I kid about something like that? Have you forgotten I live in Colorado?"

"No, but there are warm days there. In fact, I remember a few times during the summer when it got up in the nineties."

"Possibly, but I feel more comfortable in jeans or long pants. If there's a problem with what I'm wearing, I can go back by the hotel and change."

She waved off his words. "No problem. I'm fine with it. I just want you to be comfortable."

"Oh, I plan to be comfortable."

"Okay, then. Are you ready? All I have to do is—"

"Come here," he interrupted in a low, husky tone, pulling her into his arms. "You look good, and you smell good, too."

She went to him easily, willingly. Doing so reminded her of the time when things had been so good for them. A time when she had felt sure of herself where he was concerned. "Thank you. And I should also be thanking you for the flowers. Or should I say the rosebush. It's beautiful."

"So are you."

"Thank you. Now as far as the card is concerned..."

"What about it?" He continued holding her in his arms. It was as though this was where she was meant to be.

"Getting carried away, don't you think? Not giving me much room to push."

He feigned ignorance. "You think so?"

"Yes."

"You think I'm moving too fast?"

Channing sighed deeply before pulling herself from his embrace and taking a step back. He could see the irritation in her expression. "What you're doing is saying things you don't mean. So chill, okay?"

He did mean them, and he intended for her to know it. But for now… "Okay. Are you ready to go?"

"Yes, let me grab my tote bag."

As she rushed toward her bedroom, he noticed the huge plant sitting in the corner. When he'd walked into the florist shop after leaving her house earlier today, he'd seen it and wanted her to have it. He knew from the months they'd been together that she liked roses, especially red ones. Yet he'd never sent her any. On those occasions when he had sent her flowers, she'd gotten the pink-and-white carnations like all the other women he'd dated. He had been intent on not changing his course. The last thing he'd wanted was to fill her mind with the hope that things were more serious between them than they actually were. In a way, this rosebush represented all the roses he should have given her and hadn't.

"I'm ready."

He smiled at her. "Okay, then. Let's go."

Taking hold of her arm, he led her toward the door.

"It seems you thought of everything," Channing said, noting the large basket in the backseat. She wasn't sure what was in it, but she was impressed he'd brought it.

"I tried to. We can eat whenever you get hungry."

She had eaten a nice lunch right after Megan's call, and it had filled her up. But that was before she'd gotten into Zane's rental car and the basket had snagged her attention.

To get her mind and her stomach off the basket, she examined her surroundings. She saw all the cars parked facing the huge screen. A little excitement ran through her body. This was something new for her. "This is nice," she said. "And this is the first time I've been to a drive-in."

Zane let his seat back to accommodate his long legs. He glanced over at Channing. "You've never been to one before?"

"No. How old do you think I am? I understand drive-in theaters are nearly as extinct as dinosaurs."

"They aren't *that* extinct," he said, chuckling. "I used to go to one every Saturday night with my parents. They would load all of us into the van. It was fun. The one we went to even had a playground."

"Wow, you remember all of that?"

He nodded. "Yes. Those were special times for us, especially for me. After the folks died, that's all I had left. The memories. My counselor suggested I write it down."

She arched a brow. "Counselor?"

"Yes. Mrs. Harris. She was a grief counselor. Dillon and Ramsey thought it would be a good idea if we all went to see her. I think that's when I decided I wanted to become a psychologist."

She followed his lead and pressed the lever to let her seat back. Her legs weren't as long as his, but it felt nice to stretch out. "You have a degree in psychology, yet you've never used it in your work. Why?"

"Because by the time I finished college it was all hands on deck at Blue Ridge Land Management," he said. Blue Ridge was the family firm that his father and uncle had left behind. "Dillon and Ramsey were doing all they could to keep things going, and I felt my rightful place was to be there to help them. It was all about sacrifices."

He shifted in his seat to face her. "In a way, going to work for Blue Ridge was a blessing."

"In what way?"

"It showed me that I'm not suited for being indoors behind a desk. After a while, I felt boxed in. Caged. I knew that I couldn't be a psychologist. I needed to work outside."

"Then that partnership with your cousins came at the right time."

He smiled. "Yes. Mainly because Derringer and Jason were ready to bail from Blue Ridge, as well. The three of us love horses, and our fathers taught us to ride when we were knee-high. So when our cousins in Montana decided to expand their horse training and breeding business, there was no doubt in our minds that we were on board."

She nodded. One of the things she'd missed after leaving Denver was talking to Zane. They had a rapport that had made it easy to talk about anything. Or almost anything. She'd just realized he had never before shared with her why he'd pursued a degree in psychology instead of a degree in business like his brother Derringer and several of his cousins. She knew his brother Ramsey had gone to school for some type of agricultural degree since he'd always wanted to be a sheep rancher.

"Was Dillon upset because the three of you defected at once?"

Zane chuckled. "No, he understood. He'd known Blue Ridge wasn't in our blood any more than it had been in Ramsey's. Some people are born to be corporate leaders, and some are not. Besides, Riley and Stern were eager to take their places at the company. Even Canyon was gung ho once he decided being a doctor wasn't for him."

The huge screen flared to life. When it showed visuals of what they had for sale at the snack bar, Channing heard her stomach growl. She glanced over at Zane. "Sorry."

"No need to apologize. If you're hungry, just grab something out of that basket. I have a lot of good stuff in there. Better stuff than what you're seeing on the screen."

Of course after he'd said that, Channing had to check

it out and make sure. Taking off her seat belt, she rose up in the seat on her knees and reached in the backseat to uncover the basket. She was impressed. There were several meaty-looking sub sandwiches, bags of chips, an assortment of fruit and a bottle of red wine. Her favorite. But what really caught her eye were the two wine glasses. They were engraved in a beautiful gold script. One had her name on it, and the other had his.

A deep stirring spread in the center of Channing's stomach. Why would he go out and do something like that? She grabbed a couple of sandwiches, the bottle of wine and both glasses. Turning back around, she straightened in her seat but didn't put the seat belt back on.

She held up her bounty. "Nice wine glasses."

"Thanks. I happened to see them in the hotel's gift shop. I thought, wow, imagine that. Our names."

Channing threw her head back and laughed. He was lying through his teeth. "Come on. Names like Channing and Zane? You want me to believe there's another..." She stopped, coming short of saying the word *couple*. They were no longer a couple.

Zane didn't have any misgivings. He finished the sentence for her. "Couple like us? Probably not, since we're unique."

She shrugged and handed him a sandwich. He took it, and she opened the wine and poured them both glasses. She handed his to him and said, "Mmm, smell the aroma. Isn't it wonderful?"

He took a sip, met her gaze and held it. "I like your aroma better."

Channing swallowed, wishing he hadn't said that. It was bad enough sharing such close quarters with him, but to have him draw any level of intimacy into their conversation was too much. To keep things safe, she decided not to respond to what he'd said.

He'd told her often how he loved her scent, how it would turn him on. Well, she hoped he remembered their agreement about no sex. She wasn't so sure he *did* remember—the car's windows were tinted where no one could see them. Channing couldn't help wondering if that was by choice or coincidence.

Before she could dwell on it any longer, the screen blared the announcement that the first movie was about to begin. So she ate her sandwich and sipped her wine while silence reigned between them. She refused to glance over at him. Instead, she stared straight ahead at the huge movie screen.

Zane's blood pressure had spiked. He took a sip of his wine while eating his sandwich. Reaching back into the basket for a bag of chips, he ate them, as well. He enjoyed the meal all while inhaling Channing's scent. How had he gone two years without the aroma he'd become addicted to?

He knew women pretty damn well. Every woman had her own unique scent. He knew the power that pheromones could have on a man. Channing had a way of luring him in with her scent each and every time.

Trying to get his mind off Channing for the time being, he wondered if the drive-in theaters would become a fad again. Gone were the days when you had to park next to a speaker pole and pull the speaker in through your car's window. Due to modern technology, the sound was now transmitted through your car's radio. Nice.

Because they'd arrived early, the lines had not been long, and they had found a good parking spot. The view of the screen was spectacular. He wasn't a big John Travolta fan, but he knew Channing was. When he'd inquired at the hotel about where to take his lady that was casual, different and fun, the concierge had mentioned this place. Zane was glad he had.

Finally, he couldn't help himself. He glanced over at Channing, only to find that it seemed as though she was really absorbed in the movie. How many times had she seen *Grease?* He'd given her the DVD, and when it had come to Denver as a play, he'd taken her to see that, as well.

She had finished off her sandwich and the last of her wine. "Want more wine?"

She gazed over at him. "No, I've had enough. Thanks."

She turned back to the movie, but he continued watching her. Damn, he loved her. Whether she believed him or not, it had happened just the way he'd told her. The realization might have been late in coming, but it had punched him hard, first in the heart and then right between the eyes, making him see things he hadn't seen before.

If she needed to see his transformation to believe him, then a transformation was what she would get. Tonight, he was starting off slow, smooth and seductive. He reached across the seat and took her hand in his. They used to hold hands all the time, but he could tell she was somewhat surprised by his gesture. She didn't pull her hand away, but it felt stiff in his.

"Relax, Channing. I just want to hold your hand."

"Why?"

He could say he wanted to do it because he loved her and he enjoyed touching her, but he figured she wasn't ready to buy that. "I just do, okay?"

She shrugged with tense shoulders. "Okay."

"And before you get rigid and unbending, I haven't forgotten your 'no sex' rule."

She relaxed somewhat. "I was beginning to wonder."

He chuckled. "Why?"

"Because you're touching me."

He lifted a brow. "Was I not supposed to?"

She shook her head. "It brings back memories."

He smiled. "But memories are good, right?"

Her chin lifted. "Some are. Some aren't."

The last thing he wanted was for her to think about the bad memories he'd caused. "Slide over here for a minute," he said, tightening his hand on hers.

She hesitated but then slid across the seat toward him. He folded up the center console to make a bench seat. He didn't want anything separating them. Satisfied with their closeness, he wrapped his arms around her shoulders. "That's better. I like you plastered against me like this. I missed this, Channing. The closeness. The intimacy," he said truthfully. He hadn't realized just how much until now.

"It was your choice," she said, and he heard the bitterness in her tone.

"I know. My mistake," he countered softly.

She glanced over at him, and he saw the reservation in her eyes. He knew he would do anything to remove that look. "It was hard for me after you left, Channing."

"Was it?"

She asked as if she didn't believe him. "Yes. I was in a bad way mainly because I couldn't believe you'd left. You said you were leaving. You even went through all the motions of leaving, but I just couldn't get it through my head that you were actually going to do it. For a long time, I was in a state of denial."

She frowned, narrowing her eyes. "Why? Because you're the great Zane Westmoreland, and women aren't supposed to leave you? It's supposed to be the other way around?"

He didn't say anything for a minute. "I thought that was the reason at first," he said truthfully. "But then…"

She looked searchingly at him. "But what?"

"I felt the loss," he said hoarsely. "I actually felt it. And when it hit me that you wouldn't be back, I developed a bad attitude. It was so awful that no one in my family wanted to be around me. Dillon had to step in a few times to keep me and my other cousins or brothers from exchanging blows. I was filled with so much anger that just about anything could set me off."

Channing stayed silent. She'd talked to Megan a few times after moving to Atlanta, and his sister hadn't mentioned anything about Zane's bad temperament. But then she and Megan had agreed not to bring him up in any of their conversations. However, hearing what he was saying now made her ask, "Why, Zane? Why did my leaving upset you when you told me there could never be anything permanent between us?"

Zane sighed deeply as he thought about what she'd asked. How could he link the fear he'd felt at her departure to the same fear he'd felt when his parents had died? After she'd left Denver, he hadn't been able to handle the loneliness and emptiness within him. And when he had compared those feelings to the void he hadn't ever wanted to feel again, he'd withdrawn. He'd resolved never to let down his guard with any woman like he'd done with her.

"Zane?"

He could hear impatience in her voice. She wanted an answer, and he knew she deserved one. However, how could he explain it in a way that she would understand? A way where she could connect the dots the way he finally had?

Zane held her gaze and forced himself not to pull her into his arms and kiss her instead of answering her. He couldn't do that this time. He had to make sure he laid out everything she needed to see.

"You left me, Channing. At first, I convinced myself that it didn't matter, that you were doing the right thing because I couldn't give you what you wanted. But then…"

She leaned toward him. "Yes?"

He spoke truthfully when he said, "Then I began to feel like a piece of me was gone. I felt empty. My emptiness turned to anger because I had sworn I would never let myself feel such pain over a loss again."

An uneasy feeling raced up Channing's spine as she stared at Zane, the movie forgotten. Hearing him say those words had an insurmountable effect on her. Had that been when he'd realized he might feel something for her?

If what he said was true, then she could see why he'd gotten upset when she'd returned almost two years later with a fiancé. But it didn't explain or excuse his behavior at McKays. She had given him a chance to tell her he loved her, but he hadn't. Instead, he'd seduced her to prove a point.

"I had to leave," she said softly. "I could not stay in Denver and pretend I was okay in a relationship that wasn't going anywhere." She released a deep sigh. "Maybe this whole 'pushing' thing isn't a good idea, Zane."

"What makes you say that?"

"If it doesn't work, I'm the only one who'll get hurt. After McKays, I left Denver in pain for the second time with no plans to ever return or to ever see you again. Then, low and behold, you show up yesterday and the next thing you know we're having sex for old time's sake. You came back again today and convinced me that all it will take is a little push to get you to fall in love. But if I couldn't do it during the nine months we were together, what difference will it make now?"

He heard the doubt in her voice. The frustration. He wouldn't be happy until he heard certainty. Absolute and complete. When all was said and done, he wanted her misgivings to be put behind them…mainly because he wanted her to know she had his heart.

She pulled back and looked at him with a narrowed gaze. "Is this nothing but a game to you, Zane? A game to see how far you can make me go without giving me a commitment? Or maybe it's revenge. You're getting back at me for having the nerve to leave you in the first place. You like proving points."

He leaned forward. "Although I know it's hard for you, I'm asking you to trust me. I wouldn't be here if I didn't care about you, Channing." He ran his fingers through her hair. "You mean everything to me."

Channing drew in a deep breath. Zane knew exactly what he was doing. She'd always loved the feel of his hands in her hair. There was something about the way he did it that sent tingling sensations through her.

The silence between them lengthened. She closed her eyes, wishing she could pretend those two years without him had never happened and things were as they used to be. Maybe if she and Zane had stayed together, if she hadn't tried to rush things along, they might be married by now. That possibility was why she was here now. Taking another chance on him.

"What are you thinking about?" he asked her in a low voice.

She opened her eyes and looked at him. His face was right there, inches from hers. "It doesn't matter."

"Everything about this matters, Channing."

She wished she could believe that.

"Ask me what I'm thinking," he said throatily.

They should be watching the movie. Wasn't that what they'd come here for? she asked herself.

No. The reason they were here together was to see if they could repair their damaged relationship. To see if he could love her the way she needed to be loved. To see if he could really love her the way he thought he could. "Okay. What are you thinking, Zane?"

"How beautiful you are for starters."

His hand left her hair and moved to her chin. He tilted her face up to his. "Very beautiful."

"You can't see very well," she whispered. His lips were close to hers. She knew those lips well. Full and inviting, they had the ability to make liquid heat fill her. Just thinking about how well she knew those lips, her first-hand knowledge of how they tasted, had her feminine muscles clenching.

"I can see just fine, Channing. And you know what else I was thinking about?"

She swallowed tightly, knowing it was best not to respond but unable to hold back. "No, what?"

"This." And then he leaned in, capturing her lips with his.

Chapter 10

Zane knew that Channing couldn't deny that kissing was one means of communication they both enjoyed. And he wasn't about to make it a quick kiss. On the contrary. He intended to play it out for as long as he could and redefine in her mind just what a Zane Westmoreland kiss was all about. He was fighting to keep control, but the mating of their tongues made it difficult. Nearly impossible. He felt weak in the knees even when he wasn't standing.

Heat tore through him. He tightened his arms around her as his tongue danced with hers. He loved her taste almost as much he loved her scent, and he craved her with a hunger he felt all the way to his groin.

Channing's moans stirred sensual sensations all through him. They fed him. Stimulated him. Wildly intoxicated him. Nothing, and he meant nothing, was better than this—having your lips held captive by the woman you both loved and desired.

Her moans turned to whimpers when he deepened the kiss even more. Everything about her electrified him, made him feel whole and complete.

The sound of a car door slamming had him lifting his mouth off of hers. He stared at her, trying to come to terms with emotions that, until recently, had been foreign to him.

"What are you doing, Zane?" she asked in a slurred tone, as if she'd gotten tipsy from the intensity of the kiss.

"I was kissing you," he said smoothly. "And I want to kiss you some more. The Zane Westmoreland way."

He held her gaze. Saw the perceptive glint in her eyes. She knew just what a kiss *his way* entailed. Was she game? He was going to make sure that she was.

Lowering his mouth to hers, he kissed her again while wrapping her in his arms. This kiss was just as hot, just as greedy and just as intense, but this time it held more: doggedness, urgency.

Though it was hard to do so, he broke away from the kiss. He had to give her a choice. She could tell him to stop or give him the go-ahead. He watched as her expression got serious, her forehead knotted in deep consideration. He went still, not knowing what she'd decide, but knowing it was her decision to make. He would respect whatever it was.

He released a sigh of relief when she wrapped her arms around his neck, pressed her body close to his and tilted her mouth up to him. Grateful. Appreciative. Enthusiastic. He felt all of those things. Then he gently gathered her close, sliding his tongue between her lips.

He knew how much the kiss affected her when the arms around his neck tightened and her moans deepened and intensified. Her mouth was hot and delicious, and he was giving it one serious sensual assault. He wanted her.

With a deep groan, he slowly lifted his head and kissed his way down her neck to the pulse throbbing at its side.

He pressed a lever that made both their seats glide back, and then, with the other hand, he adjusted the steering wheel out of their way. He pulled her into his lap, facing him. He felt the shivers that passed through her body when his teeth grazed across her skin.

She sucked in a deep breath when he whipped the tank top over her head and undid the front clasp of her bra. The minute he saw her breasts he lowered his lips to a nipple, greedily sucking it into his mouth. His hands were busy, unzipping her shorts and inching them—as well as her panties—down her thighs.

His mouth hungrily moved to the other breast while she moaned his name over and over. He raised her up as he worked his mouth down her naked body, licking her belly, tonguing her navel and then tilting his seat back in a reclining position so that Channing's feminine mound stared him in the face.

Craving her taste in a way he never had before, he grasped her thighs and slid his tongue inside. She sucked in a breath, and he sucked on her, fastening his mouth to her most sensitive spot with no intention of letting go until she screamed his name.

He held tight, needing this as much she did.

"Oh," Channing moaned as Zane's tongue made that swirling motion it could do so well. And then that same tongue began fluttering like crazy, sending all kinds of sensual vibrations ricocheting through her. Did he know how many nerve endings were located right here? Yes, oh, yes. Right there? Oh, yes, he knew. Zane knew just about everything when it came to a woman. And he was devouring her the way only he could.

He nibbled until she couldn't take any more. Spasms ripped into her body, making her scream. She trembled all over from head to toe and at the juncture of her thighs.

He wanted to be pushed, so she pushed. Boy, did she push, and he didn't let go. Didn't let up. And then she climaxed again. Her body became electrified all over again.

When the last sensation left her body, she moaned out his name and collapsed against him. He pulled his mouth away from her and gently eased her down his body. Then their mouths connected, and she tasted the essence of herself on his tongue.

She gripped his broad shoulders and felt his hard muscles. She pulled her mouth away and heard his deep masculine growl as he gathered her close and whispered, "Mine." At that moment, the possessive word didn't bother her like it should have.

With all the strength she could muster, she lifted her head to meet his gaze. Before she could say anything, he gave a tight yet gentle squeeze to her butt cheeks and said, "No. We didn't have sex. We shared a kiss."

Physically exhausted, she didn't have the strength to argue. And when he shifted their bodies so she could sit curled in his arms, she did, dropping her head on his chest, listening to the rapid beat of his heart against her cheek.

He held her and ran his hand all over her naked body as if stroking her to sleep. Zane's kisses were what erotic fantasies were made of, and he'd given her a double whammy. Orgasms like the ones she'd just had should be outlawed.

She yawned, feeling sleepy, and as she closed her eyes, too tired to keep them open, she heard him murmur something close to her ear, but she was too far gone to make out the words.

* * *

"I love you, baby."

Zane whispered the words although he doubted Channing heard what he said. She'd drifted asleep while naked in his arms.

He studied her features. They were peaceful, satisfied. Reaching into the backseat, he retrieved his jacket and placed it over her. A smile touched his lips as he thought about how she looked more *his* than ever.

He felt the rise and fall of her chest. He'd missed this, her falling asleep in his arms. But what he'd really missed was waking up with her draped over him, their legs entwined on those nights when he had stayed at her place or she had stayed at his. Upon waking, they would make love again. And again. His body hardened at the memories, and his erection poked her in the backside.

Zane noticed the movie screen. Although there was one more movie to be shown, a lot of people had already left. Half the number of cars filled the lot than there had been an hour ago. He glanced at the clock on the car's dashboard. Was it after midnight already? This was a weeknight. A number of people would have to be at work tomorrow.

In his mind, he tossed around plans for tomorrow. He didn't intend to let a single day go by without spending it with Channing. He would ask her to ride with him to Richmond.

She shifted in sleep, and the jacket covering her slid down an inch, exposing a plump breast and a juicy nipple. His mouth twitched, and the heat of desire rippled through him like a wave. The position wouldn't have been so bad if he wasn't inhaling her scent each and every time he took a breath.

Deciding he should take a quick nap as well, he closed his eyes and rested his chin on her forehead.

"Wake up, sleepyhead. Time for me to take you home."

Channing slowly opened her eyes and blinked a few times. Zane's face came into focus. She then gasped when she realized she was naked in his arms with only his jacket covering her. She scrambled to move from his lap, but Zane's hands tightened around her.

"Where do you think you're going?" he asked, his mouth quirking in a smile.

"I need to put on my clothes." She glanced out the window. The first thing she noticed was that the movie screen was black. The next was the absence of other cars. "Please don't tell me we're the last car here."

He chuckled. "Okay, I won't tell you."

"Zane!"

"Okay, we're not the last but pretty close. I will admit we're the only one on this row and the only vehicle that's still parked. Everyone else is leaving."

"Then give me my clothes."

"Hmm, the idea of driving you home with you wearing nothing is tempting."

She frowned. "Don't play with me, Zane. I need to get dressed before someone comes over here."

He smiled as he released her and watched her ease her panties up her legs and thighs before wiggling into them. The shorts were next. Then came the bra and tank top. He always liked watching her get dressed. As a doctor, she had to be prepared for any emergency, so she had a knack for dressing quickly when she needed to.

Channing glanced over at Zane while running her hands through her hair. "What are you looking at?"

"You."

"Shouldn't you start the ignition so we can leave?"

"In a minute." He leaned over and kissed her.

She frowned when he straightened and then started the car. His lips had been warm, and she could feel her bones turning to mush. Trying to ignore the way her belly was flipping all over the place, she asked, "What was that for?"

"I want you to dream about me tonight."

She drew in a deep breath. At least he hadn't suggested that he stay the night. Zane's kisses were always the prelude to something else. Specifically, the prelude to more intense lovemaking.

She didn't say anything because her head was already filled with memories of what had happened earlier. No sex but a degree of kissing only Zane could deliver. As she focused straight ahead, they left the drive-in theater, and she recalled how he had stripped her naked and feasted on her body. Why did the man have such a skillful mouth?

"I'm driving to Richmond this morning. You want to go with me?"

Channing glanced over at him. "Richmond?"

"Yes. Last year we sold a client in Richmond a couple of our horses, ones that I trained. I thought since I was in the area I would check on them. I talked to the guy yesterday, and he's all for it. In fact, he wants to talk to me about buying several more."

Channing stared at him. When they'd been together before, he would often tell her about his work, but there had never been a time when he'd invited her to go with him on any of his business trips. She'd always hoped he would ask.

"So will you go?"

"I had planned to spend time on the beach tomorrow."

"We can do that on Thursday."

Her forehead bunched. He was making plans for them to spend even more time together? "When are you going back to Denver?"

He shrugged. "It depends."

She lifted a brow. "On what?"

"You."

"Me?"

"Yes, you. I told you why I'm here."

"Yes, but I'll be staying in Virginia for another two weeks. Surely you don't plan to hang around here all that time."

He smiled over at her as he turned the corner into her beach community. "I don't see why not."

Her belly flipped again at the idea of him wanting to stay here in Virginia to be with her. "Don't you have work to do back in Denver?"

"Yes, but I'm doing some of it here using my laptop. I'm going through files and purging a number of accounts we've closed over the past year."

She knew how much he detested any sort of administrative work, yet he was doing it. So he could stay here with her. Zane preferred working outdoors with the horses. Did being with her mean that much to him? She shook her head, rejecting the notion.

"Channing? Ready for me to walk you to the door?"

She blinked upon realizing she was home already. When she opened the door, he grabbed the basket out of the backseat. They had finished off all the food, and the only things left in the basket were the wineglasses and wine bottle. "Keep these for whenever we finish off the rest of the wine."

She didn't say anything as she took the basket from him. He was beginning to sound sure of himself. Too sure of himself.

Channing would have walked quickly to the door, but he held her hand, deliberately slowing her pace. He didn't seem in any hurry, but she already had the key in her hand. "Thanks. Tonight was fun."

"Glad you enjoyed it, and about Richmond… You will take the drive with me, won't you?"

She swallowed as she tried to decide what she should do. "Yes, I'll go."

He smiled. "Great. I'll be here to pick you up around nine."

"All right."

He leaned in close and placed a gentle kiss on her cheek. "Need me to check inside before leaving?"

Channing shook her head as she opened the door. "No. I'll be fine."

"Okay. But how about giving me a sign after you get inside that everything's okay? I'm not moving the car until you do."

"Okay. Good night."

He smiled down at her. "Good night, Channing."

She closed the door, and after placing the basket in the kitchen, she went to the living room window and looked out. Zane's car was still in the driveway. She waved to him and watched him wave back before he backed out into the street.

She watched until he was no longer in sight. Then she went to the kitchen and pulled the wine bottle out of the basket, along with wineglasses. She poured wine into the glass that bore her name, thinking how pretty the glasses were and how thoughtful and touching it had been for Zane to buy them.

Taking her glass into the living room, she eased down on the sofa, fully aware of what tonight had done to her.

It had pulled Zane deeper into her heart. She couldn't help but wonder if tonight had changed anything in his heart.

Probably not. She hadn't been the pusher this time but instead had been mainly a satisfied recipient. He had been the dominating male who took charge, and she had let him.

He needed to chill and let her handle things her way. Already he'd planned tomorrow for her, and if she let him, he would dominate the rest of her time in Virginia.

Channing suddenly realized that the one thing she'd never done before in their relationship was to take control. Whenever they'd made love, he'd been the one to initiate it.

Suddenly she had a plan.

"Not so fast, Zane Westmoreland," she muttered to herself. "Later today will be my time, and I intend to push you right off your feet."

Zane tossed his car keys on the table the moment he entered his suite, feeling good about his date with Channing. The look on her face as she'd stood at the window and waved goodbye had been priceless. His stomach had clenched tightly at the thought of actually driving away from her instead of staying the night to finish what they'd started at the drive-in.

It had been hard to keep driving without making a U-turn back to her. But she had set the "no sex" rule, and he'd given his word that he would adhere to her wishes. But like he had shown her tonight, he had no qualms about stretching the limits of that rule to his advantage whenever he could.

He was about to toss his jacket across the chair when his cell phone rang. Pulling it out of his jacket pocket, he gritted back a curse. It was Megan. A part of him didn't want to answer it, but with his luck, she would call Channing next and he definitely didn't want that. He didn't need Megan sticking her nose where it didn't belong. How he and Channing decided to work things out was no business of his sister's.

He clicked on the phone. "What do you want, Megan? It's late."

"I know what time it is, Zane. I had emergency surgery at the hospital and I'm on my way home. I also know where you are."

"And?" He braced himself for his sister's tirade. Since marrying Rico, his emotionally detached sister had been showing all kinds of emotion. She'd become expressive as hell, and for someone who'd once prided herself on having self-control, the new Megan took a lot of getting used to.

"I'm glad you've come to your senses."

He raised a brow. "Meaning?"

"Meaning, I talked to Channing yesterday, and I believe it."

He paused to lean in the doorway that separated the sitting area from the bedroom. "Believe what, Megan?"

"That you finally realize you love her."

Zane let out a relieved breath. At least his sister believed him. Too bad the woman he loved wasn't there yet. "What made you change your mind?"

"You would not have lied to Rico. You had no reason to do so. And then you dropped everything to fly out there to plead your case and surrender your heart."

"Yeah, for all the good it's doing," he said, suddenly feeling frustrated. He was glad his sister didn't consider his actions suspect, but he still had his work cut out for him. Channing wasn't making things easy for him.

"Don't give up, Zane. You hurt her, and she has to learn to trust you again. You have to give her a reason to believe in you. She has to know that she can win your heart fair and square."

"She's won my heart already, Megan. I love her. But she doesn't believe me because I made the mistake of telling her so many times that I *didn't* love her."

"Um, like the boy who cried wolf. He cried it so long that when the real wolf came along, no one wanted to believe him."

"I know, and I only have myself to blame."

"Well, we're all rooting for you."

He chuckled. "We?"

"Yes, the entire Westmoreland clan. At least those of us who understand what true love is about. After loving Rico, I can't imagine a person not being with the one person who has their heart. The one person they know will make them happy."

Less than an hour later, when Zane eased into bed and slid between the sheets, he thought of his conversation with Megan. He was grateful that she believed him. Now he had to make Channing believe.

He smiled, thinking that in a few hours he intended to turn up the heat.

Chapter 11

"Ready?"

Channing blinked at the sensations twirling around in her stomach.

They could have been caused by the deep, husky timbre of Zane's voice or by the way he leaned in her doorway, dressed in a pair of jeans and a chambray shirt, with his Stetson riding low on his head. His navigator sunglasses finished off the package, and she was convinced he was the most handsome man she'd ever seen.

Why did his smile seem so luscious and sexy this morning?

"Yes, I'm ready. Come on in," she said, stepping aside. "I just need to grab my purse. I figure we can come back here later and eat dinner. I still have a lot of leftovers."

He took off his sunglasses. She could tell he was surprised by her invitation. "All right. Sounds like a plan to me."

She was about to walk off to get her purse when he touched her arm. "Not so fast." He pulled her into his arms and let his gaze move up and down her body. "You look pretty."

"Thanks." She had taken great pains to look nice today. From the appreciative look in his eyes, she knew it was worth it. His desire caused goose bumps to form on her arms. "And you look nice yourself."

They stood for a moment, staring at each other. Channing could feel the heat and the charged air between them. She couldn't help but remember what had happened last night at the drive-in. Those same memories were what had kept her up most of the night as primal needs ripped through her.

She absently licked her lips and heard Zane's breath catch. "What's wrong?" she asked.

Instead of answering, he held her gaze. She felt the fire in every part of her body.

"Nothing's wrong, baby. In fact, everything is right." He drew her close and lowered his mouth to hers.

If he thought she would resist, he was wrong. Channing even stretched up on tiptoe to meet his mouth. His hands went around her waist, and she grabbed his massive shoulders, pressing her body against perfect abs and muscular thighs.

But what made her breasts throb was the engorged bulge pressing hard at the juncture of her thighs.

If he needed to be pushed, then she would push with all the strength she could muster.

She hoped she wasn't making a mistake.

Nothing, and she meant nothing, was better than the way Zane's mouth mated with hers. He relished her with a hunger that made her moan deep in her throat and made her wet between her legs simultaneously. A sense of intimacy that she'd fought for the past day overtook her, had her needing sexual fulfillment as much as she needed her next breath.

When her body began to quiver, he slowly pulled his mouth away and stood holding her until the last shiver left her body. As if to satisfy her one last time, he licked his tongue across her lips before nibbling the corners of her mouth with his teeth. Tingles swept through her.

"If we don't leave now, we'll never get out of here," he whispered against her lips. "My self-control is slipping, and I'm tempted to say to hell with your 'no sex' rule, lift up this sundress and ease inside of you."

She could imagine it happening. Her body was ready, aching for the feel of his shaft thrusting in and out of her. She was intensely aroused and knew there was no way he hadn't realized it. He was very acute when it came to that.

"Um," she said, backing out of his arms. She needed to put some space between them. "Excuse me for a minute."

"Take your time. I'm not going anywhere."

She moved toward her bedroom, but before opening the door and stepping inside, she paused and glanced over her shoulder. He stood there, looking so incredibly sexy that the sight was an assault on her senses in every way.

"If you prefer that we spend the day here doing nothing, our plans can be changed, Channing."

She was tempted. Boy, was she tempted. But she wanted to go with him to Richmond and do something with him she'd never done before… She wanted to see a part of his life he'd kept from her. "No. I'm looking forward to going to Richmond with you."

"All right."

Lust surrounded them, but she was determined to change all that lust into love. More than anything, she wanted to believe that she could.

"Need my help, Channing?"

She blinked upon realizing that she'd been standing there staring at him like a dimwit. She had wanted to change into new underwear, a special pair just right for the heat building between them. Suddenly, she could see him kneeling before her and easing her panties down her legs, helping her into a new, lacy pair. She opened her mouth to tell him that she didn't need his help but then decided it was time she tested his control.

"If you like."

She saw the heat that flared in his eyes. "Yes, I would definitely like."

Channing nodded before continuing to her bedroom, and he followed. She moved to the dresser and pulled out a pair of black lace panties. She held up several. She knew that was his preference.

A smile curved his lips.

She closed the drawer and brought the pair of undies to him. He took them from her fingers and slowly knelt down in front of her. Reaching out, he ran his calloused hands up her dress and between her legs. The contact with her skin had blood rushing through her veins.

Channing met the dark, heavy-lidded eyes gazing up at her, saw how his control was being stretched. His jaw clenched tight, and his nostrils flared while he eased her plain panties down her legs. She could hear the intensity of his breathing, and her breasts felt tight. When her panties were down to her knees, his hand paused, and then heated fingers inched back up between her legs to caress the folds of her womanhood. She drew in a quick breath when he slid two fingers inside of her.

"Zane…" His name eased from her lips. An intense desire stirred in the pit of her stomach when he stroked her. Automatically, her inner muscles clenched as his fingers gave her a sensuous workout. Then, as if he'd merely wanted to remind her of what gifted fingers he had, he withdrew his touch. She watched as he took those same fingers, wet with her moisture from her body, and inserted them into his mouth. He sucked hard, as if relishing the taste of her nectar.

Watching him made her weak in the knees, but before she could sink to the floor, he returned his hand to her thighs to complete the task of removing her panties. He was slow, taking his time, and the feel of the skimpy fabric easing down her legs set off primitive urges within her. The eyes staring up at her held such a fierce hunger in their dark depths that she felt drawn to him more than ever before.

"You can step out of them now."

His words floated up to her, and she lifted her legs to step out of her panties. Her breath lodged in her throat when he took the fresh pair from her and slid them up her legs. He rubbed his face against her thighs before inhaling deeply.

"I'm convinced I'm addicted to this," he said. "It always amazed me how wet you can get for me," he said, his dark eyes glinting with heated lust.

It always amazed her, as well. When he lifted her dress and took his hot tongue and drew a circle around her navel before pulling her panties the rest of the way up, she swore she felt the floor shake beneath her feet.

Sensations swamped her. When he stood and gave her backside a playful smack, those sensations vibrated something fierce, sending tremors running through her.

"Anything else you need help with before we leave?"

She took a step back and eased down her dress. "No, that's it. I would not have wanted to change my underwear if you hadn't kissed me the way you did."

He chuckled. "Do you want me to promise not to kiss you again?"

She thought about his question and immediately knew the answer. "No, that's not what I want."

Zane stared at her intently, and she felt his uncensored look. "Good, because I doubt I could do that, anyway." He reached out and took her hand. "Come on, baby, let's go."

Sipping the beer Morris Holder had given him, Zane thought the same thing now that he had thought last year when he, Derringer and Jason had met with the man. This was a pretty nice spread. But as far as he was concerned, nothing was more beautiful than Westmoreland land, and he had a special affection for Zane's Hideout. His spread was the best with the lake and the mountains surrounding it. Now that Bailey's spread was next to his, he wondered if Ramsey and Dillon meant to punish him when they'd given her that parcel. Lord, help him. At least it was still undeveloped land, and Bailey wasn't showing any interest in building anything on it.

Instead of taking the interstate, he had driven the scenic route to Richmond, making various stops along the way and enjoying lunch at a café in Jamestown. What would normally have taken two hours had taken more than three, but he hadn't wanted to hurry. He preferred spending quality time with Channing.

Turning his thoughts back to Morris, Zane took another sip of beer. A self-made billionaire at fifty-eight, Morris was in great physical shape. He had his own workout room with every piece of exercise equipment imaginable. And then there was his stable of horses, which Zane knew Morris rode often.

Zane moved his gaze to the view of the meadows, and his stomach clenched when he saw Channing. She was walking beside Morris's wife, Lisa. Lisa was a beauty in her own right, but no one, he thought, was more beautiful than Channing. He loved her yellow sundress. It looked damn good on her. Sexy.

"Channing's a nice woman, Zane."

He glanced back at Morris. "Thanks."

"Any plans for the future?"

Zane wasn't surprised by the man's question. The last time he was here, Morris had been a bachelor for more than twenty years, and Lisa had been his live-in lover. Now the two were married. "Yes, I plan to marry her as soon as I can convince her that I love her."

Morris nodded. "Good luck, and don't give up. I woke up one morning and decided I had been a single man long enough. Over breakfast, I asked Lisa to marry me. For the longest time, she thought I wasn't serious because I'd never mentioned marriage before. There was the issue of the twenty-five-year difference in our ages. That issue used to concern me, but on that morning, it no longer did. Age is nothing more than a number, and I refused to go another day without making plans for a future with the woman I loved and cared about most."

Zane nodded and took another sip of beer. "She didn't have a problem with your sudden change of heart?"

He chuckled. "Not sure she had a problem with it, but she was skeptical at first. The subject of marriage had never come up between us, so I think she thought I was dying or something. Convincing her that I wasn't was hard, but I did it."

Morris took a sip of his own beer and then added, "Women don't understand that men might be slow, but when we make up our minds about something, that's it."

Zane released a deep breath. "Yeah, that's it."

But it seemed he was having a harder time convincing Channing than Morris had convincing Lisa. A small smile stretched across his mouth. He wouldn't give up.

Morris stood. "Lisa and I would certainly love it if you and Channing stayed and had dinner with us."

Zane stood as well, an appreciative smile touched his lips. "Thanks for the invite, but Channing and I have made dinner plans already."

What he wasn't saying was that he couldn't wait to get back to Channing's grandparents' home to be alone with her.

"I like Lisa. Did you know she used to be a pharmacist? That's how she and Morris met," Channing said. "He happened to drop by the drugstore where she was working one day."

She and Zane had left Richmond and were on their way back to Virginia Beach. While Zane and Morris had talked business, she and Lisa had gotten to know each other, and Lisa had given Channing a tour of their beautiful ranch. Lisa had also told her about the twenty-five-year age difference between her and Morris.

Channing had been surprised when Lisa had said she and Morris had been married only a little more than a year after being lovers for five years. Five years! It was hard to believe that Lisa had been willing to wait five years for Morris's affections. Channing had bolted from Zane after nine months, telling herself that had been long enough.

"Yes, Lisa is a nice person, and Morris did mention how they met."

Channing's gaze shifted to look out the car window. Lisa and Morris's story was something Channing couldn't get out of her mind. She shifted her gaze back to Zane. He was hot, and she could feel the heat radiating from his body to hers. His eyes, hidden behind his sunglasses, were on the road, which was fine since she wanted to watch him.

There was no way she could have remained Zane's lover for five years without knowing for certain how he felt about her. Her makeup was totally different from Lisa's. Her parents and grandparents had always claimed she had a low tolerance for some things, that she lacked patience. She wondered if her impatience had worked against her where Zane was concerned.

They came to a stop at a traffic light, and she could feel the dark depths of Zane's eyes staring back at her behind his sunglasses. Her heart thumped hard in her chest, and her breath stopped from the intensity of his gaze.

"Is anything wrong, Channing?" he asked her.

"No, but I have a question for you. Lisa and Morris were lovers for five years before Morris asked her to marry him. Had I not left Denver for Atlanta when I did...had I remained there as your lover, where would we be now?"

She watched as a frown of concentration marred his forehead. "I honestly don't know," he said softly. "I want to think I would have come to my senses and you and I would be married, or at least engaged. But I can't rightly say. It took your leaving a second time to make me realize what you meant to me."

Channing nodded. *What she meant to him...* Even now she wasn't sure what that was and had only a limited amount of time to find out.

The car moved again, and Zane shifted his gaze back to the road. Behind the sunglasses, he tried to keep his eyes from blazing in frustration. When would she ever believe that he actually loved her? What if she never believed it?

For the first time in his life, he was dealing with the fear of losing the woman he loved. The thought that no matter how hard he tried he could still end up without her as his wife sent a rush of irritation flowing all through him.

Hey, don't even think of losing her, man. You got yourself in this mess, and you can get yourself out. You got to make her feel as if she's the most important person in the world to you, because she is.

He brought the car to a stop again at another traffic light. He glanced over at Channing to find her still looking at him, and he drew in a shaky breath. The air between them was charged.

She absently licked her lips and tucked strands of her windblown hair behind her ear. At that moment, all he could think about was just how delicious the area around her ear tasted. He'd used his tongue there a number of times.

He was a man with a healthy sexual appetite, but he knew she equated his desire with lust. How could he get her to understand that his sexual need for her was an extension of his love? He was fully aware she was fighting her own deep attraction to him.

"Got any plans when we get back to your place?" he asked when traffic began moving again.

She shrugged. "I thought I'd grab something out of the freezer for a quick meal and then I'll let you come up with ideas for ways to spend the rest of the day."

He wasn't so sure she would want to do that. If she left it up to him, they would be making love all over the place for the rest of the day and well into the night. "I guess we can spend time on the beach," he offered.

"Yes, I guess we can do that."

When traffic slowed up again, he gave a quick glance over to her. She hadn't sounded enthused about doing that. "Any other ideas?" he asked holding her gaze.

"Anything you want to do is fine with me, Zane."

His erection began throbbing again. He quirked an eyebrow at her to make sure they were on the same page. "Anything?"

"Yes, *anything*."

Shivers of anticipation raced through his body, and he broke eye contact with her to return his gaze to the road. If she thought he didn't intend to hold her to what she'd just said, she had another thought coming.

He glanced at the clock on the car's console. At that moment, he decided to discontinue driving the scenic route and hit the interstate. She had been sending out some pretty strong vibes today, vibes that all but declared that she was now in the driver's seat. And he couldn't get back to Kindle Shores quick enough to find out just how she would drive him over the edge.

Channing watched the endless stretch of two-lane road ahead of them. She'd told Zane what she wanted, and knowing him like she did, he would take full advantage of it.

And she'd be ready when he did.

Her body had been attuned to him since he'd changed her panties that morning. At the Holders' ranch, she had caught him staring at her more than once, pinning her with his dark gaze. Other than when Lisa had invited her to take a tour of the ranch so Morris and Zane could talk business, he had been there by Channing's side.

She had been fully aware of him every time his arm had snaked around her waist, every time he'd taken her hand in his, every time he'd brushed a wayward curl back from her face. Those looks and impromptu touches had ignited a flame inside her, one she hadn't been able to put out yet. So here she was, probably as aroused as Zane, and it didn't matter that he knew it.

"Did skipping out on that symposium cause problems for you at the hospital, Channing?"

She looked at him, finding it oddly gratifying that he cared. "No. I have a really good relationship with Dr. Rowe and the other top hospital administrators. I had only committed myself for three weeks, although I'd taken a six-week leave from my position in Atlanta."

"But you would have considered staying all six weeks."

She noted he said it as a statement more than a question. She could tell him that she had been leaning toward not doing the additional three weeks because being back in the same town with him hadn't been easy. She had even considered visiting her brother and his family in San Diego for a week or so. But Zane didn't need to know any of that.

"Maybe. Maybe not," she said. "I hadn't made up my mind yet."

"But what happened at McKays that night made you decide to leave."

Again, he had presented it as a statement. "Yes," she said. "It helped me to decide."

"I'm sorry I drove you away from Denver. But I'm not sorry for coming after you, and I'll do so again if I have to, Channing. To be quite honest, my real mistake was not coming after you that first time."

His words gave her pause and reminded her that the Zane she'd known had been quite the ladies' man. He would have no reason to run behind any woman, no matter how much she had wanted to be his exception.

"Just think how different things would be now if I had come after you," he added.

Channing smiled at him. "And how different do you

think things would be, Zane?" she asked and noticed he was pulling off to the side of the road.

Zane brought the car to a stop, cut the engine and turned to her. "I want to think we'd be married with a baby."

"A baby?"

Seeing the startled look on her face, a smile curved his lips. "Yes, Channing. A baby. My baby. Don't you like children?"

"Yes, but…"

"But what?"

"We never discussed children," she said softly.

No, he thought, they hadn't. Mainly because he'd never wanted to discuss a future with her. "We're talking about them now."

"Are we?"

"Yes. I like kids. What about you?"

She nodded. "Yes, I like them."

"How many do you want us to have?" he asked her. "I want several since I'm used to a big family. Hey, we can be like my cousin Quade and have three in one day."

Channing's mouth dropped open, and she simply stared at him. She knew all about Quade's babies. Triplets. "Are you crazy?"

He chuckled. "Yes, I am. I'm crazy about you." He brushed a kiss across her lips. "If you don't want triplets, I'll settle for twins."

Zane laughed at her shocked expression as he straightened in his seat. Turning the car's ignition back on, he maneuvered the vehicle onto the road knowing he'd given Channing something to think about.

Channing didn't say anything as she watched Zane switch from the two-lane road and take the ramp that led to the interstate. What *could* she say when her mind was spinning? Zane had just implied they had a future. With children. She wasn't mistaken about that. She knew he liked children. She'd seen him around his cousin Dillon's son. But Zane had never brought up the subject of children they would have together.

But today he had.

Channing stole another glance at Zane. She had to admit that over the past two days she had detected changes in him. Positive changes. He wasn't as inflexible as he once had been, and he came off as less guarded. He was letting her into his private world. A small stirring of pleasure rippled through her and warmed her insides. They were making progress.

A good twenty minutes or more passed. When she saw they were taking the exit for Kindle Shores, anticipation nipped at her heels. Although Zane's expression was well hidden by those navigator sunglasses, she knew he was just as eager as she was to get to their destination.

Within five minutes, Zane pulled the car into her driveway as all kinds of emotions churned inside of her. As he cut off the engine, she saw his fingers tap the steering wheel while he focused desire-drenched eyes on her.

"Are you hungry?" he asked in a low, sensuous tone.

His question had a mouthwatering effect…but it wasn't for food. "No. You?" The sun was shining brightly overhead, but Channing knew that wasn't the reason the interior of the car felt so hot.

"A meal isn't what I have an intense hunger for now, Channing."

Her breath caught. His words, spoken in a quiet voice, compelled every single cell in her body to ignite in an overaroused state.

She swallowed. "And what is it that you want?"

His fingers stopped tapping the steering wheel. Instead, those fingers brushed across her wrist, making every erogenous zone in her body come alive with a need she couldn't deny.

Holding her gaze, he leaned toward her and whispered, "I want you every way I can have you."

Channing felt as though every nerve in her body was on fire. She drew in a deep breath. "Then maybe we need to take this inside."

A sexy smile touched his lips. "I agree."

Chapter 12

No sooner had the door closed behind them, Zane and Channing were tearing off each other's clothes. Zane knew wanting any woman this much had to be insane, but that thought was wiped from his brain with the erotic sweep of her tongue in his mouth. Where had this intense hunger come from? How was it driving him as much as it was driving her?

She had him pinned against the door and was pushing him to do anything she wanted. He was definitely game as long as she kept kissing him this way, so deeply and completely. When she suddenly jerked her mouth free, dropped to her knees in front of him and took his engorged sex into her hands, he groaned deep in his throat.

"Ah, hell!" He threw his head back as her heated tongue swirled over his swollen shaft before she hungrily mouthed the full length of him. He groaned when suddenly it seemed as if she would swallow him whole.

She was using her mouth to infuse her ownership on this part of him. And she was doing so in the most earth-shattering way known to man.

Pleasure shot to all parts of his body. She was building a fire within him and quenching it at the same time.

While her fingertips stroked his thatch of curly hair, her mouth sucked harder. Then her fingers shifted lower to gently squeeze his testicles, causing a jolt of pleasure to tear through him. Did she know her actions were the embodiment of his wet dreams? Did she know she was bonding herself to him?

He grabbed her head, twining his fingers through the silky strands of her hair before wrapping a lock around his fist to hold her mouth right there. Yes, oh, yes. Right. There. And then he felt it, the first vibrations stirring in his groin.

"Channing," he whispered as sensations flooded through him. His heart was racing, and he couldn't get his breathing regulated. And then with one brutal yet erotic suck of her mouth, the intensity slammed into him. He felt the release gush into her mouth.

There weren't any words that could define what he felt at that moment. Though *mind-blowing* was close. He groaned her name over and over until the last sensation had swept through his body.

He didn't recall when she let go of him or when she eased to her feet. All he remembered was gazing through a haze of sensuous contentment to stare into the depths of her eyes.

"Channing—"

He wanted to tell her he loved her. But before he could fix his mouth to say the words, her soft lips took control of his, and she kissed him with such completeness it had him groaning out loud again.

He couldn't take any more. He swept her off her feet, into his arms, and headed for the bedroom.

When Zane placed her on the bed, Channing stared up at him, watching the intensity in his features. She had a feeling this lovemaking would be different from any other they'd shared. When he joined her in bed, her legs automatically opened for him. With the ease of a man who knew just what he wanted, Zane slid between them.

They stared at each other for several heartbeats before she felt him filling her with long, powerful thrusts, stretching her and going deep. When he continued moving in and out in long, languorous strokes, the rhythm caused electrifying sensations to overtake her. His hands tightened on her hips, holding her immobile while he totally possessed her feminine core.

"Ah," she groaned while intense pleasure blazed through every part of her.

Then his strokes became harder and harder, deeper and deeper, complete and absolute. The result was staggeringly powerful.

She met his gaze, and the look in his eyes took her breath away. For the first time in her life, she felt an emotion coming from him that she'd never felt before. It might have been a figment of her imagination or wishful thinking, but she decided to take the feeling and run with it.

The moment that decision was made, her body seemed to splinter into a thousand pieces. She dug her fingers into his shoulders, and it was only then that he lowered his head and took her mouth to drown out her screams.

When he withdrew from the kiss, he whispered against her lips, "That was lovemaking, *not* sex. It's never been just sex with you, Channing. Never."

Then he grasped her face in both hands and lowered

his mouth to kiss her again. Channing doubted she could ever love him any more than she did at that moment.

"I'm glad you haven't lost your touch in the kitchen, Channing."

Channing smiled at Zane while placing a plate of cookies in front of him as he sat at the kitchen table. She slid into the chair across from him. "And I'm glad you haven't lost your touch in the bedroom."

At his deep chuckle, she grabbed one of the cookies and bit into it. They had made love several times before finally getting out of bed and putting on clothes…at least some of them. He had slid into his jeans and she into his shirt. Then they had gone into the kitchen to get something to eat.

Channing had taken a few things out of the freezer before they'd left for Richmond, and all she had to do was place them in the microwave. Now she and Zane were sitting at the table enjoying cookies and milk for dessert. It seemed all the dishes she'd prepared during her cooking frenzy were his favorites. Go figure.

When she saw the way he was looking at her, she took a deep, quivering breath. It didn't help matters that he was shirtless with that powerful chest on display. A chest she had licked all over hours ago. She shivered at the memory. Lord! She needed a cold glass of water. Quick. The glass of milk just wasn't doing it.

"Excuse me," she said, getting up from the table. She strolled over to the refrigerator to get a chilled bottle of water. She quickly opened the refrigerator, grabbed one, unscrewed the top and took a huge gulp, appreciating how the cold liquid flowed down her throat. Boy, she'd needed that.

"You want to share?"

She jumped. She hadn't known Zane had gotten out of his chair and was standing right there in front of her. "Sure," she said, reaching behind her to reopen the refrigerator.

"No, I want to share yours."

"Oh." She handed him her bottle and watched him finish it off before he placed it on the counter.

He then smiled at her and said, "You make me hot, baby."

Her insides stirred. If he only knew how hot he made her. She raised her palm to his forehead. "Um, you feel normal."

His lips curved in a smile as he took hold of her hand and lowered it to his zipper. "Can you say the same here?" he asked.

She swallowed. No, she couldn't. He felt huge, engorged and erect. You would think that with as much action as they'd had earlier, more sex would be the last thing on their minds. Evidently not.

"Well?"

She cupped him through his jeans and watched desire flare in his eyes. "I can handle this."

"You're the only woman who can," he said throatily, reaching up to peel his shirt off her. "So tell me, Channing Hastings," he said, tugging out of his jeans, "have you ever been taken against a refrigerator?"

"No." She breathed the words. Blood rushed thickly through her veins at the thought of such a thing happening.

He lifted her, and her legs automatically wrapped around his waist. "Then consider this your first time… but it won't be your last, baby."

Zane lay awake, staring at the ceiling, while a naked Channing slept soundly beside him. Something flared deep within him when he thought about how they had spent their day, beginning with the drive to Richmond and then returning here.

It reminded him of how things used to be on her free days from the hospital. She would spend her time with him at the Hideout. How could he not have seen then just how great they were together? Although he'd known their relationship was good, he hadn't understood the significance of what that meant until it was too late. That was why he was here backpedaling, trying to convince her that he loved her, doing whatever it took to get that message across.

After they'd made love in the kitchen, starting out against the refrigerator and ending up on the counter, they had dressed and taken a walk on the beach. They had run into Ronald and his family. Zane had been introduced to Jennifer and their two kids. Seeing Ronald with his family made Zane long for that same thing with Channing. He'd meant what he'd told her yesterday. He wanted kids and looked forward to the children they would make together.

When they'd returned to her villa, he'd hinted that he needed to go back to the hotel to change clothes. He had hoped she would suggest he check out of the hotel altogether and spend the rest of his time at the beach house with her. But she hadn't. He'd been disappointed, but he hadn't pushed. He recalled one of his father's old sayings: "Anything worth getting is worth waiting for...." And he knew deep in his heart that Channing was worth waiting for. He was determined to rid her of any and all doubt about his love for her.

She shifted her body in sleep, and immediately he became aroused. When he felt her hand on his thigh, every cell in his body became energized. She slowly opened her eyes, and his heart pounded in his chest when she smiled at him.

"Now that you're awake," he said softly, brushing hair from her face, "I need to leave."

"To go back to the hotel?" she asked quietly.

"Yes."

He saw the slight marring of her forehead and knew she was trying to make a decision. When she shifted closer and eased her thigh between his, he knew she had made it.

"Since you're determined for me to push you into falling in love with me, then maybe you should stay here."

He cupped her chin in his hand. "You sure? Whether I stay here or at the hotel, I'm not leaving Virginia Beach until you do, Channing."

She nodded. "I'm sure. So unless you're desperate for your things, you can wait until the morning to go get them."

His hand left her chin to rub his own. "I can use a shave, but I can wait until tomorrow. If you wake up in the morning and I'm not here, that's where I'll be…checking out of the hotel."

"All right."

He kissed her and felt that special connection between them. They still had more road to travel, but at that moment, he felt that they were at least making progress.

The ringing of the telephone woke Channing. She noticed the spot beside her in bed was empty as she reached for her cell phone on the nightstand. "Hello," she said in a sleepy tone.

"Gracious. You're still in bed?"

Channing came wide-awake upon hearing her grandmother's voice. She glanced over at the clock. It was close to eleven. Typically she was an early riser, but when you spent most of the night making love, exhaustion had a tendency to creep up on you.

"Yes, I'm still in bed. How are you Gramma?"

"I'm fine, but I wanted to check on you. Our last conversation had me worried."

Channing took a deep breath. "I know, but I'm better."

"Does that mean your opinion of men is better?"

Channing thought of the past two days she'd spent with Zane and how thoughtful and considerate he'd been. But, most importantly, she thought of how he'd included her in his world. "Yes, it's improved some."

"Glad to hear it."

She and her grandmother talked for a little while longer before they ended their call. Channing stretched and then eased out of bed. Thinking of Zane checking out of the hotel, she nibbled her bottom lip. She wanted to be optimistic that she wasn't making a mistake.

She hoped she wasn't wrong, but she was beginning to feel a special bond between them, and it wasn't just about sex…although she thought that part of their relationship was super, too. She felt more.

But then, she quickly reminded herself, she had felt more the last time they'd been together, when she'd assumed he had fallen in love with her. She couldn't afford to make another mistake about something like that. So she would take one day at a time. She wouldn't rush, but she would, in her own way, continue to push him. Yes, she'd push, but she wouldn't shove. In her mind, there was a difference. If he was close, she would see to it that he got closer. She had to believe that Zane was worth taking a chance on.

The sound of a car door closing had her looking out the window. Zane was back, and she watched as he went to the trunk of the car and removed his luggage and laptop. As if he felt her watching, he glanced at the window, tilted his Stetson back and looked straight at her. When he smiled, she actually felt it radiate from him to her and she smiled back. Then he did something that the Zane she'd always known would never have done.

He blew her a kiss.

Her breath caught, and his gesture sent a warm rush of pleasure flowing through her. This was the man she loved, the man she wanted to marry and the man she wanted as a father for her children.

Suddenly, she realized that she was looking at the world through rose-colored glasses again, and Zane had once again unlocked her heart.

Chapter 13

"Zane, don't you dare! Put me down this instant!"

"Okay."

And he did so, unceremoniously dumping her into the ocean. Channing surfaced, sputtering and pushing wet hair from her face. "How dare you!"

"I dare because I thought you needed cooling off. I saw the way you were looking at me. Like you wanted to jump my bones."

"I was not, you arrogant, conceited…!"

Ignoring her ravings, he continued. "Not that I'm complaining about you wanting a little roll in the sand. But although this is considered a private beach, there are others around. What would the Farmers think? Or your grandparents' neighbors for that matter?"

Instead of answering, she shot him a venomous look before turning to swim the short distance back to shore. He let her go. There was no doubt in his mind that she was angry with him. He smiled, thinking he would have to make up with her. The thought fired his blood. Making up with Channing was always an enjoyable experience.

Since he was in the water, he might as well take a leisurely swim. Because there were so many lakes on Westmoreland land, the one thing his parents had been sure to teach their offspring was how to swim. He considered himself pretty good at it…mainly because of the swimming races he, his brothers and his cousins had held during the summer months while growing up. He'd been the reigning champ for years…until Bailey showed him up. Now the little nymph still held the title.

He glanced to where Channing lay on the towel she had stretched out on the sand. It was hard to believe it had been a week since he'd moved out of the hotel. As far as he was concerned, every day seemed like heaven.

They woke up making love and went to bed making love. In between, they spent the day on the beach or, like yesterday, shopped. She had been determined that he should purchase a pair of shorts, and, to satisfy her, he had. After she had whistled outrageously about what a nice pair of legs he had, he'd poked out his chest and decided wearing the damn things wouldn't be so bad… especially if it meant she would continue looking at him with all that sexual hunger in her eyes.

After spending enough time in the water, he swam back to shore. Smiling, he sauntered across the beautiful white sand toward Channing. She opened her eyes and eased up when she heard his approach.

"Relax, I'm not going to bother you," he said, flopping down on the towel beside her.

She frowned over at him. "You better not."

He pretended to shiver. "Now I'm scared," he teased.

She rolled her eyes and lay back down. "Your cell

phone's been ringing," she said casually, although he knew there was nothing casual about it. A lot of women had his number, and being missing in action probably had a lot of them worried about him. Evidently, no one in his family was giving out information as to his whereabouts so the women had taken to calling. For the past couple of days, he had turned off his phone. He'd cut it back on this morning to check with his family and to call the phone company to request a new phone number. The latter was something he hadn't told her about yet.

"It was someone in my family," he said, looking over at her.

She frowned. "You have *several* missed calls, Zane."

"Like I said, it's someone in my family," he said, reaching out and sweeping a lock of damp hair from her face.

"How can you be so sure?"

A smile ruffled his mouth. "Because I had my number changed this morning. No one has it but my family, and they wouldn't share it without my permission."

He saw the surprised look on her face. "You had your number changed?"

"Yes, and you're the only woman who's not related to me who has it."

She gave him another surprised look. "I have it?"

He nodded. "Yes. I keyed it into your phone while you were washing your hair this morning."

"Oh." She didn't say anything for a minute, but he knew the idea of him having a new, private phone number pleased her. He was glad that it did.

"And speaking of my hair, I'm going to have to wash it again, thanks to you."

"No problem, I'll help." He saw the way her cheeks flushed at his offer. No doubt she was remembering what had happened when he'd offered to help wash her hair the last time, three days ago.

He reached over and pulled his cell phone out of the shorts he had left on the chaise lounge with his shirt. He checked the missed calls. "Canyon. Canyon. Canyon. Canyon and Canyon," he said, grinning. "I told you."

"Sounds like he needs to talk to you," Channing said.

Zane shrugged. "He has woman issues."

"And you being *Dear Zane* like *Dear Abby* will help him solve his problem, right?"

He chuckled. "Kinda. Sorta." Then he held her gaze and said in a serious tone, "I know about women, yes. But with the one woman I should have known about and should have handled with the love and respect she deserved, I blew it."

He watched as his words gave her pause. His heart pounded when she only smiled. He didn't say anything, either. He wanted to let her think about what he'd just said.

"You want to go to the drive-in movies again tonight?" he asked her a short while later.

"Um, what's playing?"

He chuckled. "Does it matter?" They had gone to the drive-in two other times and had totally enjoyed making out in the car.

She smiled over at him. "No, it doesn't matter, and yes, I'd love to go to the drive-in with you tonight."

"What do you want, Canyon?" Zane asked his cousin later that evening. He and Channing had enjoyed their time on the beach. Then, like he said he would, he had helped wash her hair…which led to other things. They had eaten dinner, and Channing had gone next door to give the Farmers a batch of the cookies she'd baked earlier that day.

"I can't believe you're just calling me back, Zane. I could have been dying," Canyon snapped.

Zane rolled his eyes. "You're talking to me now so you're not dead. What do you want?"

"Keisha. I told her we should talk, but she says she doesn't want to have anything to do with me."

Zane glanced at his watch. He couldn't wait to go to the movies with Channing. "Either take her at her word or do something about it. Action speaks louder than words."

"I guess you would know. Word has it that you're somewhere trying to convince Channing you're falling in love with her."

Zane heard the smirk in Canyon's voice. "For your damn information, Canyon, I'm not falling in love with Channing. I just told her that."

Channing had returned from next door and walked toward the bedroom to let Zane know she was back when the words he'd blared out to his cousin stopped her. Her head spun in shock at what he'd just said.

He was not falling in love with her?

He had lied to her?

Her body quivered in pain. He had been playing a game with her all along. A game with her heart.

Not able to handle what she was feeling, she turned, nearly blinded by her tears, and rushed back out of the house.

"What do you mean you just told her that?" Canyon asked. "Megan and Bailey are convinced you're crazy about Channing and told us not to be surprised if you came back married."

Not a bad idea, Zane thought, and knew he would give

it more consideration later. "The reason I'm not falling in love with Channing is because I'm already in love with her. I realized just how much I loved her before I left Denver. But she doesn't believe me. And I'm here to prove otherwise."

Canyon didn't say anything for a long moment. "So it's true. Some woman has finally gotten to you?"

Zane smiled. "Yes. The same way a woman got to you, and once they get to you, Canyon, there's not a damn thing you can do about it. If you want Keisha, then you need to go after her."

"Damn it, Zane, she doesn't trust me. She believes the worst about me."

"Get over it, or live the rest of your life without her. There's nothing you shouldn't be able to forgive her for, even if it was her losing faith in you. From what I gather, Bonita Simpkins set you up pretty damn good, and I wouldn't give her the satisfaction of knowing her plan worked."

Zane glanced at his watch again. The movie would start in an hour. Channing had said she would be right back, and he couldn't help but wonder what was taking her so long.

"Maybe you're right," Canyon said. "I went to Bonita when it happened and tried to get her to tell Keisha the truth, but she refused."

Zane looked at his watch again. "Look, Canyon, I got to go. I've given you all the advice I'm going to give on this Keisha matter. You're on your own from here on out. Goodbye." He then clicked off the phone.

Moving out of the bedroom, he headed for the front door. Evidently Channing had gotten into a conversation with Jennifer and forgotten their date. He would just have to go next door and remind her.

* * *

Channing walked the beach as she swiped at the tears that couldn't seem to stop flowing. When was she going to stop being a fool? And for the same man!

He had played her well, and what hurt her more than anything else was that there had been no need for him to do that. Why couldn't he just let her go? Why did he have to follow her here with lies, lies and more lies? There was no way he could refute what he'd told Canyon. Words she'd heard with her own ears.

I'm not falling in love with Channing. I just told her that.

The memory made Channing cry harder, made her chest ache and her head hurt. It seemed she'd been walking the beach for hours when she knew it had only been a few minutes. Clenching her fist in anger, she turned around. It was time to go back and confront Zane, tell him he had played his last game on her …

She gasped when suddenly the sand beneath her feet gave away and she began to sink. "Oh, God!" She tried pulling her feet out, but it only made her sink deeper.

Frantically, she glanced around. It was pitch-dark, and she could barely see the lights from the homes at Kindle Shores. It occurred to her then just how far she had walked. She knew the area. It was one swimmers and sunbathers were warned to avoid for this very reason. Years ago, she had heard how a couple who had been strolling along this particular section of the beach had met their fate when they both went down in quicksand. They had drowned from the high tide before the search party had found them.

Channing willed herself not to panic. She had to try and remain calm. Each time she attempted to pull her feet free, she sank lower. What was she going to do? She didn't have her cell phone with her and hadn't told anyone where she was going. And why had she walked so close to the shoreline?

When she sank lower still, she fought back tears. Would Zane come looking for her? He should be the last person she wanted to see, but right now she would give anything to see his face. He had no idea where she was, but she had to believe he would come.

She had to believe that.

"Channing left here a half hour ago," Jennifer said to Zane. "I was standing on the porch, and I watched her go inside. After that, I came in here to give the kids their baths."

"I saw her go back out," Ronald added, coming to stand beside his wife. "Channing hadn't been inside her house more than a few minutes before she ran back out. I was still outside picking up the kids' toys when I saw her. She was walking quickly down the beach." He hesitated and then added, "She seemed upset about something."

Upset? Zane frowned. *Why would Channing be upset?*

"I wouldn't know why she would be upset," he said. "Maybe she just wanted to take a walk before we went out. We're supposed to be going to the movies."

Jennifer nodded. "She did mention that. That's the reason she said she had to rush back. So it's strange for her to wander off when she seemed so eager to go out with you."

Zane had to agree. That was strange. "Well, thanks. Hopefully she'll be back soon," he said, glancing down the dark stretch of beach. He couldn't see a thing. The thought of Channing being out there didn't sit well with him. It made him feel uneasy.

"On second thought, I think I'll go look for her," he said, walking off the Farmers' porch.

"Need any help?" Ronald offered.

"No, I'll probably meet her on her way back," Zane said hopefully.

"If you don't, you have my number," Ronald reminded him. "Call me."

"I will," Zane said over his shoulder. Ronald had given Zane his number when Ronald had inquired about the purchase of a pony for his daughter. Zane had promised to check on it when he got back to Denver and give the man a call as to whether Born Free's foal was for sale.

Zane began walking toward the beach, and that uneasy feeling just wouldn't go away. Ronald had said Channing seemed upset, but Zane didn't have a clue as to what could have upset her. Nothing had been awry when she'd left to take the food over to the Farmers. She had even given him a kiss before leaving.

He did recall that not long after she'd left to go next door he had returned Canyon's call. He'd talked to his cousin until right before he'd gone to the Farmers for Channing. That meant she returned during the time he'd been on the phone with Canyon.

Zane searched his mind for why she would have come inside the house only to leave a few moments later. Could she have overheard his conversation with Canyon? If she had, there was nothing said that would have upset her. In fact, he'd given his cousin advice about Keisha again.

Zane stopped walking when he suddenly recalled something. It was when Canyon mentioned him falling in love with Channing. Zane's response had been, *I'm not falling in love with Channing. I just told her that.*

But then Zane had proceeded to clarify what he'd meant. But what if Channing had heard the first part of his conversation with Canyon and not the second? His guts twisted at the thought that she might be somewhere

assuming he was making a fool out of her, assuming he
had no intention of falling in love with her. He could see
how that would trouble her.

Zane picked up his pace as he looked up and down
the shoreline. It was dark, so he pulled out the miniature
flashlight on his key chain.

The thought that something had happened to Channing pricked his skin. There was no way he was going to
lose her. No way.

Channing tried fighting her fear, but it was useless.
From the moon's light, she could see the ocean and it appeared to be coming closer, which meant the high tide
had started. The water's spray was hitting her in the face.
Already she had sunk down to her waist and was sinking faster by the minute. It was as though the sand was
pulling her in.

Once or twice she thought she had heard someone
walking around, but when she'd called out no one was
there. Was this how her life was to end? She felt tired,
drained; she began imagining all kinds of crazy stuff.
Didn't her brother once tell her about wild dogs that
roamed the beaches at night? Even snakes. And here she
was being held captive by the earth.

No! In protest, she tried moving one of her feet and
then cried out in frustration when it sank a foot farther
into the sand. Then the ocean water began hitting her in
the chest.

She knew without being told that the tide was coming closer.

Zane stopped walking and scanned his flashlight ahead
of him. Would Channing have come this far? What if
she'd taken another path, away from the beach, and was

walking through one of the trails to return home? He was about to turn around, hoping that was what she had done, when he heard a faint sound. Automatically he moved toward it and began calling Channing's name.

Channing tried calling out several times. "Help me! Somebody please help me." The sand had covered her up to her breasts, and she was sinking faster.

She went still when she thought she heard her name. Was she imagining things?

She listened and heard it again. It was Zane's voice. She was sure of it.

"Zane! I'm over here. In quicksand. Please help me!"

A few moments later, she saw a flash of light, and then it was aimed at her. She heard Zane's colorful expletives as he raced toward her.

"No, Zane!" she shouted. "Don't come any closer, or you might get stuck, as well. You need to go get help."

Zane had already assessed the situation. There was no time to get help, but he did pull out his cell phone and call Ronald to tell him to come quick with rope and his truck. Zane glanced around. The tide was coming in, and already the sand had covered Channing nearly to her neck.

He knew he had to keep her calm, but he couldn't just wait for help to arrive. He moved around, tentatively testing the area surrounding her and was glad the quicksand was confined to the little area where she was. That meant he could attempt to pull her out if she held on to him.

"Okay, Channing, listen up, baby. I'm going to need you to arch your body back as far as it will go. That will help spread out your weight and make it harder for you to keep sinking. I'll get behind you on hard sand. Extend your arms back to me, and I'll pull you out while you try working your legs free."

Channing heard Zane's instructions, but the minute she moved her body to arch her back she sank deeper. "Zane!"

Zane tried to stay in control of his emotions, but he was two seconds from jumping in there with her. "Channing, don't rush. Take your time. Arch your back, and extend your arms backward so I can grab them," he said, lying flat on his stomach as close as he could get to her.

"No! I might pull you in and you'll die with me."

"I'd rather die with you than live without you, damn it. You are my life, and I won't lose you. I won't. Now bend your back as far as you can, and extend your arms over your head to me."

He knew he was taking a chance because he would be relying on his strength to pull her out. "Now do it!"

The demand in his voice was sharp. She arched her back, and he could see her struggling. "Don't fight, Channing. Just arch like you're in a pool trying to float on your back."

Channing followed his directions and found spreading her weight was helping. She could even disentangle her legs a little. "My legs are loosening up some," she said with excitement in her voice.

"Arch a little bit more, Channing. We're not there yet. I need to grab your arms. Bring them back over your head as far as you can. Pretend I'm about to make love to you and I need your body shaped like a bow, lifting up off the bed."

He gave a deep sigh when he extended his hands out as far as he could without tumbling into the quicksand with her. He came close to touching her fingertips. "That's it, baby. Arch your back just a little more, and I'll pull you out."

"It hurts," she moaned.

"I know, baby, but do it. Do it for me. I'll die if anything happens to you. I can't lose you."

He sounded almost convincing, Channing thought as she closed her eyes and tried arching her back some more. But she knew the truth about how he felt. Still, she tried moving her legs. "I think I lost my sandal. It was one of my new ones."

"I'll buy you another pair," he said, knowing that she was exhausted. But he couldn't let her give up. The tide was coming in fast. He almost yelled for joy when he was finally able to catch Channing's hands in a tight grip.

Now came the hard part.

Placing all his strength on his shoulders, he closed his eyes and began his attempt to extricate her from the quicksand. A couple of times he almost lost his grip, but he refused to let go.

He pulled with all his might, trying to ignore the pressure on both their arms. He knew he was slowly pulling her free, and when he was able to catch her around her upper chest, he reached out and grabbed tight. That's when the heavy beams of a pickup truck shone on them before coming to a stop. Several men jumped out. Zane didn't take his gaze off Channing, but he knew it was Ronald and he had brought others to help.

Zane felt his grip loosen on Channing and cursed. Ronald and several guys surrounded him with huge flat lumber, which provided a bridgelike surface that let them get closer to Channing. While they held the bridge in place, Zane crawled over it and grabbed her by the waist.

He knew someone had tied a rope around him and was pulling him back, and he was bringing Channing with him. It took great effort, but when she was completely free from the quicksand, the men cheered. He gathered Channing close while she cried in his arms.

Chapter 14

Zane sat in a chair beside the bed and watched as Channing slept. He'd held her in his lap in Ronald's truck all the way home. Then he had held her while they showered, washing off enough sand to start their own beach. He'd even washed her hair because she was too tired to do it herself.

Then he had toweled her dry and dressed her in pj's and placed her beneath the covers. That was when the doctor had come, an older man who lived in the community and still made house calls. Dr. Peterson had said the pills he'd given her would make her sleep for a while. Already she'd been sleeping for four hours, and Zane was still here, sitting by her bedside.

He'd never known real fear until tonight. When he thought about how close he'd come to losing her. What if he'd given up searching earlier and turned around? What if he hadn't heard her cry for help? What if he hadn't taken that first-aid training years ago, which had taught him what to do if you become lodged in quicksand? What if—

"Zane?"

He jerked when he heard Channing's voice and was out of the bed in a flash. He moved to sit next to her. "Yes, sweetheart? How do you feel?"

"Like hell."

He nodded in understanding. Dr. Peterson had said she would be sore for a couple of days. She had strained a lot of muscles while arching her back. "Is there anything you need? Water? Juice? Milk? Sorry, you can't have any wine, thanks to the medicine you're taking."

She gently grabbed his wrist and saw the scratches her hands had made trying to hold on to him. "Why, Zane? Why would you risk your life to save mine?"

Zane sighed deeply. Now more than ever he had to make her understand...and believe. "Because I don't have a life without you, Channing. I told you while you were in that quicksand, and I meant it."

She didn't say anything for a minute and then slowly released his hand. "But I heard what you told Canyon, Zane," she said accusingly. "You told him that you were not falling in love with me. That you'd only told me that."

So he'd been right. She had overheard the first part of his conversation with Canyon. "Yes, I told him that."

He saw the crushed look that appeared on her face, and when she made a move to turn her back to him, he said, "But you ran off before overhearing the rest of our conversation, Channing. Had you stuck around, you would have heard me clarify what I meant. The reason I can't fall in love with you is because I'm already in love with you."

He shifted to lie beside her in the bed. He needed to touch her. To hold her.

"I knew when I left Denver to come here that I loved

you. And it happened just like I said. But you didn't believe me, Channing. You thought I was confusing love and lust. But I knew how I felt. It was you who had doubt. So I came up with a plan.

"Since you thought I wasn't in love with you, I wanted to let you think I was *falling* in love with you. If you needed to see the transformation, then I had no problem showing it to you. For I am a changed man, Channing. I've never loved any woman before, but I do love you. I want to give you my love. I want to give you my name, and I want to give you my babies."

He eased off the bed and went to the drawer where he'd placed the items he'd taken out of his luggage. He reached inside and pulled out the locked box and carried it over to the bed. "This box holds all my treasures. I purchased it the day after you left town," he said, taking the key out of his pocket.

"This is what kept me going after you left me, Channing. All I had were the memories."

Channing slowly eased up in bed, fighting against the pain of doing so. Her eyes widened when Zane pulled out the calendar she'd given him a few years ago. "You kept that?" she asked, surprised.

"Yes, and it was my lifeline. I would spend hours and hours looking through it and was too stupid to figure out why." He placed the calendar aside and pulled out another item. The gold chain.

Channing gasped again, surprised. "I thought…"

"What did you think, Channing? That I would pawn it? Give it to another woman? I bought it for you and only you," he said, reaching out and placing it around her neck where it belonged. "I didn't want it back, but you insisted. So I kept it in here, and this is where it's been ever since."

He didn't say anything for a long moment. "The last

item in here is something you haven't seen before. Something I purchased before leaving Denver to come here. It's something I intended to give you when the time was right. When I knew I had convinced you that I loved you."

He reached inside and pulled out a small white jeweler's box and handed it to her.

Channing held Zane's gaze as she took the box from him. Her heart began beating fast and furious in her chest. She broke eye contact with him to open the lid and then gasped at the beautiful diamond ring.

"Channing, will you marry me? I love you so much, and I don't want to be separated from you for a single night. If I have to move to Atlanta, that's fine. I have family there already. If you and I need to split our time in Denver and Atlanta in an arrangement like Rico and Megan's, then that's fine, too."

Tears Channing couldn't hold back any longer flowed down her cheeks. A misunderstanding had almost cost her her life tonight. Because she hadn't believed Zane's words of love. He'd been saying it, but tonight, in saving her life the way he had, he had shown it.

"So, do you need to think about my proposal?" he asked, breaking into her thoughts.

She swiped at her tears. "No, I don't need to think about it. I love you, and I believe you love me. Tonight you proved just how much."

"I do love you," Zane said, sliding the ring on her finger. "And I want a short engagement."

"I want that, too," she said, smiling as she looked down at the ring, thinking how beautiful it was. "I'll move from Atlanta to 'Zane's Hideout.' While in Denver, Dr. Rowe, the chief of staff, made me an offer to come back to work at the hospital. I turned her down, but she said she would keep the offer open for six months."

Zane grinned, not believing how nicely things were falling into place. "Riley's getting married in a couple of months, and I don't want to rain on his parade, so what about the month after? That would be in October."

She smiled. "What about a Christmas wedding?"

He let out a deep groan. "The wait will kill me."

She chuckled. "I'll be there to help you manage. If I start the transfer paperwork next week, I can move back to Denver in another month."

"If you did, that would make me a happy man, sweetheart. You have a home already at the Hideout." Conscious of her sore muscles, he shifted his body so he could lower his lips to hers.

He then kissed her with all the love he felt in his heart.

"Then consider it done," she whispered a short while later when he let her come up for air.

And then they sealed their engagement with another kiss.

* * * * *

*Don't miss the next two Westmoreland novels
by Brenda Jackson!*
CANYON
Available August 2013

*Years ago, Canyon Westmoreland let
misunderstandings ruin a good thing. But now
Keisha Ashford has returned—with a two-year-old son.
This time, nothing will stop Canyon from
claiming what is his—his woman and his child!*

STERN
Available September 2013

*When Stern Westmoreland helps his best friend with a
makeover he never expects sizzling attraction to
ignite between them. Now there's only one way to make
her his: have one long, steamy night together as much
more than friends!*

INTIMATE SEDUCTION

Chapter 1

Donovan Steele opened the door to his home and walked inside with a huge smile on his face. Over the weekend in New Hampshire, his best friend from childhood, Bronson Scott, one of the most popular drivers for the NASCAR Sprint Cup Series, had placed in the top five.

Donovan was proud of Bronson's success because Donovan, of all people, knew how hard his friend had worked to achieve it. Bronson was not only a skilled driver but was also a racer for the team he owned, Scott Motorsports. Donovan's chest also swelled with pride at the fact that his family-owned business, the Steele Corporation, was a major sponsor of Scott Motorsports. That provided plenty of advertising for SC and offered Bronson the financial support he needed to pursue his lifelong dream.

Another reason for Donovan's smile was that at the race he'd been among friends and had managed to unwind and not think about how busy the coming months would be for him back at the office. A new product under development at SC, the first in several years, had everyone excited; especially Donovan since he headed the Product Administration Division. But Gleeve-Ware, as it was called, had to be completed in time for the annual Product Trade Show being held in Toronto this November.

Instead of returning to Charlotte yesterday like he'd planned, he and a good friend from college, Uriel Lassiter, as well as two of his cousins from Phoenix—Galen and Tyson Steele—decided to stay an additional day to celebrate with Bronson and Myles Joseph, another good friend and a Scott Motorsports driver.

And then there had been Joanne Summerville, a racetrack groupie who'd come on to him after finding out about his close relationship to Bronson and the other drivers. Even now he could still picture her standing under the July sun in those skintight jeans and that sky-blue T-shirt that had stretched snugly across a pair of well-endowed breasts.

Joanne had been a looker, all right, and he regretted not taking her up on what she'd been offering. He hadn't the time to squeeze in a short fling, no matter how tempting, and he could still see the sexy pout on her lips and the disappointment in her eyes when he'd turned her down. His only saving grace was that he figured he'd run into her again at a future race.

Donovan dropped his travel bag on the floor by the sofa instead of taking it upstairs to his bedroom. Due to an early flight out this morning, he'd missed breakfast and was hungry. He walked toward the kitchen, deciding that in desperate times even a peanut-butter-and-jelly sandwich sounded pretty good.

The moment Donovan walked into his kitchen he could tell his housekeeper had been there. Everything gleamed, from the stainless-steel appliances to the ceramic-tile floor. He appreciated the way she kept his house clean. He was a stickler when it came to neatness, but he also liked having a good time and had no desire to spend his weekends doing chores. He was too busy spending his time doing women.

It came as no surprise to those who knew him that he enjoyed and appreciated female company. There was no crime in that and at thirty-three, he enjoyed being single. He spent his time doing things he liked, which included a lot of traveling for pleasure, and refused to be tied down to a woman who'd have a hissy fit if he left her behind or one who felt entitled to accompany him.

He'd learned the hard way that women tended to get outright possessive. Alyson Greer had been such a creature, and even now he got cold chills remembering how she had resorted to stalking him. From that point on, he'd made a conscious effort to make sure any woman he became involved with knew the score.

There were simply too many beautiful ladies out there to get tied down to just one.

His three older brothers were wearing wedding bands and that was all well and good—for them. He was happy they had found wonderful women to fall in love with and marry. But he was not the marrying kind. He wasn't even the serious relationship kind. Short-term affairs suited him just fine.

Besides women, his favorite pastime was auto racing. Not that he would ever get behind the wheel of a race car but he totally enjoyed being a spectator. He couldn't describe the rush of adrenaline that flowed through his body while watching a race. Of course, sharing an orgasm with a woman was still number one in his book, but being at a race was a close second.

He reached to open his pantry when he noticed a pair of women's sandals on the floor by the sliding glass door to his screened patio. Where had they come from and whom did they belong to?

Had the cleaning lady left her shoes? Was she still there?

He picked up the sandals to study their design. Sleek and snazzy. He'd only seen his housekeeper once or twice, and although she wasn't a bad-looking older woman, he couldn't imagine her wearing a pair of stylish and trendy shoes. But then he might be wrong. He couldn't judge every fifty-something-year-old woman by his mother and his aunt's taste in fashion.

He cocked his right brow, his curiosity piqued, and for the moment his hunger was placed on the back burner. He went back into his living room and then the dining room and glanced around, noticing that the rooms were neat as a pin, tidy as could be and well-dusted. That was enough evidence to indicate his housekeeper had been here.

On the main level, he also had a guest bedroom and a spacious bath, with the master suite and his office and another bathroom upstairs. If and when he felt inclined to invite a woman to stay for the night, the downstairs guest room was where they would sleep. He considered it his entertainment room. At one time he'd installed mirrors in the ceiling over the bed until his nephew Marcus—who would come spend the night on occasion—got old enough to question why they were there.

The master bedroom was off-limits. He considered it his personal domain. No woman could lay claim to ever sleeping in what he considered his *real* bed. A number of them had tried, considered it a challenge, their ultimate goal. But so far none had ever made it up those stairs.

After checking the other rooms, he made his way upstairs. It didn't take him long to check the bathroom and his office before heading down the hall that led to his master suite. His bedroom door was closed, which wasn't unusual, but what *was* unusual were the sensations he began feeling in the pit of his stomach, similar to the ones he felt when he was standing on the sidelines waiting for the race to begin.

He opened the door, and his eyes quickly circulated the room, stopping first on the vacuum cleaner that was still plugged into the wall and then on the feather duster that was sitting on his dresser.

He stepped into the room and held his breath when he saw a woman asleep in his bed.

What the hell?

Quickly, he crossed the floor to his bed and stared down at the sleeping woman. She was definitely not his regular cleaning lady. This woman looked to be in her early twenties and was absolutely, undeniably beautiful.

She was lying on her side but her face was angled in a way that showed an ample portion of it. What he saw flooded his gut with something he'd never felt before, a sensual attraction so hard, gripping and intense that he had to struggle to get air past his lungs.

Her skin, a beautiful chocolate-brown, looked soft, satiny and smooth. Her long eyelashes fanned her eyes, and in sleep she looked totally at peace. Her hair, a dark brown shade, flowed to her shoulders with bouncy-looking curls at the end. He had encountered beautiful women countless times but never before did one have such a gripping effect on his libido. And that very thought downright unnerved him.

Pulling in a deep breath, he inhaled, then took his time releasing it after deciding it was time to wake her. Although his first instinct was to remove his clothes and get into the bed with her. Instead of feeling his privacy violated by the woman in his bed, he was feeling something else altogether. Lust. Bone-chilling, gut-wrenching lust to a degree he'd never experienced before.

He tried tamping down the sensations by thinking that he definitely had a number of questions for her…but first he had to get her out of his bed. With that thought in mind, he reached out and gently touched her shoulder, trying to ignore the way his fingers trembled at the contact. He then watched as she slowly stretched her body before cuddling into another position without opening her eyes.

Tempted to see the rest of her, he slowly lifted the covers… His sex immediately got hard, pressed tight against the fly of his jeans as his gaze lit on her lush, shapely body. His eyes raked over her khaki shorts and cotton top, taking in her long, toned legs, small waist, curvy thighs and flat tummy. And then there was her scent. It assailed his senses the moment he lifted the covers, a totally feminine aroma that clutched him in blatant desire.

Thinking he'd better do something before he totally lost it, he dropped the covers back in place and gently shook her awake. His fingers trembled for a second time when they came in contact with her shoulder.

He stared down at her face as her eyes fluttered open, blinked a few times, widened and then stared back. The color of flowing honey, her eyes were a perfect match for her complexion. The woman was even more beautiful with her eyes wide open looking like a deer caught in the headlights.

He watched as she opened her mouth as if she wanted to say something but then changed her mind. Instead she moistened her top lip with the flick of her tongue before gnawing nervously on the bottom lip. He felt an immediate tightening in his stomach. An aura of sexual magnetism surrounded them, held them within its grip.

When he couldn't handle the sensations any longer, or the torture of imagining all the things he would love doing to her tongue and lips, he spoke up. "I believe you're sleeping in *my* bed, Goldilocks."

Though her mind was working just fine, Natalie Ford was speechless and incapable of movement. When she'd opened her eyes, the last thing she expected was to drown in the depths of the most gorgeous pair of dark-brown eyes she'd ever seen. And the man's features were so striking and breathtakingly handsome.

The sensations overpowering her midsection weren't any better. Her response to him was instantaneous and so intense that, until he had reminded her, she'd forgotten that she had fallen asleep in his bed. *His bed.* How embarrassing!

The last thing she remembered was thinking she had finally cleaned every room in the house and had saved his bedroom for last. She was about to strip the bed for fresh linen when something about it beckoned her, invited her to lie down between the luxurious covers. That, combined with the little sleep she'd gotten the night before, had her putting her feather duster aside and sliding between the sheets. The moment her head touched the pillow she had breathed in Donovan Steele's masculine scent. With all kinds of crazy fantasies playing around in her head, she had drifted off to sleep. Now she was wide awake and although she'd never met the man towering over her, she was certain he was Donovan Steele.

Her aunt had three clients who insisted that she handle their housekeeping personally—and were willing to pay extra for that request. Harrell Kelly, Jeremy Simpkins a

Donovan Steele. Kelly and Simpkins were professional football players for the Carolina Panthers, and Steele was a successful businessman whose family was well-known in Charlotte. According to her aunt, the three men liked things done a particular way and were determined to protect their privacy. They were her aunt's exclusive clients.

Until her aunt's sidelining injury.

Natalie managed a smile hoping he had a sense of humor because she felt the situation needed it. Tossing the covers aside and pulling herself up into a sitting position, she said, "Break's over. I need to finish this room, which means it's time for me to get back to work."

Thankfully, he stepped back as she eased off the bed. However, he crossed his arms over his chest, looked at her intently and asked, "Do you usually take breaks in other people's beds?"

There was that voice again. Deep, throaty, husky. It was crazy, but she felt as though the sound touched her physically, in some of her most intimate places and in very provocative ways. She wished she could ignore both him and his question as she proceeded to strip the bed. Being handsome was one thing, being over-the-top, teeth-chillingly gorgeous was another. There was no way she could forget he was standing there. He was too overwhelmingly male.

Since she was filling in for her aunt who was home recovering from a broken ankle, this man was technically her employer, and she doubted Aunt Earline would appreciate losing him as a customer. She struck a businesslike tone and said, "No, I don't usually take breaks in other people's beds. That was the first. But then I've never seen a bed quite like yours before."

And that was the truth. Although Donovan Steele was probably six-four, with broad shoulders, he wasn't what she considered big. His bed, however, was huge. There was no doubt in her mind that four people could sleep comfortably in his bed. She could just imagine what a man—a very handsome one at that—did in a bed this size. Whatever he did, she doubted he did it alone.

"Before we get into an in-depth discussion about my bed, don't you think you should at least tell me who you are, since I know you aren't my regular cleaning lady?"

Natalie stopped and glanced over at him. Not to do so would have been outright rude. The moment her gaze locked with his, she felt sensations she couldn't ignore flood her stomach and her heart rate increased. It should be against the law for any man to look so unerringly masculine.

He had chocolate-brown eyes, a chiseled jaw and a sensual mouth on a creamy cocoa complexion. His hair was cut low and neatly trimmed around his head. A pencil-thin mustache on his upper lip gave him a sexy look. He was wearing a pair of jeans and T-shirt with huge letters that said "Forged of Steele." His scent, the same one that had tempted her to cuddle even more between his sheets, surrounded them.

She inhaled deeply. "I'm Natalie Ford," she said without extending her hand. The bundle of sheets she held to her chest made it impossible to do so anyway and she was glad. The thought of touching any part of him left her off balance.

"And I'm Donovan Steele."

She nodded. "I figured as much. My aunt, Earline Darwin, is your regular cleaning lady. She broke her ankle last week, and I'm filling in while she recuperates. She tried reaching you last week, and when she was unable to do so, she left a message on your answering machine letting you know what happened and that I would be her replacement for the next six weeks."

He kept his gaze fastened to hers as he said, "I left town early Friday morning, and I'm just returning today, so I didn't get any of my messages." He paused for a brief second before adding, "That's mighty kind of you to fill in for your aunt. Will she be okay?"

Natalie was surprised he cared enough to inquire. "Yes, her ankle will be fine as long as she remains off of it for a while. Thanks for asking."

He leaned against the dresser. "Now I have something else to ask. Would you like to explain why you were in my bed?"

She met his dark eyes. "Like I told you, I've never seen a bed like yours before and couldn't help wondering if it was as soft and comfortable as it looked. Once I sat down on it and saw that it was, I was tempted to slip between the covers, and I must have dozed off. I apologize for doing so. It was very unprofessional of me, and it won't happen again."

A look she couldn't define quickly flashed across his face, and she had a feeling he wasn't accepting her apology easily. He continued to look at her for a long time with an intensity that made her throat tighten. But then she felt something else with his stare. Direct heat. And it was getting hotter by the second. She tried to recall when, if ever, a man affected her this way.

"I accept your apology, Natalie Ford."

Natalie blinked, realizing he had spoken. "Thank you, and like I said, it won't happen again."

A slow, sexy smile touched the corners of his mouth. "I think that it will. In fact, I'm counting on it."

It took Natalie a few seconds to recover from the impact of his smile to catch his meaning. When she did, she tilted her head, looked at him and fought the power of his sexuality and the way her body was responding to it.

She could tell by the look in his eyes, that deep concentrated stare, that he'd honed in on it too. So, okay, there was chemistry between them. She refused to see it as a big deal. The man evidently was a flirt. "I wouldn't if I were you, or you'll be disappointed," she decided to say.

He lifted his shoulder in a nonchalant shrug at the same time that he shoved his hands into the back pockets of his jeans. "I won't be." An assured smile touched his lips.

For a few timeless moments, their gazes held in a clash of wills. Now she understood Aunt Earline's warning about him. According to her aunt, the man was a bachelor who had quite a reputation with the ladies. Apparently when it came to what he perceived as an available woman, Donovan Steele believed in equal opportunity regardless of sex, religion, race, national origin or occupation, since for all he knew she was no more than someone who cleaned houses for a living. Definitely not the kind of woman a man of his wealth and stature would mess around with.

It then occurred to her that, yes, a cleaning woman would be just the type of woman a man like him would probably mess around with. Discreetly. Not someone he would get serious about and take home to meet his upscale family. He'd be surprised to learn that she had a Ph.D. in chemical engineering and was a professor at Princeton University.

"So, when can I take you out?"

Donovan's question intruded into her thoughts. She studied his face and saw the confidence in the dark eyes staring back at her. No doubt because of the women he'd dealt with in the past, he was pretty sure of himself. He probably figured she was an easy lay and with a few sweet words her legs would part like the Red Sea. Boy, was he wrong.

"I won't be going out with you, Mr. Steele."

He smiled. "Feel free to call me Donovan, and is there a reason why?"

There were several reasons she could give him, with his blatant arrogance heading the list. "The reason I won't go out with you is because I work for you, and I've learned that mixing business with pleasure isn't a good idea."

That response, she thought, sounded more politically correct than what she'd actually wanted to say. "And in addition to that, I'm taking a hiatus from dating for a while," she tacked on for size.

He tilted his head at an angle that made his stare even more penetrating. And then he did something she hadn't counted on him doing. He chuckled. But it wasn't just any old chuckle. It had both a seductive as well as a challenging sound to it. It immediately set her on edge and alerted her to the fact that he didn't consider what she'd just said as obstacles.

He verified her assumptions by saying. "Your aunt works for me. You're working for your aunt. It's not the same. And the only possible reason that I can think of as to why such a beautiful woman like you would want to take a break from dating is because you've dated the wrong men. You're now looking into the face of the *right* one."

Natalie wasn't sure he was the right one, but he certainly was a determined one. Deciding not to waste her time arguing with him, she tightened the bundle of linen she held to her chest and slowly backed up. "I'd better put these in the washer. I'll be back later to put fresh sheets on the bed." She quickly moved to the door.

"Natalie?"

Calling her by her first name was a liberty she hadn't given him but was one he was arrogantly taking anyway.

She slowly turned around and once again saw him looking at her. "Yes?"

"Considering the attraction between us, I feel I should
give you fair warning that I'm a man who goes after what
I want and won't stop until I get it."

She lifted her chin and looked at him while trying to
ignore the surge of desire that stirred low in her stomach.
There was no way she could deny an attraction existed
since the chemistry between them was so blatantly obvious. She of all people understood chemistry and just how
reactive it could be.

"Thanks for the warning, *Mr. Steele*." And then she
swiftly walked out of the room.

Donovan rubbed a hand down his face, trying to get a
grip. What the hell was wrong with him? To say he was
attracted to his temporary housekeeper would be an understatement. Even now he could still feel the heat that
had ripped through him when her eyes had opened and
latched onto his. And he'd been aroused ever since. Totally, irrevocably aroused.

He pushed away from the dresser he'd been leaning
against and pulled in a deep breath. He wasn't a man
who pounced on a woman so quickly after meeting her,
no matter how good she looked. Usually, when it came
to pursuing a member of the opposite sex, he was known
to be patient, allowing time for nature to take its course
since he was fairly certain how things would eventually
end. On the rare occasion when he had to shift things in
his favor, he would utilize the art of seduction.

He wondered what approach he would have to take in
this situation. For some reason being patient with Natalie
Ford just didn't work well with him. He was a goner the
moment he had checked out her legs. If he thought they

were nice-looking lying down, then they were definitely gorgeous standing up. Most men were inclined to favor a woman's breasts or her backside, but Donovan was definitely a leg man.

He had to admit, though, that her breasts and backside were definitely pleasing to the eyes, as well. He'd gotten a good glimpse of the swell of her breasts through her blouse before she clutched his bed linens to her chest as if they were some kind of shield. And when she had skedaddled out of the room, the way the material of her shorts had stretched across her shapely behind had sent intense heat flaring through him. Just thinking about all her make-a-man-hard body parts fueled his lust.

And he knew women well enough to know she was as interested in him as he was in her. Reading a woman had always been easy for him no matter how coy they tried to be. The courtship game was a phenomenon he'd never gotten right and had never really cared if he did or not. He'd discovered that getting it wrong had never hurt his cause since he usually got whatever it was he was after anyway.

There was something about Natalie Ford that he couldn't quite put his finger on. She had an air of decorum and sophistication that didn't quite mesh with the job she was doing. She had tried using the don't-date-the-employer defense on him, but it hadn't worked because like he'd told her, technically she was not his employee. He would admit that at SC he'd personally instituted a rule about fraternizing with the hired help, a course of action he'd been forced to implement after a number of female employees targeted him as the Steele man to get.

He glanced at his watch. From the look of his home, she was about to wrap things up and would probably be leaving in the next half hour. She had said her aunt would be recuperating for six weeks, and he intended to make sure Natalie didn't try doing a switcheroo on him with another housekeeper.

Just that quick his mind was made up. Natalie Ford was someone he intended to seduce.

Chapter 2

Fighting back a nervous shiver, Natalie quickly moved down the stairs in her haste to get to the laundry room. Her senses felt out of control. Overworked. And all because of one man. She was used to sparring with her students, but sparring with Donovan Steele had rattled her brain.

She should not have been tempted to lie down in Donovan Steele's bed, but her aunt had indicated he rarely made an appearance during the day due to his work schedule. Natalie had erroneously assumed she would be long gone before he got home. How was she to know the man had gone away for the weekend and would come home unexpectedly?

He had found her in his bed, and now the man had all kinds of crazy ideas. Did he really expect her to go out with him? And what she'd told him about taking a hiatus from dating had been the truth. She was yet to meet a man who wasn't threatened by all her successful academic achievements. She had graduated from high school at sixteen and had gotten her doctorate at twenty-one. Thanks to the head of the chemistry department, there had been a job waiting for her when she had graduated.

Although she loved her job, this year things had been rather challenging, trying to teach while providing assistance on a special project for NASA. The university had been glad to loan her expertise to the government but hadn't felt the need to reduce her classes.

Her thoughts shifted back to Donovan Steele, and she couldn't help but make a face. Doing so was childish at best, but at least for the moment it made her forget she was a woman who was very much attracted to him. She fought back a groan. Why her of all people? And why him?

And why did she have a weakness for men in jeans? Especially a man who wore a pair like they were tailor-made just for his body. Firm thighs, lean hips, tight abs. And then there had been those muscles beneath his T-shirt. Although she hadn't wanted to, she had checked him out. Donovan Steele was well-equipped in all the right places.

She wasn't particularly pleased she had noticed that. In fact she wasn't at all pleased that he had made her fully aware of him as a man. She had done a good job over the past few years concentrating on other things besides men. Men, more often than not, were a nuisance, and she'd found it better to go through life trying to forget they even existed.

She glanced down at her watch. It was almost noon, and she had one more home to clean that day. Deciding she needed to finish up and leave as soon as she could, Natalie loaded the washer and was about to put in the detergent and fabric softener when she heard the refrigerator open and close. She didn't have to look around to know Donovan Steele had come downstairs and was in the kitchen.

After closing the lid on the washer, she braced herself before turning around. He was there, looking good in his jeans and watching her—checking her out. And not trying to hide the fact that he was doing so.

"Is anything wrong, Mr. Steele?" She fought to keep her voice even although her stomach churned something awful. And to make matters worse, she was finding it hard to breathe.

With his legs crossed at the ankles he was leaning against a kitchen counter, staring at her and looking as relaxed as any man should be. She wished she could feel as comfortable as he seemed to be.

"No, there's nothing wrong," he finally said smoothly as he popped the cap off a beer bottle. "So, where have you been hiding, Natalie Ford?"

She raised a brow. "Excuse me?"

"I asked where you've been hiding. I'm surprised our paths never crossed before."

Natalie couldn't help but inwardly smile at the absurdity of that. Did the man actually think he should know every single female in Charlotte? Evidently he did. "I doubt we run in the same circles, Mr. Steele. Besides, Charlotte isn't a small town."

She thought about telling him where she lived and exactly what she did for a living and changed her mind after recalling other men's attitudes once she shared it with them. She was immediately labeled a mad scientist or chemistry geek. Better to let him assume she cleaned houses for a living.

"How old are you?"

Instead of responding, she asked, "How old do you think I am?"

His eyes scanned her face, as if to study her features. Her body warmed when his gaze dropped to her chest and began studying the V of her blouse like the size or shape of her breasts beneath the cotton material would tell him anything. Her throat grew tight, and she felt a hot sensation in the lower part of her stomach. And then, of all things, she felt her nipples harden against her blouse.

"So, what do you think?" she asked in an attempt to direct his gaze back to her face. It was slow in coming, and the smile that touched his lips made her wish she hadn't asked the question since she knew he would read it wrong.

"I personally think they're a nice pair."

She frowned, not believing he'd actually said that. "I was referring to my age, Mr. Steele."

"Donovan," he inserted quickly.

Ignoring his comment, she said, "You were supposed to guess my age."

"Oh, yes, that's right." A wry smile touched his lips, but not at all apologetic. He studied her face again, and she could feel herself blush under his intense scrutiny.

"I'd say around twenty-two or twenty-three."

Natalie wondered if he was being truthful or just trying to be nice. Either way she was truly flattered. "I'm twenty-six."

He took another sip of his beer, and the surprise in his eyes was genuine. "You definitely don't look it."

"Thanks, and how old are you?"

"Thirty-three."

And a very handsome and well-built thirty-three at that, she thought. His sensual chemistry mixed with a hefty dose of raw sexuality, and she was being affected by all that virility. Dragging in a deep breath, she said, "I need to finish everything upstairs and get out of your way."

A disarming smile touched his lips. "You aren't in my way."

But he was in hers, and if she didn't remove herself from his presence she would continue to think about indulging in things she shouldn't. Not only was he challenging her mentally, but he was doing physical things to her—things that no man had ever done before, without a touch, caress…or kiss.

At that moment she felt her lips tingle, and she felt butterflies in her stomach. She glanced at her watch. "I need to wrap things up here to be at my next client's home before two," she said.

"No problem. I'll let you get back to work, but first I need to ask you something."

She stepped into the kitchen and slipped her sandals on her feet. He was watching her every move, staring down at her feet. Then his eyes moved up her legs before finally meeting her gaze again. She slowly arched a brow in response. He had already asked her out, and she had turned him down. She wondered what he had to ask her now. "Ask me what?"

He took another sip of his beer. "I'm sure your aunt explained to you that I'm a man who appreciates my privacy, which is why I want personalized service from the cleaning agency. I don't want just anybody cleaning my home."

She lifted a brow. "Are you saying that you have a problem with me being here?"

"No. You've explained why you're here. You've also indicated your aunt won't be able to do any chores for about six weeks."

She looked at him, wondering where he was going with this. She folded her arms across her chest. "Yes, that's what I said."

"In that case I hope you can understand I expect you

to be the one—the *only* one—to handle things here. It would greatly upset me to discover some other person has access to my home."

She frowned. "We have a number of good employees who—"

"Won't be coming here," he said firmly. "Your aunt understood when I hired her agency that I had a problem with a lot of strangers having access to my home, which is why she took on the job herself. Now that she's not capable of doing it, either you take care of things or no one at all."

She tried to keep her frown from deepening. He was trying to be difficult. If her aunt didn't consider him such an important client she'd give him an ultimatum—either accept whatever one of the other Special Touch House-keeping Agency's employees she assigned to clean his condo or end his association with the agency.

Instead she said, "Fine."

"And I want to increase my services to once a week instead of twice a month."

She had to refrain from glaring at him. His request was ridiculous considering cleaning his home had been a piece of cake compared to the condo owned by Jeremy Simpkins.

He kept his eyes on hers, not for a single second look-ing away. "Will that be a problem?" he asked.

There was only one answer she could give him. "No, there won't be a problem. Do you want to keep your Mon-day appointments?"

"Only if I'm your sole client for that day." At her raised brow he clarified by saying, "Just in case you accidentally fall asleep again…in my bed."

Her jaw was set firm when she replied, "Like I said, it won't happen again."

He smiled. "But in case it does."

Natalie inwardly sighed. "It won't."

He nodded, lowered his voice and said, "Regardless. I want you to give this place your full attention. And if you can switch from Mondays to another day of the week. I would prefer it."

"I'll see what we can do," she said, trying to keep the frustration out of her voice.

"Thank you."

"Now I'd like to ask you something," Natalie said, fuming inside.

He waited a long moment before asking, "What do you want to ask me?" He took another sip of his beer.

"Do you normally hit on every woman who crosses your path?"

He gave her that seductive smile again. "Every woman? No. But I don't have any qualms about hitting on a woman I'm interested in. Like I told you earlier, I believe in going after what I want so there're some things I don't beat around the bush about."

"Apparently." And without saying anything else, she moved past him to go back upstairs.

Donovan's lips eased into a crooked smile. "Methinks the lady is just about ready to box my ears," he muttered before finishing off the last of his beer and placing the empty bottle on the counter. Boxing his ears wouldn't be so bad if he got to lock lips with her in the process.

While she was talking, his gaze had been fixed on her mouth. Never before had he seen a pair of lips so deliciously tempting. Just the thought of savoring them, licking them crazy, sent instantaneous heat flooding his insides. Being attracted to any woman was precisely the sort of thing he didn't need right now.

The matters of SC, specifically the product under development, were enough to occupy his attention. The Steele Corporation had been working on Gleeve-Ware and had hired a renowned chemist, Juan Hairston, to create the formula for a highly durable and flexible tubing of silicone, rubber and fiberglass. In its final form Gleeve-Ware could revolutionize the manufacturing industry and push the transportation industry into the next century by the production of a durable, long-lasting tire.

The research, which had begun over a year ago and had been deemed top secret, had gotten unwanted attention when a rival manufacturing company had learned about Gleeve-Ware. They had gone so far as to try and obtain the formula. A high degree of security was in place since SC had decided not to take any chances.

He and his three brothers—Chance, Sebastian and Morgan—comprised the managing body of SC. Chance, at thirty-eight, was CEO. Sebastian, whom they fondly called Bas, was thirty-six and held the position of SC's problem solver and troubleshooter. Morgan was thirty-four and headed research and development. His cousin Vanessa worked for the company as head of PR. The board of directors included, in addition to his parents, his aunt and his two cousins, Taylor and Cheyenne.

The Steele family was huge and close-knit. In addition to the Steeles living in Charlotte, there were a number of other Steeles spread out all over the country. They enjoyed getting together every two years for a family reunion.

When Donovan heard the vacuum cleaner start up, he decided to make the peanut-butter-and-jelly sandwich after all. He may have been overtaken by lust but in no way did he plan to starve over it.

He reached out to open the pantry at the exact moment his cell phone rang. Pulling it off his belt, he checked the ID screen and saw it was Kylie, his sister-in-law. He immediately clicked on the phone. "Tell me you're calling to invite me to dinner." Kylie loved to cook.

She chuckled. "You don't need an invitation to dinner, Donovan. You know you're always welcome. That's not the reason I called. I need a favor."

He smiled. "Anything for a slice of your apple pie."

"Um, I wasn't going to bake a pie tonight, but I'm sure that can be arranged."

"Okay, then, what's the favor?"

"My assistant has a doctor's appointment tomorrow, and there's this huge delivery I need to take over to the hotel and arrange for a business meeting on Wednesday morning. Any other time I would close down the shop while I'm gone, but one of my suppliers needs to deliver some more vases in the afternoon. Chance is picking up the baby when he gets off work, so I don't want to bother him about coming here and covering for me, especially with Alden. You and I know my son's a handful. Since you have to pass here on your way to the Racetrack Café, I wondered if you'd be willing to make a pit stop here and hold down the fort for about an hour or so?"

He'd done so before, last year when she'd been in a crisis. "Hey, that's no problem. What time do you need me there?"

Everyone in the family knew he arrived to work at six in the morning and left at three o'clock, unless some sort of emergency came up. He worked hard but liked playing even harder. The Racetrack Café was jointly owned by several drivers on the NASCAR circuit, including Bronson. It was a popular bar and grill in town and one of his favorite places to eat and hang out. It was customary for him to drop by there every day after work before heading home.

"Around three-thirty."

"I'll be there," he said, already tasting her mouthwatering apple pie.

"Thanks, Donovan, you're a jewel."

"Of course I am. And before you hang up I need to place an order of flowers to be delivered tomorrow to my housekeeper. She's recuperating from an ankle injury."

"Sure. What's her name?"

"Earline Darwin. Hold on while I get her address right quick."

"No need. I've delivered several flowers to her already. Evidently she's a well-liked lady. I'll make sure these get out tomorrow," Kylie promised.

"I'd appreciate it, and will see you tomorrow."

He smiled thinking his brothers had struck gold with his sisters-in-law. Kylie was extra special because not only did she cook mostly every day—and he knew he could drop in for a free meal—but she had made his oldest brother an extremely happy man. The family had all but given up on Chance, who had lost his first wife to cancer and had remained single after Cyndi's death for more than seven years. But he and Kylie had gotten together, had married and now—in addition to Chance's son, Marcus, who was away at college and Kylie's daughter, Tiffany, who had graduated from high school a couple months ago and was currently traveling out of the country with her grandparents—they had Alden, their active two-year-old son. Like most kids his age, Alden kept his parents on their toes. Nowadays, there was never a dull moment at Chance and Kylie's house.

Donovan finally noticed the vacuum cleaner was no longer running when he heard the sound of Natalie's footsteps. He glanced over his shoulder. She stood in the middle of the kitchen with her purse slung over her shoulder, ready to go.

"I'll be leaving now, Mr. Steele," she said in a very professional tone.

He turned to her and smiled. "I'm Donovan. Say it."

He saw the frown that lit her eyes. "I think it's best to keep things strictly business between us, Mr. Steele."

If she was trying to grate on his last nerve, he would not let her. Her attitude only made him even more determined to one day hear his first name flow passionately from her lips. "Okay, but business or otherwise you can still call me Donovan."

"I prefer not."

He moved away from the pantry to come and stand directly in front of her. "Then I plan on working hard to change your mind, Natalie. And I will succeed."

Natalie opened her mouth to give him a blistering retort, to tell him he would fall right on that nice-looking tush of his, but paused. If keeping her mouth shut meant retaining him as a customer for her aunt then she would overlook his arrogant attitude. Instead she said, "I'll discuss your request for increased service with my aunt and determine the days that will work for us and for you."

She turned and headed for the door, fully aware he was right on her heels. Before she reached her destination, he said, "I've thought about it, and I prefer Fridays if that day is available."

She paused and then turned around. "I'll check my aunt's schedule, and I'll get back with you later this week." She knew her tone of voice suggested she wasn't looking forward to doing so.

"Fine, and I'll look forward to receiving your call. And here."

She glanced down at the twenty-dollar bill he was holding out to her. "What's that for?"

He chuckled. "It's your tip. I usually leave it on the

kitchen table for your aunt, but since you're the one who cleaned up the place today, it's yours."

She backed up, refusing to take it. "That's not necessary. We bill you monthly for your cleaning service."

"I'm aware of that, but I believe in tipping, as well. Take it."

She started to refuse it again but changed her mind. She wouldn't keep it for herself but would pass it on to her aunt. "Thank you," she said, taking the money from his hand.

Their fingers touched, and the main thing she hadn't wanted to happen did. Sensual energy released in her body, rousing her senses. It had been bad enough to deal with the vibes that had been radiating between them. An actual touch was downright dangerous.

She tried ignoring the reaction and hoped he did, as well, since it wouldn't get either of them anywhere. Unfortunately, she could interpret the look in his eyes. Whereas she intended to ignore it, he planned on doing no such thing. Not only was the man arrogant but he was a rebel as well.

She fixed him a chilly look. "Like I said earlier, I'll get back with you later this week."

"I look forward to your call."

She just bet he did. Fighting back the temptation to say something smart, she turned—without saying another word to him—opened the door and left.

"How was your first day, Nat?"

Natalie smiled as she looked across the room into the questioning eyes of her aunt. When she'd gotten home after taking care of her last client for the day, she'd found Aunt Earline taking a nap. Natalie had taken the time to prepare something for dinner before her aunt had awakened. The doctors had said the medication for pain would make Aunt Earline sleep for long periods of time. And although Natalie regretted her aunt's broken ankle, she of all people knew this forced period of rest was just what her aunt needed. She'd worked too hard all her life.

It had been her aunt who had taken on the responsibility of raising her as a newborn when Natalie's mother, who'd gotten pregnant at eighteen, had taken a break from the fast life she was living out in California just long enough to give birth to her baby and leave it in the care of her only sister and her husband before taking off again. Over the years her mother had returned on occasion when her money got low, and she would threaten to take Natalie away unless they paid up.

Natalie had been in her teens when her uncle died of cancer but had been only ten when she'd seen her mother for the last time. That was the day Lorene Ford's body was shipped back to Charlotte for her funeral. According to what the police had said when they'd called Aunt Earline from Los Angeles, Lorene's boyfriend had stabbed her to death in a fit of jealous rage.

Last year her aunt, deciding she wanted to be her own boss, had given up her nine-to-five job as a secretary for the school system to start Special Touch Housekeeping Agency. Her aunt was working diligently to build a clientele looking for personalized homecare.

"Today was challenging only because I had to get familiar with the layout of each home and figure out the best way to utilize my time." Natalie finally told her aunt. She saw no reason to inform her aunt that she had fallen asleep in Donovan Steele's bed.

"Mr. Steele was out of town for the weekend and didn't get your message." She couldn't help but smile when she added, "Needless to say, I was definitely a surprise to him."

"I'm sure you were. He's very particular about who cleans up his home. He likes protecting his privacy. I understand the woman from his last cleaning service tried coming on to him, and when he didn't return her advances, she threatened to pass on information about him to the newspaper's gossip column."

Natalie lifted a brow, enlightened. No wonder he was such a hardnose about someone else coming in to clean his place. "He wants to move into a weekly slot. Preferably Fridays."

When she set the cup of tea in front of her aunt, she noticed her frowning. "He wants cleaning service every week?" Aunt Earline asked.

"Yes."

"Why? There's not much to do on the days he's paying us for now. He's a rather clean man, not a slob like Simpkins."

Natalie couldn't agree more. Jeremy Simpkins was a slob, and what was sad was the fact he had a live-in fiancée, so to be fair Natalie wasn't sure which of the two deserved the title. The house had been a complete mess. And it seemed that the two had had a fight the night before. Broken dishes had littered the kitchen floor when she'd arrived. From the looks of things, the argument had started during dinner and had been a doozy.

"Well, that's what he wants," she said, sliding into the chair opposite her aunt with her own cup of tea. It had always been a ritual for her aunt to enjoy a cup of herbal tea in the evening after dinner.

"Then we need to see how we can adjust our schedule to accommodate him. He was one of the first clients

I took on, and through him, I got a lot of good referrals. Besides, he pays well and is a generous tipper."

Natalie nodded at her aunt's words. "He gave me a twenty-dollar tip, which I put in the emergency fund jar," she said.

"You should have kept it. You earned it," her aunt replied.

Natalie shook her head. "No big deal." A smile then touched her lips. "He thinks I'm a regular employee with your cleaning service."

Her aunt lifted a brow. "And you didn't set him straight and inform him that you were a chemistry professor at Princeton University?"

Natalie shrugged. "I saw no reason to do that. He can think whatever he wants, as long as he pays for his cleaning service each month."

She took a sip of her tea and, deciding to change the subject, said, "Farrah called while you were asleep. She and I are getting together Friday night and going out."

Farrah Langley was her girlfriend from high school. While growing up they were thick as thieves, and they made a point to get together whenever Natalie returned to town. She was one of the few people Farrah had confided in when she'd suspected her ex-husband was cheating. And when her suspicions proved to be true, Natalie had been the one who'd provided Farrah with long-distance consolation and support during her divorce.

Aunt Earline smiled. "I'm glad to hear it. I feel bad about you leaving your job to come help me take care of my business. I promise to do everything I can to hurry up and get better."

"And I don't want you to worry about it, Aunt Earline. You need me and I'm here. I had a long talk with Eric last week about my coming here, and staying until you're back on your feet makes perfect sense."

Eric was Aunt Earline's son, who was five years older than Natalie and employed with the State Department as a foreign service officer. He was currently living in Australia.

"Besides, I needed a break from the university anyway," Natalie tacked on. "I did agree to be back in time to do that lecture at the start of the fall semester, and my department head was grateful for that."

Her aunt took a sip of tea and then looked at her and asked, "So what do you think of Donovan Steele? Most of the time I've cleaned his place he's at work. However, the few times I've seen him I found him to be quite a charmer."

A charmer? That was the last thing she'd thought of him. And how did they get back on the topic of Donovan Steele anyway? She shrugged. "I guess some women would find him a charmer, but I was really too busy cleaning his home to take notice."

At that moment the phone rang, and she was grateful for an excuse to get up from the table to escape a conversation about Donovan Steele.

Chapter 3

"And you actually found the woman asleep in your bed?"

The man sitting across from Donovan at a table in the Racetrack Café rarely showed surprise, but he did now. Bronson Scott had to be the most unflappable man Donovan knew, even when he was behind the wheel in a race car going close to two hundred miles an hour. Regardless of his ability to retain his cool, Bronson did have one major flaw that few people detected. He had a stubbornness that he effectively hid behind a billowy cloud of charisma and charm. He was also loyal to a fault to those he trusted and considered friends. Donovan knew he fell in both categories.

"Yes, she was in the bed upstairs," he responded and watched as Bronson's eyes widened.

"What did you do?"

Not what he'd wanted to do, Donovan thought as he

sighed deeply. "I woke her up…after checking her out first. I liked what I saw."

Bronson smiled,. "Regardless, you caught her sleeping on the job, and with your stern work ethic I'm surprised you didn't fire her on the spot."

Donovan was surprised, as well. But there had been something about his Goldilocks that had given him pause…as well as a hard-on that still had her name wrapped around it. How could he explain to his best friend that when he had gazed down at Natalie desire as hot as it could get, as deep as it could go, had blazed through him? And he doubted he could explain why he wanted her back in his bed with an intensity he hadn't felt in years, if ever.

"I could have fired her but I didn't," he decided to say after taking a sip of his beer right out of the bottle.

Bronson chuckled. "And that, my friend, says it all."

Donovan raised a brow. "And what exactly is it saying?"

Bronson leaned back in his chair. "The extent of your interest. That finding her in your bed—that particular bed—has given you what you see as a vested interest in her life."

Now it was Donovan's time to chuckle. "Not her life, Bron, just her body."

There. He'd spoken out loud the very thought that had been running through his mind ever since Natalie Ford had walked out of his door. She was a woman, a good-looking woman, a very hot and enticing woman.

A woman he wanted.

He had decided the moment he'd stared down into her open eyes that he wanted her. Sexual chemistry between them had been thick, the air surrounding them charged. Dangerously so. He would go so far and admit he didn't particularly understand that part of the equation, but he would accept it now and dwell on it later. He knew what he wanted and would act on it. In a way, he already had. She would be in his home at least once a week for the next six weeks. A strategic move that he was pretty damn proud of.

"So what do you know about her?"

Donovan didn't say anything for a moment, thinking about Bronson's question. And then he said, "In addition to having a nice-looking body and a beautiful face, she's twenty-six. Her aunt, my regular housekeeper, hurt her ankle and will be laid up for at least six weeks, and she's filling in to help out."

He then fell silent for a moment as he remembered her in his home. The most prominent memory was how she'd folded her arms beneath her breasts and stared at him with defiance in her eyes. But still, there had been something about her that certainly had his insides simmering in heated longing. He rarely gave any woman a lasting consideration, definitely never thought of plotting the sexual downfall of one, but all afternoon he'd been doing that very thing.

"And I know, by her own admission," Donovan spoke up to add, "that she is currently not seeing anyone. In fact she says she's taking a break from dating."

Bronson lifted his brow. "Why?"

"We didn't cover the details, not that it matters since she will start dating me."

"Good luck."

Donovan took another pull from the bottle and then asked, "Good luck?"

"Yes, I've never known you to get so interested in any woman. The next six weeks should be rather interesting."

Donovan held back the urge to laugh out loud. Instead he said in an amused voice, "And I assume you think that *you* can talk?"

It was a known fact between the two of them that Bronson had fallen hard for a woman named Sunnie, the oldest of the St. Claire triplets from Florida and sister to the wife of Myles Joseph. Sunnie, unfortunately, was playing hard to get, but Bronson was determined to get her anyway.

Just like Donovan planned to get Natalie Ford.

The difference was that Bronson, by a decision of his own, which still had Donovan utterly confused, had allowed himself to get snarled without even putting up a fight. That was a predicament Donovan didn't intend to ever find himself in. He enjoyed female companionship like the next guy—hell, probably a lot more than the next guy—but he knew when and where to draw the line. No woman, no matter how gorgeous her legs were, would get the best of him. In his mind she was a body to be had, pleasured and enjoyed.

"I'm thinking about going to Florida this weekend," Bronson said, breaking into his thoughts.

Donovan was unaffected by Bronson's words. His friend was determined to pursue a woman who didn't want to be pursued.

"I propose a toast," Bronson said, picking up his beer bottle. "To women. The ones we want for whatever reason we want them. May we both be successful in achieving our goals."

Their bottles clinked, and then they both took a huge gulp. The main thought on Donovan's mind as he felt the bitter-tasting liquid flow down his throat was that he would indeed be successful with Natalie Ford.

The next morning Donovan arrived at the office and discovered his calendar was full and that there was an important meeting with his brothers in Chance's office at nine.

He enjoyed arriving at work early, usually coming straight from the gym where he gave his body an intense workout for an hour before showering and dressing to arrive at the office by six.

His secretary usually got in around eight, which meant he had a couple hours to handle whatever was at the top of his "must take care of" list without any interruptions. There was a time Sebastian and Morgan would also arrive around six in the morning. But since they got married, they seemed reluctant to leave their wives any sooner than they had to. Since Chance had been a single dad with a school-age child to handle, he'd preferred flexing his hours to suit his needs, which had been understandable. Nowadays he still flexed his schedule due to Alden. Either he took him to the nursery each day or picked him up. Donovan could tell his brother enjoyed stepping back into the role of father to a young child.

Donovan sat down at his desk with a cup of steaming coffee in his hand and rolled his eyes at the mere thought of any woman keeping him in bed beyond what he deemed was necessary. Men had a tendency to get too carried away with the opposite sex. Hell, they got carried away with sex period…or in his case, as he would admit grudgingly, the thought of getting sex.

That made him think of Natalie Ford. Hell, he had thought endlessly about her last night, if the truth be told. And alone in his office with just his thoughts, he might as well tell it. He had dreamed about her and her legs. He had even gone farther than that by thinking about the juncture of those legs and how he'd love to lose himself in that section of her body. A part of him wished she had not changed the linen on his bed. Instead of welcoming the clean, fresh scent when he'd gotten between the sheets, he had longed for her scent, a reminder that she had been in his bed.

But even without her scent as a memory, he had remembered. He had remembered to the point where he'd gone to sleep with a hard-on as a result of thinking about her, recalling what he'd seen when he had lifted that bedspread off her while she slept. She had looked so damn good in her shorts and top that he couldn't help wonder just how she would look naked.

He was so enmeshed in those thoughts that he jumped, almost spilled coffee on his shirt, when there was a knock on his door. He frowned and glanced at the ceramic clock on his desk, a birthday gift from Lena, Morgan's wife. It was a joke in the family that he enjoyed watching time slip by. It was early—a few minutes past six. Who else would be in the office this early other than security?

"Come in," he yelled out.

He was surprised when Sebastian stuck his head in the door, before opening it wide to walk in with a cup of coffee in his hand. Donovan sat up straight in his chair and quickly slipped the piece of paper he'd been doodling on inside his desk. Absently, he'd been jotting down all the ways he'd like to do Natalie. He was a master when it came to lovemaking positions and wanted to try each and every one he could think of on her.

"Why are you here so early?" he asked as his brother shut the door and eased down in the chair across from his desk.

"Jocelyn has a doctor's appointment later today, so I thought I'd come in early and get a few things done before I have to leave."

Donovan nodded. It was hard to believe how things had changed for Bas since getting married. There used to be a time when the Steele Corporation was more than a company to Bas; it had been his lifeline. Bas had been the last Steele brother to come work for SC. Of the four of them, it had been Bas who'd given their parents the most grief while growing up, especially during his teen years. Bas and the old man used to butt heads all the time, mainly because trouble had a way of finding Bas at every turn.

Now Bas was a happily married man with a baby on the way.

"Everything's okay with Jocelyn and the baby?" Donovan asked.

Bas smiled. "Yes, everything is fine. Since she's due next month, the doctors are now seeing her each week."

"And you still don't want to know if you're having a boy or girl?" Donovan asked, then took a sip of his coffee.

"Nope. We'll find out soon enough."

Donovan nodded. That was the same attitude his other brother Morgan and his wife, Lena, had taken. Lena was due to deliver a month or so after Jocelyn.

"All we know is that it's one big baby. No triplets for us," Bas added jokingly. Donovan understood the punch line. Their cousin Cheyenne had given birth to triplets nearly nine months ago. The first multiple birth ever recorded in the Steele family.

His conversation with Bas easily shifted into details about the race that past weekend. Everyone was happy about Bron's win and the positive exposure it had given SC. It was good advertising dollars at work.

"Do you know what our meeting this morning with Chance is about?" Donovan asked, knowing if anyone knew it would be Bas. As company troubleshooter, he kept well informed of anything and everything that happened at SC.

Bas shrugged. "Chance will tell you everything you need to know soon enough."

Donovan rolled his eyes, wondering why he'd even bothered to ask. When it came to sharing SC's business with anyone, Bas always developed a case of locked lips.

"Well, I'd better get to my own office. I have a lot to do," Bas said standing.

Donovan inwardly smiled. It would be just like Bas to put distance between them for fear of him trying to pump him for more information.

"Okay, then. I'll see you at the meeting," he said when Bas turned to leave. Donovan lifted a brow wondering what suddenly had Bas so nervous.

Natalie sipped her coffee trying to decide when would be the best time to call Donovan Steele. She and her aunt had worked on the schedules, and after shifting a couple of customers from Friday to Thursday—with their consent, of course—they had come up with a workable solution to accommodate Mr. Steele's request.

She was working on the inside today, from the office set up in her aunt's home, doing payroll and ordering supplies, and had been, for the time being, successful in talking her aunt into taking it easy and getting some rest.

Checking the clock on the wall once again, she figured Mr. Steele should be in his office by now and decided to give his business number a try. Taking a deep breath, she picked up the phone, glanced at the business card her aunt had attached to his file, and punched in the numbers. It didn't take long for his secretary to answer.

"The Steele Corporation. Donovan Steele's office. May I help you?"

"Yes, may I speak with Mr. Steele?"

"Who may I say is calling, please?"

"Natalie Ford."

"Please hold on, Ms. Ford."

Natalie pushed away from the desk to glance out the window, trying to get her mind off the fact that in a few moments she would be hearing the sound of Donovan Steele's voice again. Maybe she was suffering from a case of concentrating too much on work and not enough on the opposite sex. Why else would the sight of a good-looking man with a sexy voice have her mind flipping around like a fish out of water?

It wouldn't take much to close her eyes, recall and visualize yesterday's encounter with Donovan Steele. After leaving his place, driving over to her next client's home had been difficult. She'd been overheated. Blatantly hot. If she could have gone somewhere and stripped down to her panties and bra she would have been tempted to do so.

And the sad thing about it was that her body's high temperature had had nothing to do with Charlotte's weather. It had been a hot day in July, true enough, but not a scorcher. She could now attribute her fever yesterday to Mr. Steele.

Mr. Steele.

He had tried several times to get her to call him Donovan, and she had refused to do so—would continue to do so. To call him by his first name sounded too personal, and she didn't want to have that kind of relationship with him. She refused to have any sort of a relationship with him.

Her thoughts snapped back to the present when she heard the phone click in her ear and then… "Hello, this is Donovan."

Immediately, her heart began pounding, and even though she didn't want it to, her body began heating up, similar to the way it had yesterday. The man had such a sexy voice.

"Hello."

At the sound of that voice again, she suddenly realized that she had not responded to his first greeting and quickly said, "Yes, Mr. Steele, this is Natalie Ford from Special Touch Housekeeping Agency."

"Yes, Natalie, what can I do for you?"

His words flowed across her body like a stroke of some explosive fluid to a simmering brushfire. She'd never concentrated on the sound of a masculine voice before, especially not to this degree. And the sound of one had definitely never even come close to giving her a sexual thrill. For her to come this unglued meant she had gone without male company too long. What had it been now? Five years?

"Natalie?"

She sighed and pushed a lock of hair back from her face while trying to ignore the way he said her name. His sensuous tone stroked something within her that so far no man ever had stroked fully before.

Passion.

While growing up she'd known about her mother's wild and reckless ways, and had gone through life determined not to make the same mistakes Lorene Ford had made when it came to men. As a teen, instead of letting the pursuit of boys occupy most of her time, Natalie had found solace in her books.

And when she'd gone off to college, being younger than the other students had been challenging. That's when she had met Karl Gaines. Like her, he had been totally absorbed in his books...or so she had thought. She had found out the hard way that he'd been just as cunning, controlling and manipulating as he'd been brilliant.

And he had been cruel. He had eroded her confidence as a woman and her ability as a mate to keep the man she loved satisfied sexually. He hadn't minced words when he'd talked about her lovemaking abilities, or lack of them.

Even with the disappointment of that brief affair with Karl, Natalie truly believed that somewhere deep inside of her an intense amount of stored-up fire was just waiting to be released. But she was determined to keep it under lock and key, although a part of her yearned to set it free.

"Yes, Mr. Steele," she finally said, determined to keep things on a professional level between them. "I'm calling to let you know that Special Touch will be able to accommodate your request to have one of our employees—"

"One of your employees?" he cut in sharply to ask.

Natalie knew why he'd done so and modified her words. "*I* will be there every Friday, and when my aunt gets back on her feet, she will resume her duties as your personal housekeeper."

There. She hoped he was satisfied. She shifted, uncomfortable in her chair suddenly, feeling as if she'd just placed herself at his beck and call for six weeks. She shrugged off the idea, thinking that she would probably be in his home no more than two to three hours each week.

"That sounds better, Natalie. A whole lot better. Thanks for calling to inform me of the change. It says a lot for your aunt's agency to try and work with her clients this way."

Natalie rolled her eyes. "We aim to please," she said tartly and immediately saw the error in doing so when he replied.

"Aim to please? Um, that's good to know. Goodbye, Natalie."

"Goodbye, Mr. Steele."

Natalie hung up the phone thinking at least she had gotten through the conversation relatively unscathed and not feeling as if she'd been stripped naked. But for some reason she had been left with the impression that she wouldn't be so lucky the next time around.

* * *

Donovan leaned back in his chair after ending his call with Natalie. It somewhat amused him that she still refused to call him by his first name: but all that would definitely change after they shared their first kiss. After that, not only would she say his name but she would be purring it.

He closed his eyes to recall some of the finer details of yesterday. He moved past the episode of discovering her in his bed—but only because that segment had consumed his entire mind most of yesterday and the majority of last night. Instead he chose to fast-forward to when he'd come downstairs to find her in his laundry room bending over while loading his sheets into the washer. He was surprised he was still breathing. Never before had a pair of legs seemed so in sync with a lush behind. He had immediately grabbed a beer out of the fridge. It was either use the cold drink to cool off or take the chance of burning to a cinder. He remembered too when he had stood in front of her, right before she'd made a fast exit for the door. He'd had come close to leaning in and kissing her.

"Mr. Steele, your brother phoned to remind you of the meeting in his office at nine."

Upon hearing his secretary's voice, Donovan opened his eyes, and his gaze immediately landed on the clock on his desk. It was ten past nine. "Let Chance know that I'm on my way, Sandra."

He quickly stood, and before reaching the door grabbed his jacket off the rack. It was unlike him to be late to a meeting. How could he let fantasies of a woman who was playing hard to get totally swamp his thoughts?

A profound edginess flowed through him as he made his way down the hall toward the elevator. He refused to let Natalie Ford turn his entire life topsy-turvy. No sooner had he made that vow when he felt heat suffuse his body at the thought of all the wild sex he planned to have with her once he seduced her. Just thinking about those legs that he liked so much being wrapped around him while he made love to her seemed to boost his energy level.

He stepped into the elevator thinking next Friday couldn't get there fast enough.

"So where do you want to go Friday night?"

Natalie resisted the urge to tell Farrah nowhere. Although she much preferred staying in and curling up with a good book, she knew she and Farrah needed to get together. They hadn't seen each other since Christmas, the last time Natalie had returned to Charlotte. Besides, Friday would be exactly a year to the date that Farrah's divorce from Dustin had been final. That wouldn't have been so bad if Dustin had felt any remorse for cheating on his wife. Instead, once Farrah had confronted him with her suspicions about his extramarital affairs, he hadn't tried to deny them, nor had he apologized for breaking his marriage vows. Instead he informed his wife of four years not to waste time forgiving him since he wanted a divorce to marry the other woman—the woman who'd had his child. And he'd done just that—less than a week after his divorce had been final.

"Natalie?"

Natalie blinked and stared down at the speakerphone on the desk, realizing she hadn't answered Farrah's question. "Doesn't matter. Wherever you want to go is okay with me."

"Um, in that case, Nat, I want to go somewhere there will be a lot of men."

Natalie could only shake her head while thinking that Friday would be one of those nights. Last July she and

Farrah had met in New York for the weekend to do some shopping and take in a play. She had let Farrah talk her into going to this nightclub in Harlem, and the two of them, along with several very handsome men, had danced the night away. Her feet actually ached at the memory. She smiled when she remembered the disappointed faces of the men who'd thought they would be getting more from her and Farrah than a few dance moves.

"That's fine. You pick the place," she decided to say, shifting her gaze to the flowers that had just been delivered to her aunt. They were from Donovan Steele. She could tell her aunt had appreciated the man for being thoughtful enough to send them.

"Um, what about the Racetrack Café?"

Farrah reclaimed Natalie's attention with her question. She had heard about the Racetrack Café but had never been there since it had opened up after she left town for college. From what she'd heard, it wasn't your typical sports bar and grill. She understood the food was good and the atmosphere friendly. And usually there were more men there than women because on occasion a well-known race-car driver would drop by.

"The Racetrack Café sounds like a winner to me as long as you don't plan to dance all night."

Farrah's laughter came through the speakerphone. "I promise I won't."

"Glad you could join us, Donovan."

Donovan couldn't help but smile at his oldest brother. Even if Chance hadn't been born the oldest, he would still be the perfect one for the CEO role. He was a born leader, and Donovan would admit grudgingly that Chance was one of the few people who could keep him in line. Most of the time. Bas and Morgan knew it was a lost cause.

"Sorry, I got somewhat detained," he responded entering the room and closing the door behind him. As he took a seat, he glanced at the others already there—Bas, Morgan and Vanessa—who no doubt had been on time. Unlike his two brothers who were staring at him, Vanessa had chosen to pass the time by messing with her BlackBerry.

She'd only been married a year, and if he were to guess by the way her thumbs were working, she was sending her husband, Cameron, a dirty little text message. The way her lips tilted at the corners in a devilish smile all but confirmed he was right; whatever message she'd sent had been hot and sleazy. He of all people knew just how that part of a person's mind worked.

Since she had been too busy texting to notice he'd arrived, he said, "I'm here now, Vanessa, so you can stop texting Cameron those pornographic messages."

She snapped her head up, glared at him and then opened her mouth as if to deny that was exactly what she'd been doing. And then as if she'd thought about it for a quick second, she closed her mouth and the glare slowly vanished from her face. She tilted her head at an angle and lifted her chin. "Doesn't matter. We're married now," she said haughtily.

"Thank God."

That had come from Morgan and understandably so. Cameron was his best friend, and he of all people knew how long it had taken Cameron to win Vanessa over. As far as Donovan was concerned, it was too long. It was his opinion that no woman had been or currently was worth all of that.

"Now that we're all here," Chance said, before anyone else could make a comment. "I'm turning the meeting over to Morgan. Since he heads the research and development department, he will bring us up to date on some information we received this weekend regarding Gleeve-Ware."

Donovan shifted his gaze to Morgan. Not for the first time he wondered how Morgan did it. He was a father-to-be, worked hard for SC and in addition to that, he was a political figure in town. He had won a council at-large seat last year. Where did the man get all his energy?

"I wanted to bring something to your attention," Morgan was saying. "I got a call from Juan on Sunday morning. Someone tried to break into the lab Saturday night. The alarm sounded but nothing was taken. He just wanted to make us aware that someone is interested in what we have going on with Gleeve-Ware and will probably stop at nothing to get the formula."

Donovan nodded. Morgan had gone to college with the chemist, Juan Hairston, they had hired to head the Gleeve-Ware project. "What do you need from us to make sure that doesn't happen?" Donovan asked.

"All the appropriate steps have been taken to protect and maintain the secrecy of the chemical process formula, but still, I'm encouraging everyone to keep your eyes and ears open and report anything suspicious to Bas since he's our troubleshooter working with security," Morgan said.

"And, Vanessa, I suggest you get with Holly Brubeck in HR to make sure we're doing periodic security checks on any employee with access to our trade secrets, and to make sure all employment applicants sign confidentiality agreements. The last thing we want is to hire someone whose goal is to steal the formula for Gleeve-Ware right out from under our noses."

Vanessa nodded. "Is there anything else you want me to do from a PR standpoint?"

"No, but don't be surprised if we suddenly start getting painted with a negative brush," Chance responded to say. "If the culprits can't get the information they want, they might resort to smear ads or negative accusations."

"Like they did a couple years ago when they put out the rumor we were outsourcing," Bas added, reminding everyone.

The meeting lasted for another half hour when other business matters were discussed. Right before Chance closed the meeting, Donovan spoke up. "Just an FYI. I will be working from home on Fridays for the next few weeks."

Bas raised a brow. "Is there a reason why?"

Donovan smiled at everyone who was looking at him. "No reason."

But he knew his brothers knew him well enough to know such a move probably involved a woman.

And they were right.

But they had no idea that he was meticulously planning the intimate seduction of one Natalie Ford.

Chapter 4

"If you need to reach me, Donovan, just give me a call on my cell phone," Kylie Steele threw over her shoulder as she quickly headed for the door. "You probably won't get many customers, and most of them will be phone orders instead of walk-ins. See you later." And then she was gone.

He chuckled as he took the stool behind the counter and watched his sister-in-law pull out of the parking lot. He'd covered for her before and knew what to do. He had an hour or so to kill until she returned so he might as well make the best of it, and with the flat-screen TV on the wall directly behind him, at least he wouldn't get bored.

To kill some time, he took his BlackBerry out of his pocket and scrolled through his text messages. Most of them were from Joanne Summerville, the woman he'd met at the races this past weekend. He hoped she wouldn't start making a nuisance of herself. He could definitely do without that type of woman.

A half hour later he had put his BlackBerry away and his attention was concentrated on the television, namely CNN, thinking it was a damn shame Soledad O'Brien was a married woman. He was about to scoot the stool closer to the television for a closer view of her when the jingle of the bell above the door alerted him that he had a customer. He glanced up and saw an elderly woman with a cane stop in her tracks when she saw him.

"Where's Kylie?" she asked him accusingly.

He lifted a brow. The way the woman had asked implied she thought he had done away with his sister-in-law. "She had to step out," he decided to answer to assure her misplaced fears. "May I help you?"

She frowned at him. "And who are you?"

The woman sure asked a lot of questions. He wondered how long it would take for her to place an order and leave. She was presently standing in the way of him and Soledad. "I'm her brother-in-law," he said, hoping that would allay whatever problems she had with him.

He watched, surprised, as a slow smile replaced her frown. "Oh, you're one of those Steele boys."

He chuckled. He hadn't heard him and his brothers described just that way in a long time. Of the four of them, most people knew Bas mainly because while growing up he'd had a reputation around town for getting in all kinds of trouble. "Yes, ma'am, I'm one of those Steele boys."

"And which one are you?"

"The youngest."

She nodded. "Oh, you're the one who likes the girls."

That was him, all right. He lifted a brow, wondering just who this woman was. One thing was for certain; she had just made a pivotal point about him and he had no problem admitting it. "Yes, ma'am, I'm the one who likes the girls."

"Just like Drew did in his day."

Donovan couldn't help but laugh. Drew Steele was one of his father's cousins, and from what Donovan had heard, thirty years ago Drew had had to leave Charlotte when a bunch of women threatened to do him bodily harm because of his notorious reputation. Drew escaped to Phoenix, eventually married and had a slew of kids.

"Yes, just like Drew," he said, not the least bit ashamed to claim such a thing. What he didn't say was that, unlike Drew, Donovan felt he had his game together and didn't intend to get run out of town by a bunch of women. Times had changed. Most men weren't seeking a woman's undying love and affection—just a chance to share her bed. He made a point to make sure the women he messed around with knew the difference.

"I take it you knew Drew," he said, indicating the obvious.

The frown returned to the elderly woman's face. "Oh, yes, I knew Drew. He would have messed up my daughter's life if we hadn't sent her off to school in Florida with my sister. She was so convinced she was in love with him and that he loved her. Everyone in town knew he didn't love anyone but himself. That was over thirty years ago. She eventually married and got on with her life."

Donovan nodded, happy for her daughter. There was no need to tell her that although Drew had pretty much settled down some of his sons were following in their father's footsteps. "Did you want to place an order?" he decided to ask her.

She slowly began moving toward the counter. "Yes, I got a sick church member, and I want to send her a bunch of those flowers over there," she said, pointing to the refrigerated glass case containing an assortment of flowers prearranged in a ceramic vase. "Any ones will do in the twenty-dollar price range."

"All right. Do you want to take them with you?" he asked, writing out the order form.

"No, I want Kylie to have them delivered for me," she said and then handed him a slip of paper.

He glanced down at it. "Earline Darwin?" he asked. Of course he recognized the name.

"Yes, you know her?" the elderly woman asked.

"Yes, I know her." *But I want to get to know her niece even more.*

"Did you get a lot of orders while I was gone?"

Donovan glanced up when his sister-in-law walked through the door. "Around three phone orders and only one walk-in. A Ms. Hayes stopped by to send a bunch of flowers to Earline Darwin."

"Like I said yesterday, Ms. Darwin is a popular lady. I'll make sure she gets them tomorrow," Kylie said, moving to the register to close it out for the day.

"No need. I'll drop them off on my way home." Donovan figured Natalie would be there taking care of her aunt since she couldn't get around much.

Kylie tilted her head to look up at him with a bemused look on her face. "Why? Did Ms. Hayes say she wanted them delivered today?"

"No, but I thought I could do that and also check on Ms. Darwin."

Kylie crossed her arms over her chest. "Okay, what's going on here, Donovan? You're a nice guy and all but what's the real reason you're dropping by Ms. Darwin's home? And I recognize the address. It's not on your way home, nor is it close to the Racetrack Café. So just what are you up to, Donovan Ridge Steele?"

Donovan tried hiding his smile by looking down at his feet. He'd gotten caught so he might as well come clean. Besides, this was Kylie. Since marrying Chance, she'd had two teenagers in the household to deal with—teens that Donovan had discovered could be as conniving as they came.

He lifted his head to meet Kylie's questioning gaze. "I told you that Ms. Darwin is my housekeeper."

She nodded. "Yes, you did mention that."

"Well, what I probably didn't mention is that her niece is filling in for her for the next six weeks."

He watched as understanding shone on Kylie's face. "She's pretty, I imagine."

"Very."

Kylie frowned. "And knowing you like I do, I guess that means you want to add her to your get-her-in-my-bed list."

He wondered what Kylie would think if she knew Natalie had already been in his bed; however, he hadn't been in it with her. "Aw, come on, Kylie. You make me sound like the rake of the year. I'm very up-front with any woman I become involved with. I tell her what to expect and what not to expect."

"But that's no guarantee that they won't fall in love with you anyway. I don't want to remind you about Alyson Greer."

Donovan rolled his eyes. "Please don't bring her up. And I did explain to Alyson how things would be, but she refused to take me at my word because she had her own agenda. What you don't want to accept, Kylie, is that there are women just like me out there who don't want a lasting relationship any more than I do. Those are the women I deal with. Plain and simple."

From her expression, he could tell his words hadn't

been too convincing so he said. "Trust me, Kylie. It's not that serious."

She lifted a brow. "I don't know about that, Donovan. I'm the mother of a daughter whom I want to be aware of men like you."

His grin didn't waver since he didn't take her words as an insult. "And your daughter has an uncle who would defend her honor to the hilt if he had to. But, again, the women I deal with know the score. If they choose not to believe what I tell them, or if for some reason they get it into their heads that I'm a man who can be caught and tamed, it's their fault and not mine."

He and his sisters-in-law had had this conversation several times before, and his stomach knotted at the awful memories. One night they had cornered him and all but made him promise to be considerate of women's feelings. It had taken him a full hour or so to convince them that he was.

He watched as Kylie sighed in frustration before walking over to open the glass case. "I hope you know what you're doing, Donovan. I have a feeling that one day will be payback for you, and some woman is going to break your heart."

He chuckled. "Trust me, sweetheart, it's not going to happen."

"Aren't those flowers just lovely, Nat?"

Natalie smiled as she placed a bowl of soup in front of her aunt while glancing at the flowers that had been delivered earlier that day from Donovan Steele. "Yes, they are pretty, Aunt Earline. But then all your flowers are simply beautiful."

And she had received quite a few from various church members, neighbors and friends. Natalie had a feeling why her aunt thought the ones from Donovan were so special. Because she hadn't expected them. There certainly hadn't been any flower deliveries from Kelly and Simpkins.

"I need to send him a thank-you card."

Natalie knew it would be a lost cause to tell her aunt there was no hurry in doing that, so she didn't.

"You got two calls today from potential clients. I got their addresses to mail them out a brochure," she said sitting down across from her aunt at the table.

"Thanks."

"And the Baxters called to cancel their service on Thursday. They're going out of town."

For the next hour Natalie brought her aunt up to speed on everything that had happened that day with the business including the bad news that they'd received a resignation from one of their employees whom they considered dependable.

"I hate that Lola will be leaving us in the fall, but I'm glad she's decided to return to school. She only has a few credits left before she gets her college degree. And at least she gave us a lot of notice for us to find a replacement."

And then it was time for her aunt's afternoon nap. After making sure she had taken her medicine and was comfortably settled in bed, Natalie was just leaving her aunt's bedroom and closing the door behind her when the doorbell sounded. Not wanting the sound to disturb her aunt, she quickly headed toward the front of the house, wondering if one of her aunt's church members had come calling.

She glanced out the peephole in the door, and her chest immediately tightened. Donovan Steele was standing on the porch. What on earth could the man want? Glancing down at her skirt and blouse, and deciding she looked decent enough, she quickly ran her fingers through her hair and then she inhaled deeply before slowly opening the door.

Before she could ask why he was there, he handed her a vase of flowers and said, "I thought I'd help out my sister-in-law by delivering these."

It took all of Donovan's self-control not to pull Natalie into his arms for the kiss he'd been aching for since meeting her yesterday. It was insane. Yet, for one tantalizing minute he wanted more than anything to pull her into his arms to find out if her lips were actually as soft and delicious as they looked.

It would be a provocative move. Bold. Totally out of line. Considering such a thing should give him pause. Unfortunately, what it was giving him was an ache right behind his zipper, which he was trying like hell to fight back.

He was fully aware of her, although he was trying so hard not to be. She looked cute in her skirt and blouse. In truth there was nothing unusual about them. Still, they stirred raw desire within him. But when you had legs that looked like hers and a body that could make a man drool, it was hard not to be fully aware of anything she wore. Even a potato sack if she chose to don it.

"You work with your sister-in-law part-time?"

Her question brought his attention back in focus and away from her legs. "Not really," he said, deciding to lean against the porch column for support. "She had something to do today, so I did her a favor by watching the store for an hour or so. One of your aunt's church members dropped by and ordered these flowers. I couldn't resist delivering them in person."

Her eyes shone bright in the fading sunlight. "And why couldn't you resist delivering them?" she asked.

He could feel her nervous tension and watched as she licked her top lip with her tongue and felt his gut tighten even more. Her luscious scent surrounded him, made him appreciate being a man who was intent on having her. "Because I figured you would be here, and it gave me a chance to see you again," he finally said, watching her reaction to his words with a steady gaze.

She opened her mouth as if not believing what he'd boldly stated. Then she closed it, paused momentarily and said, "Mr. Steele, I think—"

"Donovan. That's what I want you to call me. What will it take for you to do so, Natalie?"

He observed the narrowing of her eyes, the tightening of her lips. She wasn't too happy with him now. Just as well since if the truth be told, he wasn't too happy with her, either. She was being difficult, playing hard to get. Normally he liked the challenge, but in this case, although he'd only met her yesterday, she had made an impact, and his patience was wearing thin.

He decided to press on while he had her at a loss for words. "Are you going to invite me in?"

Her eyebrow arched. "For what reason?"

"So I can say hello to your aunt."

"Sorry, she's asleep and I don't want to wake her up."

He managed to smile. Boy, she was stubborn. "And I wouldn't want you to. Considering everything, I'm sure she needs her rest." *Just like considering everything, I think you're trying to hide the desire that's so blatant in your eyes, in the hard tips of your nipples that are pressing against your blouse. Why are you fighting me?*

"Thanks for delivering the flowers."

Natalie's voice intruded into his thoughts, and acting on pure impulse, he moved a step closer to her. The only thing separating their bodies was the vase of flowers she held in her hand. He wanted to get a clear view of the look in her eyes, to see what she wasn't yet experienced enough to hide. An image came back into his mind, the one of finding her asleep in his bed. But in this one, she wasn't fully clothed. Instead she was stark naked.

He released a sharp intake of breath, and at that moment he was more determined than ever to have her, to do all those things to her he had dreamed about last night and envisioned most of the day.

"Goodbye, Mr. Steele."

As incredible as it was at that point in time, a slow smile formed on his lips. For now he would let her assume she was calling the shots. His smile widened even more as he took in her obvious apprehension. No doubt she was concerned just what his sudden good mood was about. Especially when the air surrounding them was shrouded with so much sensuality. It was so thick he could probably wallow in it. He felt it and knew she could feel it too.

"Please let your aunt know that I dropped by," he said in a husky yet hushed tone before taking a step back.

Without giving her time to say anything—and doubting seriously that she would have done so anyway—he turned and walked away.

Chapter 5

"What do you know about Donovan Steele, Farrah?" Natalie asked her friend as she watched her check her side mirrors before changing lanes. They were on their way to the Racetrack Café for an evening of fun.

At the first opportunity she could grab, Farrah glanced over at her. "Donovan Steele?" she asked with surprise in her voice. "Why on earth would you ask about him?"

Because maybe talking about him will stop my breasts from aching whenever I think about him. She had literally been in one hell of a fix since seeing him yesterday. She hadn't expected him to drop by, nor had she expected her body's reaction to seeing him. "I'm just curious."

She figured that response would not be good enough for Farrah and wasn't surprised to find herself under Farrah's intense stare when they came to a flashing light at the train tracks.

"No, girlfriend, you're not just curious," Farrah said.

"You just got back in town last week, so why would you be asking about Donovan Steele?"

Natalie squirmed under Farrah's intense scrutiny and knew she would have to tell her the whole story since Farrah wouldn't let up until she did. "He's one of Aunt Earline's clients, and I was cleaning his home on Monday when he came home unexpectedly."

"Um, so you got to see the handsome hunk?" Farrah asked smiling as she waited for a train to pass.

"Unfortunately, I did. But that's not all I did,"

Farrah lifted her brow. "What else did you do?"

"I was cleaning his room, saw his bed, saw how comfortable it looked and wanted to try it out."

Farrah's eyes widened. "You got in Donovan Steele's bed, the one upstairs?"

Not understanding why the location of the bed would make a difference, Natalie shamefully admitted. "Yes. I was just going to try out the mattress to see if it was as soft as it looked. I hadn't intended on falling asleep."

"You actually fell asleep?" Farrah laughed. "Wow, that's rich."

"I don't know about it being rich since he found me there."

"Let me get this straight," Farrah said, wiping tears of laughter from her eyes. "You fell asleep in Donovan Steele's bed and he found you there?"

"Yes."

Farrah shook her head. "I'm sure your aunt hated losing him as a client."

"She didn't. As a matter of fact, he increased his cleaning service from twice a month to every week," Natalie informed her.

Farrah didn't say anything, but Natalie could see her friend's mind at work. She was working out everything

Natalie had told her in her head to come up with a reason for Donovan Steele's action. Natalie could have saved her the trouble. She wasn't born yesterday, nor was she the naive, brainy professor some men thought she was. She knew exactly what his motives were.

"He wants you," Farrah finally said matter-of-factly.

"Yes, that's what I figured, especially since he thinks I'm no more than a cleaning lady. I didn't bother telling him what I really did for a living."

Farrah smiled. "So, you're going to try him out?"

Natalie looked aghast. "Of course not! I know his true colors since he's been taking every opportunity to display them. I hear from Aunt Earline that he's Charlotte's number one player, and there is no doubt in my mind that he's looking for another conquest. I have no intentions of being the next notch on his bedpost."

Farrah didn't say anything for a moment, and Natalie had a feeling when her friend did speak again that she wouldn't like whatever she would say.

"You may want to reconsider that decision, Nat. A fling with him might give you a new attitude," Farrah said softly.

Natalie knew that look, and once again she squirmed accordingly. While in high school, the only time she put her books aside to indulge in some honest to goodness, off-the-wall fun was when Farrah talked her into it. Otherwise, she would have lived a relatively boring life. But this was not their school days and Farrah, who'd been thrust back into the life of a swinging single, evidently wanted her to join her.

"Don't look at me like that, Farrah. I know what you're thinking."

Farrah then gave her that smile she knew so well. "And what am I thinking?"

"That I need to take advantage of it because it's been years since I got laid." Natalie knew there was nothing Farrah could say but confirm her statement since recently that had been Farrah's constant argument. Over the years, Farrah had relentlessly tried building the case that Natalie needed to get her head out of her books and stop spending so much time in the lab and work on another type of formula—one that produced a love life, and if not a *serious* love life, definitely a fling.

"Yes, that's what I'm thinking and it makes perfect sense, don't you think?" Farrah interrupted her thoughts by saying.

Natalie rolled her eyes heavenward. "No, that's not what I think."

"Come on, Nat, what do you have to lose? You don't know what you're missing out on. You can't convince me you aren't curious."

Natalie wished she could deny what Farrah was saying but she couldn't. She hadn't slept with anyone since college and Karl. Only Farrah knew the full extent of the scars a man's emotional abuse could leave. But she had tried moving on, only to encounter men who weren't cunning and manipulative like Karl but who were weak-minded enough to feel threatened by a woman's successful scholarly achievements.

"Look, Nat," Farrah said, after glancing at the car in front of them to make sure it hadn't moved. "Seriously. I'm not saying you need to start sleeping around, by any means. All I'm saying is that you should enjoy your life and not give in to the failures of the only man you've ever slept with by thinking all men are that way."

Natalie knew she didn't think that way, but she would be the first to admit one of the reasons she hadn't been hitting the singles scene was because she felt more comfortable in her career than in the prospect of putting all that work into a relationship to nowhere.

When Farrah checked on the cars ahead of them again, Natalie decided not to let her off the hook so easily. "What about you, Farrah? Did Dustin make you think all men are that way?" Natalie studied Farrah's features. She saw a glimpse of the pain in her friend's eyes that was still there even after a full year.

"I'm trying to move on, Nat. And no, I don't think all men are like Dustin, but I will admit the next one who comes close to my heart will have a tough job convincing me that he's not. In other words, no man will ever capture my heart again."

Natalie knew Farrah meant every word she had spoken. To this day Natalie didn't understand how Dustin could have hurt Farrah the way he had. Regretting she had brought him up, she steered the conversation back to what she'd asked Farrah earlier.

"So, are you going to tell me what you know about Donovan Steele?" The cars started moving ahead, and she watched as Farrah shifted the car back in gear.

"Not much to tell. I've seen him before at a charity function or two so I know he's an extremely good-looking man. I only know what I read and what I overhear from the women at the gym. According to them, he only indulges in short-term affairs and is very selective about whom he sleeps with. Some women think it's quite an honor to be the chosen one because he's one hell of a lover."

Farrah glanced over at her when the car stopped at a traffic light. "I also hear he's very persuasive and could probably talk the panties off a nun."

Natalie couldn't help but smile at that claim. "All the more reason to keep him at arm's length," she said.

She could see him as a persuasive guy since if given

the chance he would have tried wearing down her resistance on Tuesday evening. Hadn't he told her he went after whatever he wanted and always succeeded in getting it? He'd given her fair warning. And she planned on taking it.

"We're here."

Natalie was pulled out of her thoughts to glance through the car window. The parking lot was full. "This place gets a lot of business, I gather."

Farrah smiled. "Yes, I've only been here once before with a girl from work. The food was good and the entertainment even better. And since you aren't interested in having a fling with Donovan Steele, I'm sure you'll meet some other likable guy here."

Natalie rolled her eyes. Having a fling was the last thing she was interested in.

"You want another beer, Donovan?"

"No, thanks. I'm fine, Jon. I'll be checking out in a few," Donovan said, sparing the bartender a quick glance before returning his gaze back to the flat-screen television on the wall behind the counter. They were showing a rerun of last weekend's race in New Hampshire.

When the bartender moved on, Donovan leaned back against the barstool accepting the fact that his full concentration wasn't on the race. Instead, over the course of the night, as well as the nights before, he had done a very unorthodox thing. He had allowed a woman to dominate his thoughts.

He wasn't sure how to view his meeting with Natalie when he had delivered the flowers. She'd been feisty—that was for sure. And strong-willed. But he had a feeling she was also a very passionate woman. And it was that passion he would love to get a hold on and work to his advantage. Last night he had dreamed about her. In sleep he had inhaled her scent, imagined her legs wrapped around him and envisioned her lips mingling with his.

He had awakened with sweat covering most of his body and an erection as hard as a rock. He was glad to see the work week come to an end and was looking forward to the weekend. He had a date lined up with Jean Carroll and he knew from past experiences that she would make it worth his while.

He happened to glance back up at the television screen and then looked to the mirror on the wall that picked up a clear view of anyone walking through the restaurant's door. He blinked thinking he was seeing things, but when he continued to stare at the mirror he saw that Natalie and another woman had come through the door. He was tempted to turn around but knew if he did she would definitely see him. So, instead, he sat there and watched as a waitress led them over to the table and out of sight.

Releasing the breath he'd been holding, he caught Jon's eye and beckoned him over to him.

"Another beer?" Jon asked.

Donovan shook his head. "No, but you see the two women Marisa just seated at a table in the back. I want you to give them whatever they want."

Jon strained his neck to see who Donovan was talking about. "Okay. Will you be joining them?"

"Later."

"All right." Jon then walked off.

Donovan pulled in a deep breath. What he didn't tell Jon was he wouldn't go anywhere near that table until he got himself together. He couldn't believe Natalie was here, invading his domain. It was bad enough he'd thought of little else besides her all day; now she was going to give him a reason to think of her all night. Again. And now there was a slow burn in his belly, and he seriously doubted even a cold beer would be able to put it out.

He glanced back at the television screen, trying to ignore the fact she was there, but everything in front of him seemed to blur while a current of electricity seemed to charge the air.

Donovan glanced at his watch as heat flowed through his midsection. It was barely eight and too early for him to think about going home. And why should he? He had never ducked the other way when it came to a woman. Goldilocks had once again invaded his turf, so the way he saw it he had rights—rights he intended to exercise. He had given her fair warning.

Getting off the stool, he headed in her direction.

"Everything on the menu looks good," Natalie said to Farrah. "What are you going to have?"

"Um, that guy who just walked in looks pretty good."

Natalie glanced up, followed Farrah's gaze and nodded in agreement. "Yes, he does look good but, unfortunately, he's not on the menu."

"What a shame. I wish he was."

Natalie chuckled, but her laughter was cut short when she saw the man in question approached by another man. "I don't believe it," she said in an annoyed voice.

Farrah, who had gone back to studying her menu, glanced up. "You don't believe what?"

"Donovan Steele is here, and he's talking to your guy— the one you wished was on the menu. Hopefully, he won't look over this way and see me."

As if those very words had damned her, Donovan glanced her way. His gaze settled on her face and held her eyes captive. She barely had time to draw in a ragged breath when she felt white-hot desire whisk through her veins and settle deep in her limbs. So deep she had to place her glass of water back down on the table.

"Natalie?"

She heard Farrah call her name but was too caught up in the intensity of Donovan's gaze to break eye contact. She finally answered nonetheless. "Yes?"

"Are you sure you told me everything about your relationship with Donovan Steele?"

That question made Natalie meet Farrah's curious expression. She swallowed deeply. "Yes." When Farrah continued to look at her, she finally asked in a strained voice, "What do you think I didn't tell you?"

"How much you want to jump his bones."

Hearing Farrah speak aloud what she had refused to acknowledge in her thoughts caused a blush to color her cheeks. Did she really want to do that? Was that the reason why every morning since meeting him she'd waken with sensuous aches in her body and dreams too scandalous to mention to anyone?

"Natalie?"

She knew she had to say something or Farrah wouldn't let up. "I plead the fifth."

Farrah chuckled. "You can plead the fifth all you like, but it's not going to help you since both men are headed this way."

Natalie refused to turn her head to see if Farrah was teasing her. She knew she wasn't. There was no way for her and Donovan Steele to be in the same place without him trying to use his power of persuasion on her. "Remember what I said. He doesn't know what I actually do for a living and I want to keep it that way," she whispered.

Farrah smiled. "I'll keep your secret, but from the way he's looking at you, I doubt what you do for a living is what's on his mind right now."

Natalie couldn't resist temptation any longer, and she shifted her gaze to see the two men walking toward them. Farrah was right.

Xavier Kane glanced over at Donovan. "Hey, man, are you sure those ladies don't mind being interrupted?"

Donovan smiled as they kept walking toward where Natalie and a friend were sitting. He liked Xavier. Known as X, he was a close friend and personal attorney to the man who'd married his cousin Vanessa last year, Cameron Cody, and was the godbrother to Donovan's friend from college, Uriel Lassiter.

"We'll find out soon enough, X. Doesn't she look happy to see us coming?"

X chuckled. "Depends on which one you're focused on."

"I've got my eye on the one in blue. We have a little matter we need to resolve."

X let out a sigh of relief. "That's good because she's the one shooting daggers at us. I'm glad I'm focused on the other one. She's smiling. I can work with that smile. All I have to do is turn up the heat."

As Donovan got closer to the table, he decided regardless of the cold look Natalie was sending his way, he intended to turn up the heat, as well.

Chapter 6

"How are you tonight, Natalie?"

She would be a lot better if he didn't seem to be in such a good mood. He was smiling, and his white teeth against his creamy cocoa complexion made his smile even sexier. And then there was the sound of his voice—throaty, husky, just enough to feel like a caress across her heated skin. This man had the ability to stir every nerve-tingling sensation in her body and was doing so. Probably intentionally.

"I'm fine." And then she asked, "What are you doing here?"

He chuckled. "I could ask you the same thing since this is my hangout. I'm here every Friday night unless I'm out of town. My best friend is one of the owners. Considering all of that, it's my turn to ask. What are you doing here?"

Telling herself it would serve no purpose to argue with him, she glanced over at Farrah and quickly recalled her manners. "I'm here with my friend from high school. Farrah, this is Donovan Steele."

Donovan quickly took up the introductions by taking the hand Farrah offered him and said, "It's nice meeting you, Farrah, and I would like the both of you to meet a friend of mine, Xavier Kane."

Pleasantries were exchanged and handshakes were made. "Do you mind if we join you?" Donovan asked.

Natalie was about to say yes, she did mind, but Farrah spoke first. "No, of course not. We'd love for the two of you to join us."

Donovan, Natalie noted, was already pulling out a chair before Farrah had finished issuing the invitation. She also noted that he took the chair closer to her while Xavier sat beside Farrah.

"So, have you ladies ordered yet?" Xavier asked, smiling at everyone but especially at Farrah.

"No, we were checking out the menu. We've never been here before so what do you guys suggest?" Farrah asked. Farrah glanced over at her, and Natalie merely raised an arched brow—her way of sending a silent message that she was not happy. Instead of being bothered by her soundless threat, Farrah merely smiled sweetly over at her, and at that moment Natalie knew Farrah was up to something. That had her worried.

"Since you asked," Donovan said, "for appetizers I would suggest their coconut shrimp if the two of you like seafood."

"We do," Farrah quickly spoke up for the both of them. "And especially shrimp."

Donovan smiled. "Then you're in luck because for the main course it's all the fried shrimp you can eat tonight. They also have a variety of other seafood dishes that are just as delicious."

Natalie pretended to concentrate on the menu. Out of the corner of her eye she saw that Donovan had leaned back in his chair as if listening to the getting-to-know-you conversation between Farrah and Xavier. He was also pretending, because she was fully aware his attention was focused on her.

"How is your aunt?" he asked.

His question made her glance at him over the top of the menu, and she wished she hadn't. Tonight he was sitting under a light fixture that seemed to highlight all those features she had tried forgetting this week but had found herself dreaming about anyway. He had a beautiful pair of eyes. She had noticed them before, but for the first time she allowed herself time to literally drown in their dark depths.

"She's fine. Thanks for asking," she heard herself say before returning her attention back to the menu. Suddenly feeling hot, she reached for her cold glass of water and took a sip.

"Better?"

She glanced over at him again. "Excuse me?"

He smiled. "I asked if you felt better. Did the water quench your thirst? Cool you off?" he leaned over closer and asked silkily.

She stiffened at the underlying assumption. Okay, it was true that she was hot but not necessarily in the way he assumed. Although he was probably right. "As a matter of fact, yes, I do feel better."

At that moment the waitress returned to take their order, and Natalie had a feeling before the night was over she would be drinking plenty of cold water.

Given the way that he and Natalie had parted on Tuesday, if anyone would have told them that on Friday night they would be sitting next to each other sharing a meal he would not have believed them.

She didn't have a lot to say; her friend was the talkative one. She seemed satisfied just to eat and listen. And he was content just to sit and watch her. She was affecting him more than he'd ever imagined any woman capable of doing. In a way that bothered him; actually it frustrated the hell out of him.

The only reason he could come up with for his obsession was the fact that he'd found her in his bed. The same bed no other woman had ever lain in. Relying on his memory of those psych classes he'd taken in college, he knew there had to be an underlying meaning, a valid connection, between his fixation and her in his bed. His theory? She'd stepped into a part of his space that no other woman had ever invaded, and because of it, he was determined to get her back in that bed.

Whatever the reason, it really didn't matter, he inwardly conceded, taking a sip of his beer. Natalie Ford was in his system, buried deep, and he only knew one way to get her out. It was only then that he could move on to other things—specifically, other women. Until then...

"So, your best friend is one of the owners of this place," she said as if finally deciding to make small talk. Xavier and Farrah had just excused themselves to go to the game room to shoot some pool, leaving them alone. He could tell by the way she'd glared at her friend that she hadn't wanted to be left alone with him.

He met her gaze, held it a moment and then said, "Yes. He and several other race car drivers. I would introduce you to Bronson but he left this morning for Florida."

To pursue a woman, Donovan thought, shaking his head. Bronson was the one man he'd figured would never do something as crazy as chasing after a woman, but he'd been proven wrong. No one had really been surprised when Myles Joseph had gotten married earlier that year. After all, they'd heard for years about the woman Myles had left behind in Florida but who still had his heart. But for Bron, a man who could basically have any woman he wanted, to willingly settle on just one—especially one determined not to even give him the time of day—had shocked the hell out of Donovan mainly because Bronson used to be an even more devout player than he was.

She must have felt him staring at her and looked up. A sensuous flutter automatically traveled up his spine. At the same time he was aware of the slight shiver that touched her body although she didn't know he'd seen it. A man as experienced and well-versed in women as he was didn't miss too much of anything.

The lighting in this particular section of the restaurant was low, and her features, especially her eyes, seemed more profound in the candlelight gleaming from the table.

He wondered if they were playing a game, a test of wills, to see who could hold whose gaze the longest. Who would be the first to look away? If that was the case, they could sit here all night. He was a master at seduction, and for her he intended to be on top of his game.

"Are you sure you don't want to go join X and Farrah in the game room?"

She tilted her head but didn't shift her gaze. "I don't know how to play."

"It's not hard. I could teach you. Give you a quickie."

The moment he'd said the word *quickie* he felt the lower part of his body harden, felt a spark ignite in his gut. And he could tell she'd also picked up on that single word, although she'd tried keeping all traces of a reaction from her face. But he had seen the slight widening of her eyes. He had heard her sharp intake of breath and had locked in on the judicious quivering of her lips. He didn't have her just where he wanted her by any means, but he knew his play on words was getting to her, would eventually break down her resistance. But first he had to calm her fears about being uncomfortable with him, while at the same time continuing to let her know where he stood and exactly what he wanted. Suddenly his mind was filled with all those lovemaking positions he had jotted down on a piece of paper earlier in the week.

He took a sip of his beer, licked his lips and still holding her gaze asked, "So, Natalie, are you interested in learning something new?"

Natalie's mouth tightened at the challenge since that's exactly what she saw his question as. Heaven help her, but she was seriously giving his suggestion some thought. Not that she would do anything other than let him teach her how to play pool, of course. But she was very well aware that his mind was on something else. She knew a play on words when she heard it, and if he thought he would get the better of her, he had another thought coming.

"It depends on what I'm learning and who's doing the teaching," she finally replied.

Was it her imagination or did his eyes just darken? Either way, she suddenly fought a tightening in her stomach and a warm feeling between her legs. She broke eye contact with him long enough to reach for her glass of water to take a cool refreshing sip. At the moment, she didn't care what he was thinking.

"What if I promise to make any training session worth your while? And it doesn't have to be learning how to play pool. Is there anything you want to learn how to do for the first time or learn how to do better?" he asked, his voice deep, strong and quietly seductive.

While deep longing and need seemed to wrap her in their strong embrace, Natalie studied his eyes with the same intensity that he was studying hers. She could not deny that something was building inside of her, an urgency she wasn't familiar with or used to.

Her eyes shifted from his eyes to his lips—full, sexy and kissable. It was then she remembered something that Karl had once told her; she couldn't kiss worth a damn. It had only been his opinion but it had still hurt, and she hadn't felt inclined to kiss another man for fear of him rendering that same verdict. Karl's remarks about her kisses had been rather kind compared to the score he'd given her lovemaking skills.

"Tell me," he repeated, his tone remarkably patient, "is there something you wish to learn how to do or learn to do better?"

Natalie swallowed. She had to regain control of her senses or else she would be spilling her guts to him, telling him about every deficiency Karl claimed she had and asking him to prove her ex-lover wrong. Further complicating matters, she would probably go as far as asking him to disprove some men's belief that a woman who possessed a high IQ was nothing more than an intellectual geek who didn't have a sensuous bone in her body.

For one instant she was tempted, but then she realized her limitations with this man. He wanted an affair, which was something she could very well do without. That pushed her to say, "No, there's nothing new I want to learn and nothing I want to improve at, although that doesn't mean I'm perfect in everything."

He continued to look at her as if he was trying to read her mind. "If you're sure…"

"I am."

"All right, but if you ever change your mind, let me know."

She opened her mouth to tell him that wouldn't be happening when Xavier and Farrah returned to the table. She could tell by the smile on her friend's face that she was enjoying Xavier's company.

"Who won?" she asked.

Farrah made a face. "He did, of course. But I think I surprised him."

Xavier laughed. "You most certainly did."

At that moment music from the live band began playing, and before Farrah could settle into her seat, Xavier had captured her hand and was pulling her back to her feet. "Come on, let's dance."

"All right," Farrah said smiling and off they went.

"Let's not allow them to outdo us this time," Donovan said, pushing his chair back and standing up.

Natalie stretched her neck to look up at him. The band was performing a slow number, and she wasn't sure it would be a good idea for them to dance together. The thought of their bodies connecting, rubbing against each other, while the smooth, often sensuous melody of slow music surrounded them was too much to consider.

She opened her mouth to decline when he held out his hand to her. "Don't be afraid of me, Natalie."

His tone was quiet, not challenging nor mocking. There was no way she could explain to him that at the moment her emotions were too strong for a slow dance. "I'm not afraid of you, Mr.—"

"No, not tonight. I am not Mr. Steele tonight, or are you afraid to call me Donovan?"

"I'm not afraid of anything," she said drawing in a controlling breath.

"Then prove it."

A part of her felt she didn't have to prove anything to him, but another part knew she had to prove something to herself. It had taken her months to get over Karl's mental abuse, to build up her self-esteem. She would be the first to admit that other than her co-workers at the university, her students, her professional affiliations and the few neighbors she'd gotten to know, she basically lived a solitary life, and in a few years she would be turning thirty with no plans to change the way she existed.

So, she would get through this dance not for him but for herself. With that thought in mind, she placed her hand in his. The moment their hands touched there was a spontaneous reaction. Fire and passion seemed to rush through her veins and settle in every finger in her hand. She made an attempt to pull her hand away but he held it in a tight grip.

She recalled very little about crossing the room to the dance floor or the smirk she saw on Farrah's face. But she did remember the exact moment Donovan pulled her into his arms, settled her against his rock-solid muscular form to bury her body into his heat and his scent.

He wrapped his arms around her waist, and she instantly responded and then tried to bring some semblance of control to the clamoring going on inside her body. As if it belonged there, her head automatically settled against the firmness of his chest.

A warning alarm went off in her head, a warning she decided not to heed. She rarely stole moments for herself to just chill and relax, enjoy the moment. She'd never taken time to enjoy a man. However, she intended to do so now.

She closed her eyes not wanting to think. Instead she allowed her mind and her senses to drink in the perfection of this moment on the dance floor in the arms of a man who was as handsome as handsome could get.

And he was caring, although such a depiction might be stretching it a bit. For all she knew, his current show of tenderness was just part of his ploy to get inside her panties. But still, the large hand gliding softly across her back was tumbling her into a myriad of sensations and feelings she hadn't counted on. For the moment, she didn't have to think about her class load for the fall and how many lab projects she would have to assign. The only thing she wanted to think about was the here and now in Donovan Steele's arms.

It didn't take long for the music to stop, and with the ending came the return of her senses. She lifted her head from his chest and retreated a step, noting he kept a firm hand on her back. "Let's take a walk," he suggested softly.

"A walk?"

At his nod, she asked, "Where?"

"Outside. For just a minute. I need to catch some fresh air."

She was about to tell him that he didn't need her to go with him to catch some fresh air, but the hand in the center of her back was propelling her forward, through the double doors that led out back. The moment their feet touched the porch, he turned her into his arms to face him.

The moment she looked up into his eyes, she knew. And it had nothing to do with getting fresh air but had everything to do with him getting her.

Donovan tried drawing in a controlling breath and knew it was a waste of time. As calm as he might have looked, he was totally out of control. And he placed the blame solely at Natalie's feet. He wasn't sure if it was the way she was dressed, in a pair of snug-fitting jeans that were molded to her hips and to her backside with flawless precision and the blue blouse that had a few buttons undone to show the rounded curve of her full breasts. Or it could have been the perfume she was wearing that made his body think of hot sex every time he sniffed it. But then it could have been the way she was wearing her hair, pulled back in a cute ponytail with ringlets of curls crowning her face. He felt a naughty urge to remove that rubber band from her hair to see it tumble around her shoulders and then run his fingers through the lustrous locks.

Those were just some of the reasons his heart was now beating erratically in his chest and he had an erection. They were also the reasons his tongue felt thick in his mouth, filled with a greedy desire to mate with hers.

But the main reason he was in such a bad way was how she'd felt in his arms and how with every sway of her hips against him he'd had to take a steadying breath—and each breath only intensified his desire for her. So now, although he was fighting like hell to remain calm, he was feeling every amorous bone in his body tilting over the edge. And it wasn't helping matters the way she was looking up at him, with an expression that said she was waiting for him to do something, even though she didn't have a clue what he'd be doing.

Deciding not to keep her in suspense any longer, he lowered his head to hers, his lips delivering minimum pressure on hers, fighting back his desire to devour them to the full extent. He nibbled at her, used his tongue to lick the corners of her mouth over and over again.

And then under their own will, her lips parted, eased open slightly, enough for his own tongue to slip inside and claim her mouth fully with a possessiveness that had him moaning deep in his throat. And then he confronted something else he knew that would do him in. Her taste.

He felt his erection throb. He felt the tips of her nipples press hard against his shirt, and immediately his hand went into action and drifted lower from her back and beyond the smallness of her waist to settle on the curve of her butt. Amazing and magnificent all rolled into one single piece of hot flesh.

He groaned again, and the tone of the kiss changed. He became greedy as sensations washed through him, sensations he felt all the way down to his toes. He heard her sexy little moan, and he couldn't help wondering how it would feel to share an orgasm with her. To ease his throbbing erection. To press the hard strength of his body inside her all the way to the hilt. To thrust into her with the same rhythm he was using on her mouth.

In his bed.

He wondered if he were to ask whether she would go home with him tonight, sleep in his bed, make love with him as many times as the two of them could handle. All night long sounded pretty damn good right about now. With his hand on her backside he pressed her closer, knowing there was no way she could not feel his hard-on pressed against her stomach.

He slowly pulled his mouth away from hers but it didn't go far. It nibbled around her lips, kissed the corners of her mouth. "Natalie, come home with me tonight," he whispered hotly against her moist lips.

Natalie wasn't sure why she allowed Donovan to kiss her, why even now she wasn't resisting while he continued to kiss her, other than by doing so she was proving Karl wrong. If she couldn't kiss worth a damn like Karl had claimed then someone had forgotten to tell Donovan Steele. He appeared to enjoy locking lips with her as much as she did with him. If he hadn't liked it he wouldn't have let it last so long. He sure wouldn't be still messing around with her mouth the way he was, licking it, greedily nibbling on it like it was better than any candy he'd eaten. And it sure wouldn't have him hard to the extent that she could feel his aroused shaft pressing against the lower part of her.

But more than anything, he wouldn't be asking her to go home with him if she was such an awful kisser. However, she wouldn't be going anywhere with him since she wasn't fooled, not for a second, what he was all about. He wanted a wham, bam, thank you, ma'am, and unfortunately she didn't know the first thing about engaging in short, meaningless affairs. But then the one she thought was going to be a long, meaningful one with Karl had left a bad taste in her mouth…a bad taste she had to admit Donovan had just replaced with a pleasant one.

"Natalie."

He whispered her name again in this deep, husky voice that could make the area between her legs ache, make her panties get wet. She could barely resist the urge to reach out and undo his zipper and take that aroused part of him in her hand to see how the thickness would feel touching it.

How could she think of doing such a thing? She was actually contemplating playing out what her mind had dreamed several times. For the first time in years her body felt ravenous for a man.

Her lips parted with a groan. That was all the opening it seemed that he needed to slide his tongue back into her mouth in an attempt to kiss her into agreeing to go home with him. She wouldn't change her mind about it. But he could try.

And he did.

This time his lips were hard and demanding yet at the same time persuasive. So persuasive that she had to grip his shoulders to keep her knees from buckling beneath her. Never had she been kissed like this, being rendered helpless to do anything but to kiss him back.

At that moment the back door flew open and they quickly pulled apart and glanced over at the intruder. One of the cooks stood in the doorway with an apologetic look on his face. "Oops. Sorry. I just wanted to come out here to grab a smoke." And then just as quickly as he had appeared, he was gone back inside.

But his appearance had given her just enough time to clear her head and make her take a step back. She glanced up at Donovan, met his gaze and swallowed deeply. He had desire in his eyes, deep, dark, seductive, and she knew if she wasn't careful she would be falling under his spell.

"We need to go back inside, as well," she managed to say. "And I won't be going home with you tonight, Donovan." There, she'd said his first name. To call him Mr. Steele now wouldn't make much sense, especially after the torrid kiss they had just shared. So much for keeping things on a professional level. All she could do at this point was make sure things between them didn't escalate any further.

"Well, at least you're not calling me Mr. Steele anymore," he said, mimicking her very thoughts. "And you're sure you don't want to go home with me?"

She tilted up her chin, met his gaze. "Positive. I know when and where to draw the line."

A smile touched the corners of his mouth, and it was so magnetic she almost felt her lips being pulled in its direction. "And I know when and where to turn up the heat, Natalie," he countered.

There was no doubt in her mind that he did. Nor did she doubt that he would. "Donovan," she said, hearing his name a second time and trying to downplay how much she liked saying it. "I think we need to make some decisions."

He lifted a brow. "About what?"

"Whether I should remain your housekeeper. Like I said on Monday, we have a number of other ladies who can—"

"No. And if you're basing your suggestion on the kiss we've shared, forget it."

She glared up at him. "You're being difficult."

He raised what she thought was an arrogant brow and said, "Sweetheart, you've never met a Steele at a time when he's being difficult, and trust me, you wouldn't want to. What I'm being is realistic. I know what I want, just like I know what you want. If I didn't before, I do now. Your kiss said it all. Stroke for stroke. Lick for lick."

She tilted her head back and she knew that defiance—in all its glory—was shining in her eyes. Fine! So she'd never met a Steele being difficult. Well, he was about to meet a Ford when she was. "I'm not one to act mainly on physical attraction. I will not be pushed into an affair with you."

He chuckled. "I don't plan to push, Natalie. I plan to seduce, and when I do, babe, you won't stand a chance."

Natalie inhaled a deep breath. In all her twenty-six years, she had never met a man quite like him. He actually thought he was all that. He figured all he had to do was snap his fingers and they would go tumbling between the sheets. Maybe that was how easy it had been for the other women he'd encountered, but he would see that she was cut from a totally different mold. Because of her mother's wild and reckless ways, she'd grown up with a very sensible mind. She'd done without sex for over five years and could very well do without for another five—even ten or twenty if she had to.

She was about to open her mouth to give him the dressing down that he deserved when he said, "No more arguing tonight, Natalie. Come on, let's go back inside."

A moment of indecision raced through her. Should she not argue anymore with him tonight and let him have the last word, or should she give a blistering retort? She had a feeling any type of rejoinder from her would fall on deaf ears. Besides, her aunt always said that with some people you have to show them rather than tell them. "Fine, let's go inside."

And without waiting for him to say anything, she headed for the door.

"Don't try and get tight-lipped on me now, Nat. What is going on with you and Donovan Steele?"

Natalie glanced over at Farrah. As soon as she had gotten back inside, she had waited only long enough for Farrah to return to the table from off the dance floor with Xavier to announce that she was ready to go.

"Trust me. You don't want to know," she said, glancing out the window at all the bright neon signs they were passing.

"Yes, I do. You tell me about you and Donovan, and I'll tell you about me and Xavier."

Natalie glanced back over at her. "Is there a *you* and Xavier?"

Farrah laughed. "Not the way you make it sound, no.

Like I told you earlier tonight, after what Dustin did I won't ever let another man get close to my heart again."

Natalie nodded. "He seems nice."

"He is, but I was married to a nice man, remember? Or at least we thought he was nice. To some he might still be nice, but Dustin's main problem was that he didn't know how to keep his pants zipped for anyone but his wife."

The bitterness was still there in Farrah's voice, and Natalie wondered if it would ever go away. "Would you see Xavier again if he were to call you?" Natalie asked.

"Depends on the reason. If he calls because he's interested in a long-term affair then, no. But if he contacts me for a booty call, then maybe."

Natalie knew her friend actually felt that way, and that was sad. Farrah had always been the dreamer, the one who wanted marriage and kids, the house with the white picket fence. The one who'd believed in forever after.

"But I won't have to worry about Xavier wanting to pursue anything serious," Farrah said. "I recalled hearing his name before and then I remembered where. He's one of those men in the Bachelors in Demand Club."

Natalie raised a brow. "What's the Bachelors in Demand Club?"

Farrah glanced over at her when the car came to a stop at a traffic light. "I heard some of the single women at work talking about it one day. It seems that years ago, six close friends from Morehouse made a pledge to each other the day before graduation that not only would they stay in touch but they would become godfathers to each other's children, and that the name of each of their first sons would begin with the letters U to Z. They kept their promise, and all six sons became godbrothers to each other. Most of them are now in their late twenties or early thirties. A few years ago, for some reason the six decided to form the Bachelors in Demand Club. In other words they are bachelors in demand, men who aren't interested in settling down until they've sown their wild oats, so to speak. Rumor has it that each of them has his own heartbreak story to tell so now they intend to go through life making sure there isn't a repeat by guarding their heart."

Natalie pushed a curl out of her face and asked, "And you think Xavier is one of these men?"

"Pretty sure of it, but of course I didn't ask him about it to be certain. I do recall that there are two of them living in the Charlotte area, Xavier and a man by the name of Uriel Lassiter. The other four are spread out over the country."

Natalie didn't say anything for a moment and then she asked, "What do you think is Xavier's story?"

The traffic light changed to green and Farrah put the car in gear to begin moving. "Don't know his hang-ups, and I'm not going to worry about what they could be. In addition to being pleasing to the eyes, he was also great company tonight, but that's about it. He didn't suggest that we see each other again so I'm leaving it at that."

She quickly glanced back over at Natalie when traffic slowed again. "Enough talk about Xavier Kane. I want to know about you and Donovan and what went on when the two of you went out back."

Natalie rolled her eyes. Did Farrah not miss anything? "What do you think went on?"

"A quickie perhaps?" Farrah asked with a smirk.

Natalie couldn't help but grin. "No. Sorry to disappoint you."

"Heck, I bet the one who's really disappointed is Donovan Steele. When Xavier and I got back to the table and you announced that you were ready to leave, he actually looked like he could throttle you."

"Whatever."

"At least I know he kissed you," Farrah said, grinning. "And real good."

Natalie frowned. "And how do you know that?"

Now it was Farrah's time to roll her eyes. "Good grief, Nat. Take out your compact and look at yourself. Your lips are still swollen."

Not knowing whether Farrah was teasing or serious, Natalie took out compact and looked at herself in the mirror. "Oh," she said, touching her lips while at the same time feeling a tint of embarrassment touch her cheeks.

"Yes, oh," Farrah said smiling. "But don't worry. Your aunt will probably be asleep when you get home tonight and your lips will be back to normal in the morning."

Natalie closed her compact wondering what Xavier Kane had thought. What had anyone thought who'd seen her lips? Probably the same thing Farrah thought. She had been well and truly kissed. And they were all right. Donovan had kissed her in a way she had never been kissed before and had made her feel things that until tonight had been foreign to her.

"Will you be seeing Donovan again, Nat? So he can kiss you again?"

Natalie tried ignoring the flash of pleasure that shot through her body at that possibility. "That was our first and last kiss. I won't be going out with him, which means the only time we could possibly see each other is when I'm there to clean his house. But those are the days he'll be at work, and I plan to get in and out before he comes home."

"Good luck, Nat."

Natalie glanced over at Farrah. "And why are you wishing me luck?"

"Because I think you're going to need it. You asked me what I know about Donovan, and I didn't finish telling you everything. What I didn't say that I've heard is that he's a man who gets whatever he wants, and tonight the look on his face made it pretty clear that he wants you."

Chapter 7

"Hey, man, you weren't at the top of your game today. What's up with you?"

Donovan shot his brother a frown. "There's nothing wrong with me Morgan, so get off my ass."

Bas dropped down on one of the bleachers and took a huge gulp from his water bottle, and then said, "Sounds like we might need to play another game since that one didn't seem to work out your frustrations, Don."

Donovan glared at his brothers, all three of them. It was a tradition that they play basketball at the gym every Saturday morning to work off any competitive frustrations that might have built up that week. For the four competitive adult males it was their way of not butting heads Monday through Friday at SC.

As much as Donovan didn't want to admit it, Morgan was right. He hadn't been at the top of his game. And it was all Natalie Ford's fault. There was no reason the woman should not have slept with him last night. No reason at all.

"Do you think we need to play another game for your benefit, Donovan?"

Chance's question interrupted Donovan's musings. He glared at his oldest brother. "No."

"Good, because I need to get home and get Alden," Chance responded glancing down at his watch. "Kylie is hosting a baby shower for Lena and Jocelyn, so Alden and I are getting lost for a while."

"Can I get lost with the two of you?" Morgan asked grinning.

"Include me in," Bas readily said. He glanced over at Donovan. "What about you, kid? You want to hang around with a bunch of happily married men?"

"No, I have better things to do with my time. Things married men only dream about doing," Donovan said, using a towel to wipe the sweat off his face.

"Don't be so sure of that, Donovan," Chance said grinning. "We hate to disappoint you, but married men can have just as much fun with their wives as single men have with their girlfriends—probably even more. Why is it that we, the married Steeles, are the ones in a good mood today, while you're the one who still needs a frustration adjustment? Doesn't sound to me like your girlfriend is doing her job."

Donovan's eyes narrowed. "I don't have a girlfriend."

"Hmm, then maybe you should consider getting one," Chance threw over his shoulder as he, Bas and Morgan headed into the locker room, leaving Donovan glaring at their backs.

Donovan stared at the phone for a moment after hanging it up. He could not believe that he had just broken a date with Jean Carroll of all women. Jean, the one who came ready with her own set of handcuffs. And it was Natalie Ford's fault.

Ever since he had kissed her last night, his mind and body had started playing tricks on him. First, he had awakened after a night of dreaming about Natalie with a hard-on that wouldn't go away, even after he'd relieved his bladder and taken a cold shower. He had finally gotten it to act right by the time he had slipped into a T-shirt and jogging pants to meet his brothers for a game of basketball.

Then it had been the taste of her in his mouth that wouldn't fade. He had brushed his teeth, gargled several times and still whenever he smacked his lips he could taste her—that sweet, sensuous taste that had electrified his mouth while kissing her.

And lastly, it was the way she had felt in his arms, how soft and cuddly her butt had felt beneath the palms of his hands. He didn't want to touch another woman quite that way any time soon. His erection was throbbing for just one woman. If he didn't know better he'd think Natalie had cast a spell on him.

He was about to get up and head toward the kitchen when the phone rang. He checked the caller ID to make sure it wasn't Jean calling him back to try and change his mind about their date tonight. He sighed in relief when he saw it was his roommate and friend from college, Uriel Lassiter. Over the years, he and Uriel had maintained a close relationship.

He picked up the phone. "Uri, how are things going, man?"

"I'm still tired from last weekend at the races, but I called to give you some good news."

"What?"

"That publishing company in Colorado that we had our eye on last year is back on the market."

Donovan rubbed his chin thoughtfully. "Hmm, so what do you think?"

Uri chuckled. "I think that if you're still interested, I'll have an updated portfolio on your desk by Monday morning."

"Hey, that'll work because I'm still interested." His cousin Taylor was his wealth-asset manager and she was doing a fantastic job of managing his finances, but right out of college he and Uri had formed their own co-op. They'd started out flipping houses, and it became such a moneymaker that they expanded and began buying small companies and reselling them for a profit. The co-op had become so successful that they had invited a few select others to join in over the years. Uri had left his job as an insurance executive to handle the business end of things on a full-time basis.

Donovan talked to Uri another fifteen minutes before they ended the call. Standing, he stretched his body before heading toward the kitchen to grab a bite to eat. For the first time in years, this was a Saturday night and he didn't have anything to do.

He gave her a slow, sexy smile as he moved toward the bed, his gaze moving over her naked body, seeing everything but zeroing in on the area between her legs. The nipples on her breasts automatically hardened and she released a deep breath. He was pretty potent if the size of his erection was anything to go by. And his muscular body was masculinity at its perfection.

She watched as he began to move closer and closer, and without waiting for him to join her on the bed, she

pulled up and willingly went into his arms. Together they
tumbled back onto the covers.

Natalie's eyes flew open as she inhaled a long, deep
breath. She'd just had another dream about Donovan. She
couldn't believe she was letting him interrupt her sleep
this way. Typically, she wasn't a hot and bothered woman,
but there was something about Donovan that unleashed
a sexual desire she had never encountered before. Never
before had she dreamt about a man making love to her. Or
almost making love to her, she corrected, since so far in
none of her dreams had they finished the act. She would
always wake up moments before their bodies joined as
one.

She inhaled deeply not sure if that was a good thing
or a bad thing. In a way it was bad because she woke up
curious as to how it would have been if they had. And
it was a good thing because a part of her felt she really
should not want to know.

But she did.

And that area between her legs was tingling to find out.

She glanced over at the illuminated clock on the nightstand. It was two in the morning.

Releasing a frustrated sigh, she pushed the covers aside
and eased out of bed. She had brought her laptop with her
to work on a few items for NASA while she was here. Last
year she had received a national award for her work on
stratospheric chemistry and ozone depletion. Her report
had been embraced by the NASA Ames Research Center
which had led to her working closely with the center last
summer. Her findings had been put in a book that was
doing quite well on the academic circuit. Now she was
working again with NASA on a project to increase the
rate of nitrous oxide in the atmosphere.

These studies had been her lifeline. When most people

curled up at night with a good mystery novel, she much
preferred curling up with her laptop to work on chemistry formulas. Very seldom did anything else consume
her mind while working—definitely not the likes of any
man. But Donovan Steele had somehow managed to seep
inside the very essence of her brain that had always been
off-limits. He had managed to invade a space that had always been kept reserved for all her subscripts. Somehow
she needed to get back in sync.

Her aunt needed her so she didn't have the option to
leave Charlotte. And she couldn't have her aunt drop
him as a client because he headed the dependable list.
He paid his bill on time and had few, if any, complaints
or last-minute changes in the schedule that could cause
the agency loss of revenue or manpower. In other words,
he was a model client, one you didn't drop just because
he intended to sleep with the cleaning lady's niece.

Of course, as far as she was concerned, it was wishful
thinking on his part. But still, those dreams wouldn't go
away. And to make matters worse, her conversation with
Farrah last night still weighed heavily on her mind. It
constantly reminded her that it had been years since she'd
been intimate with someone and all because of one man.

At least Donovan had proven that Karl's kissing claim
was wrong. Could he prove the other claims were wrong,
as well? Was she as terrible in the bedroom as Karl had
accused her of being?

As she sat down at the desk in the room and booted up
her laptop, she couldn't help but inwardly call herself a
fool for letting Karl mess with her confidence years ago.

Logging in to her internet account, she went into the
project folder that stored vital information when she
wasn't on-site at the campus lab. And just in case someone tried hacking into her computer base, she had all the

information coded in a way that only she could decipher. Usually when she worked on formulas she felt she was in her element. But tonight she knew deep down she was using her work as an escape.

In fact if she was completely honest with herself she would admit to having used it as a way of escaping for a very long time. At that moment she couldn't help but think about the vast differences between Karl and Donovan. Karl had been too brilliant for his own good and assumed because of his high IQ that everyone else was lacking. It had taken her years to realize that he hadn't been comfortable with his own skin, which was probably why he took great pride in downgrading others.

The complete opposite was true with Donovan. He was arrogant but he was also comfortable in his own skin. It was obvious that he was a man comfortable with who he was and what he represented. Manly, in and out.

Sensations flowed through her stomach when she thought about just how manly he was. That was what had her in a bad way. She had five days to get herself together. On Friday she would return to his home, and she wanted to make sure that she was in and out of there before he got in from work. She had six more weeks to go, and she intended to avoid the man at all costs.

"You're pregnant?" Donovan asked, looking into the smiling face of his cousin Vanessa. She had come into his office first thing Monday morning and dropped the bombshell, and he wanted to make sure he'd heard her correctly.

"Yes," she responded, bubbling all over with joy. "Cameron and I found out this morning. I'm sure Cameron has told Morgan already, and I talked to Mom, Taylor and Cheyenne on my way to work. But since Chance and Bas haven't arrived yet, you're the first here to know."

Feeling happy for his cousin, Donovan stood up and came from behind his desk to give her a huge hug. "I can imagine how happy Cam is," he said.

Vanessa smiled while at the same time wiped tears from her eyes. "He's extremely happy. I think we decided how much we both wanted a child the night we took on the role as babysitters for Little Dane," she said of her best friend Sienna's son. "He was such a joy, and we knew then we wanted a child of our very own."

"Let's just order up one baby this go-round, please," he said grinning. "I don't think the family will be able to handle it if you follow in Cheyenne's footsteps and have multiple babies." Vanessa's sister Cheyenne had given birth to triplets last year.

Vanessa chuckled. "Yes, but you have to admit Chey is doing a grand job with them along with Quade's help. I'm glad he convinced her to make North Carolina their home and use the house she owns in Jamaica as a vacation home."

Donovan nodded, thinking his brothers had all gotten married and now all of his girl cousins—at least the ones living here in Charlotte—were having babies. Taylor and Dominic's son had been born the first of the year.

"So when are you going to settle down, marry and start a family, Donovan?"

His answer was quick. "Never. I happen to like being single."

"I thought I did, too until I fell in love. So beware, your time is coming," she warned.

He frowned. "Don't hold your breath, sweetheart. Just glow in your own happiness and leave mine alone."

Vanessa studied his features. "But just think how much happier you could be curling up with the same person each night, someone who you loved."

"Love? I'll pass. There's not enough love in the world to make me fall in love with any woman."

He went back around his desk and sat down, thinking that he was beginning to feel smothered by all these Steeles who were either getting married or having babies.

Chapter 8

Humming her favorite tune, Natalie unlocked the door to Donovan's home around nine o'clock Friday morning. She had called when she'd been a block away hoping he didn't answer, an indication that he'd left for work already. Her plan was to get in and out before noon just in case he decided to come home for lunch.

Placing her purse down on the sofa she moved toward the hall closet where he kept the cleaning supplies. She was in a good mood. Her aunt's visit to the doctor yesterday had gone well, and during Natalie's restless nights she had been able to finish the first part of the project she was working on with NASA.

She still had her nightly dreams and figured there was no help for them. She was a woman whose needs were letting themselves known, but she was determined to ignore them like she always had, although they were more prevalent now than ever before.

She had finished cleaning the kitchen and had started in the living room, establishing her rhythm as she dusted the furniture while the sound of Ne-Yo blared through her earbuds. She liked music and enjoyed dancing, although her moves on Friday night had been different. She had been on the dance floor with Donovan, in his arms while moving to a slow tune. It had been a long time since she'd been held by a man that way. And even now she was experiencing aftershocks from when he'd taken her outside and kissed her, practically devouring her mouth.

Suddenly there was a tap on her shoulder. Startled, she yelped then spun around only to collide with a wide, solid chest. She jumped back, almost losing her balance in the process while placing her hand over her furiously beating heart. Donovan was standing there in bare feet and wearing a pair of jeans and a shirt that was completely unbuttoned and hung open showing a beautiful muscular chest. He looked as sexy as sin.

She snatched the earbuds from her ears as her gaze shifted from his face and moved lower to where a path of hair trailed from beneath his navel past the waistline of his jeans. She felt the heat of embarrassment rush to her cheeks when she looked back to his face and knew he was aware what area of his body had grabbed most of her attention.

Natalie wished he would button up his shirt and was tempted to suggest that he do so, but this was his house and he had the right to dress as he pleased. She swallowed, momentarily at a loss for words until she remembered he had just scared her out of her wits. She opened her mouth to speak, but he beat her to it.

"I tried to get your attention to let you know I was here, but you were too busy dusting and dancing around." He smiled. "And those were some pretty good moves, by the way."

She frowned, not in the mood for any of his humor. "What are you doing here, Donovan?"

A slow, deliberate smile touched his lips. "I live here."

She rolled her eyes. "Why aren't you at work?"

"I'm working at home today."

"Why?"

"Because I felt like it."

She wished she could throw her feather duster at him.

"I have a lot of work to do, and I promise to stay out of your way. The only reason I came downstairs was to grab a piece of fruit."

"So you won't be leaving for work today?" she asked.

"No."

"I wish you would have contacted the agency to let us know. We could have changed your cleaning to another day," she said.

"Why would you want to do that?"

She gave what she thought was an obvious answer. "You're here."

He lifted a brow. "Is that supposed to be a problem?"

She tilted her head while crossing her arms over her chest, leveling him with her gaze before asking smartly, "What do you think?"

A rumble of a chuckle erupted from his throat. "I think you're making too much of it. I'm upstairs in my office out of your way, so you can skip that room today. I have work to do and I'm sure you do, as well."

Her eyes narrowed as she watched him turn and sprint up the stairs.

Donovan closed his office door behind him, leaned against it and let out a deep sigh. He was not accustomed to retreating from a woman that he wanted, a woman he intended to have. But Natalie had him rethinking his strategy, polishing his approach and modifying his tactics—and all with one final goal in mind. Seduction. He intended to get her back in his bed and make love to her, all day and all night. Only then would he effectively get her out of his system and move on.

With the Product Trade Show in a few months, he had too much work to do to let any one woman tie up his time with her continued rejections. He should be seducing her to his will, making love to her until he got enough, and once he got his fill he would walk away.

And not look back.

In the meantime, he would do whatever he had to do. If she thought she would eventually wear out his patience, then she was wrong. The woman had definitely underestimated his determination.

He drew in a deep breath. How could any one woman look so desirable? Those shorts and tank top she was wearing definitely weren't helping his libido. It was a different outfit from last week but it was hard for him to ignore just how good she looked in it. When he had come down the stairs and seen her move her body in a provocative dance while dusting, he had immediately gotten turned on. Hell, if he was totally honest with himself, he would admit that he had been turned on since waking up that morning and knowing that she would be coming today.

Now that she was here, the first thing he planned to do was break through her defenses. That was something he'd done Saturday night when they had shared a very intense kiss, a kiss that had blood rushing through his veins. A kiss that had kept him awake that night, fueling his lust.

Almost a week later and his lust was still getting fueled. Sighing again he went to sit behind his desk. He had brought work home. He had reports to read, and he had a conference call with Morgan and his research and development team in a half hour regarding Gleeve-Ware.

Donovan checked his watch. He would concentrate on work for a while, and then his full focus and attention would shift to Natalie.

Natalie was on her knees in the master bathroom, scrubbing the tile around the shower when she heard the door open to the office where Donovan had been sequestered for the past two hours.

She hoped if he was headed downstairs he wouldn't enter his bedroom but would keep moving down the stairs. She only had his bedroom left to clean and much preferred that he wasn't around while she did so, considering he'd found her asleep in his bed the last time she cleaned in here.

She listened to the steady footsteps and knew the moment he had entered the room and was standing there, in the open doorway, staring down at her. She might be imagining things, but she could feel the intensity of his gaze on her backside. So, let him look if that's what he wanted to do. She would just ignore him.

She tried. However, when seconds ticked into minutes and he didn't say anything, she shifted around, leaned back on her haunches and looked up at him. "Did you want something?"

She realized her mistake too late. The darkening of his eyes told her she was asking the one question better left unanswered. He evidently didn't agree and responded, "Yes."

Natalie swallowed deeply. She could just imagine what he wanted. The way he was looking at her said it all, but she knew the polite thing to do was to ask anyway, just in case she was wrong. After all, he was the client. "And how can I help you?" She grimaced thinking that question didn't sound much better.

"You can start off by getting off the floor. Does it really take all of that?" he asked.

His response wasn't what she expected, and she rolled her eyes, while at the same time trying to ignore how sexy he looked leaning in the doorway. "You're paying for cleaning services," she stated.

Donovan frowned. She didn't have to remind him, yet he still thought it didn't take all of that. He thought of how she'd looked on her knees with her backside tooted up in a cute way toward him. A tingle of desire had oozed through his stomach as if he hadn't been filled with wanting her already. It had been like adding kerosene to a flame already out of control when he thought about all the things he would like to do to that behind.

"Mr. Steele?"

His thoughts were pulled back at the sound of her voice. Then he concentrated on what she'd just called him. "You're starting that back up?"

"Starting what back up?"

"Calling me Mr. Steele."

"That's your name," she said, getting to her feet and pulling off the plastic gloves and tossing them into the trash can before washing her hands.

"For you, it's not. I'm Donovan. I thought we had straightened that issue out on Friday."

She dried her hands. "Had we?"

"I was certain that we had," he said, watching her put

his cleaning supplies back under the cabinet and appreciating how she bent over to do so. He glanced around and sniffed the air. The placed looked clean and smelled good.

"Then I guess it's gone back to being business as usual," she said smartly, coming to a stop in front of him and tilting her head back to look up at him.

He wanted to show her just how wrong she was by pulling her into his arms and kissing that agitated look off her face.

"Excuse me."

It was then that he realized she needed to get by and expected him to move out of he way. It would have been the gentlemanly thing to do. But all he could think about was that his bed was less than six feet behind him, and he would love to take her over there, strip her naked and then make love to her.

"You want me to move?" he asked, knowing she did but liking her standing in front of him, closer than she even realized. Her scent was sensual and set off a flutter of desire in his stomach. And like Friday night, her hair was pulled back in a cute ponytail with ringlets of curls crowning her face.

On sudden impulse, he reached out, and with a flick of his wrist, while ignoring the look on surprise on her face he sent her hair tumbling around her shoulders.

"What do you think you're doing?" she asked, indignant.

Her indignation was something he could handle. What he couldn't handle—at least not much longer—was desiring her so much he could no longer think straight. His erection was growing heavier by the minute. "I just did something I was tempted to do Friday night. I wanted to see your hair tumble around your shoulders, and then I wanted to do this." He reached out and ran his fingers through the lustrous strands.

It was a bold move, and she stared up at him like he'd lost his mind. Maybe he had. While she seemed at a loss for words, totally stunned, he figured he might as well push the envelope and take things to another level.

On that decision, he lowered his mouth to hers and swept his tongue between her startled, parted lips. She moaned, which triggered his own groan, and his erection grew harder. Like the last time, this kiss was hot. It was also something desperate. Their tongues mingled and then began dueling, and in the process he felt his senses get shredded to pieces. When he felt her trembling, he wrapped his arms around her, needing to hold her as much as he wanted to believe she needed to be held.

He could tell she was too overtaken by the kiss to notice he was slowly walking backward, pulling her with him. And he continued to kiss her provocatively, without any restraints, not thinking of letting up and with a hunger that astounded him. He claimed her mouth with a free-for-all kiss as all those dreams that had tortured him this past week came surging back with megaforce. When the back of his legs touched his bed, he deepened the kiss and pulled her closer to him, gathered her tighter into his arms. Together they went tumbling backward, actually free-falling into the sheets.

But he didn't let up. In fact, knowing he had her where he wanted her actually made him sort of crazy, and it wasn't helping that she was responding to him with a passion that he felt all through his body.

He deepened the kiss to drown farther in the sweet recesses of her mouth, but that wasn't enough. He wanted to touch her all over, taste her until he got enough...which wouldn't be any time soon. She had become an itch he needed to scratch—but way below the surface. The stark reality of just how much he wanted her loomed in the back of his mind, but he couldn't deal with that now. For him to desire any woman to this degree was unheard of, totally crazy. Insane. And he simply refused to admit to the possibility that he, the master of seduction, was the one getting seduced.

And with that possibility flashing through his mind like a bold warning, he suddenly freed her mouth to draw back to look at her, observe her in silence. Her eyes were closed, she was breathing heavily and her lips looked liked they'd been thoroughly kissed. But the main thought in his mind, what he considered as a major accomplishment, was that she was in his bed, flat on her back beneath him.

He knew at that moment that she was fully aware, just like he was, of what could or would happen next. Here, in this bed with her, a bed he'd never shared with another woman, the thought of which had fueled his lust since meeting her.

She slowly opened her eyes and looked up at him. He looked back and what he saw was a beautiful woman whose hair was tumbled around a flushed face, and whose honey-brown eyes had a degree of warmth that symbolized a level of passion he rarely saw in a woman.

Enthralled, he held her gaze, wanting more than anything to get naked and sink into the deep, luscious depths of her. On his tongue he tasted her, even while imagining another taste of her he wanted to become familiar with. Her intimate taste. The thought of doing so made his sex surge, and he knew she felt it when it did.

"You're trying to seduce me," she whispered as fragments of passion exploded bit by bit, inch by inch in his stomach from the sound of her voice. He was getting turned on even more seeing her lips move.

There was only one response he could give her, one of complete honesty. "Yes, I am trying to seduce you." And then helpless to do or say anything else at that moment, he lowered his head to kiss her again.

Chapter 9

This, Natalie thought, was a deliberate seduction, as calculated as it could get. And just as shrewd. Vastly intimate. There was no doubt in her mind that he was a master at it, had years of experience and had sharpened his skills just for her.

His tongue was having a field day with hers, driving her to the brink of madness by bringing forth ideas in her mind that she'd never considered before. A part of her desperately wanted to believe that his kissing her this way was a waste of his time, that she was immune to such seductive tactics. But another part of her, the one that was enjoying the feel of his tongue mating with hers, wasn't sure just how strong her willpower was.

Over the years she had encountered a number of men who'd wanted to take her to bed to not only dissect her mind but to break it down in the process. They'd felt threatened by her intellect, and when she refused to let their ruse work, they began feeling intimidated and saw her as a bother. She had handled their rebuff by displaying her competency even more. As far as she was concerned, not wanting to accept her as an equal was their problem and not hers. As a result, she'd been labeled problematic. That, coupled with her desire not to ever encounter a man close to Karl in attitude and temperament, had forced her long ago to take herself out of the game. That was one of the reasons she thought Donovan Steele was as lethal as they came.

There was nothing typical with him. Everything seemed out of the ordinary. She was way out of her league with him, beyond her limited experience with men.

Through the heat consuming her with their kiss, she was instantly aware of him lifting her tank top and knew she should resist him. Instead she moaned deep in her throat when she felt a tingling sensation flood her belly beneath the warmth of the hand he placed on her stomach. Moments later, his hand moved, shifting upward and unfastening the front clasp of her bra. And then, without missing a beat, his mouth followed to her breast.

That's when she lost touch with reality and lost her grip on any control she had. His tongue stroked her nipples and she became engrossed, totally, irrefutably absorbed in the sensations ripping through her. He was devouring her breasts with the same greed he had bestowed on her lips. Each suck and lick to her nipples elicited a deep pull in the area between her legs. She suddenly felt sensitive there as sensations deluged her. And at that moment she felt the need to whisper his name.

"Donovan."

Donovan was fully aware of the moment Natalie said his name, and the passionate tone had his erection throbbing. He wanted to hear her say it again, but right on the

verge of having an orgasm. Her scent was hot and enticing, and was getting to him in the most primitive way.

He moved his hand to the elastic waistband of her
shorts and without giving himself much time to think
about what he was doing, he eased his hand inside and
quickly moved past the silky panties she was wearing,
going straight to her feminine mound.

The moment he touched her there, his fingers making
contact with her wetness, he heard her release a litany of
deep moans. The sound, as well as her intimate response
to the area he was touching, drove him over the edge.
His desire to taste her became overwhelming. Elemental.

Giving a final thorough lick to her breasts, he quickly
went into action by pulling her shorts and panties down
her legs. Before she could deny him access, he lowered
his head between her thighs, and his mouth went straight
to the heated folds of her femininity.

On instinct her hips thrust upward, and he grabbed
her hips to hold her there, needing to devour her with a
hunger that focused his senses on this particular part of
her body. With practiced licks and precise flicks of his
tongue, he tasted the invigorating sweetness of her blazing fire, her steamy passion, and he didn't plan to let up
any time soon—not until he made her come.

That didn't take long. When her thighs began trembling, he knew she was about ready to detonate. Every
nerve and muscle in his body was poised, prepared and
primed for the experience. And when it happened and she
screamed out his name, he continued the intimate kiss,
claiming this part of her as his. Intense pride filled his
chest at the sounds of pleasure she was making. He held
nothing back and neither did she. The next time, he si-
lently vowed, he wanted to be staring her in the eyes when
it happened. And there *would* be a next time.

He continued kissing her while at the same time giving her body time to recover. It was only then that he withdrew his mouth, eased back up her panties and shorts before sliding up her body to look at her. Her eyes had a glazed look, and she seemed momentarily at a loss for words.

She moved her mouth as if she was going to say something, and he quickly decided that he wasn't ready for her to say anything. So he leaned closer, bent his head. Her lips parted and he slid in his tongue and kissed her, sharing her own taste with her. Moments later he reluctantly pulled his mouth away.

She looked up at him. "That should not have happened, Donovan."

He figured she would say something like that. "But it did. You and I both wanted it to happen. We enjoyed it. Admit it," he countered.

Natalie wasn't ready to admit anything. Her mind had practically turned to mush, and she couldn't even think straight. She'd arrived this morning to clean his house, not to be the recipient of mouth sex. And especially not to the point at which it had made her scream. She was the most disciplined person she knew, and she had screamed.

"Admit it, Natalie."

She narrowed her gaze and wished she could ignore what had happened between them. Ignore him and that smile curving his lips. So she glanced around the room and said, "I need to finish up in here and leave."

The smile curving his lips widened. "So that's the way you want to play?"

She had news for him; she hadn't wanted to play at all and had been doing just fine remaining on the sidelines. He and his naughty tongue had definitely thrown a monkey wrench into things. The vivid memory of his head between her legs had her blushing.

"Like I said, today was a mistake," she reemphasized.

Donovan quirked a dark brow and recognized her ploy for what it was. She still wasn't ready to acknowledge what was between them, what he wasn't about to let slide by. She had said she thought today was a mistake, but she hadn't said it wouldn't happen again. Evidently she had missed that fact and he was glad.

Deciding he had pushed her buttons enough for one day, he eased into a sitting position. He glanced around the room when she got up off the bed. "There's nothing else you need to do in here," he said.

He noted she tried looking everywhere but at him when she said, "There's plenty I need to do. I haven't dusted, vacuumed the floor or changed the linen," she said briskly.

"Don't worry about dusting or vacuuming in here today. And I don't want my linen changed, Natalie. Your scent is absorbed into the sheets, and I want it to stay that way for a while."

She tilted her head and met his gaze. The air suddenly became charged again. Intimate. Sexually explosive. She moistened her lips with the tip of her tongue before replying, "Suit yourself."

He gave her a slight smile. "I did and I'm extremely satisfied."

She began backing up toward the door. "Well, if you're sure you don't want me to do anything else in here, then I'll be going."

"I'm sure."

"And I'll be contacting you sometime next week to discuss my replacement," she added firmly.

"No, you won't. There will be no replacement, Natalie."

Her eyes widened and then glared. "Surely you don't

think that I can continue to be your housekeeper after what happened here today."

"I'm afraid that's exactly what I think. It's what I know."

He knew his words sounded arrogant, more than a little presumptuous and selfishly cocky. He watched her body stiffen and would not have been surprised if she had thrown some object off his dresser at him. Instead, after glaring at him for a second, she moved closer to his bedroom door.

"If you get restless and edgy later, just come back. I'll be here. And if not tonight, I'm available any night. If I'm not here just let yourself in." Donovan heard himself give the invite, and a part of him couldn't believe he'd actually done so.

Instead of answering him, she rushed out of the bedroom and hurried down the stairs.

Just as well, he thought, easing off the bed. Other than his cousins and sisters-in-law, no other woman had ever been given unlimited access to his home. It was evident that he had it bad for Natalie. But he inwardly assured himself he could handle this temporary bout of madness and that the only reason he was being so indulging with her, so abnormally reckless, was because they had only five weeks left to be together. He was confident by the time her aunt was back on her feet and had resumed her position as his housekeeper that he would have worked Natalie out of his system.

The sound of the front door opening and closing signaled that she was gone.

"How did things go today, Nat?"

Natalie glanced over at Aunt Earline as they sat together at the dinner table. The question was one her aunt asked every day, and Natalie thought that if she was truthful and told her just how things went today, Earline Darwin would be mortified. Aunt Earline must never know that although she and Donovan hadn't gone all the way, she had been in his bed and together they had practically made kissing an art form, and that in the end he had lapped her up pretty good. Right into an orgasm. Even now her inner thighs felt extremely warm, and she had to hold her legs together real tight just thinking about what Donovan had done between them.

She plastered a smile on her face. "Everything was okay." There. She'd given a short answer. That was that.

Apparently not when Aunt Earline further asked. "So this change in days works for Donovan Steele?"

She couldn't help recalling how he'd been conveniently home when she had gotten there and the somewhat smug look on his face when she'd left. "Yes, apparently it does. I was in and out of there in no time." *But not before he got me on my back and did some scandalous things to my body.*

"That's good."

Yes, she inwardly admitted, although she didn't want to do so. It had been good. Too good. The inner workings of her body were now clamoring for a repeat performance. The unshakable Dr. Natalie Ford had been shaken to the core.

An hour or so later she was pacing around the house like a caged bird that needed its freedom. She and Farrah had planned to go out again tonight, somewhere other than the Racetrack Café, but Farrah had canceled their plans because she had to work late.

It was early but Aunt Earline had already retired for the night. She planned to watch her all-time favorite movie, *Dirty Dancing,* for the umpteenth time before going to sleep. Her aunt had encouraged her to go out and have some fun tonight, with or without Farrah.

As she paced, she couldn't get Donovan's invitation out of her mind. "If you get restless and edgy later, just come back. I'll be here."

The man definitely had some arrogant nerves in his body. What woman would even think about taking him up on his offer? Natalie dropped her face in the palms of her hands and ashamedly admitted that *she* was.

She slumped down on the sofa. Should she really be ashamed? What was wrong if she did consider having a fling with him? At least she knew where he stood. She definitely wasn't looking for love and neither was he. In fact if she was thinking about a fling then he would be the perfect candidate. He was probably an expert at flings.

In addition to that, she didn't have to worry about him getting all crazy on her if he somehow found out she was a chemistry professor at an Ivy League university instead of a bona fide cleaning woman, not if the relationship was sexual and nothing more. And when it was over— for however long it lasted, which would be no more than five more weeks at best—she would return to Princeton, New Jersey, feeling renewed and energized. Farrah had been right Friday night. A meaningless fling with Donovan would give her a new attitude.

She was twenty-six, a professional, a woman who deserved to indulge in a fling or two. She had realized a long time ago that it would be close to difficult to find a man willing to come into her world, and most of the male counterparts she'd found were too stuffy and boring. None had ever come close to attracting her attention the way Donovan had. Besides, he could be the one to prove whether or not Karl's verdict on her skill as a bed partner was true. A part of her always wondered. Donovan had proved Karl wrong with the kissing, and she couldn't help wonder if he would prove the other part false, as well.

Natalie eased to her feet. There was only one way to find out.

Donovan tightened his grip on the telephone in his hand. "Okay, Morgan, thanks for keeping me in the loop. We figured sooner or later word of what we were doing would leak out," he said. "We're good as long as the trade secrets don't get into the wrong hands."

"You're right," Morgan said. "But I'll feel a lot better when that Product Trade Show is over."

Donovan talked to Morgan a few minutes longer before hanging up the phone. For any business, the exploitation of trade secrets was a serious matter and the protection of them was complicated at best, especially when chemical formulas were involved. One of their competitors had again tried obtaining information, which meant SC was determined more than ever to make sure that didn't happen.

He glanced at his watch and saw it was close to eight. He had thought about going over to the Racetrack Café for a while to hang out with Bronson and the guys, but for some reason he wasn't in the mood. What he was in the mood for was sex. Even now, his manhood was twitching for release of the most elemental and primitive kind. He had a list of women who were amenable to a booty call tonight, but he only wanted one particular woman. Natalie.

He sucked in a deep, satisfying breath when he recalled how earlier that day he had gone down on her, but not before feasting on her breasts. Every muscle and every fiber in his body had been attuned to her.

He then pulled in a frustrated breath at the thought that what he'd done today might have scared her away.

He didn't want to think about the possibility that he had pushed her to the limit, and she would make good on her threat to send in a replacement, or better yet, convince her aunt to drop him as a client.

With nothing better to do, he was about to head back to his office to finish reading the Gleeve-Ware report he'd started on earlier when there was a knock at his door. Thinking it was probably Bronson, Myles or Uri dropping by, he crossed the room in his bare feet and opened the door. His jaw almost dropped.

Standing at his door was Natalie, and she was wearing a black miniskirt and a low-cut white blouse that clearly showed she wasn't wearing a bra. Not that she needed one with her full and round breasts.

He took in her outfit and how gorgeous her legs looked in it before returning his gaze back to her face. He stared at her while his manhood, which had been twitching earlier, broke out into a full-fledged throb.

She stared back before saying in what he thought was a soft, ultra sexy voice, "You said to come back if I got to feeling restless and edgy." She took a minute to breathe in before adding. "And I'm here."

Chapter 10

Everything happened in such rapid succession that Natalie wasn't sure who made the first move. The thing she did remember was Donovan reaching out and pulling her inside and slamming the door shut behind her. After that she recalled the moment he lowered his mouth to hers, which resulted in a heated exchange of lips and tongues. And she did remember the moment he swept her into his arms to carry her up the stairs, not breaking the kiss in the process.

But what was kind of fuzzy was what brought on what was happening now. He had stopped halfway up the stairs and lowered her bottom to the step to lift up her skirt where he then proceeded to rip off her drenched panties.

"I need one quick taste," he said huskily and with an intensity that she felt all the way to her toes. And before she could blink, he had knelt between her legs and lowered his head to penetrate her deeply with his tongue.

She fought for control, but the only thing she could do was grab the wood railing, totally helpless against the myriad of sensations that shot through her as he used his tongue to stroke her wetter. She was on the verge of exploding when he suddenly withdrew his mouth and stood up, towering over her.

"Can't wait to make it upstairs," he said, lowering his zipper and then quickly removing his jeans and briefs. He held on to his jeans long enough to pull out a condom packet that he ripped opened with his teeth. Then he tossed the jeans away.

Through passion-glazed eyes, she watched as he put the condom on his engorged shaft. She'd never seen Karl perform such a task, and watching Donovan prepare himself inflamed her senses. He was big, a lot bigger than Karl, which had her wondering if perhaps she should be worried.

She quickly dismissed the notion from her mind when he dropped back down to his knees in front of her. He then reached out and grabbed hold of her hips in a firm grip, lifting her bottom off the step while inching his body toward hers, opening her legs wider in the process.

A quiver of anticipation raced through every part of her body. When he leaned closer and began easing his shaft inside of her, holding her gaze while doing so, for one unguarded moment she allowed herself to let go.

Donovan, however struggled for control. It took everything within him not to thrust hard in the wake of the excruciating pleasure being inside of her brought. Never would he have thought that passing through territory he had never been in before would give him such exquisite pleasure. Her body was tight but was stretching to accommodate his size. And his hands continued to hold tight to her hips while tilting up her bottom for a more perfect fit.

A soft whimper, which he hoped was the result of intense pleasure, escaped from between her lips when he finally reached the hilt. Then she threw her head back and released an intense feminine groan. The sound was electrifying and sent shivers down his spine, propelling him to move within her.

He began riding her slowly at first, absorbing her scent through his nostrils and fighting to retain control while waves of intense pleasure washed over him with pulsating intensity.

Adrenaline rushed forward, gushed through his veins and swelled his erection inside her even more. He heard her breath catch at the same moment her inner muscles clamped down on him. They tightened, holding his shaft hostage, and he nearly lost control. He regained it and began moving within her again with a possessiveness he'd never demonstrated toward any other woman.

He lifted her hips higher off the step, not allowing his hold to ease even the slightest bit while establishing a rhythm that taunted her and challenged him. He heard her moans, and they threatened to drive him over the edge as he thrusted back and forth inside of her with lightning speed. And she was meeting his thrusts, stroke for stroke. They were making love on the stairs of all places, but the place didn't matter—only the outcome.

And the outcome was more than he'd bargained for. He released a guttural moan just seconds before she screamed his name as she was plunged into a state of ecstasy. Her orgasm ignited bursts of pleasure within him at the same time his body shattered in a huge explosion of its own. She clung to him and wrapped her feet securely around his back. Desire sank deep into his pores, and he felt himself being thrown into some unknown abyss.

He bent his head to capture her lips. Refusing to leave

her body, he kept a firm grip on her hips as sensations rammed through him nonstop until his release left him feeling drained but completely satisfied. He knew he was in deep trouble when, moments later, he started getting hard again.

This time he wanted to make love to her in a bed. His bed. He withdrew from her body, gathered her into his arms and carried her the rest of the way up the stairs.

Natalie wondered if she would ever be able to move again. She seriously doubted it. After making love with Donovan on—of all places—the stairs, he had brought her up to his bedroom where he finished undressing her and had made love to her all over again. He made love as intensely and thoroughly as he probably did everything else, and more than once he had whispered in a deep, husky voice just how much he enjoyed it. She believed he had, which meant Karl had said all those things only to hurt her.

"You're awake from your nap," that same deep, husky voice said now.

She found the strength to glance over at Donovan. He was lying beside her, one of his legs was thrown over hers as if holding her captive. She couldn't miss the fact that they were both naked. After making love with him, she had drifted off to sleep, too exhausted to keep her eyes open any longer. To most people dozing at this hour would equate to retiring for the night, but since she intended to sleep in her bed at her aunt's house, Donovan was right: she had only taken a nap. A much needed one. But now she was wide awake.

She glanced over at the clock on his nightstand. "It's late. I need go."

"Not yet. We need to talk."

Tension settled in the back of her neck. She had a feeling she knew what he wanted to talk about. Given his reputation, she was surprised they hadn't had the discussion before he'd taken her on the stairs. "I already know what you want to say," she said.

"Do you?"

"Yes. You don't want me to assume what we've done means anything of substance and that you aren't the marrying kind and prefer short, meaningless affairs."

He stared at her and didn't say anything for a moment. Then he asked, "Knowing all of that, where does it leave you?"

She couldn't help but smile. Lord help him, but the man actually thought every woman would be forever scarred because of his rejection. "That leaves me with what I want most, too."

"Which is?"

"A good life without any man cluttering it up."

His brow rose before he responded. "I recall you saying you'd taken a break from men."

"It's more than a break, actually," she said, widening her smile. "I'm no more interested in a serious involvement with a man than you are with a woman, so you can lower your guard and sleep peacefully tonight."

He would, Donovan thought, although for some reason it bothered him that she could so easily wipe him off. Why did she have to be so accepting of his stance on affairs? Why did he feel so annoyed by hers?

She made a move to get up, but his leg hindered her progress. She frowned. "Do you mind?"

Yes, he did mind—about a number of things that he really wasn't even sure about. One thing was for certain, though. He didn't like how easy it was for her to dust off what they'd just shared. Maybe he should be relieved that she wasn't the clingy type, that she was mature enough to engage in a meaningless affair and know how to move on. That she wouldn't be entertaining any lingering side effects from it. But still. He had made her scream—several times. He'd given her multiple orgasms. Her leg print was probably a permanent imprint in his back. He had been inside her so much tonight that his shaft would probably be suffering from withdrawals starting tomorrow. He was beginning to get awfully pissed that the one woman who affected him like none other was acting as if he hadn't made an impression on her at all, lasting or otherwise.

"Donovan?"

He met her gaze deciding she had underestimated a Steele. "Yes?"

"Would you move your leg?"

"I don't think so." Instead of moving his leg, he shifted his body to straddle her.

Her gaze narrowed up at him. "And just what do you think you're doing?"

"About to get some more of you."

"And if I don't want to give you more?"

An arrogant smile touched the corners of his lips. "Then it's up to me to convince you that you really do. Seduction is my specialty." He leaned down and captured her mouth with his.

Just that quick desire spiked up his spine. When she began kissing him back with a need just as ravenous as his, he knew he had her convinced. But that wasn't enough. Not by a long shot. He wanted to hear her scream some more.

Moments later he broke their kiss only to trail his mouth down the base of her neck toward her chest and greedily latched onto a breast. Both were pretty, shaped with perfection, appealing to any man's eyes, definitely a tasty treat to his tongue. As he worked that tongue to her breasts, taking the nipples in his mouth, sucking for a while and then using his tongue to give unadulterated pleasure, her moans began coming and the sound taunted his control. He knew women well enough to know she was almost over the edge, and he wouldn't be happy until he was tumbling off the cliff with her.

Feeling a heady rush of pleasure at the sensuous state he now had her in, he moved away from her breasts to trek further south when, in one heck of a surprising move and totally catching him off guard, she slid from beneath him and with a shove to his chest sent him tumbling on his back. He blinked to find she was now the one straddling him.

"Are you ready to be punished, Donovan?" she asked.

He swallowed deeply. "Depends on how you plan to dish it out." The look in her eyes warned him that whatever she had in mind would probably be brutal and that he was in for a lot of suffering.

"So, you want some more of me, huh?"

He couldn't tell a lie although admitting such a thing could be tantamount to acknowledging something he'd rather keep to himself. He was becoming addicted to her. "As much of you as I can get and then some," he said, actually with little regret.

"And you think you can handle whatever I give you?" she asked as her hand skittered over his chest. His reaction to her touch was instantaneous, and he watched a haughty smile touch her lips when his shaft got even more engorged. Before he could answer, she swept her hand downward and captured him in a firm, yet painless, grip.

He suppressed the urge to groan, but that didn't stop the shiver of arousal that shot through his body knowing she held him in her hand. He barely got the words out in a strained voice. "Yes, I can handle it," he said, when in fact he wasn't so sure.

"Um, I hope for your sake that you can." And then in a quick and surprising move, she lowered her head and went down on him.

Chapter 11

There was no way she was going to let him know she was a novice at this, Natalie thought, using her mouth in a way she'd only heard about and hoping she was doing it right. Apparently she was, if the way his fingers were clutching her hair was anything to go by.

And then there was the way he was breathing—ragged, choppy and at times uneven while making a number of groaning sounds. She tried to ignore all of that while her tongue did all the things to him she would secretly admit to fantasizing about in her nightly dreams. She had never considered doing this to Karl or any man, but with Donovan there was something about his scent that enticed her to sample his taste.

"I can't take any more," he said in a jagged breath while at the same time clenching her shoulders in an attempt to pry her enthusiastic mouth from him. He pulled her up over his body, and lifting his head from the pillow he met her mouth, taking it with a greedy intent and a voracious hunger.

Supported by an arm on both sides of him, Natalie let him plunder her mouth at an insatiable will, returning the kiss with the same fervor that he was delivering, not believing that after all they'd done already that night they still were going strong with no thoughts of letting up. At least she wasn't, and by the way he was avidly feeding on her mouth, neither was he.

But she wasn't through with him yet. She was determined to make her brand of torture bittersweet. Ignoring his protest, she pulled away from the heated kiss and licked her lips before saying. "You weren't supposed to do that."

He flashed a wicked grin that held no remorse. "Sorry about that."

"I'm accepting no apologies. You're going to pay."

The look he gave her was one of incredulity. "With more torture?"

She smiled sweetly. "I'll let you decide. Now hand me a condom, please."

Shifting slightly, he reached over into the nightstand and pulled out a condom packet and ripped it open with his teeth. He handed the condom to her before tossing the opened foil packet to join the others littering the floor.

"Look at the mess you've made," she said, grinning. "I'm sure your housekeeper thinks you're a slob."

Donovan couldn't help but chuckle. "Then I'm going to have to convince her otherwise," he said, trying to retain his composure as he watched her sheath his erection and noted how fascinated she seemed with the entire process. That wouldn't be so bad if the hands touching his shaft weren't so warm. They reminded him of the warmth of her mouth on him.

"There." Finished with the task, she then eased her body in place over his and centered her feminine mound right over the head of his engorged member.

"That's right, sweetheart, take me on home," he said in a tormented breath. "Lead me right inside of you."

"Um, what if I say that I don't want to?"

He arched a brow. "Then I would say you've got to be kidding."

She couldn't help but smile at that. "No, I'm not kidding," she said, while deliberating easing the lower part of her body down a little so that her feminine mound could lightly brush against his shaft. He sucked in a deep breath at the fleeting contact.

"What's the matter, Donovan? Can't you handle it? Can't you handle me?"

For the first time in his life, Donovan actually wondered if perhaps there was a woman he couldn't handle, and he was flat on his back staring up at her. The thought of that was absurd, ludicrous at best. But then, he was the one who seemed to be suffering, and she appeared to be having the time of her life increasing his misery.

Donovan inwardly sighed. His mama always told him you could catch more flies with honey than with vinegar, and he was willing to put it to the test. He reached out and wrapped his arms around her neck. "Are you sure you want to keep agonizing me?" he asked, lifting his head up to lick the corners of her mouth with his tongue. He then used that same tongue to trace the outline of her lips and watched the simmering fire he was igniting in her gaze.

He took a breast into his hand, fondled the nipple with his fingertips. He sensed the moment when passion instead of punishment took over her mind. Now it was time to put the icing on the cake by seducing her with words of what he wanted to do to her and how he intended to do it. He spoke deliberately low but made sure he could be heard as well as understood. He was explicit, described everything in detail, every single position, giving her an unscripted idea of just what his plans were for her. His words were breaking through. He could tell by the darkening of her eyes and the unsteady sound of her breathing. He could also tell by her feminine scent. His words had lubricated her even more.

She tipped her head back and stared at him, and he wondered if she realized that her lower body had inched down a little, and that the blunt head of his shaft had penetrated her somewhat. It was inching forward, stretching her again to make the intimate connection possible.

He continued talking, making promises, while their bodies connected. But that didn't stop him from cupping her backside in his hand to hold her in place, or locking his leg around her just in case she had a change of heart. Their bodies were now locked, and he didn't intend on letting her go anywhere. With that thought in his mind, he lifted his hips off the bed to fill her even more.

Now it was time to deliver on all those promises he'd made.

Before she had time to react, he thrust in hard, almost retreated and then thrust in hard again. In response she moved her body to the rhythm he'd set, riding him as hard as he needed to be ridden. Never had he made love to a woman with so much intensity, an all-out assault on delivering passion to her on a silver platter. The same way she was delivering it to him.

Somehow with their vigorous entanglements they had changed positions, and he was now the one on top. He tilted her hips at an angle to drive relentlessly into her. He was never into drama, but as far as he was concerned, you couldn't get any more dramatic than this. This was lovemaking at its finest, the kind that made multiple orgasms commonplace. She was bringing something out of him that he'd not known had been inside of him.

"Donovan!"

No matter how many times he heard her scream his name, it always did something to him. It triggered his engorged sex locked inside of her to react. To explode in one hell of a release. She grabbed hold of his shoulders. Her nails dug deep into his shoulder blades, but pain wasn't the dominant factor right now. The passionate flames burning through his veins were. And even as he felt her come apart in his arms and he exploded in an orgasm that had rocked him to the core, he couldn't stop thrusting into her, needing this. Needing her.

He quickly pushed away the thought that he would need any woman, no matter how enjoyable the lovemaking was. Tomorrow he would deal with all these foreign emotions swamping him now. But not tonight. Tonight he wanted only to deal with this. Immeasurable pleasure.

Natalie glanced at the clock as she eased out of bed from under Donovan's arms. She was glad her aunt was a sound sleeper and probably didn't know that it was close to five in the morning and she hadn't returned home yet.

She glanced around for her clothes and then quickly remembered Donovan had stripped her naked on the stairs. The memories had sensuous shivers moving up her spine. The man had more passion in his little toe than Karl had had in his entire body. Donovan may be a tad arrogant, but the man could certainly deliver. He had made good on all those promises he had whispered and had introduced her to lovemaking positions she hadn't known existed. Her body was sore but she felt good. She couldn't even count the number of orgasms she'd had tonight. To say she had made up for lost time was an understatement.

She wrapped her arms around her naked body as she glanced over at Donovan sleeping peacefully in the bed he'd found her in that day. Leaning back over to the bed, she brushed a kiss first on his cheek and then his lips, being careful not to wake him.

One and done.

At least she knew where she stood with Donovan. He had spelled out his expectations—or lack of them—loud and clear. One night of extreme pleasure and it was done, never to be repeated. A one-night stand, nothing more, nothing less. He had definitely gotten rid of her restlessness and had taken the edge off. She would always have memories of their night together.

Backing away from the bed, she turned to slip out the door but not before glancing back over her shoulder at him. Whether she wanted him to or not, Donovan had a special place in her heart.

Donovan nearly jumped straight up out of bed at the ringing of the phone. With hazy eyes, he glanced around the room trying to recall what day it was. Then he remembered. It was Saturday morning.

He leaned over and snatched the phone out of its cradle. "Hello?"

"Hey, we thought we'd get together and have breakfast at your place before heading over to the gym," his brother Morgan said in the phone. "I'll make a pit stop at Mary's Diner. You want the usual?"

Donovan raked a hand down his face in an attempt to wipe the sleep from his eyes. "Yes, the usual will be fine." Then his stomach growled, and he remembered the intense sexual activities from the night before. "Make it a double order for me, though."

He hung up the phone and slumped back down in bed. Jeeze. What a night. If there was such a thing as having a sexual hangover then this was it. He shifted his body to look down at the floor. There were condom packets everywhere. Damn. How many of the blasted things had he used? If he thought all that action last night was a result of a dream, then he was looking at viable proof that it wasn't. And just when had Natalie left? How could he have slept through her slipping out of bed? She at least deserved a walk to the car.

Knowing he needed to get up since his brothers were on their way over, he eased out of bed and headed toward the bathroom. And he needed to get rid of any evidence of his activities of the night before or his brothers would never let him live it down. He chuckled thinking that they actually thought they could share such things with a wife. Not that he thought any of his sisters-in-laws were prudes by any means, but still. Some of the positions he had introduced Natalie to last night were scandalous at best. But she seemed to have enjoyed them as much as he had.

A half hour later he had showered, dressed, discarded all those used condom packets off his bedroom floor and picked up his clothes that had been scattered all over the staircase.

By the time his brothers arrived, he figured he looked like a man well-rested with no signs of what had happened the night before. Apparently not. Bas walked in, took one look at him and said, "Damn, Donovan, what's with all those passion marks on your neck? Rough night, huh, kid? No wonder you wanted a double order."

Donovan rolled his eyes. Leave it to Bas to notice such things. Of course Chance and Morgan were now giving him their full attention. "Don't worry about any marks on my neck," he growled, taking the breakfast bag from Bas's hands.

Still, he couldn't help walking over to the mirror on his foyer wall to take a look for himself. Bas was right. He did have passion marks all over his neck. Usually he was the giver of such things, never the recipient.

"Evidently you had a wild one on your hands last night," Bas said, laughing, clearly amused.

Normally, any jokes his brothers made about his conquests wouldn't bother him in the least, but since his bed partner had been Natalie, for some reason it did bother him. Yes, she had been wild but he had driven her to it. He had been relentless to see how often he could make her come. "I'd rather not discuss it," he said to the three and saw the surprised look in their gazes.

"Okay." Chance nodded. "If that's how it is."

In all honesty, Donovan wasn't sure just how it was, but until he sorted everything out in his head, he merely said, "Yes, that's how it is." And then he tacked on something he figured he would never, ever say about a woman. "She's different."

Farrah raised a brow as she gazed across the table at Natalie. "That's the fourth time you've yawned in fifteen minutes. Didn't you get any sleep last night?"

Natalie couldn't help but shift in her seat under her friend's intense stare. And she was sure she was blushing. Instead of answering, she tried changing the subject. "Do you remember Gail Porter, that girl who used to sit in the back of the class and not talk to anyone, until that day she got up in front of the class to do her report and told us her parents had taken her to a nudist camp? I wonder what happened to her."

Farrah simply smiled over the top of her menu. "I understand she moved away, got married and now has some top-level job at the White House."

A surprised expression touched Natalie's features. "Really?" she asked, incredulously.

With a straight face, Farrah simply answered, "No."

Natalie narrowed her eyes. "That was mean."

Farrah laughed out loud. "What's mean is you not answering my question about your lack of sleep last night. Now are you ready to tell me where you went last night?"

No, she wasn't. Instead, Natalie took a sip of her water. Luckily, her aunt had been asleep when she had returned home this morning just moments before the delivery boy had thrown the paper in the yard. Without taking a shower, she had crawled between the sheets with the scent of Donovan still clinging to her skin and memories of their lovemaking in her mind.

"Natalie?"

Knowing Farrah wouldn't let up until she was given an answer, she looked across the table, met her inquisitive gaze and said, "I was with Donovan."

Farrah lifted a brow. "And?"

"And what?"

Farrah rolled her eyes. "What do you mean you were with him? Did the two of you meet up at the Racetrack Café? Did you go out on a date someplace else? Did you—"

"I was at his house. I spent the night."

The corners of Farrah's lips curled up in a smile. "By spending the night do you mean you slept in a guest room? Did the two of you sit on the sofa all night watching movies and holding hands? Did the—"

"We slept together," an annoyed Natalie leaned over and whispered curtly. Farrah liked getting details. "But we didn't get much sleep for mating like rabbits all night long." She narrowed her gaze and snapped, "Satisfied?"

A smirk of a grin appeared on Farrah's face. "Forget about me. Are *you* satisfied?"

Natalie blinked, not expecting Farrah's retort. Natalie leaned back in her chair. Relaxed. Settled. Not as sore as she had been that morning. She couldn't help but smile. "Yes, I'm satisfied. Extremely. Exceedingly. Enormously. Tre—"

"Cut! I got the picture."

Natalie knew that Farrah really didn't. There was no way anyone could get the picture of what had gone on inside Donovan's bedroom last night, and in a way that was a good thing. The picture would have been erotic, X-rated at best.

"So he was worth all those years of holding out?" Farrah asked.

She nodded. "Every single moment I spent with my head in a book, working on projects and trying hard to forget men existed. Yes, he was worth it."

Farrah smiled. "Then I'm happy you got the experience. When will you see him again?"

Natalie shook her head. "I might see him again but not that way. What we shared last night was a fling—a one-night fling. It won't be repeated. That's what we both agreed."

Farrah didn't say anything for a moment and then said. "That might be easier said than done, Nat."

Natalie was glad the waitress appeared at that moment to take their order or she would have been forced to admit Farrah was right.

Donovan pulled his damp T-shirt over his head and tossed it in the dirty-clothes hamper. Today the basketball game between him and his brothers had been brutal. Evidently there had been a lot of frustrations to unleash. Still, he felt good. Not that he'd had to work off much masculine energy since he'd done so last night.

He left the laundry room and walked into the kitchen where he immediately headed for the refrigerator and opened it up. He pulled the beer from the six-pack Uri had left a few weeks ago, popped the tab and then took a long pleasurable gulp.

A satisfied smile touched his moist lips, which he wiped with the back of his hand. Life couldn't be better. Then he glanced around the kitchen and thought that life couldn't be lonelier.

He frowned, wondering where in the hell that thought had come from. A lonely Steele? How could that be when he had brothers and cousins living in the same city? And he could always catch a flight to Phoenix, Chicago, Miami or Boston and visit his relatives there.

He went over to the window and glanced out. What would it be like to come home to a house he shared with someone? Not just someone, but the woman with whom he'd spent the night in bed. Could he even imagine building a life with one woman, building a family and having children, building his own dynasty like his brothers were doing?

It didn't take a rocket scientist to see they were happy, had eased into the roles of husbands and family men without a hitch. He'd always figured he was different, didn't want the things they did and totally enjoyed his freedom. So why was he even considering otherwise?

He took another gulp of beer, emptying the can. Moving away from the window, he placed the empty can on the counter. He'd promised Bron and the guys that he would drop by the café tonight since he hadn't shown up last night, as was the norm. But he had no regrets. Last night he was here in bed with a woman that still had his heart pounding each time he thought about how his body had plummeted into multiple orgasms while inside of her.

Natalie had shown him, proven beyond a shadow of a doubt that no two women were the same. He had met his match, and even after making love to her last night, he wanted her again.

Chapter 12

Natalie sat at the desk in her aunt's office as she worked on the schedules for next week. It had been a week since she had made love to Donovan in his huge bed. She hadn't heard from him, but she hadn't really expected any contact. Like she had told Farrah, she and Donovan fully understood each other. He didn't want anything beyond what they'd shared Friday night and neither did she.

She'd been keeping herself pretty busy. The agency had taken on three new employees, and she'd been busy working them into the schedule. Her aunt's doctor visit this week indicated she was healing nicely, and Natalie was happy for that. So it was her opinion that life was good.

But that didn't mean she didn't have those dreams each night in which Donovan had a starring role. And now that she knew how it felt to make love with a man who was just as giving as he was taking, she knew he had tilted the scales and she doubted another man would ever affect her the way he had. She'd been dealing with elements of chemistry since she'd won her first science fair in the eighth grade, but Donovan had the ability to ignite a totally different kind of chemistry, the type she wasn't accustomed to dealing with. And then there were those funny little feelings that would start fluttering around her heart whenever she thought of him. They were feelings that could grow into something more than she wanted them to be. They were feelings that had more to do with the human anatomy than with chemistry.

She'd gone to pull one of the client's records from the file cabinet when her cell phone rang. She quickly picked it up. "Yes?"

"Dr. Ford, this is Dr. Stanley."

Natalie lifted her brow in surprise. Dr. Miriam Stanley headed the global study of the troposphere for NASA, and they had worked closely on various projects over the past two years. "Dr. Stanley, this is a pleasant surprise. Is anything wrong?"

"No, everything is fine. However, I was hoping I could request your assistance on short notice."

"In what way?" Natalie asked, leaning back on the desk. She was already reviewing formulas for NASA that could imply a continental pollution source for industrial emissions.

"We will be hosting a number of government officials on the Princeton campus next Friday, and we were wondering if you could be included on a panel for a discussion on global warming."

Next Friday? Natalie nibbled on her bottom lip trying to determine if it could work. Her aunt was doing fine so flying back to Princeton for a couple of days wouldn't be so bad. She could fly out Thursday night and fly back Saturday morning. "Yes, I'd love to participate."

"Thank you. I'll e-mail you a number of the key discussion topics," Dr. Stanley said.

A few minutes later Natalie hung up the phone, still smiling. She knew her name had been tossed about as a possible person who could sit on the Global Warming Commission. To do so would be an outstanding accomplishment. She needed to start jotting down the key points she intended to discuss, and hopefully, doing so would keep her mind occupied for a while.

Donovan released a deep breath when he heard the sound of the front door opening. That meant Natalie had arrived for the weekly cleaning of his home. And again he'd taken a work-at-home day. He hated admitting that he'd been looking forward to this day all week long—and had even contemplated calling her during the week. But then he would remember their agreement. What they'd shared had been a one-night stand and nothing more.

Still, he couldn't discount the fact that she had been on his mind every day and night. Since he had yet to change his bed linen, he drifted to sleep breathing in her scent and filled with passionate memories of their one night together.

The thought that Natalie was downstairs had his shaft hard. He could, and he would now admit that he had it bad for her. The last seven days had been pure torture. More torturous than the agony she'd delivered that night. But in the end she had relieved his suffering in a way that could still make him tremble inside. She had delivered continuous pleasure over and over again—for someone not as experienced in the art of lovemaking like most women he'd encountered. He had surmised as much from the way her eyes lit up when they tried varied positions. He had introduced her to a lot of things in that one night and like a zealous and devoted student, she had been eager to learn.

And then there had been the way she had taken him into her mouth. What she'd lacked in skill she had made up in enthusiasm. Just thinking about what she did and how she'd done it made his shaft even more engorged and sent a rush of desire racing through his body.

Leaving his office he went into his bedroom and began stripping off his clothes deciding what he needed more than anything before coming face-to-face with Natalie was a cold shower. Otherwise, he wouldn't have any control and would be tempted to try to seduce her for another day and night of pleasure as soon as he set eyes on her.

A short while later, he stepped out of the shower and grabbed a huge velour towel to dry off. He heard the sound of her moving around right outside his bedroom door and wondered what she would think if she were to see him just as he was. He wouldn't shock her with his nakedness but would come close. With just a towel wrapped tightly around his middle, he crossed the room and flung the door open.

The woman let out a scream.

It wasn't Natalie. Collecting his wits, he ducked behind his bedroom door, cracking it open with just enough space to talk through it. She was still screaming and he knew he had to take hold of the situation by first calming the woman down. He could just imagine what she was thinking seeing a half-naked man suddenly appear.

"Would you please calm down, lady? I live here," he said with a little irritation in his voice. The woman appeared to be in her late fifties. Where the hell was Natalie?

"You're Mr. Steele?" she asked once she'd finally stopped screaming.

"Yes, I'm Mr. Steele."

"Sorry that I screamed like that but you scared me half to death. The agency said you would be at work."

Donovan knew that in all essence there was no reason for him not to be at work. He had worked at home last Friday with the clear intent of seducing Natalie. Now that he'd slept with her there was no reason for him not to have gone into the office today. But deep down he knew there was a reason. He had deliberately stayed home with the sheer purpose of seducing her again. Sleeping with her hadn't gotten her out of his system.

"I decided to work at home today. And where is my regular cleaning lady?" he asked, annoyed.

"Ms. Darwin hurt her ankle, sir."

Out of respect for the woman's age, he tried not rolling his eyes. She was old enough to be his mother. It was bad enough she'd seen him undressed, and now she was referring to him as *sir*. Natalie was going to pay dearly for this little fiasco. "I'm aware of that," he said, trying to keep his voice calm. The woman had been frightened enough. "I'm talking about the woman who's cleaned this place for the past two weeks. I believe she's Ms. Darwin's niece."

"I don't know. I'm new. I was told to come here today. Is there a problem, sir?"

"No, there isn't a problem." *At least not with you. But I will deal with Natalie Ford. She will pay dearly for this, especially since I told her I didn't want another house-keeper.*

"Please continue your cleaning," he said, plastering a smile on his face. "I'm going to get dressed, and I'll be out of your way shortly."

"Yes, sir."

He closed the door. If Natalie thought she'd seen the last of him then she had another thought coming.

* * *

Placing a client's file aside, Natalie reached out and answered the phone on the desk. "Special Touch Housekeeping Agency."

"You've underestimated me, Natalie."

Natalie pulled in a deep breath. She recognized the deep, husky voice and knew the identity of the man on the other end of the call. And he didn't sound like a happy camper. "Is there a problem, Mr. Steele?"

He didn't say anything, but she swore she could hear his teeth gnashing. And then. "What have I told you about calling me Mr. Steele? If I remember correctly, I was Donovan last Friday night."

He'd been a number of things last Friday night, she thought. He was also the best lover she'd ever had, granted she hadn't had many to compare him with, but the one comparison she could make pushed him off the charts. "Mr. Steele, is there a reason you called?" From his tone she knew there was.

"Yes, there is a reason. I thought we understood that no one but you or your aunt would be responsible for the cleaning of my home."

Natalie smiled politely, although he couldn't see it. She had received good news earlier from Dr. Stanley and had no intention of letting him ruin her day. "As you know, my aunt is recuperating, and considering our relationship—specifically what happened between us last Friday night—there was no way I could return to your home."

"Did I force you to have sex with me, Natalie?"

His question came as a surprise. "No, of course not."

"So there's no way you can claim there was any type of sexual harassment involved, right?"

"Right, and neither am I trying to. But the key word is *involved*. We slept together, of our own free will, but we slept together nonetheless, and in doing so, we've taken our relationship from a professional one to a personal one," she tried pointing out.

"If I remember, we didn't get much sleep that night. And one has nothing to do with the other. And you were forewarned what would happen if my requests weren't followed. I enjoy my privacy and—"

"For crying out loud, Donovan," she said, annoyed enough at this point to forego professionalism. "Ms. Harris is old enough to be your mother. She has been married for over twenty years and is not aspiring to become a cougar. She's harmless. And we did a thorough background check. The woman is trustworthy."

"Probably. But still, you defied my wishes. Meet with me at the Racetrack Café at seven tonight to discuss the situation."

Natalie frowned. "There's nothing to discuss."

"I think there is. You've made me an unhappy client. If you check the files of several of your other clients—namely Jeremy Simpkins, Harrell Kelly, Uriel Lassiter, Myles Joseph and Colin Ashford, they are clients based on my recommendations and referrals. All it would take is a phone call from me and they'll drop the Special Touch Housekeeping Agency like a hot potato."

Natalie's frown deepened, and she sat up straight in her chair. "You wouldn't do that."

"I wouldn't suggest that you try me. I'll see you tonight at seven."

Natalie slammed down the phone.

Just who does he think he is? How dare he!

She began pacing the floor. He would ruin her aunt's company just because he couldn't have things his way? So, he wanted to meet with her to discuss things. Fine. She'd meet with him, and she'd give him a piece of her mind.

* * *

Donovan drew in a long breath as he hung up the phone. Desperate times called for desperate measures, and he'd just displayed a sign of a desperate man. Of course he wouldn't do anything to hurt Natalie's aunt's business but she didn't have to know that. Besides, he couldn't think of any other way to get her to meet with him tonight. And because he didn't want her to think it was all about sex, he'd decided it would be best if they met someplace other than his home.

Now that was another mystery to be solved—that it wasn't all about sex. The intensity of their coming together had been as miraculous as it could get. Even when he hadn't wanted to think about it, when he hadn't wanted memories to invade his brain and accumulate in his mind, they had anyway.

But now he wanted to get to know the woman who had him biting at the bits. What was there about her that he found obsessive? Why had he denied himself the opportunity to bed Jean Carroll on more than one occasion because the thought of being inside any woman's body other than Natalie's, was a turnoff?

Admittedly, he was as intrigued as he was horny, and tonight he was determined to place his highly sexual state on the back burner to find out more about Natalie Ford.

Chapter 13

Still furious, Natalie walked into the Racetrack Café and glanced around. It didn't take her long to spot Donovan standing at the bar talking to another man. Her lips set in a frown, her eyes narrowed to a slit, she walked up to Donovan, got right in his face and snapped, "I'm here. Are you satisfied?"

"If he's not, I most definitely can be."

Natalie turned to the man standing with Donovan at the same time his gaze traveled over her features. She inhaled deeply. Did all Donovan's acquaintances have to look so breathtakingly handsome?

She opened her mouth to apologize for her brash manner when Donovan spoke up. "Get lost, Uri. She's spoken for. But I guess I will introduce the two of you. Natalie, this is Uriel Lassiter, a good friend of mine."

Natalie summoned a smile while extending her hand. "Sorry for being rude. Nice meeting you, Uriel."

"Apology accepted, and please call me Uri. And it's nice meeting you, as well, Natalie. Now I guess I better get lost before Donovan forgets just what close friends we are." And then after giving her one last smile, Uriel walked off.

"Come on, let's get a table," Donovan said, recapturing her thoughts while grabbing his beer off the counter.

"You may want to make it someplace private so others won't overhear what I have to say to you," she warned.

He lifted a speculative brow. "Sounds serious."

She gave him an exasperated look. "And you didn't think that it would be?"

"A man can hope. Come on, I know just the place."

She followed as he weaved through the crowd, and before she noticed just where he was leading her, he'd opened a door and ushered her inside a room that appeared to be someone's office. "This is my friend Bronson's office," he said. "He won't be here for another hour or so."

She turned on him with narrowed eyes. "I didn't mean *this* private, Donovan."

"Relax, I promise not to bite. Have a seat and get whatever is bothering you off your chest."

At that moment he looked at her chest. Except for the lone button undone at the top, her blouse was decent enough. She had dressed appropriately, not wanting to give him any ideas. But right now her nipples were hardened peaks pressing through the material of her blouse. And the man didn't miss seeing anything.

The darkening of his eyes made her pulse rate increase. "Okay, I'll sit," she said. Anything to shift his attention from her chest.

"So what's on your mind, Natalie?"

She rolled her eyes. "You tell me since you're the one who demanded this meeting."

"Oh, yes, the issue of my replacement for a cleaning lady. I expected you to come today."

"And I told you why I didn't. We slept together so I can no longer work for you. You can stand here all day and all night and say that you employ my aunt not me, but it doesn't matter. In my mind I've slept with the boss."

"And that bothers you?"

"Yes, it bothers me." She wished he would sit down. *He* was bothering her. Standing made her totally aware of how sexy he looked.

As if he'd read her mind, he moved away from the door to lean against the edge of the desk, facing her. He slipped his hand into his pockets, and her gaze shifted first to his pockets and then to his zipper. Did the man always have to look aroused around her?

"How long have you worked for the agency?" he asked.

"Why?" She returned her gaze back to his face, certain that a blush flamed her features.

"Because you're a very beautiful woman, which accounts for the reason I'm very attracted to you," he said. "And I find it odd that none of your other male clients have ever hit on you before."

The sound of his deep and husky voice sent shivers down her spine. She inhaled deeply, thinking that now would be a good time to tell him that she did not clean houses for a living and that she was a chemistry professor at an Ivy League university. But a part of her couldn't risk that he would act like all the others and feel threatened by her achievements and see her as an intellectual geek.

"Natalie?"

"Well, believe it. All my other clients have been nothing but gentlemen."

He chuckled. "And I'm sure none of them ever found you in their bed. But still, I'm curious as to how long you've been with the agency."

She shrugged. "Long enough."

"And before that what did you do?"

She wondered why he was asking these questions. "I was in school," she said, which wasn't an all-out lie.

"Do you ever plan to go back to school?"

That question was easy enough to answer. "Yes, I plan to go back in the fall."

He nodded. "That's good, because I'm a proponent of education."

He didn't have to know it but so was she.

"How far along are you in your studies?"

She tilted her head back and looked at him. "Why all the questions?"

"I'm trying to get to know you."

His response surprised her. "Why?"

Her question was a good one, Donovan thought. Why did he want to know more about Natalie Ford? And especially now when he needed to stay focused on SC. They'd had another meeting in Chance's office yesterday, and Bas had reported that suspicious activities were still going on and that the Gleeve-Ware formula was still in high demand.

"Donovan?"

His thoughts were pulled back to Natalie. He knew it was insane, totally unreasonable to want a woman so much, but then, maybe it wasn't. That night his body had responded to her in a way it had never responded to another woman, and even now he wanted to pull her into his arms and kiss her with a passion that had his heart racing. But the wanting, the desire, had to be mutual. It had to be what she wanted too. There was only one way to find out. She had resisted his seduction once, only to come to him on her own terms. Would she do so again? It was a challenge worth probing.

"Yes?" he finally answered.

"Why do you want to get to know me?"

"Come here and find out," he said, straightening his stance and holding out his hand in an invitation.

Natalie sucked in a deep breath, disgusted with the way her body was responding to Donovan. She moistened her lips before saying in a not so convincing tone of voice, "No."

"You sure you're not as hungry to taste me the way I'm hungry to taste you? I want to taste your breasts again, put a nipple in my mouth and make love to it with my tongue. And then the icing on the cake is when I taste you there in your very feminine place. You don't know how much I want to savor that particular spot again."

The man was killing her softly with his words. She could feel herself getting drenched between the legs. "We agreed that night was supposed to be one and done. It was just a one-night fling," she heard herself say in a breathless voice.

"Did we? Was it? And don't we have the right to change our minds if it suits our needs, our purposes and our wants?" he asked.

Should they change their minds? she wondered. And who would they hurt if they did? They were both adults who had to answer to no one. And there was no way she could deny how much she enjoyed him as a lover. So why was she fighting her desire for him? Farrah thought a full-fledged affair with him was just the thing Natalie needed, an affair that lasted as long as they wanted it to, at least until she returned to Princeton. And like Farrah had said, denying him was easier said than done.

But then there were those emotions she was trying hard to keep at bay, emotions that swamped her whenever she thought about him, or was around him, like now. She studied his features and saw the intensity in his penetrating gaze. Yes, they had the right to change their minds. She eased out of the chair and took a step toward him and placed her hand in his.

"No promises," he said, pulling her closer into his arms.

She understood and she agreed. "No promises," she repeated, realizing at that moment with a sinking heart that she was slowly drowning in emotions he was stirring within her. Emotions she'd never felt for another man since Karl. Emotions she couldn't fight any longer.

A moan flowed from her throat when he captured her mouth with his. Immediately his taste set her entire body on fire. When he deepened the kiss with a greediness that she felt all the way to her toes, she wrapped her arms around his neck and pressed her body closer to his. The bulge behind his zipper was potent, an indication of where things could be headed, and she knew if he led her there she would hopelessly follow.

The ring of his cell phone had them pulling apart, but he didn't intend to let her go too far. He held on to her elbow while fishing the cell phone out of his jeans pocket.

"Hello." His tone was one of irritation at being interrupted.

She watched as his eyes widened and heard the concern in his voice when he asked, "When?"

And then he responded to whatever he was told by saying. "I'm on my way."

He quickly put his phone back in the pocket of his jeans and then said to her. "Come on, let's go." He had a firm grip on her hand.

She blinked. "Go where?" she asked, while letting him guide her out of the door with him.

He glanced over his shoulder. "To the hospital. One of my sisters-in-law, Jocelyn, has been rushed there."

Natalie stopped in her tracks, which caused him to do the same. Her eyes widened in alarm. "Oh, my goodness. What happened? What's wrong?"

A smile touched the corner of his lips when he said, "She's having a baby."

The rush was on, and within minutes Natalie found herself strapped into Donovan's two-seat Mercedes convertible sports car. He was racing down the interstate, most of the time not adhering to the speed limit, but she couldn't help love the feel of her hair blowing in the wind. Adrenaline was flowing through her veins. At the moment she didn't want to think about how much emission from his car was probably polluting the air. Nor did she want to consider just how the emissions were being absorbed in the upper troposphere at mid-to-high latitudes.

She glanced over at Donovan. What had he been thinking to ask her to come with him to the hospital where his family would probably be gathered? How was he going to explain her presence?

One thing she knew about being placed in unexpected

situations was to be prepared whenever possible. That propelled her to say, "Tell me about your family, Donovan."

He glanced briefly at her and smiled before turning his attention back to the road. "That's a tall order since the Steele family is a big one. My grandparents had six sons and two daughters. Two sons moved from Arizona and settled here back in the sixties and started the Steele Corporation; a manufacturing company. My father was one of the brothers, and my uncle was the other. Uncle Harold died of lung cancer around twelve years ago, leaving his share of the company to his wife and three daughters, Vanessa, Taylor and Cheyenne. My father retired eight years ago and left his share to his four sons. My brother Chance is the oldest and CEO. Sebastian, whom we call Bas, is the second oldest and is a troubleshooter in the company. Morgan is brother number three and heads the research and development department, and I'm the youngest. I manage the product administration department."

She nodded. "Your cousins, the three females, do they work for the company, as well?"

"Only Vanessa. She's over our PR department. Taylor and Cheyenne have seats on the board of directors. Taylor is a wealth asset manager and she and her husband live in DC, and Cheyenne is a retired model. She and her husband live here in Charlotte and had triplets less than a year ago, so she's pretty busy these days."

Natalie chuckled. "I can imagine. Triplets. Wow. So who's having a baby now?"

"Bas's wife, Jocelyn. But in another month we'll be doing this scene again since Morgan's wife, Lena, is expecting, as well and is due to deliver in September."

He continued talking about his family, and Natalie heard the warm affection in his voice. He also told her about his other cousins that were spread all over the country and how close all Steeles were. She drew in a deep breath when he pulled into the hospital's parking lot, still not sure why he had asked her to come. But at the moment she couldn't think of any other place she'd rather be than with him.

Chapter 14

The miracle of life always amazed him, Donovan thought, gazing into the very happy and smiling face of his brother as he held his newborn baby daughter in his arms. They had named the baby Susan after Jocelyn's favorite aunt. Jocelyn's sister Leah, who'd given birth to a daughter earlier that year, had named her daughter after their mother who'd passed away when Jocelyn and Leah had been young girls.

Donovan glanced over at Natalie who was sitting in a chair next to Kylie, Vanessa and a very pregnant Lena. All four women, who'd had tears in their eyes earlier were talking to Jocelyn, who looked rather relaxed after giving birth. He looked at Chance and Morgan to find both of them staring at him instead of their newborn niece, and he knew why. They were still in shock. This was the first time he'd ever brought a woman to a family gathering of any kind, and they were curious as to why. Hell, he was trying to figure out the answer to that question himself. All he knew was that at the time he'd gotten the call from Chance to tell him that Bas was on his way to the hospital with Jocelyn, he hadn't been ready to let Natalie out of his sight.

And then he'd talked her ears off while en route to the hospital. She'd asked about his family, and that had opened him up. Instead of sticking to the basic facts, he had ended up telling her practically everything, including information about the Steele brothers' weekly Saturday morning on the basketball court. He also told her about how Chance had met Kylie, how Bas had met Jocelyn; how relentlessly Morgan had pursued Lena; how far Cameron had gone in his pursuit of Vanessa and about Cheyenne and the triplets. Never had he shared so much information about his family to any woman.

And then there were the women in his family who'd latched onto Natalie the moment he had walked into the waiting room with her by his side. He hadn't had to introduce them since they had proceeded to introduce themselves. It didn't take a rocket scientist to see they were just as shocked as his brothers.

"So what do you think about my baby girl, Donovan?"

He glanced over at Bas, who was still wearing a proud smile even after the nurse had come to take baby Susan and place her back Jocelyn's arms. "She looks tiny, not as tiny as Athena, Venus and Troy looked when they were born, of course," he said of Cheyenne's triplets who'd been born premature. "But she's still a tiny thing."

He chuckled. "It will be fun watching her grow up, and I hope when she gets older that you don't play the big bad wolf of a daddy to her dates."

Bas grinned. "I won't unless she brings home a man like her uncle Donovan."

It was a joke but Bas's words were still on Donovan's mind when he and Natalie walked out of the hospital to the parking lot. Was he really that bad that his own brother found his ways with women despicable? Bas hadn't been an angel before he'd married Jocelyn. In fact his engagement to Cassandra Tisdale gave Donovan the shudders every time he thought about it. No one knew how glad the family had been when Bas had come to his senses and broken off the engagement.

But still, Donovan knew that he would be the first to admit that none of his brothers had ever been die-hard bachelors, at least not with the concentration that he had. He was a proud playa card member. Did he have any regrets about keeping one close to his hip? Not really. But he knew that although he'd claimed otherwise, eventually one day he would settle down. He had just refused to think about doing so.

Deciding to switch gears, he thought back on his family, namely his parents. They had arrived, and thanks to his mother, there was no chance of anyone else holding the baby any time soon. And after introducing Natalie to his parents, he wanted to get her out of here before his mother could start the inquisition, which he figured would happen had they lingered.

After pulling out of the parking lot and merging with traffic, he glanced over at Natalie. She was quiet, and he couldn't help wondering what she was thinking. Like everyone else, she'd taken a turn holding the baby and he doubted he would ever forget the way she looked with the infant in her arms. She'd had that maternal look on her face, and he'd known at that moment that motherhood was definitely in her future.

"You have a nice family, Donovan."

He glanced over at her briefly. "Thanks. What about you? I know you have your aunt. Any parents or siblings?"

She shook her head. "No, I was an only child. However, I was raised by my aunt and uncle. Their son, Eric, is five years older than me. My mother gave me to my aunt and uncle when I was just a few days old and kept trucking back to California. She would visit on occasion but did nothing but cause trouble whenever she did so—usually to get money out of my aunt and uncle by threatening to take me away if they didn't pay up."

She paused for a moment, and he figured she was regrouping her thoughts, reliving the past. He couldn't help wondering if she felt deprived of her mother's love and attention.

"Her boyfriend stabbed her to death when I was ten," she said, continuing. "It had been four years since I'd seen her, and when they sent her body back here for burial she was nothing more than a stranger to me. My aunt, uncle and cousin were all the family I had and all that I needed."

"Where's your uncle?"

"He died when I was in my teens. And my cousin, Eric, is in the State Department and works for the embassy in Australia."

When the car came to a traffic light, he tilted his head to look over at her at the same time she glanced at him. Their gazes locked, held for a second. He knew he had to ask what he should have asked her before they'd made love, but he hadn't because at the time it really hadn't mattered since it was a one-and-done sort of thing, as she liked putting it.

"Who broke your heart to make you take a hiatus from men?"

She didn't answer right away. Instead she broke eye contact with him and looked ahead through the shield.

"Karl, the heartbreaker and manipulator. He practically stripped me of my self-confidence when it came to relationships by convincing me I was lacking in certain areas." She glanced over at him. "You proved him wrong."

He remained silent for a moment and then he said, "I'm glad I was able to do so."

Natalie smiled. "I'm glad, too."

The interior of the car got quiet again, and she would have loved to know what was going on inside Donovan's head. Why had he taken her to a place where he'd known his family would be congregating? Everyone had been nice but more than mildly curious. She could tell. That only led her to believe bringing a woman around his family was not his norm. She had liked everyone—his cousins, his sisters-in-law, his brothers and his parents. They'd made her feel right at home. Included. No one had asked her a lot of questions, and she was glad of that. She would not have wanted to lie to them.

She hadn't lied to Donovan just now. She'd told him about Karl. What was her rationale in doing that? It wasn't like it would mean anything to him in the scheme of things. But for some reason she had wanted him to know sharing a bed with him had been therapeutic as well as pleasurable.

"Do you mind if I drop by my house a minute to get something before I take you back to the café?"

She glanced over at him and shook her head. "No, I don't mind."

"Thanks. I appreciate it."

The clock on the car's console indicated it was a little after ten. She figured once she got back to the café she would get her car and go on to Farrah's where she would be spending the weekend. Tonight they planned to do facials and watch romantic movies until dawn if they could last that long. Usually, they would both fall asleep by midnight.

Moments later Donovan pulled into the garage attached to his condo. He closed the garage door behind them and then turned off the car's engine. He glanced over at her. "Would you like to come inside?"

She shook her head. "No, thanks. I'll just sit here until you come back."

"That might be a problem."

She stared at him a moment before lifting a brow. "And why might that be a problem?"

"I told you I needed to drop by the house to get something."

She nodded, confused. "Yes, you did say that, and what of it?"

"What I needed to drop by the house to get is *you*. So will you come inside with me, please? I want you so bad I can barely stand it."

She frowned, started to tell him that sounded like a personal problem, but when she glance down at his lap, she saw that it *was* a personal problem for him. A rather huge one.

She stared back at his face. She'd never known a man to want her this much. "Bringing me here was rather presumptuous of you," she said, her frown deepening.

"I did ask."

"No, you led me to believe you needed to get something."

"I do need to get something."

She opened her mouth to argue at his logic but then closed it, knowing it wouldn't do any good. The man gave arrogance a whole new meaning. "I'm staying put right here," she said stubbornly.

He smiled and leaned over the console, very close to her mouth and said, "Then I guess this place will have to do. At least for this."

Before she could draw her next breath, he had mingled it with his in a kiss that was so potent she felt it all the way to her toes. His tongue was dueling with hers, stroking varying degrees of desire within her. She knew the exact moment he slipped his hand underneath her skirt, expertly moving under her panties to insert his finger into the warmth of her. And then his fingers began moving to the same rhythm his tongue was using on her mouth.

Nothing about the kiss was civilized. It was as untamed and wild as it could get, and when an orgasm threatened, his mouth on hers and his fingers inside of her boldly pushed her over the edge.

"Now are you ready to go inside?" he asked a short while later, pulling his fingers out of her while greedily licking the corners of her lips.

His words, a hoarse whisper, inflamed her body even more, and at that moment she couldn't deny him anything, especially after what he'd just given her.

"Yes," she all but whispered back. "I'm ready to go inside."

Getting out of the car, he quickly came around in front to open her door. The moment she alighted he swept her into his arms and proceeded to carry her into his home.

Not wasting any time, as soon as they passed through the back door he began stripping her naked right there in his kitchen. He then placed her on her back on his kitchen table, and then after practically tearing off his own clothes and putting on a condom, he crawled on top of her.

He gazed down at her. "This is what I wanted to come here to get. Thank you for letting me have it."

He drew in a huge breath, and in one smooth thrust he entered her, then he pulled out slightly, only to thrust into her again.

Over and over. Nonstop. Even when he felt her inner muscles clenching him and heard her soft sounds of sexual pleasure, he kept going and going. He couldn't stop. Even the pain of her fingernails digging deep into his back couldn't slow him down. And when an orgasm struck the both of them, he began giving and giving until he had nothing left to give.

At least so he thought. He began getting hard again while buried deep inside the warmth of her body. "Natalie." He'd lifted himself up slightly to say her name and then it was on again. The only thing he could think of was that he might never get enough of her.

Natalie eased from the bed, careful not to awaken Donovan. After he had talked her into staying overnight she had called Farrah. Without going into a lot of details she cancelled their sleepover with a promise they would do lunch next week.

She glanced over at the clock on his nightstand. It was close to five in the morning.

They had finally given the kitchen table a rest only to come upstairs to wear down his bed. Then a few hours later he had carried her back downstairs and after collecting their clothes off the floor and tidying up the kitchen, they had shared cooking duties and made omelets and coffee.

After they had eaten and were headed back up the stairs, Donovan had gotten an unexpected visitor, a man he introduced as his best friend, Bronson Scott. Just like Xavier and Uriel, Bronson was handsome as sin, and although she wasn't into auto racing, she recalled seeing his face a number of times in the newspapers as well as on the cover of *Sports Illustrated* magazine as part of a NASCAR spread. When Donovan had mentioned her car being left at the café, Bronson had offered to bring it to her and leave the keys under the mat.

After Bronson left, they had gone back to bed to make love again and had eventually drifted off to sleep. But as was the norm with her, she found herself waking up with chemical equations in her head that she needed to jot down. She didn't have her laptop, but she always kept a notepad in her purse.

Slipping Donovan's T-shirt over her head she padded in her bare feet down the stairs to get the notepad out of her purse. Then she headed back upstairs to his office. She sat down behind his huge desk and inhaled deeply, thinking that sleeping with Donovan again had not been in her plans. But the man was a master at seduction.

She glanced around the room. This was only her second time in here. The first time she had been concentrating too deeply on cleaning the room to pay close attention to the plaques on his wall and the trophies in a cabinet.

Getting up from behind the desk, she walked over to study the plaques. All but one had been presented to him for his volunteer work in the Special Olympics. The other had been presented to him for being a mentor with the Charlotte public school system.

Then there were all the basketball trophies he'd gotten while in college. She wished she could have been in the bleachers when he was running up and down the court. With his fine physique, that would definitely have been a sight to see.

Returning to the chair behind the desk, Natalie knew she had to tread very carefully where Donovan was concerned or else those emotions within her which were al-

ready teetering close to the edge, would soon lose their
balance and topple over. The last man she'd thought she
loved had ended up hurting her badly. She knew that, because of her mother, she didn't take rejection well, so she
avoided it at all costs. Karl had taught her a lesson of what
could happen if you were to let your guard down, and she
could see herself falling for Donovan if she wasn't careful.

She had been working on various formulas for almost
an hour when she heard a sound and glanced up. Donovan
stood shirtless in the doorway wearing a pair of jeans, un-
zipped, and riding low on his hips. His shoulders looked
powerful; the wide span of his chest was masculine, sexually compelling. His appearance was doing a number on
her senses, and the degree of his sexuality set off a dis-
tinct throb in her body.

She could vividly recall everything they had done since
entering his home, and the memories made sensuous shudders flow through her. And it wasn't helping matters that
she was pinned by the deep intensity of his gaze.

"I woke up and you were gone. You okay?" he asked
in a concerned voice.

She knew why he was asking if she was okay. Their
lovemaking had been intense. She smiled. "Yes, I'm fine."

He glanced at her notepad. "What are you doing?"

She closed the notepad and pushed it aside. Now would
be a good time to tell him about the chemical equations
she was working on for the global warming panel, which
would lead into what she did for a living. But for some
reason she wasn't ready to reveal that to him now, especially when she remembered how other men had reacted,
calling her a chemistry geek. She couldn't handle it if he
acted the same way. But she would have to tell him soon,
especially since she would be flying out on Thursday for
Princeton.

"I couldn't sleep," she said, "and thought I'd come in and kill some time until you woke up."

A smile touched the curve of his lips. "I'm awake now."

He slowly crossed the room, and the closer he got the hotter the desire burned within her. "Are you sure you're fully awake?" she asked, watching his approach and thinking just how undeniably handsome he was.

"Why don't you come from behind that desk? I'll show you just how awake I am."

She couldn't help but chuckle. "Haven't you gotten enough of me already?"

"Afraid not. I have the desire to make love to you for the rest of the night. In fact I want you to spend the rest of the weekend with me."

She lifted a brow as she came from behind the desk. He scooped her up in his arms and set her down on the edge of it. "You want me to stay with you all weekend?" she asked, to make sure she'd heard him correctly.

"Yes. But that means you'll have to go to the Steele brothers basketball game tomorrow morning."

Earlier she had imagined how it would be to see him work a basketball court. "I'd love to go watch."

"It can get brutal," he warned, reaching out and sliding his hand up her legs. "Depending on how much frustration we have to work out."

She leaned in, close to his face. "Do you think you'll be frustrated?"

His hand went farther up her thigh. "Not as long as I go to bed with you tonight and wake up with you in the morning," he said huskily. "You, Natalie Ford, are the best frustration-reliever there is."

"Glad I can help, Donovan Steele."

Donovan leaned closer and captured Natalie's lips with his. Kissing her had a way of stripping his senses, making

him lose control. He liked the way her tongue mingled
with his, the way her taste always made him more aroused
than he already was. The way he could rouse her just by
touching her in a certain sexy spot, like he was doing now.
She groaned deep in his mouth. He pulled back slightly,
enough to break off their kiss, but then he used his tongue
to trace a trail around her lips, lips he loved kissing.

He then nibbled a path close to her ear. "I need some
more of you," he whispered huskily.

"Greedy," she accused in a deep moan, and he retali-
ated by inserting his fingers deep inside of her. Her next
moan sounded deeper than the last.

"Only with you." And that was so much of the truth
that it had him trembling inside. Every cell in his body
was attuned to her. He never imagined being this connected to any woman.

"Then if you want me, take me," she invited.

"Gladly."

And then he went back to her mouth, fed on it greedily,
while her fingers sank deep into his shoulder.

Pulling back, breaking off the kiss, he yanked his
T-shirt over her head and tossed it aside, exposing her
beautiful breasts. He bent his head and took a nipple in
his mouth, teasing the hardened tip with his tongue.

But that wasn't enough. He wanted to be inside of her.

He drew back, looked into her face and saw her passion-
glazed eyes. He then eased out of his jeans, kicked them
aside and put on a condom before sweeping her into his
arms and heading for the nearest wall. By the time she
felt the hard surface at her back, she parted her thighs.
Before she could take her next breath, he had entered her
and was moving inside of her, holding her in a way that
allowed him to penetrate deep.

The legs that curved around his back were tight, urgent, but not as urgent as the movement of his thrusts that were going in and out of her. When he felt her inner muscles clamp down on him, he threw his head back and actually growled.

As if the sound was what she needed to hear to push her over the edge, he heard Natalie cry out his name. She thoroughly lubricated his sex while at the same time she milked it for all it was worth.

His teeth clenched when another orgasm hit on the tail of the last, and he knew as he heard her orgasm follow his that when it came to undiluted passion, Natalie was in a class by herself.

"Aren't you the one who said you would never bring a woman to watch us play?" Bas asked his brother as they took a time-out. "What's going on? Are you and Natalie joined at the hip?"

Donovan didn't say anything as he took a huge gulp of water. After last night, they might as well be joined at the hip…as well as a number of other places. After making love in his office, he had taken her downstairs and they made love in the other rooms, as well. By the time she left tomorrow, he wanted them to have christened every room.

But to get his brother off his back, he said, "Think whatever you'd like."

He took another swig of water as he glanced up in the bleachers. Natalie sat talking to Kylie, who was there with Alden to support Chance. An uneasy feeling spiked up his spine. She looked good with his family. Like she belonged.

She had agreed to spend another night with him after checking on her aunt. But she wanted to keep their relationship a secret from the woman. Because that's what she wanted, he had agreed.

When the break was over and it was time to play another round of basketball, he glanced in the stands again. Natalie waved. He smiled and waved back.

"A gift? For me?" Natalie asked, looking at the prettily wrapped gift box Donovan had just handed to her when he joined her on the sofa.

"Yes, it's for you." A naughty grin touched his lips. "And in a way it's for me, as well."

She lifted a brow while unwrapping the gift. After the basketball game he had dropped her back off at his house when she'd felt sleepy and wanted to take a nap. That was fine since he had agreed to drop by the mall where Bronson was autographing T-shirts at a sports shop.

For some reason she wasn't surprised to open the box and find Victoria's Secret tissue paper. Then she smiled when she uncovered a very pretty sexy blue-and-white lace nightie with spaghetti straps.

"A lingerie shop was right across from where Bronson was signing," he explained. "This particular item was on a mannequin in the window, and I kept staring at it and imagining you wearing it."

He paused a second, looked up at her and then added, "I've never bought a woman something this intimate before."

Natalie didn't say anything at first. Knowing that he had done something for her that he had never done for another woman touched her deeply. And at that moment, she knew she could no longer deny the emotions she was feeling for him. She had fallen in love with Donovan.

She looked back down at the beautiful gift and knew she would cherish it always. She then glanced back at him. "Thank you, Donovan. I'll wear it tonight just for you," she said softly.

A grin touched his lips. "Just as long as you know it won't stay on you long."

She couldn't help but chuckle. "I didn't think it would."

She placed the box aside and crawled over into his lap to give him a very special kiss. Although she couldn't tell him how she felt, she wanted to show him.

Chapter 15

It was Wednesday morning, and for the first time in Donovan's life, he arrived to work late. His secretary stared as he passed her desk. He smiled. "Is anything wrong, Sandra?"

"No, sir. Are you ill?"

He couldn't help but chuckle and said over his shoulder. "No, in fact I couldn't be better."

"That's good to hear because your brother called, and he didn't sound like he was in a good mood."

Donovan stopped before opening the door to his office to ask, "And which brother is that?"

"Mr. Morgan Steele. And he wants to see you right away."

"Okay. Let him know that I'm here."

Donovan entered his office, tossed his briefcase on the leather loveseat and immediately walked over to the window. It was a beautiful day because the last five days had been perfect, beginning with Friday night.

Never had he made one woman the focal point of his weekend. And he couldn't recall, if ever, when he'd drifted off to sleep with his body still inside of one, connected in the most intimate way. He could only blame it on that negligee he had bought her. She had looked sexy in it, just like he'd known she would. Blue was definitely her color.

He chuckled, remembering how he'd tried making love to her in every single room in his house and, he thought smugly, he had succeeded.

In addition to Friday, Natalie had spent Saturday night with him, as well. She had left for a short while on Sunday and returned on Sunday evening when they had prepared dinner and watched a movie together, first a chick flick and then one of his action movies.

She had left late Sunday night, and he had missed her like crazy. Luckily he'd been kept busy at work on Monday but had looked forward to seeing her in the evening. He hadn't been able to talk her into staying over on Monday, but last night she had succumbed to his powers of seduction without much of a fight. The results, although he'd been late for work, had been most rewarding.

"Mr. Steele, Mr. Morgan Steele is here," his secretary interrupted his thoughts by saying over the intercom.

"Thanks, Sandra, please send him in."

Donovan turned from the window, and the moment his brother walked in he could tell there was trouble. "What's going on, Morgan?"

Morgan slumped down in the nearest chair. "There is a spy somewhere, Donovan. Devonshire Manufacturing Company knows too much about Gleeve-Ware not to be getting information from someplace. In Bas's absence I'm ordering a detailed security report on everyone who has access to the formula. This is serious."

Donovan nodded. Yes, it was serious. SC had a major product breakthrough on their hands, and others were trying to be the first to claim it before it reached the market. Troubleshooting was Bas's specialty, but he would be out of the office this week to spend time with his wife and newborn daughter.

"You still have your copy of the report, right?" Morgan asked, reclaiming his attention.

"Yes, but all those formulas are Greek to me."

"Well, destroy the copy you have since everything has practically been revised, thanks to Juan. We're keeping an updated version under lock and key, and only the four of us and Juan will have access to it."

"No problem."

Morgan turned to leave and then paused and said, "And just so you know, we like Natalie."

Donovan chuckled. "Thanks, Morgan. I happen to like her, too."

"So when are you going to tell Donovan what you really do for a living?" Farrah asked at Natalie from across the table. The two had met for lunch, a promise Natalie had made when she'd canceled their plans for the weekend to spend time with Donovan instead.

Natalie shook her head, remembering this past weekend when he'd walked in on her in his office. "I'll see him later tonight, and I'll bring it up then—especially since I need to tell him I'm leaving to return home to Princeton tomorrow."

"Considering how those other guys acted once they discovered you had a working brain, do you think Donovan will have an issue with it?"

Natalie had thought about it a lot. In the beginning a part of her wasn't sure what his reaction would be, so she had kept the information to herself. But now after spending time with him and getting to know him better, she refused to believe he would feel threatened by her achievements like all the others had. "I really don't think so."

Assuming she was a housekeeper, he hadn't placed much importance on her profession before introducing her to his family. Donovan, she believed, was a man comfortable in his own skin and would have no reason to be intimidated by her career.

"Do you think he'll be upset that you haven't been completely truthful to him?" Farrah asked, taking a sip of her tea.

Natalie shrugged. "I don't know why he would be. I began feeling deep emotions for him the first time we made love. He was so different from Karl. I couldn't help but acknowledge those differences to myself, but I refused to admit I was falling in love with him."

"Why?"

"Because in my mind that was a one-night stand, so I didn't want to put my emotions out there on a lost cause. Karl, as well as those others who felt threatened by my academic achievements, made me wary."

Farrah reached across the table to take Natalie's hand in hers. "I like Donovan, and I could tell that night at the café how much he was interested in you. I truly believe things will work out between you two, although I don't know how he's going to feel knowing you'll be returning to Princeton for good in a few weeks."

"Now that's the part that scares me," Natalie said. "I'm not sure he'll be interested in a long-distance affair." She inhaled deeply. "We'll find out his thoughts on everything tonight."

* * *

The Product Trade Show couldn't get here fast enough, Donovan thought, entering his home that afternoon. He, Chance and Morgan had met with Juan Hairston for a demonstration of Gleeve-Ware, and they'd been amazed at how much progress had been made. In addition to the wear-free tires, he envisioned a number of other ways the products could enhance the lives of consumers.

It was late but Natalie had agreed to drop by. The moment he went up the stairs and stepped into his bedroom, memories of the past few days came flooding back. He still wasn't sure how it was possible to feel so happy, and a part of him was afraid he would pinch himself to find it was all a dream.

After taking a quick shower, he slipped into a pair of jeans and went into his office to get some work done before Natalie arrived. Settling into the seat behind his desk, he noticed a small notepad on the floor and recalled it was the same one he'd seen Natalie scribbling something in Friday night when he had awakened to find her missing from the bedroom and in here. He reached down and picked it up, wondering if she had a penchant to doodle like he often did.

He opened the notepad and frowned. The first page was filled with several chemical equations that looked similar to the ones Juan had been sharing with them on Gleeve-Ware for the past eight months or so. Why on earth would Natalie have a notepad filled with various formulas?

At this stage of the game, you basically can't trust anyone. Your competitor will pay top dollar for someone to steal the formula right from under your nose, using any technique they can and anyone they can.

Juan had spoken those very words to him, Chance

and Morgan during their meeting today. Now those same words came down on him like a ton of bricks.

He wanted to believe that this was a coincidence, but there was a big GW on the first page above the list of equations. GW for Gleeve-Ware. And his mind was flashing one question: Why would a cleaning lady spend her time writing formulas?

He closed his eyes as several reasons came to mind—none of them he liked. That night he'd found her in this room, had she been copying the formula from the papers he had locked in his desk drawer? It would have been easy to get the key off his key ring, and he would be the first to admit she had acted rather strangely that night.

At that moment he felt as if someone had punched him in the gut. Pain of intensity he'd never felt before chilled him to the bone, and time stood still as he sat there and stared at the notepad, trying to come up with reasons she would have it. He tried like hell not to jump to conclusions.

But the more he thought about it, the more his mind was doing just that. By the time he heard the doorbell, intense anger had replaced desire.

Natalie knew something was wrong the moment Donovan opened the door, and stood back to let her enter and then all but slammed the door shut behind her.

"What's wrong, Donovan?"

"You left something behind the last time you were here," he said in a hard tone, holding up the notepad for her to see. "Out of curiosity, I thumbed through it and couldn't help noticing it was filled with formulas, something I wouldn't expect from a person claiming to be a housekeeper. Why is that, Natalie?"

She swallowed hard, wishing she had told him Friday

night like she'd been tempted to do. "Because I don't do housekeeping for a living."

"Evidently." He rubbed a hand down his face and then looked back at her. "So, how much were you paid?"

Paid? "Excuse me? What are you talking about?"

"I'm talking about the fact that this notepad is filled with Gleeve-Ware formulas."

"Gleeve-Ware? I don't know what you're talking about, Donovan."

Donovan inhaled deeply, trying to quell his anger. How could she stand right in front of him and claim she didn't know what he was talking about when he had the proof right in his hand? Anger mixed with the pain of betrayal and he wanted her out of his sight now before he said or did something he would regret.

"Here." He offered the notepad back to her. "This is really useless to you since those equations are outdated. The Steele Corporation was one step ahead of you."

She refused to take it. "Donovan, I have no idea what you're talking about, but if you just listen to me for a second, I'll be able to clear—"

"The only thing you can do right now, Natalie, is leave and don't come back. You got what you came for. Funny thing, though, it was a wasted effort on your part."

A cruel smile then touched his lips. "But not on mine. My goal was to get you back in my bed, and I succeeded in doing that."

"Donovan, I—"

"No! Please leave now, Natalie. I don't want to ever see you again."

Natalie knew that in his present state there was no way she could get through to him, so she turned and walked out the door.

* * *

"Let me get this straight. Donovan thought your note-pad with those chemical equations on global warming had something to do with this project his company is working on?"

Natalie wiped the tears from her eyes. "Apparently."

She had left Donovan's house and had gone directly to Farrah's, nearly colliding with Xavier, who just happened to be leaving when she was arriving. And with Farrah still in her bathrobe and naked underneath, it didn't take a rocket scientist to guess what the late-night visit had been about.

"He actually thinks I'm a corporate spy. Can you believe that, Farrah? Just how crazy is that? And what hurts more than anything is that he didn't give me a chance to explain. How could he so easily assume the worst about me after all the time we spent together?"

Farrah regarded her carefully. "So, what are you going to do, Nat?"

Natalie lifted her chin stubbornly. "Nothing. Eventually he'll see he made a mistake."

"And then what?"

Natalie inhaled deeply. "And then, still nothing. I refuse to love a man who can think the worst about me."

"But you already love him," Farrah pointed out.

Fresh tears appeared in Natalie's eyes. "I know, and that's why I'm hurting so bad."

Donovan paced the confines of his living room. His pain was almost unbearable, and he fully understood why.

He had fallen in love with her.

Hell. Him? The playa of all times? The man who swore no woman would ever have his heart? Yeah, well, one had definitely gotten it.

He didn't even try to figure out how and when it had happened. He was far from being a romantic, but he would guess it had been the day he had found her asleep in his bed. Something inside of him had cracked the moment she had awakened and he had gazed down into her honey-brown eyes. From that moment on, he had wanted her like he'd wanted no other woman.

And now that woman had betrayed him.

He would have to meet with his brothers in the morning and tell them everything. He could just imagine what they'd think to discover the one woman he had brought around had been nothing more than a corporate spy.

He glanced at the clock. It was past midnight but more than likely Chance was still up. He dialed his brother's phone number.

"Hello?"

"Chance, I need you to call a meeting with everyone in the morning."

"Why? What's going on, Donovan?"

"I'd rather not say right now."

There was a pause and then Chance said, "All right, I'll arrange the meeting."

"And it would be a good idea if Juan was included."

Chapter 16

"Okay, Donovan, what's this all about?" Chance asked his younger brother when everyone had arrived for the meeting that they decided to hold in the lab. Even Bas had decided to come in, refusing to be left out of anything of importance when it came to the Steele Corporation.

Donovan stepped forward. "It's about this," he said, holding up Natalie's notepad in his hand.

Morgan lifted a brow. "What is that?"

"Something Natalie left at the house."

Chance looked confused. "Natalie?"

"Yes."

"You still haven't said what it is," Bas pointed out, no doubt trying to follow Donovan but having a hard time.

"It's a notepad filled with chemical equations."

"And your point?" Morgan asked.

Donovan was tempted to throw the notepad across the room and hit Morgan with it. "My point is that I found it very strange that she would have something like this in her possession. And with the letters GW written on every page."

Bas stared at him. "So let me get this right. Are you saying that you think your girlfriend—"

"She isn't my girlfriend. At least not anymore," Donovan snapped.

Bas rolled his eyes. "Okay, then. Are you saying that the woman you brought to the hospital last week, and the same woman you brought to our game on Saturday, could be a corporate spy?"

"Why else would she have something like this in her possession?" Donovan countered.

"Did you bother to ask her?" Chance asked.

Donovan shrugged. "I didn't want to hear anything she had to say."

All the men in the room, including Juan, stared pitifully at Donovan for a moment before shaking their heads. Bas spoke for the group. "Donovan, you have a lot to learn about women, especially if it's a woman you care deeply about. You never accuse her of anything unless you have concrete proof."

"But this is proof," Donovan said in a frustrated voice. He could tell by his brothers' and Juan's expressions that they weren't totally convinced.

"What does she do for living?" Juan spoke up for the first time to ask.

"Her aunt injured her ankle, and she's been helping out for the past few weeks as a cleaning lady. We met when she came to clean my house," Donovan said, deciding they didn't need to know he'd found her asleep in his bed.

"And when she's not cleaning houses, what's she doing?" Chance asked.

"She said she was in school," Donovan responded, folding his arms across his chest. "And before any of you ask, I did consider the possibility that this was homework, but she claimed she was out for the summer, so she had no reason to be scribbling down chemical equations."

No one said anything for a moment and then Juan spoke up. "May I see the notepad, Donovan? It won't take me but a second to decipher the equations and tell if you're right about her."

Donovan handed it to Juan, who browsed through the pages a few minutes in silence, then looked up at Donovan. "I hope she's a forgiving woman."

Donovan swallowed. A funny feeling stirred in the pit of his stomach. "Why would you hope that?"

"Because these formulas have nothing to do with Gleeve-Ware."

"B-but the GW—"

"Stands for global warming." Juan browsed through the notepad again. "What's the name of your used-to-be girlfriend again?"

"Natalie. Natalie Ford."

A surprised glint appeared in Juan's eyes. "Natalie Ford? *The* Dr. Natalie Ford? Renowned chemistry professor at Princeton University, who just last year received a special award from the federal government for her work with NASA? And," he added, reaching across his desk to retrieve a book from a nearby bookcase, "*The New York Times* bestselling author of this book?"

Juan flipped the book to the back where a color photo of a young, but professional-looking, Natalie was on the cover. "Nice photo of your ex-girlfriend, don't you think?"

Donovan's jaw dropped, clearly stunned. "She never told me."

"Um, probably because she wasn't one hundred percent

sure about you just yet, Donovan," Chance said smartly. "Makes one wonder why."

Donovan was already headed for the door.

"If I was her, I wouldn't take you back," Morgan called after him.

"I'd never give you the time of day again," Bas added.

"I'd definitely make you suffer a little bit," Chance threw in, chuckling.

"If she does forgive you and you get back in her good graces, I'd like her to autograph my book," Juan couldn't resist saying.

Donovan didn't bother making a comment. His mind was filled with a question of significant magnitude: How was he going to win back the woman he loved?

Natalie opened her mouth to argue a point made by one of the other panelists, only to snap it closed when she saw Donovan enter the auditorium and take a seat in the back. What was he doing here in Princeton?

Refusing to let his presence unnerve her, she turned her attention back to the discussion, rebuffing her desire to look out over the crowded audience and seek him out. Their eyes had met when he entered the room, so he was fully aware that she'd seen him.

Her mind sifted through all the global warming ideology her colleagues were presenting, and she was able to rejoin the discussion and provide some opinions of her own, as well as answer several questions that were presented to her. It didn't bother her in the least that for the next hour Donovan saw just what a chemistry enthusiast she was.

After Dr. Stanley officially brought the workshop to a close and everyone began filing out of the auditorium, Dr. Lionel Walker turned in his chair and smiled at her.

"Great job, Dr. Ford. You have some very interesting concepts. I would like to invite you out to dinner so we can discuss a few."

She smiled back, recognizing a hit when she heard one and inwardly wishing that she could experience with this man the same sudden electricity she'd felt with Donovan. He was young and handsome but not as handsome as Donovan.

"Thank you for the invitation, Dr. Walker, but I'll be catching a flight back to Charlotte in the morning to check on my sick aunt," she said, ignoring Donovan. Out of the corner of her eye she saw him walk up the aisle toward the stage.

"Perhaps another time? I plan to be back in Princeton in October."

She didn't want to give the man false hope. Besides, she needed to leave the stage before Donovan reached it. She wasn't ready to hear anything he had to say. His presence meant he'd discovered he had accused her falsely, but she didn't want to discuss anything with him.

Quickly easing out of her chair, she kept the smile plastered to her face when she told Dr. Walker, "Perhaps. Please excuse me for running off but I have an appointment."

She rushed down the side aisle but she wasn't quick enough.

"Natalie, wait up."

She would have kept walking, but a number of people who were still hanging around had heard Donovan call her name and were glancing in their direction.

Inhaling deeply, she turned the moment he came to a stop in front of her. She plastered another smile on her face and said in a demure tone, "Donovan, what are you doing here?"

"I owe you an apology."

"Apology accepted. Now goodbye." She turned to walk off.

"Wait," he said, reaching out and touching her arm.

She turned back to him and wished he hadn't touched her. His touch sent sensuous chills through her body, making her remember how things used to be with them. "Wait for what?" she asked, trying to keep her voice calm.

"Can we go somewhere and talk?"

She chuckled lightly. "Why would you want to do that? You've apologized and I've accepted, so you can return to Charlotte now since we have nothing further to talk about."

"Natalie, I—"

"No, Donovan. Please leave. Go back to Charlotte."

"I won't go back without you. I have the company jet to take you home in the morning."

She shook her head. "No, I won't be returning to Charlotte with you. I have my own airline ticket."

He frowned. "Why are you acting this way? I thought you said you accepted my apology."

"I do, but that doesn't mean things will resume as they were between us," she pointed out. "In fact I think it's best if they didn't. It was nothing but a mistake."

"Don't say that."

"Why not when it's true?" she countered.

"Will you at least let me explain? Please."

She couldn't help but remember the tears she'd cried over him, the pain she'd endured over his rejection, his accusations. All of this could have been avoided if he had let her explain. But he hadn't, and now he wanted her to grant him the same courtesy he'd denied her Wednesday night.

"There's nothing to explain," she said, feeling her heart harden. "In fact I think it would be in both our interests not to see each other again like *you* suggested Wednesday night."

And before he could say anything to that, she quickly walked off and darted into the ladies' room.

Donovan watched her go, feeling a heavy blow to his heart. He was never supposed to fall in love. But he had. And regardless of what Natalie thought, they did need to talk. There was a lot he needed to understand, like why she hadn't been completely honest with him about what she did for a living. And he needed to explain why he had been so quick to think the worst about her. No excuse. Just the reason.

There was something different about her, something he had immediately picked up on. The Natalie he had gotten to know had never lacked fire. The Natalie he had just spoken to didn't display any emotion. His lack of trust and faith in her had hurt, and he had expected her anger. That he could deal with. But this unreceptive, unemotional Natalie was someone he could not.

If she truly expected him to walk away and leave her this way, then there was a lot she had to learn about him, about a Steele in general.

He turned to walk out of the auditorium. More than anything he was determined to bring her fire back.

Natalie glanced around her house—the first time she'd been back in almost a month. There was no use getting too comfortable since she would be leaving again in the morning. At least she didn't have any plants to worry about watering while she was away.

Princeton was a college town, bucolic yet intellectual. She had purchased the house three years ago and never regretted doing so. It was close to campus and located in a really nice neighborhood. And it was just the right size for her.

She hadn't bothered bringing more than a garment bag since she'd only planned to stay last night and tonight. She had already showered and was in her nightgown ready for bed. She had called earlier to check on her aunt, and since Aunt Earline hadn't mentioned anything about Donovan, that had her wondering how he'd known where to find her since she hadn't told him anything Wednesday night about leaving town. He hadn't given her the chance to do so. More than likely he had gotten information out of Farrah, which wouldn't be hard to believe since her best friend was convinced Donovan was the man for her. Farrah didn't know just how wrong she was.

Natalie's thoughts shifted back to that afternoon. When she'd come out of the ladies' room, Donovan was gone. She could only assume he had taken his company jet and returned home, like she'd told him. It was for the best.

She was about to head up the stairs when her doorbell rang. She felt a sudden fluttering in her stomach at the possibility it was Donovan. How would she handle it if it was? Trying to keep her cool, she crossed the room and looked out the peephole. Instead of a face, all she saw was a bunch of balloons.

"Who is it?" she called out.

"Donovan."

It *was* him. Her fingers on the doorknob began to shake. She leaned into the closed door. "What do you want?"

She wanted to kick herself for asking that question. Doing so had gotten her into trouble with him before— several times.

"Please open the door. I have a delivery for you."

She should tell him what to do with his delivery, but she

wasn't that kind of person. Instead, she slowly opened the door and took a step back. He entered carrying a bunch of balloons and a bouquet of red roses.

"These are for you," he said, handing her both.

She set the flowers on the hall table and then glanced around for a place to put a dozen colorful balloons. "What are these for?"

"No special reason," he said, glancing around. "I had a hard time getting them. It seems most businesses in this town close at dinnertime."

After placing the balloons down she folded her arms over her chest. "What are you doing here, Donovan?"

He inserted his hands into the pockets of his slacks. She thought that he looked good, as usual. "You said you accepted my apology, but you didn't say it with passion."

"Excuse me?"

"Passion, Natalie. That's the one common denominator we've had from the beginning. I have a feeling it's slipping away."

She had news for him: it was already gone. She lifted her chin. "I don't want to talk about it."

"That's good because I don't want to talk about it, either," he said, walking into her living room. He dropped down on her sofa and began to remove his shoes and socks.

"What do you think you're doing?"

He glanced up at her. "Bringing the passion back."

His lips curved into a smile, the kind that always gave her goose bumps. Made her wet. It was the smile that made her want to do naughty things with him. She stiffened at the thought. "I'm going to have to ask you to leave, Donovan."

"You can ask, Natalie, but that doesn't mean I'll do it. In fact, I can guarantee you that I won't."

That spiked her anger. "You think you can just stay here, against my wishes?"

"Pretty much, mainly because the rift between us is just as much your fault as it is mine. I admit that I should not have jumped to conclusions," he said, standing up and pulling the shirt out of his pants. "But you aren't completely blameless. Had you told me the truth from the beginning, that you were a chemistry professor, I would not have had a reason to think you were a corporate spy. Granted, I was swift to make a judgment and I apologize for that, but there's a reason why I did it."

She tried not to notice he was now unbuttoning his shirt. "Is there?"

"Yes. I felt myself falling for you. You were too good to be true, and deep down, a tiny part of me wanted to believe you really weren't true. So when I found what I thought was proof that you weren't the woman I thought you were, I jumped on it. I apologized for it and you said you accepted my apology. Yet, you're acting cold, unemotional and dispassionate toward me. I want the old Natalie back."

"You can't have the old Natalie back."

He stood in the middle of her living room, shoeless and shirtless. "Do you care to bet on that?"

No, she didn't care to bet on it, not when he was looking at her like she was a piece of chocolate he planned to gobble up. She took a step back. He actually assumed—even after everything—that he could just walk in here and expect things to be as they were before.

"I don't think that," he said as if he'd read her mind. "There are a number of things we do need to straighten out—like why you didn't tell me everything in the beginning. We will get to that. But first, we need to get to this."

His hand went to the zipper of his slacks. She saw the huge bulge there and remembered the last time she'd seen him in such a state and how she had taken matters into her own hands. Literally. But she didn't want to think about that. She didn't want to remember.

But when he began easing down his zipper, memories flooded her—every tantalizing detail—and her mind became jammed with all kinds of thoughts, jumbled with all sorts of memories.

"Will you come over here or do I have to come over there?"

She knew what she wanted to say but she couldn't form the words. He took her silence as indecisiveness and said, "Before either of us takes a step, I think you ought to know something, Dr. Natalie Ford."

She swallowed. "What?"

"I love you very much. I didn't think I would or could say those words to a woman, but I'm saying them to you."

He loved her? Actually loved her? Before she could let her heart fill up with joy, she had to know one thing. "And what about what I do for a living?"

"What about it? Should it matter?"

She shrugged. "It did to other men. They considered me a chemistry geek."

Donovan held steadfast to her gaze. Now he understood, at least he thought he did. But to make sure, he asked, "Did other men find what you do for a living a turnoff or something?"

She nodded. "Yes."

"It's their loss for not getting to know the real you. The passionate you. I don't care about you being a chemistry geek because in my bed you are a sexual goddess. You make me feel things no other woman has ever made me feel."

He took a step forward. "You're mine, Natalie. You became mine the first day I saw you in my bed. I later made you mine in that same bed. The first for me and any woman. And you've technically christened my entire house. There's not a single room I can go in without thinking of you, without remembering making love to you in it."

He glanced around. "And now I want to do the same for yours. I want to leave my mark in every room in this house, so whenever you're here without me, you *will* remember."

"That's an ambitious goal, don't you think?"

He chuckled. "Yes, but one I plan to achieve, starting now. In here."

She stood there, watching as he removed his pants, his briefs and then sheathed himself in a condom. Her mind barely registered what he was doing. Instead it was still fixed on the words he had spoken earlier. *I love you very much.* How could he possibly mean it? She knew how she felt about him, but how could he love her back?

"Natalie." She blinked and then realized he was there, standing right in front of her. He had come to her. Naked. For several long moments his eyes studied her, and she felt the intensity of his gaze throughout her body.

"Now for your clothes. Strip for me," he suggested in a soft, taunting tone.

She wouldn't know where to start. But for him, she knew it would come naturally. She took a step back and eased her bathrobe off her shoulders, letting it fall in a pool at her feet. Her gown wasn't anything sexy, definitely nothing like the lingerie he'd purchased for her last week. Instead she wore white-cotton baby-doll pj's. But from the way he was looking at her, she could have worn another Victoria's Secret creation.

"You're slowing down, Natalie."

She blinked, realizing she had.

"I'm not sure how long I can hold out and behave myself," he said.

Her gaze traveled past his chest down to his middle and saw what he meant. Amazing. She smiled. Her pj's might be simple, but he was making her feel sexier by the minute. It didn't take her any time after that to remove her sleepwear. Then she stood there, facing him and just as naked as he was.

He didn't say anything, but she knew what he was thinking. He took another step forward, and her heart began beating fast. Then faster. And then he was there, right in front of her, wrapping his arms around her, sliding his palms all over her back, cupping her bottom and then returning his hands to the center of her back. And before she could blink, utter a single word, he had her off her feet and into his arms.

He stared down at her. "There's one thing you need to know about me. About any Steele."

"What is that?"

"We love forever," he said.

And then he lowered his mouth to hers, kissed her in a way that only he could, giving her all of his love, his emotions, his heart.

She kissed him back, tasting his urgency. She murmured a soft moan when he placed her on the sofa, breaking off their kiss.

He dropped to his knees and gazed down at her. "I will cherish you and your body for as long as I live, Natalie. That is my promise to you. I will love you, be there for you and I will always be proud of what you do. Adm

your work. Honor you. And belong to you. Only to you."
Then he leaned closer to reclaim her mouth, as he continued to stoke the flames of desire. Doing what he'd said
he would do, restirring her emotions.

Donovan kissed her with all his heart. If he was doing
so with the fervor of a starving man, it couldn't be helped.
He was starving for her, to savor her, taste her, claim her
irrevocably as his. After tonight there wouldn't be any
questions, no lingering doubts about what they meant to
each other. They still had some talking to do, reassur-
ances to make, but right now, at this moment, more than
anything he wanted to restore her passion, passion he had
foolishly taken from her.

He broke off the kiss and settled his mouth near the
curve of her neck and placed a passion mark there, officially claiming her as his. And then his mouth moved
lower to her breasts. The moment he latched on to a nipple, her lips parted and she released a soft moan.

Hungry for her in a way that he had never been hungry
for another woman, he sucked her nipples shamelessly and
with a desperation he felt in his engorged sex. She began
shifting restlessly about as passion began to build. Then
his hands, which had brought her to climax so many times
he'd lost count, stroked her feminine core. She was wet.
She was hot. She was ready.

With the force of a magnet, his mouth was pulled lower,
down to the center of her legs where he buried his tongue,
replacing his fingers deep inside of her. She nearly came
off the sofa but he held tight to her hips, refusing to let
her go anywhere.

He heard her say his name over and over again, coher-
ently and incoherently. It didn't matter. What mattered
was the fact that she was no longer emotionless with him.

He had rebuilt her fire, her passion, with one hell of an intimate seduction.

And when her body seemed primed for an orgasm, he pulled away and joined her on the sofa, positioned his body in place over hers. He glanced down and whispered softly, "I love you, Natalie."

And then he eased his body into her, penetrated her hot, wet folds, lifting her hips with his hands to assure a snug fit.

He threw his head back. Being inside her felt good. It felt right. This was where he belonged. And then he began moving, thrusting in and out of her, losing himself in her passion.

The more he stroked, the more she squeezed him, clenched him with her inner muscles, pulled everything out of him.

"Donovan!"

"Natalie!"

They climaxed together. Simultaneously. And with an intensity that took his breath away. The orgasm shook him to the core, as waves of pleasure washed over them. And he knew inside of her would forever be his home.

"Will you marry me?"

Natalie opened her eyes and looked up to see Donovan gazing down at her. They had moved from the living room and were now on her stairway. Their bodies were still connected and not surprisingly, he was still hard inside of her. He had an intense sexual hunger, and she enjoyed feeding it.

She wrapped her arms around him tight. "Only if we can have a long engagement."

He lifted a brow. "How long?"

"Um, at least until June. I need to wrap up the school year here before I can move to Charlotte."

"You don't have to. I can move here and telecommute. That shouldn't be hard to arrange."

She appreciated him considering doing such a thing but he didn't have to. "No, I want to move back to be close to Aunt Earline. With Eric out of the country, it's for the best and besides, it's time I come out of the classroom and do other things. I like babies."

He smiled, thinking about his newborn niece. "I like babies, too."

She shifted to sit up, and he couldn't do anything but ease himself out of her. For now. She looked over at him. "Tell me why you thought I had betrayed you, Donovan."

As best as he could, he told her about Gleeve-Ware and, not surprisingly, with her chemical background, she understood and gave Juan high praises for his achievement. "That product will revolutionize the rubber and plastics industry," she told him. "That's wonderful. I can't wait to see everyone's reaction come November."

They talked some more, and she shared with him why she had been reluctant to tell him that she was a college professor, about how in the past men had always felt threatened by her achievements.

"Where they felt jealousy toward your work, Natalie, I can only feel admiration."

"Oh, Donovan."

She fell into his arms and he held her tight. She twisted her head a little and met his lips. Pleasure tore through her the moment he inserted his tongue in her mouth.

Moments later, he pulled back. "Time to make it to the bedroom, sweetheart."

She chuckled. Just as well. They had made love in the

kitchen, dining room and bathroom downstairs. "Which one? I have three."

He chuckled as he stood with her in his arms. "Tonight we will hit all three."

And she had no reason not to believe him. She had a man who was forged of steel.

* * * * *

YOU HAVE JUST READ A

⬡ HARLEQUIN®

Desire

BOOK

If you were taken by the strong, **powerful hero** and are looking for the ultimate destination for **provocative and passionate romance,** be sure to look for all six Harlequin® Desire books every month.

⬡ HARLEQUIN®
entertain, enrich, inspire™

HALOHDINC13

REQUEST YOUR FREE BOOKS!
2 FREE NOVELS PLUS 2 FREE GIFTS!

H HARLEQUIN®

Desire

ALWAYS POWERFUL, PASSIONATE AND PROVOCATIVE

YES! Please send me 2 FREE Harlequin Desire® novels and my 2 FREE gifts (gifts are worth about $10). After receiving them, if I don't wish to receive any more books, I can return the shipping statement marked "cancel." If I don't cancel, I will receive 6 brand-new novels every month and be billed just $4.55 per book in the U.S. or $4.99 per book in Canada. That's a savings of at least 13% off the cover price! It's quite a bargain! Shipping and handling is just 50¢ per book in the U.S. and 75¢ per book in Canada.* I understand that accepting the 2 free books and gifts places me under no obligation to buy anything. I can always return a shipment and cancel at any time. Even if I never buy another book, the two free books and gifts are mine to keep forever.

225/326 HDN F4ZC

Name	(PLEASE PRINT)	
Address		Apt. #
City	State/Prov.	Zip/Postal Code

Signature (if under 18, a parent or guardian must sign)

Mail to the Harlequin® Reader Service:

IN U.S.A.: P.O. Box 1867, Buffalo, NY 14240-1867
IN CANADA: P.O. Box 609, Fort Erie, Ontario L2A 5X3

Want to try two free books from another line?
Call 1-800-873-8635 or visit www.ReaderService.com.

* Terms and prices subject to change without notice. Prices do not include applicable taxes. Sales tax applicable in N.Y. Canadian residents will be charged applicable taxes. Offer not valid in Quebec. This offer is limited to one order per household. Not valid for current subscribers to Harlequin Desire books. All orders subject to credit approval. Credit or debit balances in a customer's account(s) may be offset by any other outstanding balance owed by or to the customer. Please allow 4 to 6 weeks for delivery. Offer available while quantities last.

Your Privacy—The Harlequin® Reader Service is committed to protecting your privacy. Our Privacy Policy is available online at www.ReaderService.com or upon request from the Harlequin Reader Service.

We make a portion of our mailing list available to reputable third parties that offer products we believe may interest you. If you prefer that we not exchange your name with third parties, or if you wish to clarify or modify your communication preferences, please visit us at www.ReaderService.com/consumerchoice or write to us at Harlequin Reader Service Preference Service, P.O. Box 9062, Buffalo, NY 14269. Include your complete name and address.

HDI3R

SPECIAL EXCERPT FROM

 HARLEQUIN

Desire

*Canyon Westmoreland is about to get the
surprise of his life!
Don't miss a moment of the drama in
CANYON
by* New York Times *and* USA TODAY *bestselling author*
Brenda Jackson
*Available August 2013
only from Harlequin® Desire®!*

Canyon watched Keisha turn into Mary's Little Lamb Day Care. He frowned. Why would she be stopping at a day care? Maybe she had volunteered to babysit for someone tonight.

He slid into a parking spot and watched as she got out of her car and went inside, smiling. Hopefully, her good mood would continue when she saw that he'd followed her. His focus stayed on her, concentrating on the sway of her hips with every step she took, until she was no longer in sight. A few minutes later she walked out of the building, smiling and chatting with the little boy whose hand she was holding—a boy who was probably around two years old.

Canyon studied the little boy's features. The kid could be a double for Denver, Canyon's three-year-old nephew. An uneasy feeling stirred his insides. Then, as he studied the little boy, Canyon took in a gasping breath. There was only one reason the little boy looked so much like a Westmoreland.

Canyon gripped the steering wheel, certain steam was coming out of his ears.

He didn't remember easing his seat back, unbuckling his

seat belt or opening the car door. Neither did he remember walking toward Keisha. However, he would always remember the look on her face when she saw him. What he saw on her features was surprise, guilt and remorse.

As he got closer, defensiveness followed by fierce protectiveness replaced those other emotions. She pulled her son—the child he was certain was *their* son—closer to her side. "What are you doing here, Canyon?"

He came to a stop in front of her. His body was radiating anger from the inside out. His gaze left her face to look down at the little boy, who was clutching the hem of Keisha's skirt and staring up at him with distrustful eyes.

Canyon shifted his gaze back up to meet Keisha's eyes. In a voice shaking with fury, he asked, "Would you like to tell me why I didn't know I had a son?"

CANYON
by New York Times *and* USA TODAY *bestselling author*
Brenda Jackson
Available August 2013
only from Harlequin® Desire®!

Copyright © 2013 by Brenda Streater Jackson

HDEXP73258

Kick back and relax with a

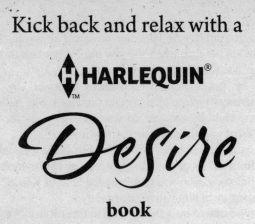

HARLEQUIN®

Desire

book

Passion, wealth and drama make these books a must-have for those so-so days. The perfect combination when paired with a comfy chair and your favorite drink or on the subway with your morning coffee. Plunge into a world of **hot cowboys, sexy alpha-heroes,** secret pregnancies, family sagas and **passionate love stories.** Each book is sure to fulfill your fantasies and leave you wanting more.

HARLEQUIN®

entertain, enrich, inspire™

HDINCAD